D0327405

The Manhattan Island Clubs

The Manhattan Island Clubs

Brent Monahan

ST. MARTIN'S MINOTAUR ❧ NEW YORK

THE MANHATTAN ISLAND CLUBS. Copyright © 2003 by Brent Monahan. All rights
reserved. Printed in the United States of America. No part of this book may be
used or reproduced in any manner whatsoever without written permission except
in the case of brief quotations embodied in critical articles or reviews. For information, address St. Martin's Press, 175 Fifth Avenue, New York, N.Y. 10010.

www.minotaurbooks.com

Library of Congress Cataloging-in-Publication Data

Monahan, Brent, 1948-
    The Manhattan Island clubs : a novel / by Brent Monahan.—1st ed.
      p.   cm.
    ISBN 0-312-30413-7
    1. Le Brun, John (fictitious character)—Fiction.   2. Morgan, J. Pierpont
(John Pierpont), 1837-1913—Fiction.   3. Manhattan (New York, N.Y.)—
Fiction.   4. Men—Societies and clubs—Fiction.   5. Sheriffs—Fiction.
I. Title.

PS3563.O5158M36 2003
813'.54—dc21

                                                          2003041294

First Edition: August 2003

10   9   8   7   6   5   4   3   2   1

FOR

GLORIA AND BILL

AND

DOLORES AND JACK

The Manhattan Island Clubs

JOHN LE BRUN walked slowly across the lawn path between the Brunswick train station and the Oglethorpe Hotel. From years of habit, the ex-sheriff cast a practiced eye around the area, making sure all was as it should be. He regulated his pace so that he would neither lead nor follow Nicodemus, one of the hotel porters.

"Saints alive!" Nicodemus protested, laboring under the weight of twin carpetbags. "I got to be totin' books."

"You are. I've been up to Atlanta on a shoppin' expedition."

"Books and books and mo' books. Someday they bring yo' house to da ground," the porter warned.

"I believe I shall collapse before my floor does."

At sixty, the black porter was a year older than Le Brun. Like the white man whose luggage he carried, he had lived in Glynn County all his life. He had known Le Brun for more than forty years.

"Bad trip back?" Nicodemus asked, reading the grim set of Le Brun's face.

"No. It was tolerable."

The porter refrained from pursuing further inquiry. He knew from rich experience that John Le Brun could not be coaxed into revealing private thoughts.

"Harry N. Pillsbury died," John volunteered.

Several years earlier, John had recruited Nicodemus to chess, but the porter showed only an average aptitude. They had mutually agreed to suspend the unbalanced competition, but so few citizens of Brunswick showed any interest in the game that John continued to bend the porter's ear about his passion practically every time they met. One of Le Brun's heroes was the American chess champion, Harry Pillsbury.

"Well, I'm sorry to hear that," the porter commiserated. "He was young."

"Yes, he was. Apoplexy. A tragedy as great as the insanities of Morphy and Steinitz. Genius exacts a great price."

"Nothin' I got to worry about," remarked the porter, stopping to lower the carpetbags to the ground for several moments.

John paused and transferred from his left to his right hand the suitcase he carried. "Any news since I left?"

"They caught the man who was robbin' them houses. He was workin' with a new postal carrier."

At last Le Brun smiled. Just as he was leaving Brunswick, a week earlier, he had been approached by Warfield Tidewell. Tidewell was the city's current sheriff and John's personal protégé. He was also the son of the man who had been one of Brunswick's most powerful judges. He had expected a bright legal future following degrees from Princeton University and the University of Pennsylvania. However, because he was southern the junior lawyer had been selected as the scapegoat when his Philadelphia law firm's dirty practices had been exposed. He had retreated to Brunswick late in 1898 and had been foisted upon Sheriff Le Brun by his father. John had admired Warfield's intelligence, his education, and his honesty and had immediately begun grooming the young man to become his replacement. As such, Tidewell had served efficiently for the past year. Unlike Le Brun, however, he did not show special aptitudes for criminal deduction. Whenever a crime was not cut-and-dried, John could expect Warfield to hunt him down and pick his brain.

So it was when four Brunswick burglaries occurred within three weeks. The crimes all took place inside private residences of the city's "better folk." Each house had been entered in broad daylight, two with no sign of forced entry. In every case there was no one at home. In two instances, the entire family was away; with the other two, everyone in the household was gone for at least an hour. Warfield's hunch was that the mastermind was someone in Brunswick society, a person with intimate knowledge of the comings and goings of the well-off households.

John had thought otherwise. "Check with Farrell Brown," he had told Tidewell at the station, just before boarding the train for Atlanta. Brown was Brunswick's postmaster. "This time of year, they put on a couple of part-time carriers, to fill in for the full-time boys on vacation."

Tidewell's face had brightened. "I see! The replacement walks up to the front door and knocks. If someone answers, he delivers the mail and earns himself high marks for personal service. If no one answers, he signals to an accomplice waiting down the street."

John had apparently been right.

The ex-sheriff and the porter started off again, making their way through the deserted grand hotel and out to the front veranda.

"You want I should fetch somebody to carry you home?" Nicodemus asked.

John shook his head and gestured for the porter to set down the bags. "Someone will happen by in a few minutes and make the offer. I believe I'll have my usual while I wait."

"I'll fetch it," Nicodemus said as he accepted the coin from Le Brun's hand. He moved back into the hotel with energy.

"Not that I have anythin' to do anyway," John muttered to himself in an unhappy voice.

Not a single soul other than Le Brun occupied the wide veranda. He put himself down in the spot that he habitually used to ambush potential chess opponents. As he crossed one leg over the opposite knee, he vacantly surveyed the north end of his hometown. Brunswick, Georgia, was the fifth busiest seaport in the South, but it also prospered by attracting the vacation savings of upland southerners and lots of Yankees during the winter and spring months. The Oglethorpe Hotel and most of the other resort services had officially closed for the season on the last day of May. John figured the hope of finding a worthy new chess opponent might as well be tucked away with his Christmas ornaments, because Advent was about when the out-of-towners returned. The only group of Brunswick natives who played chess well were of a status who would not deign to socialize with a former sheriff.

The chair John sat on was not a rocker, but he rocked it nonetheless, working off his pent-up energy. The summer solstice sun was setting over Glynn County in painterly glory. Part of the hotel facade sheltered John from the direct rays, which was just why he always laid claim to that particular seat. He was not, however, sheltered from the grandeur of the sunset reflected on the western walls of nearby buildings or glimmering in liquid orange off hundreds of windowpanes.

John let the chair's front legs settle to the veranda planking. He straightened up and felt in the small of his back the annoying pressure of his hidden derringer. Giving up his police revolver after fifteen years of service had made him feel defenseless enough; he would not remove the two-shot derringer from the little holster on the back of his belt, even if it meant some discomfort. But this evening he would gladly swear at it under his breath.

Just as John's bourbon-fortified tea arrived from the hotel bar, Sheriff Warfield Tidewell appeared on Newcastle Street. He sat tall in his buggy, driving it at a pace that indicated some urgent agenda. John sampled his drink as Warfield alit athletically and tied the reins to a hitching post. Le Brun remained placid in his seat and let the younger man come all the way to him.

"Evening, John," Warfield greeted.

John noted that the sheriff's eyes burned with excitement. Beads of perspiration dotted his brow; more than his horse had been moving with speed. "Evenin' is what it is."

"I meant 'Good evening,' " Warfield said, having already registered Le Brun's sour expression.

"That's debatable."

Warfield glanced down at John's luggage. "I stopped by your house and saw you weren't home yet, so I came here directly." His hand went to his vest pocket.

"It's quarter past nine," John said. "What's your rush?"

"Twenty minutes ago, I received a call from Charles Lanier."

Warfield needed to drop only the name. To the financial world, Charles Lanier was the senior partner of Lanier, Winslow & Company, one of the country's top banking establishments. The locals knew him as the president of the Jekyl Island Club, the fabulous resort just across Brunswick Sound whose members were limited to one hundred but who collectively controlled more than one-sixth of the entire nation's wealth. The current and ex-sheriffs knew him personally from their murder investigation at the club in 1899.

"How nice. He makin' you another job offer?"

Warfield ignored the dig. "He telephoned your house first, and when no one answered, he called the sheriff's office. He figured we'd know where to find you."

"For what?"

"He wants to hire you as a detective. Not here. Up in New York. Immediately."

John maintained his casual face. "Go on."

"They've had a murder in the Metropolitan Club. Just an hour and a half back."

John reached down and opened one of the carpetbags. "Not interested."

"You should be. The club will pay *one hundred dollars a day* for up to a week of your services, with a minimum of three hundred even if the crime is solved before you arrive."

John extracted a book from the bag and looked at its cover. "Who was murdered?"

"A member. But the apparent solution seems impossible. Just the sort of problem only you can solve."

"That is ridiculous flattery. New York is filled with detectives."

"Mr. Lanier commented on that. New York detectives take payoffs from the press. They need someone discreet as well as highly competent. You proved your discretion during and after the Jekyl Island Club investigation."

John yawned and stretched theatrically. "Still not interested. I just spent the better part of the day on two trains. I'm not in the mood to get on another."

"It's the same train. If you go around the back of the hotel, you'll see that the one you came in on is sitting there waiting for you. Another locomotive with a Pullman sleeper and private club car will arrive at eleven-twenty at Thalmann Junction. All you have to do is turn around and walk back to the station. Lanier basically said that heaven and earth would be moved in getting you to New York. His chauffeur and limousine will be waiting for you at Pennsylvania Station tomorrow evening. If you arrive at the club's front door by nine-fifteen tomorrow night, you will receive a one-hundred-dollar bonus."

"You ought to be ashamed of yourself, Warfield," John said, staring hard into his friend's eyes. He watched with satisfaction as the younger man blushed. "Charles Lanier tried to play you for a turncoat six years ago. Now you're his pimp? Why don't you say that *two* seats have been reserved to New York?"

Warfield sat down quickly on the chair next to John. "You needed me to deal with the club members on Jekyl Island. You yourself said you were too rough-hewn to handle them with the delicacy required."

"True enough. But, more important, this provides you a free ride up to that classmate of yours. The one who can underwrite the motorcar agency you so hanker for."

"That's not something one negotiates over the telephone," Warfield replied, knowing that anything less than total candor was useless with Le Brun. "I have some vacation time coming," he argued. "The council won't fire me if I take four or five days, even on short notice; the town is like a morgue this time of year."

"Tell me about it. And has Aurelia given you leave to go?"

"I haven't asked her. Why waste the time, when I know you're just contrary enough to cut off your nose to spite your face."

"I wouldn't cut off my nose. What would I perch my spectacles upon?"

Warfield's eyes narrowed, and a sly smile curled the corner of his mouth. "I know precisely why you're saying no."

"Do tell."

"You should be jumping at the opportunity. You've been wandering around this town like a marble in a tin can. Had to run to Atlanta to keep from going plumb out of your mind. My Lord, you've even tried your hand at acting! You've had a taste of London and Paris, and you told me yourself that you would have loved to tour New York as well if your money hadn't run low. This is a free ride being offered to you, John Le Brun, and you have no excuses to say no. *Except* that you understand it wasn't Charles Lanier behind the call."

"And who was it?"

"I have mentioned to you several times that J. P. Morgan created and built the Metropolitan Club. You have stood on your soapbox more often than I care to remember concerning his running of the Southern Railway System. He's one of the only men who can alter existing time-tables and commandeer the system for a private run to New York."

"Bravo, War. That was *excellent* extrapolative thinkin'. But your other thinkin' must be confused. You know that durin' the Jekyl Island

Club affair I came to loathe the man. I will not lift a finger to help him. In fact, I shall applaud from this chair if I hear that the crime has hurt him and his club."

"That's not the *real* reason you're saying no."

"Oh, is it not? Pray, enlighten me."

"He wanted the murder on Jekyl Island declared an accident because of President McKinley's impending visit. You outfoxed him and had your way. But Glynn County was *your* playing field. What was more, at that time you had nothing to lose. No one had any expectation of your solving that murder. Now you've been successful in solving club murders both here and in London. Two home runs. By the time you arrive on the scene in this case, the murder will have been a full day cold. The chance of succeeding a third time is remote. You are a proud man afraid of losing his reputation."

Le Brun flipped open the book. Without looking at Warfield, he said, "That psychology course you took at Princeton was a complete waste of time."

"Yes, I do want to get up to New York, and this free ride is very tempting," Warfield admitted. "But I also believe what I just said is true. You'll have to go up there if you want to maintain my unmitigated respect."

Le Brun answered with a shrug.

"All my speculation is actually beside the point," Tidewell, added, drawing on his ace card. "It's not me you need to say no to; it's Mr. Morgan. Won't it be delicious to have him move heaven and earth to bring you to New York City, just so you can look him in the eye and tell him to go to hell?"

John closed the book and cocked an eyebrow at Warfield. "Your forensic classes, on the other hand, were well worth the price. Carry me home so I can get some fresh clothes. Then go and inform your wife that you will be accompanyin' me to New York for several days."

THURSDAY

J U N E   2 1 ,   1 9 0 6

Y OU COME TO NEW YORK two years from today, and you
won't have ta be ferried across the Hudson."

The words of Charles Lanier's chauffeur came through in
an Irish brogue. He tootled the automobile's horn as he maneuvered
boldly into Ninth Avenue traffic. The small, craggy-faced man, who
had called himself merely Aloysius when he had met them on the train
platform, was multitalented, capable of driving in heavy New York
traffic while hemorrhaging tourist information.

"The train will run t'rough the Palisades, under the river, and right
into Pennsylvania Station. Some feat, eh?"

Warfield held up his pocket watch for John's inspection, making
sure he placed it directly in front of John's left eye. Le Brun had lost
the sight of his right eye from a detached retina while on vacation in
England the previous fall. He had gamely accommodated himself to the
affliction, so that most casual acquaintances were still unaware of his
loss.

"I wish they had the tunnel already. That ferry ride cost us the
hundred-dollar bonus," Warfield lamented.

"Don't fret yourself," John replied. "Morgan will be payin' more
bonuses than that if I accept this case."

Warfield regarded his friend and mentor, the man who had exerted more influence on his thinking in six years than his father had in thirty. He tried to imagine the reunion of J. P. Morgan and John Le Brun, like the irresistible force meeting the immovable object. It was sure to occur in private; he would only hear John's side of the meeting. He returned his attention to the *Herald,* attempting to read paragraphs whenever the car passed under a light. The *World,* the *New York Times,* the *Sun,* and the *Journal* lay on the seat between the travelers, still unperused.

Warfield whistled softly. "Incredible the stuff these reporters dig up. All this can't be coming from the police alone. Too inside. Members must have been blabbing."

"Members flapped their gums in London, too," John said.

"Besides," Warfield added, "the cops reserve their dirt for *Town Topics.* Its editor pays the most for secrets."

"They're nearly finished digging the tunnel under *both* rivers," the chauffeur prattled on. "But not wit'out a price. Did ya find an article in any of those papers about the blowout under the East River yesterday?"

"I saw the headline," Warfield obliged.

"Killed two men. They call themselves 'sandhogs,' but I call 'em heroes. Talk about dangerous work!"

Instead of holding up their side of the conversation, Warfield returned to his reading. He had visited New York City many times as a Princeton student. The images beyond the windows were not novel enough to win against news of the Metropolitan Club murder. The extent of John's experience in the city, however, had been a fleeting glimpse of the southern tip of Manhattan Island the previous fall, when he had sailed from the great port. He stared now with eager anticipation and was disappointed to view nothing but rows of tenements. Their facades were slightly varied from those of London and Paris, but he was sure they concealed similar misery. The difference was the hope in the immigrants' hearts that they could quickly jump off from these first moorings to weave their way brightly into the ever-expanding American tapestry. John was sure that the "land of opportunity" would allow the stronger and more ruthless success. The crowding, the stinging air, and the perpetual noise reminded him that he could muster little passion to accommodate himself to a world-class city, despite the attractions of great libraries, museums, and palaces of entertainment. He understood that he was able to get most of what he craved out of life right in Brunswick ... at least during the tourist season, when interesting, urbane characters delivered themselves to his doorstep. What he could not seem to find in his hometown, however, no matter the season, was a permanent female companion. Until he had visited London and met Veronica Godwin, he had been only vaguely discontent in this regard. Even though she had been much too young for him, her attentions had kindled a need that refused to flicker out. The crush of humanity that surrounded him now virtually guaranteed that there existed a perfect companion within a mile or two of where he sat. He determined to keep his one good eye open to the opportunity.

Summer dusk settled over Manhattan. The miracle of artificial light escaped from thousands of windows. The limousine's uptown travel had brought them among more stately, expensive buildings, where the better-off but not yet rich lived in neat stacks. John watched for the view to become increasingly grander.

The limousine turned right. John labored to discern the landscape of Central Park, beyond the low wall that surrounded it, an oasis of green among the brown and limestone of the buildings, the black of asphalt, and the gray of cobblestone. Two minutes later, the motorcar crossed Fifth Avenue. The panoramic view was abruptly obscured by an enormous building. Its four-story white Tuckahoe marble exterior was startling, even though it was virtually a rectangular box but for four small balconies and an imposing cornice cap. The image was something of déjà vu to John because it looked so like the club buildings on London's Pall Mall and most especially the Reform Club. From his readings on architectural styles, John recognized it to be Italian Renaissance palazzo revival. Its 142-by-90-foot bulk, at Sixtieth Street and Fifth Avenue, seemed to anchor the southeastern corner of Central Park. Beyond the club, to the east, lay a large, open tract of land. The limousine continued parallel to the building's longer side and turned into a large courtyard fronted by towering iron gates. The vehicle came around in a full counterclockwise circle, past a smaller annex, and then directly up to the main entrance.

"Magnificent, isn't it?" Warfield commented as the motorcar lurched to a halt.

"It's just one more monument to the unequal distribution of wealth," John replied.

"I've been instructed to bring your luggage down ta the Hotel Sa-voy," the chauffeur said.

John opened the car door. "I believe those who own the luggage should give those instructions. Take it all inside if you will, sir. We haven't decided if we are stayin'."

Warfield wisely refrained from comment. John took the lead through the outer club doors and up eight steps. As he climbed, his eyes swept left to a window in the otherwise solid wall. An alert face studied him. He glanced to his right and found a matching window on that wall. John's memory flashed back to a French castle he had visited the pre-vious fall, to its gatehouse just beyond the portcullis. There had been slit windows there as well, from which to shoot at invaders in case they breached the castle's moat and drawbridge. He snorted to himself as he drew the parallel between the medieval lord's fortress and this modern-day equivalent. He pushed through the inner set of doors, into the entrance hall.

While John and Warfield were admiring the large vestibule's ornate barrel-vaulted ceiling, a thin man wearing dress black and an insincere smile approached them from behind, out of the concierge alcove. John recognized his face as the one belonging to the man in the window. He was consulting his pocket watch as he walked.

"You must be Mr. Le Brun and Mr. Tidewell. I'm Theodore Cham-pion, evening manager. Welcome to the Metropolitan Club."

John thrust out his hand. Champion regarded it for the briefest mo-ment, then accepted it and allowed his to be pumped.

"Glad to make your acquaintance, Mr. Champion," John said.

"If you'll follow me into the Strangers' Waiting Room," Champion said, indicating a hallway just to their left. He went not more than twenty feet, into a good-sized anteroom. "Mr. Lanier is expecting you. I'll just fetch him and then see that your belongings are stored." He backed out and closed the door behind him.

John made a 360-degree turn. "Ever been inside this pile of rocks?"

Warfield shook his head.

His mentor laughed. "Would you have believed that a simple Rebel from Brunswick, Georgia, could manage to get you inside two of the most exclusive clubs in the world?"

"It's up to you to decide just how long we stay at this one," Warfield countered.

John studied his own image in a large mirror on the south wall of the room. He straightened his tie. "Yes, that is true."

Warfield seemed content to examine minutely the details of the room. John was less patient. He plucked up the nearest printed material on the countertop in front of him. It was the 1905 edition of *Rossiter's Club Men of New York*. The front matter indicated that it was published every other year. John estimated that its 1,138 pages contained the names, credentials, and coded club memberships of more than sixty thousand men. There were also short descriptions of dozens of New York clubs. John shook his head at the mania of club membership. New York's elite males were just as insane for clubbing as were those of London. He was most struck, however, by the nature of those allowed to advertise in the publication. He counted forty-eight ads. Nine were for custom tailors, five for banks, three for French champagnes, but no fewer than eight large ads had been placed by detective agencies. One spelled out the reasons for their presence: corporate surveillance, employment background checks, pilferage reduction, strike protection, identity investigation, family lineages traced. They all catered to fears prevalent among the rich—that partners were out to cheat them, employees were bent on earning more than a subsistence wage, and unfit suitors were scheming to wed their daughters for great dowries. Investigating murder was not a specialty listed by any of the eight.

Charles Lanier entered the room. He appeared even more clean and polished to John than he had on Jekyl Island, a bit softer but still good-looking and vital. He was closely followed by a man clearly into his eighties, with flaring nostrils, a down-turned mouth, and heavy eyelids. Lanier offered a wide smile. "Gentlemen! Good to see you again after all these years."

Tidewell and Le Brun returned similar remarks.

"This is Mr. Levi Morton," Lanier introduced, stepping back. "The president of our club."

"So kind of you to come all this way to assist us," Morton said, in a deep and gravelly voice. "Was your journey north satisfactory?"

"Quite," Warfield hastened to respond before his companion could give offense.

"Excellent. I expect you'll want to get right to business."

"So the crime has still not been solved," John said.

"Unfortunately not. This way, gentlemen."

Morton led the parade from the antechamber with a slightly shuffling stride. They returned to the entrance hall. Lanier moved ahead to press an elevator call button on the opposite side of the space. While they waited, John and Warfield drifted toward the center of the club, which was the Great Marble Hall. It was a looming space, open two stories to a forty-five-foot height. After passing through a Palladian, columned threshold, they looked on walls of pavonazzo marble, white mottled with black, and a checkerboard marble floor, largely covered by an Ardebil carpet. The ceiling was deeply coffered and gilt. On the north side, two flights of stairs, each fifteen feet wide, turned gracefully toward each other to meet on a landing halfway up, then part again. More than a dozen men occupied the hall, grouped in twos and threes. All had either come to a halt or slowed their pace to look at the strangers.

"They know exactly who you are," Warfield said, hardly moving his lips. "Look at all those respectful stares, from some of the most influential men in America." John made no reply but smiled broadly at their audience and made a small Continental bow.

"Gentlemen," Charles Lanier summoned. All four men entered the elevator. Lanier closed the outer door and inner gate and pressed the Ascend button. "There's a police detective waiting for us upstairs. Naturally, we can't exclude them just because you're now involved."

"Naturally," John agreed.

Morton said, "The victim was a long-time member of the club. Mr. Edmund Pinckney."

"They say in the *Herald* that he belonged to the South Carolina Pinckneys," Warfield reported.

"Yes. The same family. Although not the distinguished branch," Lanier imparted.

As both southerner and student of American history, John was well acquainted with the "distinguished branch" of the South Carolina Pinckneys. Elizabeth Lucas Pinckney had been a colonial planter of indigo, so sought after in Europe for royal blue dye. Her championing of the plant among other plantations in the state had led to South Carolina's initial economic growth. President George Washington had volunteered to serve as pallbearer at her funeral. She had been the mother of Thomas Pinckney, a major in the Revolutionary War, governor of South Carolina, and U.S. minister to Great Britain. Her son Charles

Cotesworth was a signer of the Constitution of the United States.

"How old was this Mr. Pinckney?" John asked.

"How old?" Morton looked at Lanier, who hunched up his shoulders. "I believe the police said fifty-two. Neither of us had much intercourse with him. He had his own circle of friends here. It's not an uncommon situation."

The elevator was ponderously slow. It was still climbing twenty seconds after the doors shut. "He was murdered on the top floor," Lanier told them. "We call it the Mezzanine Floor. Nothing up there but member bedrooms and suites."

"And did one of these bedrooms belong to Mr. Pinckney?" John asked.

"I'm sure not," Warfield interrupted. "He lived two blocks north of here, on East Sixty-second."

"Why don't we dispense with secondhand information," John suggested, gently relieving Warfield of the newspaper, "bein' as how we have direct sources at our disposal?"

At last, the elevator shuddered to a halt. Lanier pulled the doors open. As Tidewell and Le Brun emerged, they were greeted by a square-jawed man with a mop of light brown hair, close-set blue eyes, and the unmistakable bearing of a cop. He was an inch and a half taller than Le Brun. John observed that he wore a suit that was expensive but well worn. Either he had paid top dollar for it new and had worn it to death, or he had purchased it at a secondhand shop. What it told John was that this was a man whose purse did not match his pride of appearance. It suggested that he was an honest policeman.

"Ah! The out-o'-town professionals, is it?" the detective said, through a warm grin. Lanier and Morton had stepped back to allow Tidewell and Le Brun to exit first. The detective thrust out his hand, first to John and then to Warfield. "The name's Kevin O'Leary. Welcome ta New York City!"

Greetings were again exchanged.

"Step this way, gentlemen," O'Leary bade, without further ado. They walked around a corner and into a long hallway. Halfway down stood an opened trifold dressing screen, fashioned of black lacquered wood with rice-paper panels displaying authentic Japanese artwork. When they came to it, the city detective closed the screen and leaned it against the wall. Behind it, a large patch of carpeting was stained pale red.

John gave out a little laugh. "I had half expected to see the body." He looked at Morton. "You must have members with very delicate sensibilities if they can't stand a trace of blood."

"It's ta discourage the parade," O'Leary said, coming to the president's rescue. "Anyone with the feeblest excuse has found his way up here. At any rate, this is where Mr. Edmund Pinckney was found."

"By whom?" asked Le Brun.

"Two gentlemen of the club," supplied Lanier. "One of whom *does* rent a room on this floor."

"What time?"

O'Leary said, "Fourteen minutes ta eight."

"Was he dead when they found him?"

"They said so. He was definitely dead when the police arrived. And you're right about this being but a trace of blood. He took an attack ta the t'roat. His right side. Must have been on the order of a stiletto . . . narrow and t'in. Severed the right carotid artery but went in too deep and was too flimsy ta get across ta the other side."

"The killer's left to right," John said.

"Spot on. He used his right hand. The artery sent out quite a powerful spray. Decorated the wallpaper real good. The paper has some kind of treatment that allowed it ta be t'oroughly expunged. I believe the killer made one swift attack and jumped back."

"So as not to get blood on his clothing," Warfield interjected.

John regarded his protégé with the faintest of smiles but said nothing.

"Indeed," replied O'Leary, his smile patronizing. "When he saw the spurting, he knew Mr. Pinckney was a goner. The victim staggered forward for a good twenty feet. Partial handprints in blood on the wall showed that he tried ta hold in his blood first, then used his right hand ta steady himself as he moved toward the elevator. Then he collapsed and finished leaking. It sank right t'rough the carpet. The staff did a brilliant job of cleaning. Half the man's life poured out here before his heart stopped pumping."

Warfield faced Charles Lanier. "You said on the telephone yesterday that you had a suspect but that it was impossible for him to be guilty."

"And that's still the case," Lanier returned.

"Wait," John said, raising his hand. "Let's set that aside for a moment and begin with Mr. Pinckney's entry into the club yesterday. When was that?"

"A bit before seven in the evening," Morton supplied.

"Alone?"

"Yes. I am told that he came and went from the Metropolitan with frequency and erratically but that he was here on Wednesday evenings like clockwork."

"Why is that?"

"I asked the same question," O'Leary said. "Apparently, he liked the Wednesday night menu. Nothing more special ta the ritual."

"At least at face value," John replied. "So, he arrived by seven. What did he do from seven until seven-thirty?"

Lanier said, "He approached members of the club and harangued them about considering the creation of a new club."

"A new club?" Warfield echoed, with a degree of surprise that indicated he thought the notion heresy inside the exclusive Metropolitan Club.

"Yes. 'An abstemious club' he called it," Lanier answered. "He was rebuffed by several of the men. Then, in the Marble Hall, he met his murderer coming down the stairs. This man was seen at the same time by four other members standing in the hall. They all identified him as Witherspoon King."

Warfield caught John's good eye and pointed toward the newspaper.

Morton said, "King is a member from Philadelphia. Usually comes in when he's up here on business."

"Insurance business," John said, repeating what Warfield had told him in the cab.

"That's right," confirmed Lanier. "The same business Edmund Pinckney was in."

"The same company?"

"No."

John rocked on his heels. "Did either sit on the other's board? You know, interlocking directorates? Your usual New York business shenanigans?" He cocked an eyebrow at the Irish detective as he pronounced his last word.

"That would be your job to ferret out," Levi Morton said coolly. "But it will probably lead you up a blind alley."

"Why's that?"

Morton squinted his already half-closed eyes. "Because the Witherspoon King who descended the stairs was not the real Mr. King."

"An impostor," Charles Lanier echoed. "And a very credible imitation he was. The real Mr. King was an honoree at an insurance symposium twenty blocks south of here. He was with eighty other men at the moment Mr. Pinckney was murdered. One of the members had read about the dinner and award a few days earlier and thought it quite strange that the man would be lingering in the club here only half an hour before the dinner was to start. Then he saw the same fellow pass through the foyer in a great hurry at about twenty to eight and rush out the front doors."

John stopped rocking. "Has it been determined if Mr. King has an identical twin?"

"He does not," Kevin O'Leary said. "I've been in touch with his family. But"—he raised his eyebrows, widened his eyes, and lowered his chin—"Mr. Pinckney does."

John turned to Warfield. "Why didn't you tell me that?" he asked in a mock-stern tone, waving the newspaper.

"Well, I only got to the fourth paragraph."

"The killer actually went t'rough a great deal of trouble ta look like Mr. King," said O'Leary. "Expensive suit and shoes, identical spectacles, a false beard and mustache."

"Good enough to fool the eagle-eyed Mr. Champion."

"No," Morton answered. "He didn't enter through the front door."

John asked, "How did he manage that?"

"I'll show ya," said O'Leary.

John was the last to step into the elevator, which cranked ponderously downward. "Precisely how many were inside the club durin' the crime?" he asked the group.

"Twelve staff and sixty-two members," Mr. Morton supplied.

"Those who did not have at least two others vouching they were never above the second floor have been minutely interrogated," O'Leary added. "But I'd welcome you giving any of them a second going-over."

"That will be *my* job," Warfield volunteered.

John lifted his forefinger in warning to Warfield. He looked up at the overhead lights that indicated floor level.

"It's important to know that there are only t'ree doors into this establishment," O'Leary said. "On most nights, the main entrance has Mr. Champion vigilant."

"Cerberus guardin' the gates of Hades," John commented as the elevator bounced lightly to a halt.

"He is acquainted with every member and records his arrival," Charles Lanier said, ignoring the dig.

"But not the man's goin'," John countered.

Lanier's eyebrows knit for the briefest moment. "No."

"His charge is to keep riffraff out, not to observe when riffraff leaves," John remarked. No one replied directly, although the clearing of the New York City detective's throat had a slight trace of appreciation in it.

While the club president shoved back the inner gate and outer door, O'Leary said, "The second door, across the far side of the turnabout, opens into the Ladies Restaurant."

"You have a ladies' restaurant?" John asked Morton and Lanier with frank amazement.

"They are also granted admission to some of the downstairs club rooms on rare occasions," Levi Morton replied. "Times are becoming more liberal. We accommodate as much as is reasonable."

"It is very unlikely the impostor could have used either of these doors and gained entrance," the banker shared.

"And, in fact," added the city detective, "all the evidence points ta his use of the back-alley door. The one used by both staff and purveyors. We are going there now." He led the way out of the elevator to the left and swiftly left again. Within a few paces, his path was barred by a countertop that divided a doorway at stomach height. Directly behind this stood an attendant. President Morton gestured for the man to raise the counter and retreat. The procession moved through the club's coatroom, around the back of the members' elevator, into a small service alcove, through the long wine room, and to an anteroom with hooks and other provisions for the staff to stow their umbrellas, overshoes, coats, and hats. They were obliged to wend through another doorway, around a corner, through yet another doorway, and finally down a short flight of steps to the service door. Another member of the staff sat on a stool, guarding this door. He leapt up when he saw Levi Morton and Charles Lanier.

"It's all right, Albert," Morton said.

"Alvin, sir."

"Sorry."

O'Leary turned and smiled at the group. "I'm surprised I remembered every turn. A regular rabbit warren behind all the grandness, eh?" He pushed the sturdy outer door open. "Here is where our murderer gained entry. He got in posing as a delivery man from Europa Wines and Spirits. It's a top-end booze shop that stocks the best vintages, bubbles, and blends for the rich."

"He acted so sure of himself," Alvin defended.

"How so?" John asked.

"He walked in complaining loudly about having to make a delivery at night."

"When was that?"

"A little after seven o'clock." The old, stoop-shouldered staff member winced at having to recall his failure one more time. "I was just about to ask him where the regular gent from Europa was when he shoved an order form in my face, said he was new, and asked where he should deliver three cases of Moët for the Rebecca Childers coming-out party. Well, that party is going full swing as we speak, so I figured he had to be genuine." The old man shrugged. "I gave him directions to the wine room but told him he'd have to seek out the sommelier to get his bill signed. He said the order was fully paid already. With that, he dashes outside and grabs a hand truck. On it are three wooden cases from France." He looked at John Le Brun, the man studying him most intently, and asked, "I mean, would you suspect someone who was delivering so much valuable champagne?"

"I probably would not," John told him, eliciting a wan smile. "Was the champagne genuine?"

"It was," O'Leary verified. "Today we checked every shop in the city that stocks French champagne. The only ones that have sold t'ree cases or more of Moët this month sold 'em ta established customers. No off-the-street citizens ordered such quantity. He must have gotten his cases one by one, from various places over a period of time."

"You might check those established customers and see if they have three cases missin' from their stock," John suggested. He showed the doorkeeper the copy of the *Herald* that he held. "And did he look like this?"

The staff man glanced at the photograph of Witherspoon King.

"He did. Except without the spectacles, beard, and mustache. He was burly. About five foot ten. Jowls. Thinning brown hair. A pug nose."

"Was the invoice left behind?" John asked the detective.

"Yes. A very credible forgery. We're trying ta ascertain where it was printed, but that's a tall order in this city. Lots of little presses run illegally, ta avoid taxes. We can make many assumptions from this point," O'Leary said. "The first is that he rolled his hand truck inta the wine room and deposited two of the cases there. They were found on the floor, just inside the door. The t'ird case—which was no doubt on the bottom should his delivery be scrutinized—went with him down into the bowels of the building."

"You found the case empty," John said.

"No. His delivery duds were in it."

"Right. You have the articles locked up?"

"At the station house. You're welcome ta see them whenever you've a mind, but they're remarkably free of clues. Handmade stuff."

"Fingerprints on the bottles or hand truck?"

O'Leary shook his head. "We checked. He came in wearing t'in work gloves. The smarter criminals are hearing about fingerprinting and being careful."

John started back toward the wine room, causing the other men to follow him. Over his shoulder, he said, "So, he drops off his excuse for getting into the club, then nips downstairs with the bottom case to find a place to change into his disguise."

"There are several dark nooks down there," said O'Leary. "Again, not a clue left behind except for the case and the duds."

"And how does a man dressed like a member get back upstairs from the staff area without arousin' attention?" When no one answered, John paused and turned.

The two club men stared at O'Leary. He said, "Pure nerve. Let me show ya what I t'ink." He pressed past John, went out the door on the opposite end of the wine room, made a quick left, then a right. "It's possible he knew he could only get out inta the lobby by going t'rough the coatroom attendant. Did ya notice a single door between the stairs in the central hall?"

"Yes," John said.

"He couldn't risk that entrance either, because it's just on the other side of the door that Alvin guards. So what's left ta him? Here's the service elevator. It goes down ta the basement. Now, the kitchen and dining rooms are up on the t'ird floor, so the staff traffic by elevator from Floor One to Floor Two is lighter than one might expect. I watched the flow for ten minutes or so while waiting for you gentlemen. He took the lift up ta the second floor, exited quickly, and made his way down ta where he wanted ta be via the grand staircase. Who should be standing at the bottom of the steps but his victim? The two strike up a conversation that others observe. Very quick one, they tell me. The murderer turns around and begins climbing, with Mr. Pinckney right beside him. I doubt if they climbed all the way ta the fourth floor. More likely, they got in the elevator on the second."

John lowered his head in thought. The other four men waited for his next words.

"But no one saw the murder. Everyone *assumes* it's done by this King impostor." He emphasized his statements by giving O'Leary and Tidewell hard looks. "We must keep our minds open to other possibilities, however remote, as we pursue this path. Let's go into the main hall and climb those stairs," John said.

"You younger men do that," Levi Morton said. "I'm superfluous from here on. Good hunting, Mr. Le Brun."

"Thank you, sir," John replied.

When the four remaining men stood on the second-story promenade that ran around the outside of the Great Hall, John said, "If I were the killer, I wouldn't risk gettin' into any elevator once I'd committed the crime. There is always the chance the machine or the electricity would fail. He did not reclaim his work clothes and use the same door he entered through. Too much time had elapsed. He had to believe that Mr. Alvin would tire of waitin' for his reappearance and alert the rest of the staff. If he chose the ladies' entrance for his escape, he would have stood out like a sore thumb. He must have walked out the front door just as brazen as Beelzebub. Which conforms to what that one member saw."

"So, what will be your next step?" Charles Lanier asked.

"Out that door with just the same speed," John replied, "unless I speak with J. Pierpont Morgan. He is in this building, is he not?"

"Yes, he is," said Lanier.

Le Brun already knew the answer to his question. He had insulted the club several times in front of its president, and the man had swallowed the pointed words in silence. Levi Morton was not the man who had decided to bring John Le Brun from Georgia, and he would not be the one to dismiss him, no matter the insults. "Then would you please let Mr. Morgan know that my handlin' of this case rests on his meetin' with me."

Lanier worked to keep his smile from growing too large. "I told him you would insist."

"You have not risen to your place in life by luck, Mr. Lanier."

Lanier dipped his head. "Not by luck *alone,* Mr. Le Brun." He looked at the sheriff and the city detective. "Gentlemen, why don't you wait in the library?" He pointed east.

John touched Warfield on the shoulder. "You know where to find the society columns in all the New York papers. Check back through the past week and find which ones mention Mr. King bein' honored at that party."

The sheriff nodded and started off with vigor, followed by the city detective.

John turned again to Lanier. " 'Lay on, Macduff,' " he said.

They walked west, toward the Central Park side of the floor. "He's in the Writing and Reading Room," Lanier told John. "It's the second door. Just there."

John entered the room alone. It was less ornately decorated than the first-floor rooms, but it still shouted of money. The windows were large, looking upon a line of stately street lanterns and dark trees beyond. Several cabinets stood between the windows. A large fireplace occupied the northeast corner. Tables had been arranged around the space, with tufted leather chairs buttressing either side. Banker's lamps threw puddles of light on the tables' multilacquered surfaces.

"My whole house would fit in here," John observed from the doorway.

John Pierpont Morgan sat at one of the tables. He looked up from his newspaper. A cigar glowed from beneath his linen-colored walrus mustache. The custom-made smoke's red tip reinforced the rugose color of the man's grossly misshapen nose. His eyebrows remained as dark as they were the first time John had met the titan of finance, seven years earlier; his eyes were just as piercing and intelligent as John remembered.

Morgan set down the paper and stood with a grunt. He had lost a little height, so that he now stood less than six feet tall, but his girth was just as great. He was a man long unused to physical labor. John noted the blackness of the financier's suit. Where he hailed from, such a suit would have been worn only by an undertaker.

"Mr. Le Brun," Morgan said in his booming voice, without bothering to come around the table.

"Mr. Morgan."

Morgan gestured for John to take the chair directly across from where he stood. "We assumed when you got on the train that you had accepted this case." He sat again.

John circled behind the chair and placed first one then the other hand lightly upon its back. "Not at all. I agreed to come and have a look-see. Y'all were so intent on gettin' me on that late train that there wasn't time to discuss anythin' else. Perhaps if you had telephoned on your own behalf I might have made that clear."

The cigar was less than half its original length. Morgan plucked it from his mouth and ground it to death in a nearby ashtray. "Is this to be between you and me, or between us and a murderer?"

"Well, you and me don't exactly exchange Christmas cards," John said, giving his left ear a casual scratch.

Morgan held his celebrated temper in check. "You need to put the past behind you. Will it help if I admit you were right and I wrong down on Jekyl Island?"

John sat by throwing his right leg over the arm of the chair, then dropping himself onto its cushion. "It might help *you*."

Morgan did not rise to the bait. His voice and appearance remained calm. "You were summoned because you are the best man for this job. I recommended you, but from this point on I am stepping back from the affair. Let me be crystal clear: It is this club, not I, who needs your talents."

Le Brun cleared his throat. "The fact is I am not an admirer of clubs. Not this kind of club anyway. I find them pretentious, snobbishly exclusive, and self-serving. And what truly irritates me is that you again want a crime solved not to punish the murderer but to protect one of your creations."

The prolonged frontal attack finally compelled a reaction. The muscles worked under the loose skin of Morgan's throat. "You're right. I do want it protected. But not for selfish reasons. If it were possible for you to remove the cataracts of your prejudice, you'd see that this organization serves as an important incubator. It is a common meeting ground where men of accomplishment and vision plan this nation's destiny."

John crossed one leg over the other. "Foolish me. I thought that happened inside the Capitol buildin' in Washington."

"You're not half that naive," Morgan affirmed, having regained his equilibrium. "The death of a member is heinous enough; attacking a bastion of capitalism compounds the crime. It's a very interesting case. The sort a man with your skills lives and breathes for."

"Don't think I couldn't walk away from it."

Morgan flicked off the table a mote invisible to John. "I understand why you would. This was done by a very clever man. He won't be easy to catch. After your triumphs on Jekyl Island and in London, why risk your reputation?"

"A better fellow than you has already tried that ploy with me."

The most powerful man in America leaned forward across the desk. His resonant voice softened to an intimate tone. "But you're still here, aren't you? And you asked to speak with me. So, what precisely do you want?"

Without hesitation, Le Brun answered, "You recently gave a young photographer a five-thousand-dollar tip for not wasting your time durin' a sittin'."

"Mr. Steichen. Another legend begins. It was five hundred," Morgan replied. "Is five thousand your price?"

"No. If I said ten thousand, you still wouldn't blink. You want this club protected for unselfish reasons? I'd like to help you define that unselfishness."

Morgan shook his head slowly and offered a slight smile. "You *will* insist on making this personal. What's in your head?"

"When I solve this case, you shall personally conduct me to Philadelphia on the current version of your yacht."

Morgan gave an appreciative grunt. "My time is indeed worth more than money to me."

"We shall play chess while we sail. Best of three games. And I do mean best. No headaches, like the one you developed on Jekyl Island. I will allow you a reasonable period of time to fulfill this obligation. If you cannot agree, I will turn around for Georgia tonight."

"You want *no* money?"

"Oh, I didn't say that. Your offer of one hundred per day is more than fair. You will also pay the one-hundred-dollar bonus to my associate, Mr. Tidewell, for his troubles. We should not suffer if you can't make your trains run accordin' to your schedule."

Morgan scowled. He relaxed back into his chair and looked as if he were actually enjoyed the tweaking. "I am the commodore of the New York Yacht Club. This week begins its annual regatta. I cannot spare a day sailing up and down the New Jersey coast this week."

"You flatter me. I suspect this crime will take at least a week to solve . . . if indeed it *can* be solved. Besides, I intend to nose around your town a mite before I return to Brunswick."

"Very well. If you insist, let this bargain be between you and me and not the club." J. P. Morgan extended his hand across the table. Le Brun accepted it. "But *I* must insist that you misunderstand me, sir. When I seek control, it is for a purpose greater than my own. My aim is to develop your country and mine into the world's preeminent power, so that we may extend the blessings of democracy everywhere. This club is a tool for that end. I want it protected for greater reasons than my own vanity. You are my best chance of doing that."

"I will accept you at your word." John stood. "You and I now have a verbal deal."

"My word is my bond," Morgen vowed.

"As is mine."

Morgan rose from his chair. "A large part of your value, Mr. Le Brun, is your proven discretion."

"I'm not sure that will count for much, Mr. Morgan. From the newspapers we picked up in Pennsylvania Station, I would say members of this club are not nearly as anxious as you to protect its reputation."

"You're right. Some men cannot keep their mouths shut. You are fashioned of better cloth."

John said no more on the subject. He knew he would not be talking to any reporters about the case. But his intention was to consult with the prince of newsmen, the editor of the *World.*

Joseph Pulitzer was the most unusual member of the Jekyl Island Club. As a Hungarian immigrant Jew and a member of the press, he should have had no chance for membership in the Anglo-Saxon, Protestant symbol of exclusion. Some said the other ninety-nine members—men like Lanier, Morgan, the Cranes, John D. Rockefeller, the Goulds—liked the irony; Pulitzer had grown so rich attacking the wealthy and privileged that they were the only ones with whom he could associate. Others said that his acceptance was the embodiment of the old adage "Keep your friends close and your enemies closer." Whatever the case, he had been a godsend to Le Brun during the Jekyl Island investigation, willing to deploy from a distance the full force of his staff in uncovering vital facts. John anticipated that he would again require such help, in a city where his own trustworthy resources were limited to Warfield Tidewell. Pulitzer would insist on knowing everything John knew in return for his help. Consequently, the whole story would eventually be out on the street, no matter what J. P. Morgan wanted.

Morgan pulled a cigar from his breast pocket. "From my plantation in Havana. Enjoy it."

"I shall. Good evenin'." John left Morgan standing in the doorway. He worked his way toward the club library by means of a circuitous route, stopping first in the Small Card Room, then the Large Card Room, then the Billiard Room. Each was quite filled with members. The talk was lively, and John had no doubt it was about the murder. He counted more than seventy men in the three rooms. The number was greater than the total of members in the entire club the night the murder had been committed. Sixty-two men in a structure this huge seemed to John an alarmingly low figure.

When he entered the library, he found only Charles Lanier, Kevin O'Leary, and Warfield Tidewell. Apparently, the many printed admonitions against talk had convinced the gossipmongers to collect elsewhere.

"Well?" Warfield said, closing the distance to the door. "Did you work out a deal?"

"We did indeed."

Warfield smiled broadly. "Good!"

"I'm so glad you're pleased," John said.

Lanier asked, "Did he tell you that he and I were inside the club when the murder occurred?"

"No."

"That's how we ended up calling you so quickly. Once we heard about Mr. King's impostor, we knew this would be a tricky affair. Just made for someone of your abilities."

"Thank you for your confidence."

Warfield held up an edition of the *Times*. "I found a small article on Mr. King's award. Tucked away in this lower corner. Couldn't find it in any other paper."

John looked at the page. "Interestin'," was all he was willing to respond. He swung around to direct his good eye on Charles Lanier. "I will require a note from an officer on club letterhead authorizin' me as a private investigator."

"I can have that done before you leave tonight."

"Very well. For how many members was this club designed?"

"Two thousand."

"And how many does it have today?"

"About thirteen hundred."

"That can't be good."

"No, it isn't. We actually have as many men from the city as we originally expected. We've had trouble attracting men from Boston, Chicago, St. Louis, and so forth. We had hoped they'd want a club to use when in New York, but apparently they find even the reduced fees too steep."

"And the expenditures can be scaled back only so far without offendin' the current members," John surmised.

"That's right."

"So if you were to lose even one hundred of those thirteen hundred members, the Metropolitan Club would be in trouble."

"What's your point, Mr. Le Brun?"

John guided Lanier away from the other two men and lowered his voice. "Mr. Pinckney has been campaignin' to create another club. If that club were born, it could conceivably yank away that hundred members."

Lanier nodded his understanding. "First of all, with men like myself and Mr. Morgan willing to underwrite losses, we would have to lose three hundred members before we were in serious financial straits. Second, many men belong to more than one club. If they joined a new club, it wouldn't necessarily follow that they would give up their memberships here."

"I understand. I was educated to that fact in London."

"Which brings us to the third point. There is, in fact, a history of new clubs developing out of old ones without the old ones disappearing. In the late 1860s, a dispute among members of the Union Club resulted in the formation of the Knickerbocker. Yet the Union went on to greater strength. Again, some problems in the Union Club around 1890 prompted the Metropolitan's founding."

"Mr. Tidewell keeps me up on these things, against my own wishes. He tells me it was the blackballin' of a minister friend of Mr. Morgan's."

"That and several other incidents. But the Union is as strong as ever, and Mr. Morgan is still a loyal member."

John exhaled loudly. "So I should not suspect too strongly that the motive for this murder was stoppin' a new club."

Lanier held up his hand. "I'm unwilling to confirm that. For all I know, one of our members might have taken enough offense at Mr. Pinckney to have him killed over this new club. It's not out of the realm of possibility."

"And what precisely did he mean by 'an abstemious club'?"

"Pinckney did not smoke, drink, swear, or gamble."

"Mercy! He should have been a priest."

"He was riding on the rising tide of sentiment for a sober and smokeless society. Moreover, he wanted to cater to the women's-rights faction. To allow women into his club on a more regular basis. He was calling his idea 'the Twentieth-Century Club.' "

"I shouldn't think he would elicit much favor among your current membership."

"Nor I."

"And for how long had he been campaignin'?"

"One member said he believed Mr. Pinckney first spoke of it inside these walls six weeks ago."

Le Brun pulled on his lower lip. "Now tell me somethin' about Detective O'Leary, other than that he has a reputation for bein' an honest cop."

Lanier shied an involuntary glance in O'Leary's direction. "He's known to be very discreet. Mr. Morgan asked that he be transferred temporarily from the Chinatown division. He usually works vice. Opium dens. White slavery. Illegal aliens."

"But not murders."

Lanier laughed. "Murders, too. There are murders all over Manhattan, Mr. Le Brun. We are the gateway to the New World, and that attracts the most ambitious, daring, amoral characters on the face of the earth. You were the sheriff of a seaport town; you must know what slithers off boats."

"I do."

"Mr. O'Leary may conduct himself with discretion and style, but he's known to be . . . well, frankly, a tough son of a bitch."

"Good. I like workin' with my peers. I understand that Mr. Tidewell and I are to stay at the Hotel Savoy."

"Exactly. You will both enjoy covered accounts for the next week. I would have liked to put you up at the Plaza, which is just catercorner to the club, but it's being demolished to create a more splendid version."

"This far uptown, it couldn't have been more than twenty years old," John speculated.

"Try seven."

John shook his head. "If I had a few million lyin' around, I'd invest it in New York City real estate. They're not makin' any more of it, are they?"

"No, sir."

John crooked his finger to summon Warfield again to his side. "I believe we've absorbed all we can after such a long journey. We shall make a concerted start in the mornin'."

Kevin O'Leary sauntered up to the group. "Will ya be needing anyt'ing more from me tonight?"

"I think not, sir," said Le Brun.

With a flick of his wrist, the detective produced a business card. "There's the precinct address, along with the telephone number. I've scribbled me own telephone number on the back. My boss actually pays the bill so he can bother me all hours of the night. Don't hesitate ta bother me if something breaks. I live on the island, up in Morningside Heights, so I can be down here in two shakes of a lamb's tail. Stay in touch, won't ya?"

"We will indeed," John promised.

The Irishman dipped his head, gave a little salute, and continued his saunter out of the library.

"Other than your letter, what more do you need from me?" Lanier asked John.

"Have all the Wednesday-night staff assembled here tomorrow so Mr. Warfield can interview them. I know it will be a tall order, but if you could also assemble as many of the sixty-two members as charm and bribery can manage."

"And where will you be?" Lanier asked.

"Out and about." John thanked the financier, bade him a good evening, and walked with Warfield around the second-story promenade and thence down through the Great Hall and out to the vestibule. As they went, he asked his protégé, "What do you think?"

"If it's an attack on the club and Mr. Pinckney was chosen at random, we'll have the devil's own time solving it."

"Do you think it *is* an attack on the club?" John pursued.

"No. If it were, the man would more likely have set the cellar afire."

"Then what should be our focus?"

"On Pinckney."

"I agree. Therefore, when you interview the staff and members, don't just focus on who was where last night. Find out what all of them knew and thought about Pinckney. Whom he associated with. What kind of a man he was. Whether he ever voiced fear for his life." John handed Warfield back the newspaper. "Are you tired?"

"Somewhat. The excitement of the investigation and being inside this club, however, has given me a second wind."

"Well, I am dog-tired. If you still have your second wind when you reach your hotel room, do study all those papers you bought. They may save us some lost time. Now, let's get out of here. The smell of starch is about to overwhelm me."

FRIDAY

J U N E   2 2 ,   1 9 0 6

THE REPEATED SHRILL BLASTS from the doorman's tin whistle caused John to wince. An unengaged motorized cab was evidently not the easiest vehicle to find in the morning traffic rush. While John waited, he stared across Fifth Avenue at the residence of Cornelius Vanderbilt III. The block-long, five-story building was clearly patterned after a pre-Revolutionary French château and could have housed a major museum.

The immediate area held little else but hotels and mansions. Because he had been cooped up in a train the previous day, John had longed to exercise his legs. His habit since retirement had become a brisk morning walk of three to five miles, depending on his mood, his health, and the weather. Before breakfast John walked down Fifth Avenue past St. Patrick's Cathedral and back, a mere stroll to him but at least enough to get his blood pumping. Heading south from the columned front of the Hotel Savoy, he immediately passed a tall building with an apothecary on the ground floor. Across Fifty-eighth Street stood what seemed a white marble fairy-tale palace but which John realized was a number of connected homes done in a uniform French château style. Stretching south to the cathedral were homes of lesser price but still behemoths that beggared anything in coastal Georgia. They were square and built of stone or brick, four stories high, two to a block, set back a bit from the sidewalk, with walls around them just high enough to prevent passersby from gawking into the windows. Looking at them, he was reminded of illustrations depicting the blocks of palaces, temples, and monuments in ancient Egypt's Thebes and Memphis. The conspicuous ostentation had dampened John's appetite.

John had developed a metaphor that he liked to use whenever conversation touched upon the disparity between the rich and poor in the Land of Opportunity. He likened living in America to sitting in an athletic stadium. The ones who had arrived first took the best seats down next to the field. The ones who arrived last sat way at the top. All the bounty of the country had been laid out on the field of competition, and a whistle had been blown. By the time the last arrivers struggled their way to the field, everything had been claimed. Only the most ruthless and brilliant among those last arrivers managed to wrest bits of the treasure from the first. Better-than-average talent, willingness to work long hours meant little when those who had claimed the land— the source of all wealth—held to it with a tenacity that being in control and wanting to stay there fostered. The metaphor never failed to win Le Brun admirers among those newly arrived to North America. He wondered as he strolled along Fifth Avenue how well his story might be received by those hidden behind its walls and grand facades.

At last, a cab pulled to the curb in front of the Hotel Savoy. John tipped the doorman and climbed in. The cabman awaited orders in silence.

"I want to go down to the *World* newspaper buildin'. It's at the bottom of Broadway, just south of City Hall," John said, repeating what the doorman had told him.

"I know where it is," the driver said, in a voice still rough from the previous night.

"Good. And would you happen to know where J. P. Morgan lives?"

"Yep. Thirty-sixth and Madison."

"Much of a detour?"

"None."

"Then drive by it if you would."

The cabman turned the corner and went east for one block, then south. John enjoyed the lack of comments, so different from the chauffeured ride of the previous evening. The blue morning sky promised a day of pleasant warmth. John noted the large number of horseless conveyances compared to Brunswick, Paris, and London. He reflected that Warfield showed prescience in his long-held desire to own a motorcar agency.

Presently, the cab slowed and pulled to the curb.

"J. P. Morgan's house," announced the cabman.

"That one on the corner?" John asked, askance.

"Yep."

The house took up only a third of the block and was but three stories high. Moreover, its exterior was inexpensive brownstone. The surrounding fence was wrought iron, so that windows and lawns alike could be seen from the sidewalks. The windows were large but of simple casement design. As if all this relative modesty were not enough, it was covered in ivy. None of the king of American finance's self-apologetic arguments, either on Jekyl Island or inside the Metropolitan Club, had improved John's opinion of the man as had this view.

"Thank you," John said in a quiet voice. "You may drive on."

T HE *WORLD* BUILDING provided Le Brun with another shock. It was the commercial equivalent of Vanderbilt's mansion on Fifth and Fifty-eighth. Its sixteen stories towered over all other buildings in the immediate neighborhood. It was layered and decorated like a colossal wedding cake. Atop the sixteenth floor sat a huge gilt rotunda, reminiscent of St. Paul's Cathedral in Rome.

John paid his fare and walked across the street to the park. Out of the cab window, he had caught a glimpse of the tallest buildings he had ever seen. His view south was like gazing upon a man-made version of the Himalayas. Even Pulitzer's *World* building was dwarfed by the structures at the bottom of the island. The streets, like canyon floors between them, lay in dark shadow. John realized that the physical evidence of the Wall Street financial district symbolized his country's recent ascendance to Most Powerful Nation in the World status. Pride filled and warmed him.

John lowered his gaze and studied the two buildings immediately to the right of the *World*. They were the headquarters of the *Sun* and the *Tribune*. The knowledge and opinion of millions were daily formed within one city block. He entered Pulitzer's building and danced his way through the human bustle, up to the information counter.

"Good mornin'," he said to the man at the desk. "I would like to speak with Mr. Joseph Pulitzer. My man is John Le Brun."

Recognition registered on the man's face. "Yes, Mr. Le Brun! Mr. Pulitzer left word that you would probably be calling."

John broke into a laugh, simultaneously surprised and unsurprised at the genius editor's depth of knowledge. "Did he indeed?"

"He rarely visits the offices."

John listened to the hubbub around him and knew why. The nearly blind and highly neurotic newsman could not abide noise unless he was the one making it.

The deskman handed John a slip of paper. "He asked you to visit at his home. Fifteen East Seventy-third Street. And here's a complimentary copy of our morning edition."

John scanned the newspaper on his return trip to the northeast corner of Central Park. It contained a lead story about a murder that had resulted from a turf war between the "Five Pointers" and the "Eastmans," two south Manhattan gangs. Once he had determined that there was little new information of value on the Metropolitan Club case, he settled down to read the articles Warfield had clipped and underlined from the previous day's papers. When he looked up, he realized the cab was turning onto Seventy-third Street.

Again, John was surprised. The home of the defender of the common man looked like the headquarters of a great Italian bank. It was not simply 15 East Seventy-third but actually occupied four lots. Its limestone-and-granite exterior rose four stories above the sidewalk and was even more ornate than the newspaper building's. Corinthian columns framed the Palladian windows on the second and third stories. Every floor had a cornice, upon which ran small stone balconies. John could not refrain from shaking his head at the irony that its all-but-blind owner could not even enjoy the view.

John knocked on the door and was soon greeted by a man in an impeccably tailored suit. John offered a greeting and presented his card.

"Yes, sir. Mr. Pulitzer said you might call today. I am Arthur Billing, one of Mr. Pulitzer's secretaries," the man said in an English accent.

From an upper story came the familiar bellow of Joseph Pulitzer's voice.

"He wants to be more inde-goddamn-pendent? He still spends my money. He repays me with abysmal grades at Harvard. But he wants the reins held more loosely? No, put it aside. I will not respond today . . . and probably not tomorrow."

Billing offered John an apologetic look.

"Don't bother sayin' anythin'," John told him as he handed over his derby. "I know Mr. Pulitzer's temper well enough."

"Let me announce you," the secretary said.

While John waited, he glanced into the rooms off the front hallway. To his right was a stylish greeting room. To his left, he found a music room that could easily have held an audience of a hundred. Against one wall was a pipe organ, and toward the front of the room stood a full concert grand piano, with a harp just behind its raised wing.

Billing came all the way down the wide staircase before speaking. His feet made no noise on the carpet runner. John listened for the noise of the street and could not hear it. He was sure Pulitzer had had the house made every bit as soundproof as the vacation "cottage" the blind and hypersensitive newspaperman had built on Jekyl Island.

"He'll be calm by the time we reach him," Billing assured. "He received a letter from his son, Joe."

"Not a welcome one, evidently," John observed as they began the long climb.

"It's not easy being the child of any genius," Billing shared, "but one as demanding as Mr. Pulitzer is a terrible burden. He does not think it unreasonable to require everyone around him to perform at his level."

"A very complex man," John observed.

"Indeed."

They entered the second-story sitting room. Unlike the downstairs chambers, where every item was in its place and arranged for display, this room was clearly Joseph Pulitzer's working office. The room held two long tables, which were covered with books, magazines, and reams of paper. Newspapers, both the *World* and its competitors, lay in piles in two corners. A writing desk sat in a third corner, and a chair with a writing platform was positioned in the center of the room, facing an overlong couch.

Joseph Pulitzer sat on the edge of one couch cushion. He was alert, with his ear cocked toward the door. Despite the fact that this was his home, he was dressed as if expecting to receive dignitaries. His suit was charcoal gray, of a light woolen weave. Across his vest depended a gold watch chain. Large gold links glittered from his gleaming white shirt cuffs. He appeared to have aged more than the seven years since John had last seen him. His red hair had gone more toward chestnut, and his hairline had crept back so that his already-high forehead was quite pronounced. He seemed even more gaunt than he had been in the last year of the previous century. The hook of his nose was more prominent. His fingers looked even more skeletal. Traces of silver flecked his Vandyke beard and mustache. But, almost supernaturally, his unseeing eyes seemed as vital and piercing as ever, still acting as the windows of his intelligent mind. It was the one physical trait that Pulitzer shared with his nemesis, J. P. Morgan.

Pulitzer stood. "John Le Brun?"

"Here, sir."

Pulitzer put a careful foot forward and extended his hand. "What a great pleasure, after all these years!"

"An equal pleasure on my part."

"I often hoped you would make the trip over to Jekyl Island to visit me, but I hoped in vain."

"Well, you know I have a—-"

"Yes, a justifiable aversion to the place. But you're up in New York now."

"My every move is apparently known to you."

"That will be all for now, Billing," said Pulitzer. He was smiling from John's remark. "Well, this is my town. So, how is your health?"

"Fine. I've mostly given up the hard liquor. Developed a taste for wine in France. It seems to agree with me more. Taken to long walks now, so I'm a few pounds lighter than I was years back."

"But we now share a common affliction," Pulitzer said, lifting his chin. "You, too, lamentably, have lost the use of your right eye."

Of all John's surprises that morning, this was the greatest. "Now, who told you that?"

Pulitzer's head moved slowly up and down. "It would be an understatement for me to say I have many sources. Which, of course, is the real purpose of your visit. Come! Sit! Be glad you have a good left eye, to look upon this wretched creature before you. Asthma, nerves, diabetes, insomnia, constant headaches. I'd kill myself except that so many people depend on me." Pulitzer eased himself back down onto the couch and patted the unoccupied side. John moved several of the many pillows and bolsters. "I stay alive to help worthy men such as yourself. So, old Jupiter hired you to investigate this Metropolitan Club murder," he said, speaking of J. P. Morgan.

"Mr. Lanier called me," John said, carefully.

Pulitzer laughed. "Indeed. Why bark yourself when you have a dog? You've been to the club already?"

"I have."

"And how would you like me to help?"

"I need to figure out as quickly as possible why the murder was committed inside that club. Surely, if the man alone were the target, there must be a hundred easier places to have ambushed him."

"I agree," said Pulitzer. "At face value, it would seem to hinge on Edmund Pinckney's lobbying for a new club."

"Warfield Tidewell's up here with me, workin' the case from the inside."

"I remember him. The young man with the honeyed voice."

"Right." Seeing that Pulitzer was at ease, John allowed himself to rest against the couch back. "I want to work on the angle that the club was used as a diversion. I'm sure you can save me a lot of time and legwork concernin' background on Mr. Pinckney."

"Oh, that I can. The *World* has had interest in that family for many years." Without warning, he turned his head and shouted, "Billing!" Then he looked in John's general direction. "It's the morning, but since you say you've acquired a taste for wine, let me share something you're sure to enjoy."

"Sir?" Billing said, appearing with what seemed to John impossible speed.

"Bring us a bottle of that Clos de Vougeot that arrived last month." The editor refocused his attention to Le Brun. "When Billing returns, he'll assemble the notes I've had made in anticipation of your visit. So you can just listen."

John folded his arms across his chest and prepared himself for a performance. John was well celebrated in his own circles for a prodigious memory, but he knew his was nothing compared to Pulitzer's. He likened it to Wolfgang Amadeus Mozart's musical abilities, all-too-rare evidences of the full potential of his species.

"We need to begin quite a way back. The story starts in 1827. That is when Edmund's father, Chriswell Pinckney, was born. In Charleston.

He was bad business from the first. Through various underhanded means, by his mid-twenties he had parlayed a few thousand dollars into several highly leveraged properties and a dry-goods business.

"In 1852, he married Weda Rhett, the daughter of another first family of South Carolina. In her own way, Weda was as damaging to her family name as Chriswell was to his. She was a vocal abolitionist . . . anathema to their cherished way of life. She also did not believe in smoking or drinking and declared that every educated woman should have the right to vote. As I'm sure you will understand, the Rhetts were only too eager to pay a dowry to change her last name. She came to the marriage with several stunning rings and bracelets, along with a few European cameos, worth a small fortune." As Pulitzer spoke the words, his right forefinger absentmindedly circled his left cuff link. "In later years, her prosperous husband would buy her a bracelet owned by Marie Antoinette and a necklace worn by Lady Caroline Lamb. The jewels' reputations provided the pair with entrée to parties and cotillions that their owners' reputations would not."

John glanced at a nearby desk clock, which miraculously kept time without audible ticking. "Do we need to go back this far, sir?"

Pulitzer held up his bony hands. "Absolutely. I promise I won't take more than half an hour of your time. I understand that you are late to the hunt and need to ride fast to catch up. In 1854, a pair of identical twin boys were born to Chriswell and Weda. They named them Edmund and Miniver. A girl was born in 1856, but she died soon after. Sarah Rhett Pinckney completed their family in 1860. The next year, they moved to New York City."

"Weda's tongue forced them out of South Carolina?" John guessed.

"That was the excuse used, and it was not difficult to believe once Lincoln was elected. But I suspect it was more due to Chriswell's foresight. The instant England and France declined to back the Southern states in the War of Secession, he saw the handwriting on the wall. He knew the South could not prevail against Northern industry and immigration. So he sold off his two Carolina rice farms, a Mississippi cotton plantation, his Georgia lumber company, and his dry-goods store and rental properties. He immediately invested in a Michigan iron foundry. He had heard the roar of cannons before the first shot was fired."

"Sounds like a smart man."

"A fox if ever there was one. Later, he invested in Pennsylvania oil.

After the war, he took the first train south and bought six plantations at distress prices, along with a Birmingham steel mill."

"An opportunist."

"I believe you called them 'scalawags,' " said John's host.

"Correct. Turncoat Southerners, as opposed to Yankee carpetbaggers."

"But that was only the beginning of his infamy, Mr. Le Brun. In 1872, he and a miscreant named Charles Howard, from Baltimore, came up with one of the worst scams perpetrated on American citizens. For some reason, the people of Louisiana love to gamble. Pinckney and Howard conceived a Louisiana lottery. They paid the legislators three hundred thousand dollars in bribes to be let in and to operate with a tax exemption. To give the operation legitimacy, they hired General Pierre Beauregard, hero of Fort Sumter, Manassas, and Shiloh, to front them. At least Beauregard had the decency not to wear his uniform, but he was the man who periodically picked the tickets out of the drum. Only half of the thirty million dollars collected across more than a decade went back to the people. I had a hand in bringing them down and in preventing them from moving their scam to the Dakotas. From that point on, I watched the Pinckney family closely."

Billing entered with the wine decanted. He poured each of the men a glass, pressed them carefully into their hands, then saw that John was provided with the notes Pulitzer had promised. Moments later, he was gone.

"That brings us into the 1890s," prompted Le Brun.

Pulitzer was still sniffing his drink and had yet to sample it. "Not quite yet. You do understand that when I finish telling you what I know, you are obliged to report to me or one of my editors the progress of this case. I will, naturally, continue to feed you any new information we uncover." Pulitzer paused with the glass near his lips, waiting.

"As I am hired by the Metropolitan Club," answered John, "you understand that I must see to their interests first. However, I anticipate no conflict."

Pulitzer nodded his head forcefully. "Nor I." The liquid in his glass sloshed dangerously close to its rim but settled quickly. He sipped, chewed the dense liquid briefly, and swallowed, making an appreciative noise in his throat. "The true nectar of the gods."

"Very good indeed," John agreed.

"We continue! Now a multimillionaire, Chriswell Pinckney sought what every successful pirate seeks: respectability. He began joining clubs in the 1880s. Two that he joined were the Union and the Century. Now, look around and tell me what else a very wealthy man who was once poor does to give himself legitimacy in the public eye."

"He builds a fine home."

"Precisely! In 1880, a man by the name of Henry J. Hardenberg . . . an architect by profession . . . built a luxury apartment building seven stories high on the corner of West Seventy-second and Central Park West. It was so far north that some jokingly said it was in the Dakota Territories. Others said that the Dakotas could be seen from its top floor. With both tales circulating, the building became known as the Dakota. Prominent New Yorkers were not deterred by its high uptown address; in no time at all, its suites were filled. This gave the parsimonious Chriswell the courage to build his mansion in the relatively inexpensive 'far north.' He bought the parcel of land on the corner of East Sixty-second and Fifth Avenue. Built the first true mansion up here and named it Whimsy House."

"Why that name?"

"That I don't know. Amazingly, all three of his children moved in. I suppose Chriswell refused to give them money to build anything that could rival the luxury to which they were accustomed." Pulitzer took another sip, then reached forward and gingerly set the wineglass on the coffee table. John observed the many residual stains on the plush carpet immediately in front of where his host sat.

Pulitzer settled back, decided the bolsters did not please him, and paused to do a major rearrangement.

"Can I help you?" John volunteered.

"No need. A prisoner comes to know his cell, even in the darkness. We are now at 1885. Pinckney sells off all his southern holdings and oil interests and consolidates into Midwest iron and steel. Miniver manages these interests. The twins become a study in the power of parental influence. Miniver comes under his father's wing and develops an outgoing and aggressive personality. He is a drinker, smoker, womanizer, and gambler. Like his father, he evinces a caustic and abusive wit. At university, he was noted for his pranks and practical jokes.

"Edmund was his mother's favorite. Through her tutelage, he became soft-spoken, abstemious, and courteous. But note this carefully:

Nature, it seems, prevailed in their shared appetite for female conquests. Edmund's tastes, however, and his approach to women were more refined. What is most strange about the two is that Edmund evolved into a staunch Republican, and Miniver, perhaps purely to take the other side of the fence, became a Democrat."

John glanced down to the bottom of the second page of notes. Pulitzer was reciting a longer, annotated version without having missed one fact.

"Also in 1885, Edmund takes a bankroll from his father, to buy a quarter interest in the three-year-old Western Horizon Insurance Company. It is chartered in California and licensed in Oregon as well. In the next two decades, it grows rapidly with the exponential expansion of those states. Edmund travels to the San Francisco headquarters twice a year, but he mainly acts as the New York reinvestor of the policy payments. The East Coast partner, as it were.

"In the next three years, Edmund and Miniver begin vying with each other in seeing how many clubs will have them. They sometimes bid for entry into the same club, but once one is accepted the other withdraws. They never join the same club."

"Curious," John remarked. "Quite a rivalry, it would seem."

"Indeed. In 1888, Miniver marries Agatha Belknap, a celebrated Christy girl. At last, he moves out of Whimsy House. Even though a bachelor, Edmund follows his brother's example. Those who profess to be his closest friends . . . more like good acquaintances in my opinion . . . say that he has told them he was frightened at the prospect of marriage by his parents' bad example. His modus operandi is to seek out poor but beautiful women who come to New York to make their fortune. Unfairly, women have so few opportunities of profession that a good marriage becomes their best hope. Edmund leads them on with his wealth, seduces them, and drops them when they press for a legitimate relationship."

"Now *that* sounds like a reason for murder," John noted.

"Do you dislike the family enough by now?"

"My like or dislike is inconsequential," John replied. "I can't let personal feelin's get in the way of an investigation."

"I tell my reporters the same thing," Pulitzer averred. "If you have read my editorials, you will find them filled with passion but always informed by a diligent quest for the truth."

"I will say that I would not invite the people you describe for tea," John allowed.

Pulitzer snorted his delight. "Good enough. In 1890, Weda dies. As Sarah is the only daughter, she is expected to stay at home as a spinster and care for her father in his declining years. This expectation is met.

"Miniver and Agatha have two children. They are born, I think, in 1891 and 1893."

"Accordin' to these notes, your recollection continues perfectly."

Pulitzer allowed a smile. "Both of them die before school age. Of fevers." Pulitzer stopped abruptly. His lips tightened, and he blinked back an incipient tear. John remembered that the man had lost a daughter, his favorite child, to typhoid fever, which she contracted during her coming-out party. John shared the pain in silence; he had lost his wife and their unborn child to yellow fever, and it had turned his world completely upside down.

Pulitzer cleared his throat and regrouped. "During this period, Chriswell's drinking, smoking, gourmand eating, and gambling reach proportions he would never have dared while his wife lived. He who gained a fortune from gambling loses it the same way. An all-too-common and fitting occurrence. One day, he telephones the police and declares that Whimsy House has been broken into and his wife's jewels have been stolen."

"And they believed him?"

Pulitzer shrugged. "The jewels were uninsured. Everyone who knew his habits and losses said that he had had them broken up into individual stones and sold. The report of the theft was purely to save face. All the jewels, by the way, were left by Weda in her will to her daughter. This was evidently the last straw for Sarah. Her brief releases from servitude came on Sundays, when she was allowed out for church activities. She found her forte in acting in the church dramas. Without telling her father, she enrolled in a Sunday-afternoon theater program. One of her performances was viewed by a Broadway showman named Benjamin Topley. His real name is Horhovitz. He's Jewish. A romance blossomed.

"In June of 1892, Sarah broke the news to her father that she and Topley were engaged and that she would eventually marry him. Chriswell had the impresario's background checked and disinherited his daughter the next day. She immediately moved in with her lover."

At that moment, John felt as if he had asked his host the time and was now being told how to build a watch. Since a good deal of the promised thirty-minute limit remained, however, and since Pulitzer had never steered him wrong on Jekyl Island, Le Brun said nothing. He was sure the country's most respected newsman understood, as did John from seventeen years' experience, that there was no such thing as too much information when investigating a crime. On most occasions, the opposite obtained; there was almost nothing to go on. Pulitzer piled the sand high; John's job was to sift through it for the answer.

"So now the old bastard needs another slave," Pulitzer went on. "July of 1892, he brings up from Charleston a poor relative of Weda's, a Miss Lordis Goode, with an *e*. She becomes the mansion chatelaine and is still there today. In September, Sarah marries Ben. Her brothers attend the ceremony, but Chriswell does not.

"Skip ahead to the new century. In 1900, our mutual friend Morgan buys Andrew Carnegie out and begins his run at steel. The next year, he incorporates the U.S. Steel Corporation and concentrates on making it a monopoly. Chriswell resists being taken over, to his further financial decline." Pulitzer reached out, found Le Brun's knee with his spidery fingers, and lightly patted it. "He was not as good as you and I at fighting the old dragon."

"Evidently."

"On October fourteenth, 1902, after a second heart attack, Chriswell dies. He leaves the approximately thirty thousand dollars remaining in his estate tied up with his mansion. The mansion goes jointly to his sons, stipulating that one cannot deny living space to the other so long as both are alive. His will says that the mansion goes to the survivor of the pair upon death and that the house cannot be sold until one dies. If it is sold prematurely, half the proceeds are to go to charity: the rehabilitation of New York City prostitutes. I am sure an irony on his part but a worthy cause nonetheless, since we have some twenty-five thousand poor souls plying that trade even as we speak."

John filed away the terrible statistic without comment, concentrating on a fact even more interesting to him. "How the devil did you get such minute details of Chriswell's will?"

"It's street knowledge. Both brothers complained to whoever would listen to them. From whom do you think Miniver learned to play pranks?

"We jump ahead again, to December of 1902. Spurred by a failing steel mill, the drain of the aging mansion's upkeep, and a bad marriage, Miniver divorces Agatha."

This did not make sense to John. "Would that not end up costin' him more than if he stayed married?"

"No. She was mirroring his behavior and having an affair. He hired a detective, who caught her in flagrante delicto. Since they had no children and since she thought her wealthy lover would marry her on the rebound, she agreed to a fairly cheap monthly settlement. It seems her stupidity and self-centeredness were bearable only when she was young and beautiful. At this time, she was thirty-five and, I am told, rather hard looking from drink and constant smoking.

"Miniver moves back into the mansion," Pulitzer went on.

"And Edmund, to protect his interests, moves back also."

"He does," Pulitzer confirmed. "I am not sure of his motivation, but you are probably right. Another consideration is that, since he must now sustain half of this white elephant, he elects to save on hotel rent. I *do* know that by this year, Miniver and Edmund have even less use for each other than they had before. Those who know them say that they are cordial in public but invariably go their own ways."

"But is Edmund havin' the same financial problems that Miniver is havin'?" asked John.

Pulitzer held up his hand. "Ah! *I* can skip ahead, but *you* shouldn't. Be patient. In 1903, Edmund defines his Republican allegiance more pointedly by joining the Metropolitan Club. Miniver is already a member of the Manhattan Club, which is the Democratic bastion. A club to which I and several of my editors belong. This is one way I have amassed so much of this information.

"Last year, Miniver was finally forced out of his steel company. He received a small percentage of what his share of the business would have been five years earlier. Once rebuffed by Miniver's father, Morgan refused to purchase the firm and rather concentrated on ruining it."

John took his pencil and jotted a note on the papers. "So Miniver Pinckney and John Pierpont Morgan are not the closest of friends."

"Mortal enemies is more the phrase . . . at least from Miniver's perspective. To him, Morgan is the dragon to be slain. To Morgan, Miniver is the mosquito to be slapped." Pulitzer clapped his hands together.

"*Now* is the time to ask your question about Edmund's finances. What disaster occurred on April eighteenth of this year?"

John nodded with understanding. "The San Francisco earthquake."

"And what business is Edmund engaged in, and where is that business's headquarters? Western Horizon Insurance not only had its building severely damaged, but it was also all but sucked dry from payouts. Three thousand died in that earthquake; two hundred fifty thousand lost their homes; twenty-eight thousand buildings were destroyed. The losses exceeded five hundred million dollars. Are you aware of the *World*'s investigations of Equitable Life Assurance last year?"

"Warfield kept me up-to-date. He is a great admirer of yours and reads your newspaper on a regular basis." John watched Pulitzer beam. Until he returned from Europe the previous fall, John had had too many priorities above New York newspapers to read the several stocked by the Oglethorpe Hotel. Of late, he had become, out of boredom, an avid reader. Even the *World,* newspaper of the common man, did not escape his good eye now.

Far off in the house, a telephone rang. Pultizer's head swung sharply at the sound, as if it had been just behind him. He overcame his annoyance and said, "As you may recall, Equitable went from returning one hundred ten dollars per share to seven dollars within a few years. They were paying their officers and officers' children outrageous salaries and bonuses and at the same time paying off politicians like Chauncey Depew millions to look the other way. Western Horizon was better, relatively speaking, but they also paid their directors too much and invested in assets that were not liquid. When the earthquake came, they could only pay forty cents on each dollar insured. If your business has just collapsed and everything in it has burned to a cinder, that's not good news."

Pulitzer eased back, raised his eyebrows, and interlaced his fingers, indicating that his recitation was at an end.

"So, I have a number of reasonable lines of inquiry to pursue," John said. "The first is the outside possibility that a jilted lover plotted to kill Edmund for failure to make her an honest woman. Second, the lack of love between brothers and the mansion that stands to be inherited. Third, Miniver's hatred of J. P. Morgan. Then the insurance investors who would gladly see Edmund and his partners dead. Finally, the daughter who spends years in servitude to her father, only to have him lose her jewels and disinherit her."

"My money is on Miniver," Pulitzer said. "He has investments but no supporting business. He finds himself sinking under his half of the mansion payments. His brother stands in the way of selling the place. Edmund is indeed making enemies by pushing his new club idea. Miniver sees a way to redirect the blame toward the members of the Metropolitan Club and to punish Morgan, the club's founder, at the same time. How many men with five motives are not guilty?"

"I hope that's a rhetorical question, Mr. Pulitzer, for I have no answer." John rustled the papers to indicate that he was ready to go.

Pulitzer stood. "Another glass of wine before you leave?"

"It was excellent, but no thank you. I must keep my wits sharp."

The owner of the *World* turned and shouted for Billing.

Before their silent wait could become awkward, John offered, "You have an exquisite home."

"Thank you. I'm *told*," his host said, in an ironic tone, "that it has a music room, a ballroom, and an indoor swimming pool. All at my wife's insistence. I need barely more than this." His arms extended in a broad sweep. Billing failed to make his usual quick entrance, so Pulitzer continued. "It was designed by Stanford White, the same genius who designed the Metropolitan Club." His mouth curled into a devilish grin. "He's a truly amoral character. I heartily disapprove of his personal habits. In fact, several years ago I published an article revealing a licentious party he threw. Had a female model jump out of a plaster cake, covered by nothing but the ceiling. But that didn't stop me from hiring him, or him accepting the work. Genius is genius, and money is money." Pulitzer suddenly reached the end of his patience. His jovial expression transmogrified into one of Old Testament wrath. Just as he opened his mouth to shout again, Billing made his entrance, puffing slightly.

"Ready to leave so soon?" he asked.

"Yes," Pulitzer answered for his guest. "Mr. Le Brun has a very full day ahead of him." John had purposely put himself between Pulitzer and the room windows, so that the newspaperman could see his outline with the little vision remaining in his left eye. Pulitzer focused on it. "You will remember to report in to me often, won't you?"

"I will."

"Or call my managing editor, Mr. Frank Cobb. Sterling young man. I've put him personally in charge of this story."

"Very good."

"Any chance of having Mr. Tidewell read to me?"

"I can ask," John said, wondering if he could describe the house with enough excitement to inveigle Warfield to endure the torture of reading to the irascible newsman one more time. Pulitzer maintained six secretaries mainly because he demanded to hear the printed word at least six hours every day. Most vexing to his readers was his impatience with adjectives, adverbs, and long descriptive passages, requiring them to edit on the fly.

Pulitzer pointed his forefinger in Le Brun's general direction. "Do that. His voice was so soothing. Good day to you, sir, and don't be a stranger. Billing, get Ponsonby back in here!"

By the time John passed through the front doors, Pulitzer was ranting again.

B ECAUSE WHIMSY HOUSE lay only eleven blocks south of Pulitzer's town home, John elected to walk. The breeze wafted the summer scents of Central Park grass and tree leaves across Fifth Avenue. Many broughams and landaus still operated on the broad thoroughfare, and smartly dressed men and women rode prancing mares and stallions with practiced form.

John strolled by one elegant, impressive residence after the next. When he finally came to Sixty-second Street and gazed across at the Pinckney mansion, he felt somewhat disappointed. It was not by any means the biggest, highest, or most fancy home within view. The exterior was fashioned of the same homely brownstone that had been used so commonly from Greenwich Village up to Thirtieth Street. Its first story sat five feet above the sidewalk, necessitating a broad front stoop that split the structure on the Sixty-second Street side. Counting the basement, the tops of whose windows could be seen below a low brownstone wall, the house had four levels. The uppermost one was inset, losing even more space to a mansard roof. Aside from carved leaf patterns in the cornerstones which were already showing wear, the exterior offered very little decoration. The most interesting features were a pair of turrets of perhaps eight-foot diameter that hung out several feet from the top story. Each had bowed-glass windows, but they were so high that John could not see what lay behind them. At the moment, they were reflecting the blue sky and fleecy clouds. Only the wealth of tall windows kept the place from looking like a medieval fortress. John reminded himself that the residence had been the first in the area and that it must have been quite impressive when new and not shoulder to shoulder with neighbors. Considering the price of uptown Fifth Avenue real estate, he estimated that it had to be worth at least $150,000. *About what three common laborers earn in their entire lifetimes,* he thought. He could have filled a notebook with names of the men he had met over the years who would gladly have killed to own it outright.

John climbed the seven front steps, walked into the alcove that protected the doors from the weather, and rapped with one of the polished brass knockers. Each door held a long panel of acid-etched glass with Victorian floral motifs. Enough clear glass remained so that John could make out the advance of a figure. Just before the door opened, he realized it was a female.

"Yes?" the woman said as she focused on the stranger.

John opened his mouth, but words failed him for a moment. He was too intent on drinking in his greeter's image. She was only an inch shorter than he, but she was no amazon. She wore a house wrap and apron just tight enough to define her figure. It tapered from broad shoulders to a narrow waist, with pleasantly shaped prominences interrupting the journey. Long fingers poised gracefully on the edge of the door. Lovely as they were, John noted that they had seen manual labor in their time. Her nails shone with a clear polish. She possessed high cheekbones below keen blue eyes, a retroussé nose, and small cupid-bow lips devoid of lipstick. The feature that arrested John's voice, however, was the woman's crowning glory. She had a wealth of light brown hair piled so high on her head that John expected it would cascade down to the small of her back when unpinned. Moreover, it was wavy and luxuriant, the sort of hair one expected on a girl of eighteen. But this woman was clearly in her early or perhaps mid-forties.

"I'm . . . I'm John Le Brun," he said, finally finding his tongue. "I'm here regardin' the murder of Mr. Edmund Pinckney." He dug into his inside jacket pocket, produced his letter of introduction from the Metropolitan Club, and thrust it toward the woman.

Before reading the letter, she took one step back and gave John the once-over. Her expression betrayed that she had decided he was genuine. Once she had come to that conclusion, her eyes swept back and forth across the typed note. As they did, her lips pursed. She did not look pleased by John's unexpected appearance. She made a small, neutral noise in her throat when she finished reading.

"I'm Lordis Goode," she said, stepping aside and creating space for John to enter. She left in her wake a subtle scent of spring, like lilies of the valley. She had a low but feminine voice, which maintained just a hint of her South Carolina heritage. Her pose was feminine as well and carried with it poise and self-assurance. "I run the house for . . . well, it used to be for the two Mr. Pinckneys. Come in."

"Much obliged, ma'am," said Le Brun as he walked into the foyer.

"You're originally from the South," Lordis observed.

"I still live there."

"You *still* live there?" she echoed, cocking one eyebrow.

"Yes, ma'am. Brunswick, Georgia."

"The club brought you all that way to investigate a crime?"

John made a self-deprecating gesture. "I seem to specialize in club murders."

"If you say so." Something tinkled lightly from her left wrist.

John's good eye glanced down and saw a golden bracelet with half a dozen charms dangling from it. His survey moved to her ring finger and found no metal or gem gleaming there. Pulitzer had described her as "the mansion's chatelaine and still there," but he had not revealed whether or not she was married. He could not believe that such a bounty had not been claimed by some sharp man. But, he counseled himself, his opinion was still based on looks alone. For all he knew, she was a domineering harridan.

A white Persian cat came bounding down the wide central staircase and across the foyer, which was the same size as a squash court laid sideways. The cat brushed into Miss Goode's skirt and continued to wind itself in a familiar manner through and around John's legs.

"This is Neko San," she said, capturing the cat and gathering it into her arms. "The true master of the house." The cat looked boldly at John and began purring.

"An unusual name," John observed.

"It means 'Mr. Cat' in Japanese. Are you allergic to cats, Mr. Le Brun?"

"No, ma'am."

"You're shying back a bit."

"I'm a dog person. When I'm at home, I guess the neighborhood cats smell my dog on me and either hiss or scratch."

Miss Goode nodded her understanding. "Well, Neko is very friendly. Close the door if you would. We can talk in the living room." She moved with an easy grace to John's right and led the way through a deep archway into what was more a chamber than a room. John estimated it to be at least twenty by forty feet. It had ten-foot windows on the north and west walls and a large fireplace on its south side. A pair of couches faced each other close by the archway. The woman set the cat down first, then sat on one of the couches. John put himself directly across. He noted that the furniture, wallpaper, and draperies, although all of quality, were Victorian and visibly timeworn, the original furnishings from a quarter century past.

"You must be very good at what you do, Mr. Le Brun, to be summoned from so far away," the hostess observed.

"I have had my successes. My condolences on your loss."

Miss Goode let her left arm drift out so that it occupied the back of the couch. "You say my loss. Being accomplished at what you do, you already know that I am more than a servant."

"I know you've been here quite some time," John replied. "That you're a relative, and that you run this enormous place. That's about the extent of my knowledge."

"Then you do not know that I have always dealt with the two Pinckney sons on a professional level. There has been no intimacy between me and either of them." Her voice was extremely calm and even as she spoke.

"I appreciate anythin' you can share with me that you feel might solve this crime. I apologize for havin' appeared unannounced. You let me know when my welcome has worn out and when I can call by appointment, Miss Goode."

"Call me Lordis if you care to. I'm not given to formality in my personal life." Lordis glanced at a clock sitting inside a glass cylinder on the low table between them. "I can spare perhaps ten minutes . . .

unless someone else appears at the door. As you can imagine, we've been in turmoil since the murder."

The cat, as if unwilling to endure the interview, chose to rise and bound away, through another archway at the far end of the room.

John leaned forward slightly and rested his forearms on his knees. "I'm sure you've given this question a good deal of thought in the past day: Who would both want to and be capable of killin' Edmund Pinckney?"

"I have no new ideas since I spoke with Detective O'Leary. I'll tell you what I told him. He had had no death threats. He voiced no fear that he was in mortal danger. He had jilted a few women with whom he was intimate. His business was insurance."

"I know about Western Horizon and the earthquake," John revealed.

"Then you're farther along than the city detective was when he called. I'm sure that created many murderous thoughts and comments among policyholders. But if one of them were the culprit, we should have seen Edmund's partners in the newspapers by this time as well. They both survived the quake and were much more public figures."

"What about his campaign for a new club?"

Lordis drew her lower lip into her mouth, then let it slowly slip past her teeth. She seemed to stop breathing for a second. "It seems ridiculous to suppose, but then again he *was* murdered inside the Metropolitan Club."

John had spent a lifetime learning much about people from their smallest gestures, their pauses, the working of the muscles beneath their skin, how they stood and sat. Beneath what was a cloak of natural composure and self-assurance, Lordis Goode was betraying the hem of edginess.

"Puttin' aside revenge or hatred," John said, "who stands to benefit financially from Mr. Pinckney's death?"

Tension now showed plainly in Lordis's eyes. "His brother, of course. And, unless Edmund was lying . . . which he rarely did around me . . . I benefit in a small way."

"How small?"

"Several thousand dollars. We haven't had time to worry about his will."

"I see. Are you married, Miss Goode?"

"No."

"Do you have a steady . . . swain?"

The choice of word clearly amused her. "You are most definitely from the South, Mr. Le Brun."

"Please call me John."

"John. Was the question professionally or personally motivated?"

Le Brun blinked at both her directness and the unexpectedness of the question. "Both, to be frank. On a professional level, I would like to know if you have a close male friend to whom you might give money if you had it, or who might at last be convinced to wed you if you found a sudden dowry."

"Expend your energies elsewhere, John," Lordis replied, reverting to her assured demeanor again. "There was never such a man."

John longed to ask what kind of men there had been, but such boldness was not in him. "Would you say you were closer to Miniver than to Edmund?"

"No. I felt it was necessary to keep a distance between myself and them in order to maintain my position here. I like my job. I love this house and this city. I will have lived here fourteen years next month. Both brothers had moved out by the time I arrived. They only returned three and half years ago, after their father died. By that time, my relationship with them had been established. If anything, they think of me as their sister."

"They have a sister."

"Yes, but . . . Do you know about Sarah's disinheritance?"

"A bit."

"It strained the relationships. It's . . . complicated."

John abandoned his tack for another one more simple and direct. "Are you aware that the majority of murder victims know their killer?"

"That's another blind alley," Lordis declared. "This was not fratricide."

"What evidence can you offer?"

"Haven't you consulted with the police?"

"I don't rely on secondhand testimony if I can help it."

"I don't need to provide evidence," Lordis answered. "He has his own alibi." The edge was back in her voice and the tension in her posture.

"If you mean his presence elsewhere durin' the murder can be corroborated, that doesn't mean much in this case. The rich seldom do their own dirty work," John said. "Alibi or not, Miniver Pinckney is under suspicion." John looked up and around. "How could he *not* be, standin' to inherit so much?"

Lordis's eyelids batted up and down several times. "You need to take this up directly with Mr. Pinckney."

"I appreciate your delicate position, Miss Goode. Every house has its secrets. I will indeed need to speak with him. However, it would be much less embarrassin' to him and me if you could answer this one question: Did Edmund entertain women inside the house?"

"Edmund brought women into Whimsy House to impress them. They were never invited to stay. His brother was a different story."

"Thank you." Out of pure curiosity, he asked, "You showed no moral indignation as you revealed that. Do you consider yourself a modern woman?"

"If you mean open-minded, I try not to judge other people's behavior. Life punishes them enough for their acts; they don't need my judgment to suffer."

John laughed. "And you do want to maintain your position."

"I do indeed. I would be at sea outside these walls. Frankly, I've refused to think about it. There will come a time, I suppose." She smiled. "As no one has banged on the door, I believe I can give you a few more minutes, John. Would you care for a cup of tea?"

"That would be right fine, Miss Goode."

"Lordis." She stood and indicated that he should as well. "And thank you for not commenting on my name."

"You mean the biblical sound of it."

"Precisely. My father was a frustrated vaudevillian. He named me. He was the first of many who've delighted in saying things like 'Hallelujah, *the* Lordis Goode' whenever I appeared."

They passed again through the deep archway into the foyer. "Reason enough to marry," John prodded.

"You seem stuck on that point," Lordis returned. "Are you hunting for a wife?"

"I *am* single," John admitted. "Have been for a very long time. But I can't deny that I think of connubial bliss when confronted by a woman of both beauty and brains."

Lordis lifted her head a degree and smiled. "That is the one thing that I do miss about the South: the flattery of its men."

"Oh, I'm no flatterer; I'm bluntly direct." John looked up at the balcony rail that ran around the sides of the second floor. He spotted a blond, square-faced girl-woman in a maid's uniform. The moment she was seen, she stepped back out of view.

"Well, that's not southern. But it is a compliment," Lordis observed.

They had crossed the foyer and were walking through an identically deep archway into a library. John noted that, again, the furnishings were grand and well maintained but old. Midmorning sunlight poured through the windows that flanked a medium-sized fireplace, making the library seem more friendly than had the gargantuan living room.

"Were you anxious to leave the South?" John asked.

"No. I was a typical South Carolina girl, loathing the Yankees. I had no desire to visit New York City, much less live here. But, like my relative, Weda, I was a very opinionated and outspoken young lady. As you have noted, too modern for the South. I was, to speak plainly, a constant embarrassment to my family. No young man of quality would have such an independent, sassy female for a wife. So they shipped me north. It was a trial move, actually. Do you play chess?"

John had paused to look at a chessboard on a table in front of one of the library windows, causing Lordis to halt as well. He had taken a couple steps toward it while she was speaking, as if magnetically drawn.

"I do." John saw that the board was set up for an endgame, the black side maintaining its king, two pawns, a bishop, and a knight. White's survivors were its king, a rook, and three pawns. One of the pawns was close to promotion.

"Checkmate in five moves," Lordis declared. "For which side?"

John walked up close to the board. He studied it for almost a minute. "Who moves next?"

"Black."

"The answer, then, is black. But I believe it will take seven."

"Black is correct, but seven is not."

"Can you show me?" John asked. "I have the positions memorized, so you won't have any trouble replacin' them."

"Oh, I would have no trouble," Lordis said. "I've been staring at that board off and on for more than three and half years." Lordis made the requisite moves, pausing for a few seconds between each so that John could assess the possibilities for white.

"I'll be confounded. You're right! Were you playin' this game at that time?"

"Yes. With Chriswell Pinckney. On October second. His first heart attack halted the play where you see it. He died of a second attack on October fourteenth."

"And you were black?"

"I was. It would have been only the third time I beat him in many years of play. I sometimes fear the prospect of the loss gave him the attack."

John replaced the pieces in their original positions. "But you know in truth that his habits caused his death. Did he play much?"

"As often as he could once he was retired. He used to walk across the street to the miniature yacht basin, where there are chess tables and some extraordinarily talented players. He also entertained certified masters from time to time. He even paid a grand master to play him in a private series of five games. He tied two of the games."

John finished replacing the pieces where they had been. "Who was the grand master?"

"A man named Harry Pillsbury."

John looked at the woman with even more admiration in his eyes. "You met Harry Pillsbury?"

"I did. Very nice gentleman."

"And you beat a man three times who tied Pillsbury twice?"

"Two times. This would have been the third." Lordis centered the rook on its square. "But I haven't played since."

"If I can finish this investigation in quick order, would you consider playin' me?"

Lordis regarded John with an equally new regard. "I'll just bet you're no slouch."

"You'll have to try me to see."

"If you solve the case. Now you have a new incentive." Lordis looked down at the leather armchair on her side of the table. She lifted its antimacassar and studied it, decided it was dusty, unpinned it, and carried it with her toward the back of the room.

They entered the house's pantry, a large space that served as preparatory connection between kitchen and dining room. In one corner was a stove, intended to keep food warm. While they spoke, Lordis filled a kettle from a nearby sink and placed it on a burner.

"Sally," Lordis continued speaking of Sarah, "had recently moved out when I arrived, to live with the man who became her husband. She had twice visited Charleston. We took to each other there like honey to bread. The elder Mr. Pinckney thought that I could act as a liaison between him and his daughter."

"Did you?"

"Yes." Lordis lit a match and adjusted the gas burner. "Quite successfully. I visited her almost every weekend. Picked up her news and carried it back to him and vice versa."

"But you were unable to patch things up."

"Absolutely. There was no negotiating with Chriswell Pinckney. And he would never apologize. When it became clear that neither would budge, he ordered her to take all her belongings out of the house." Lordis gestured to the small table for two set under the room's east-facing window. John turned the café chair so that he could sit with one leg crossed over the other. Lordis fetched a pair of teacups and saucers and then produced a sugar bowl from a cupboard and cream from an icebox. While she spoke, she ladled one spoonful of sugar into her cup and poured a spot of cream. "I was encouraged to continue playing messenger. I kept the role until Mr. Pinckney died. By that time, Sally and I had grown extremely close. Like fond sisters. I eventually became godmother to her two children."

"An adopted family."

Lordis smiled gently. "For an aging spinster." Before John could protest, she added, "Of course, when Edmund and Miniver didn't try to contest the will on Sally's behalf, the rift between brothers and sister grew to the same proportions as father to daughter. I reassumed the role of go-between. And I am still holding this unique family together." She sat.

"Sounds like a dubious profession," John volunteered.

"Rather like a circus lion tamer."

"Wouldn't havin' your own family be more satisfyin'? You won't tell me that a bounty like you hasn't attracted a passel of men."

For a moment, Lordis stared blankly at John. She rose and had turned her back on him by the time she spoke. "The irony is that I liked New York City much more than I had expected, but I didn't like its men. At least not the sort of men in this social circle. I found myself dealing either with the snobbishly wealthy who thought themselves too good for me or their surly servants and unctuous purveyors. Just couldn't find a good man in between."

"Not at some church, or in a museum or choral society?" John suggested.

Lordis shook her head as she lifted the whistling kettle from the flame. "What I like are men of southern rearing and disposition." She brought the kettle to the table and sank a metal tea ball into the churning water. "I once had a suitable . . . *swain*. Back in Charleston. But he followed his brother to Colorado in a silver-ore rush, and I never heard from him again. I don't know if he was killed, died of some disease, or merely found another young woman to his liking. He looked very much like you. Was clever like you, too." She offered him a devilish smile.

"Now you're havin' me on," John said, feeling a blush rise to his neck and face.

"Am I?" Her continued smile told him nothing.

Rather than dare her unswerving stare, John looked around the pantry. "How many people are needed to keep this house up?"

"Eight. But we have four. I live upstairs. Mr. William Hastings lives above the carriage house, with his wife and child. He is the handyman and chauffeur. Butler as well, on the rare occasions when a party is thrown. There's also Mrs. Lassiter, who prepares breakfasts on Mondays through Saturdays, dinners on Sunday, Monday, Tuesday, and Thursday, and also helps me with the shopping and laundry. Miss Minna Gottfried is our current maid. Off the boat from Hamburg last fall. She cleans and tidies. We have a gardener in when our little bit of grounds deteriorate to the point of shame, and other professional men"—her arms swept out theatrically, embracing more than just the immediate room—"when this old lady needs some major lift."

"Money has not flowed freely of late, I understand."

"That's true," Lordis admitted.

"You said Mrs. Lassiter does not prepare dinner on Wednesdays?"

"Correct. She's been attending a civics class since January. She's pursuing citizenship, and the brothers and I applauded her taking the class." Lordis shook her head. "However, Miniver wanted to dock her ten percent of her pay for the time off. I wouldn't hear of it."

"That would explain Mr. Edmund's habit of goin' to the Metropolitan Club every Wednesday."

Lordis lifted the kettle to pour the tea. "Yes. He ate there on Wednesday nights."

From the foyer echoed a male voice calling Lordis's name. John registered the look of tension that sprang back onto her face.

"That's Miniver," she said. "Stay seated! I'll bring him in to you."

Before John could offer an alternative, she was up and away into the library. John stayed on his chair for only a few seconds. He made up his mind that it did not look right for the master of the house to find a stranger sitting so cozily in his pantry. He got up and walked into the library. A rather tall and thin gentleman dressed in a dark gray suit and wearing a black armband entered the room. His black hair was streaked with silver. He had sunken cheeks. His face was clean-shaven. He carried a briefcase in his left hand. His head was inclined to the right. Lordis walked beside him, speaking in a low tone. When he saw John, he came to a dead halt. Lordis's head whipped around, and she stopped speaking in midsentence.

"Mr. Pinckney, I am John Le Brun, consultin' detective for the Metropolitan Club," John declared, moving forward with his hand outstretched.

The man accepted the handshake and offered a "How dee do." John noted that his expression was grim and haggard. Dark half circles lay under his hazel eyes. This did not look to the experienced lawman like the face of a man who had had his brother murdered. He looked more like the hunted than the hunter. Then a sudden thought came to him. He wondered if Miniver had been told that a lawman who never failed to solve murders had been brought an amazing distance for the investigation.

"Miss Goode has been quite helpful and cordial," John said.

Pinckney managed a wan smile. "Yes. She is the treasure of this house. I heard that you were coming up from Georgia," he confirmed. "Whatever you can do to find my brother's murderer, I will be eternally grateful." His tone sounded sincere.

"Gentlemen, I have chores to attend to," Lordis said, excusing herself to the pantry.

"You do understand that, as the inheritor of this house," John said, "you are a prime suspect?"

"I do," Pinckney said, "but it's just not the case. You need to be looking within the Metropolitan Club, at those strongly opposed to Edmund's championing of a new club."

"Did your brother mention any of these men?"

"I have a list." The smell of peppermint came through his straight white teeth.

"Really? From whom did you get this list?"

"I made it. Based on conversations I had with my brother."

"And may I have it?"

"I have a copy for you. I gave the original to Detective O'Leary yesterday afternoon. You might want to divide the list between you. It's in the living room. If you'll follow me."

As they walked the length of the house, Miniver said, "I've also prepared a list of men with a professional grudge against Edmund."

"Regardin' the earthquake and his insurance company."

Pinckney arched a brow. "You *are* on top of this. There are eleven living in New York City, but certainly someone living in San Francisco could just as easily have hired a killer."

"But not as easily have known about Witherspoon King's membership and that he would definitely not be in the club that night."

"True."

"And how do you suppose this killer knew the layout of such a private club?" John asked.

"I've considered that question. While entering the actual building is very difficult, it wouldn't be hard to learn its blueprints. The club isn't that old. When it was being built, there were drawings in the newspapers and in several architectural and design magazines. It would simply be a matter of a little research."

They entered the living room. John's host crossed to a high table and snatched up two pieces of stationery. On the way back, he slid aside a pair of wide doors, exposing a dry bar that was recessed into the wall that lay between the room's two archways.

"Care for something to drink?" he asked, reaching for a carbonated water siphon.

"No, thanks. I was already talked into a glass of wine this mornin'. That was more than enough for me." John came up alongside his host.

Miniver handed over the lists, then sprayed half a glass of bubbling water into a cut crystal tumbler.

"If it's not a club member or a furious claimant, who else might the killer be?" John pursued.

Pinckney shook his head. "I truly can't think of anyone in the world with enough animus against my brother to do this. That's what makes it so frightening. Whoever it is might actually be holding a grudge against our family. In which case, I am in danger." He swung to face John straight on. "You are now staying at a hotel."

"Yes. The Hotel Savoy. Myself and my assistant."

"That's a waste of money. Why don't you both stay here? We have plenty—"

"Thank you, but we're bein' put up by J. P. Morgan. We enjoy runnin' up the tab on the old monster." John grinned.

Miniver neither grinned nor laughed. "I thought perhaps you might protect me. If indeed I, too, am a target, you could be on hand to catch the killer. Then we'd have our answer straightaway."

"I think you can rest assured that that is a remote possibility," John asserted, laboring to sound definitive enough to end the discussion. "Have you had any conversations with your handyman, maid, and cook regardin' this murder?"

"Yes. Detective O'Leary has as well. No one previous to the murder had approached any of them to extract information. They have seen nothing suspicious. It's such a complete mystery."

"Perhaps if I just fired off a lot of questions, somethin' you've overlooked might pop into your head. I have a carte blanche tab at the Savoy on Morgan's account. Could I interest you and Miss Goode in dinin' with me tonight?"

Pinckney downed the rest of the water. "That sounds like a good idea. But I have so many details to attend to. We're burying my brother tomorrow. There's the viewing and ceremony here beginning at eleven. There's—"

"I understand. Would you object to me takin' Miss Goode out?"

"No, indeed. I will suggest it to her, in fact. Of course, she is her own woman."

"I have already ascertained that. Decidedly so." John glanced down at the two lists. "Oh, and might you have a photograph of your brother that I could borrow, to show around?"

"Yes. I've collected several in the foyer, to show at the viewing. Let me get you one on your way out." Miniver led John back into the foyer.

There were more than a dozen pictures lying on a cherrywood lowboy. He gave John one that was unframed.

John held up the photograph and regarded it. It was clearly a recent shot, showing the same peppering of gray at his temples, the same sunken cheeks. He lifted the picture so that his host's face was just to its side. The investigator whistled. "Are you sure this isn't you?"

Miniver's haggard countenance seemed to pinch in another degree. "No. It's Edmund. We are . . . were . . . identical to look at."

"My sincere condolences," John offered. "Rest assured that I will do my level best to track down his murderer."

"I depend on it, sir." He reached for the front door, opened it, and ushered John into the sunlight.

L E B R U N ' S next stop was at the local precinct station. He found Detective O'Leary sitting at a desk sandwiched into a file storage room that he had commandeered for the investigation. O'Leary leapt to his feet on seeing Le Brun.

"Solved the case yet?" he asked with a mock-serious face.

"I have," John returned.

O'Leary blinked in astonishment. His disappointment was patent.

"Don't pitch a fit. I'm just havin' you on," John said, waving his jest away. "Nobody's easier fooled than the inveterate fooler."

O'Leary relaxed. "True enough. Ya got me."

"Important that you solve the case, is it?" John asked.

"To be truthful, yes. T'row those files off that chair and set yer carcass down, why don't ya?"

John made himself a seat.

"Let me tell ya something about meself," said the city detective. "I came to New York City seven years ago as a runner. A professional at'lete, hired by one of the breweries to win races for 'em. That didn't pay much, but it did get me over here. As soon as I could, I got a job as a beat cop. T'wasn't hard. The Irish take what's beneath the other Europeans: policing, ditch digging, and politicking. I made my bones with a few tough pugs and got a reputation for nerve. That and honesty. I don't take graft from nobody. That got me my present position as vice detective in Chinatown. It's okay, but I'm aiming for something even better. Solving this case would do it for me."

"You've never taken a payoff, even once?" John probed.

"So help me God." O'Leary raised his right hand. Then he looked at it and crossed his fingers. "Well, sometimes I take home stuff we confiscate. You know, hookahs, carpets, parrots, monkeys."

John laughed. "You must have quite a house."

O'Leary waggled his forefinger. "But only because the stuff would disappear or be t'rown out anyway at the station."

"I don't give a damn who gets the credit," John said, "so long as the case is solved. I'm here to compare notes so that happens."

"Then let's get to it."

In a bit less than two hours, both inside the station and continued at a corner restaurant, the two men covered every bit of background they had assembled. No breakthrough materialized.

"You know, it could have nothing to do with the Pinckneys," O'Leary suggested as John paid the check. "It might be somebody with a hatred for the Metropolitan Club, and Edmund Pinckney was the first person to walk his way."

"If that's the situation," John replied, echoing Warfield's words from the previous night, "we probably won't solve this."

"And it's back to Chinatown for me. *Nee how mah.*"

John set his napkin on the table, brushed himself off, and pushed back his chair. "Let's see what Mr. Tidewell has uncovered."

O'Leary yawned. "I'm nipping home for forty winks. I've been at this hard for the past forty-eight hours. I want to be fresh for that wake tomorrow. You know, you can often find the pyromaniac at the fire."

"Is that an Irishman's sayin'?" John asked.

"It's this Irishman's saying."

WHEN JOHN RETURNED to the Hotel Savoy, he was handed a note from Warfield directing that he meet him and Witherspoon King at the Metropolitan Club at three o'clock. Ever since serving in the Civil War as a teenager, John had learned to catch naps whenever he could, so he could work well into the night if required. He lay down for ninety minutes and drifted in and out of sleep. Images of Lordis Goode and speculations about her secrets punctuated the time.

John took himself over to the club at ten to three and was directed to the West Lounging Room. It was nothing so much as a French baroque ballroom. Every cliché of the period, from frescoed ceiling to carved and gilt woodwork, from bas-relief panels to matching vein-marbled fireplaces, choked the room with business.

Directly in John's path stood four men holding a conversation. They seemed at the same moment relaxed and striking the sort of ramrod, chest-high poses that military men did for statues. John had witnessed similar physical posturing down at the Jekyl Island Club and in London clubs. Just as girls who had practiced ballet for many years could not help standing with their toes pointed out, these men could not help carrying themselves with attitudes of power and self-importance. What made John wince was that they were to a man soft and overweight, not at all the sort of specimens who looked good posing. The image of emperor penguins came into his mind, and he had to struggle to keep himself from laughing out loud. Their conversation took a hitch as he passed them, and he could feel their eyes assessing him.

Tufted red leather armchairs were paired in front of each window. Two that faced Central Park held Witherspoon King and Warfield Tidewell. They chatted amiably. Both men stood as John approached.

"Mr. Le Brun, I am Witherspoon King." He looked precisely like the photograph in the newspaper that Le Brun had tucked into his trusty notebook. He offered John his hand. "A pleasure to make your acquaintance."

"And I yours."

"I have delayed my return to Philadelphia in order to cooperate, but I really must be on the five-ten train."

"We will not prevent you, sir." John looked around and saw that Warfield had dragged one of the leather armchairs from its proper place at another window. The group in the center of the room glared at him for his breach of etiquette. He plopped it down facing the other two chairs, and all three men sat.

"Mr. King was telling me that he has never in his life seen a man he thought could be mistaken for him," Warfield shared.

John studied the man. "What may happen by chance and what did happen by plan are two entirely different matters."

"Everyone says I should not consider this a direct attack," King said.

John nodded. "I believe you just happen to look the most like the murderer among this club's many members. You came to New York City this past Tuesday."

"That's correct. I had several business matters to conduct. Wednesday, of course, I was honored at the banquet."

"And you do not recall a man of even remotely similar facial structure and build shadowing you on Tuesday or Wednesday?"

"No, sir. Not those days or ever. I must say that I am now very curious to see how closely this man does resemble me. I wonder if he is, as the Germans say, my doppelgänger."

"Trouble is, take away your spectacles, your hair, beard, and mustache and put him in a dustman's clothes, and you might pass him in the street today without noticin'."

"Perhaps." King's brows knit. "Do you believe I am in any danger?"

"I shouldn't think so. Your insurance firm has nothin' to do with Western Horizon Insurance?"

"No. We reinsure. But not for them."

"Do you have involvement in any enterprises that might currently be considered risky or dangerous?"

"Well," King said, bobbling his head as if he had to shake the words out of himself, "there is . . . You two have been sworn by the club not to let out anything said in confidence here, correct?"

"Absolutely."

"We have some involvement with insured ships that might be jeopardized by this Russo-Japanese thing. I'm sure you've heard others in the club talk about it. We're working behind the scenes to see that it doesn't get out of hand. You know, pulling the strings on our marionettes down in Washington."

"To be sure," John said neutrally. "Anythin' else?"

"Not that I can think of."

"Did you have anythin' to do with Chriswell Pinckney?"

"Nothing at all with the Pinckney family. I cannot recall ever having met Edmund Pinckney."

"And how long have you been a member of this club?"

King thought. "Five years, I believe. Of course, I am not a regular."

"May I have your business card, in case we need to communicate further?" John asked.

King dug into his jacket and took out his wallet. "Certainly. My home telephone is also noted at the bottom."

John clapped his hands together lightly before taking the card.

"That's it, sir. I feel that you can safely put this behind you, except for readin' about its conclusion in the newspaper."

"You do believe you will solve it?" King said as he struggled to his feet.

"Oh, Mr. Le Brun will solve it," Warfield assured, rising with athletic grace.

"Don't get up, Mr. Le Brun," said King. "I do know my way out." He made a little bow and left the room with a slow, rolling gait.

Warfield extracted a newspaper from between his chair's arm and its seat cushion. It was the previous day's copy of the *Herald* with King's photo. He turned it toward his friend. "Not the face of a murderer, eh?"

"It was on Wednesday night," John countered. He produced from his pocket the photograph of Edmund Pinckney. "Speakin' of doubles, I talked with the spittin' image of this dead man this mornin'."

"That's different. He was an identical twin."

"Two too many look-alikes for my taste," John remarked. "And what of the staff and other members?"

"The event was so bold and unexpected that no one took careful notice until it was over. There was one interesting observation made by two of the members. Not of the King impersonator but of Edmund Pinckney. They said he was much more aggressive in haranguing them than he had ever been before. Almost rude. He accosted them without using their names, delivered a pithy lecture about sobriety and women's rights, enjoined them to consider his Twentieth-Century Club, and moved on before they could respond. He didn't even come up that close to them, but they both said he reeked of peppermint, which made him all the more noisome."

"His brother also sucks on peppermint," John said. "Any guesses from them about what had made him more aggressive?"

"None. Oh, I also inadvertently learned that a group within the club is pushing Congress to send troops into Cuba because a liberal faction is threatening to tax farms and estates owned by foreigners."

"They never change."

"What about *your* morning?" asked Warfield.

"Remarkably little." John sighed. "You shouldn't have jinxed me with that remark about never failin' to solve a case."

"Sorry. At least my lunch went well."

Warfield ordinarily glowed when he delivered good news, so John knew that it would be tempered by some caveat. "That's good. Tell me about it."

"Reggie and his father are over on Broadway and Fifty-eighth. Those few blocks around Columbus Circle are becoming the automobile center of the country. Really exciting. Anyway, they are very much in favor of backing me in the agency."

"Excellent."

"But they want me to wait until January of next year."

"Why's that?"

"They've invested in a fellow named Henry Ford. An inventor and mechanic out in Detroit. He's been making cars since 1902, but he believes the way for him to eclipse his many competitors is to build his automobiles on long assembly lines. One man who is narrowly skilled does one or two operations, and then the machine moves to the next station. The start-up cost for all those men and the long building is enormous, but Ford believes they can pay it off quickly by selling at much lower prices."

"That's a novel idea. Profits by volume."

"Everyone wants a car." Warfield smirked. "Everyone but you. If he can get his current asking price down by two hundred dollars, he can double demand. They naturally want me to hitch my star to Ford as well."

"You don't lose much waitin'," John judged. "You're well employed, and January's only six months away."

"That's what I thought." Warfield looked more at ease with his mentor's approval.

"In the meantime, I'd like you to hang around here one more day before goin' home. Aurelia won't murder you over five days, will she?"

Le Brun had been the matchmaker who had brought Warfield and his niece, Aurelia, together.

"Five's the limit," Warfield said. "Otherwise, we share almost no vacation this summer."

"Then one more day it will be. Concentrate on the cabmen who deliver people here. Try to find the one who carried the false Mr. King away Wednesday night. See if any other suppliers saw him arrive with that champagne. Press the people at Europa Wine and Spirits for why the man chose them. And Detective O'Leary tells me that they've started takin' photos of New York's most hardened criminals whenever they're arrested. See where those photos are kept," he said, poking the edition of the *Herald,* "and try to find a face that looks like that."

"That's a lot to do in one more day," Warfield complained.

"Ah, but you're a lot of man."

"And you will be doing what?"

"Tomorrow, I attend Edmund Pinckney's viewin'. And tonight, I hope to have dinner with a woman who I suspect is hidin' somethin'. As Pulitzer calls her, 'the chatelaine of Whimsy House.' "

"Pulitzer," Warfield said with distaste. "How is the fire breather?"

"Askin' for you to read to him."

"No chance. I have more than enough to do for you."

JOHN CONSULTED HIS WATCH from under a lamppost on East Sixty-second Street. The time was quarter to six, hardly a fashionable hour to arrive to ask a woman to dine out. But he had secured no confirmation before leaving Whimsy House that morning, and he did not want Lordis Goode making other plans. John took in several fortifying breaths and marched across the street to the brownstone castle. Just as he was about to rap with one of the knockers, a large tabby cat, long of tooth and with a piece of its left ear missing, appeared beneath him and meowed loudly.

"Another one, eh?" John remarked. "Well, as one old tomcat to another, give me some room." He let the knocker fall and brushed his suit with his open palms while the tabby paced.

Again, a female figure advanced from the other side of the frosted window glass. Lordis opened the door. Gone were her work dress and apron. In their place, she wore a dazzling white shirtwaist blouse with an extremely narrow waist and puffed sleeves. A line of golden buttons ran up its left side, angled across her clavicle, and followed the cloth up to just below her chin. She wore a navy skirt with an elaborately embroidered center panel. Pointed-toe blue patent leather shoes with faux diamond motifs peaked out from under the skirt. If there had been a wife or sister in the house, John would have suspected that Lordis had raided a closet. It was not a housekeeper's outfit.

"Waif!" Lordis exclaimed, looking down at the cat. "No one heard you at the pantry door?"

The cat did not pause to reply but ran around Lordis and disappeared into the library.

"He's a neighborhood cat. Makes the rounds but seems to prefer our fare the most. Come in."

"You look beautiful," John said. "I mean, even more beautiful than this morning."

"Why, thank you, sir! Miniver told me you had invited me to dine, but he neglected to get the time."

"My fault. I neglected to give it to him. If I'm too early—"

"I'm frankly too hungry to wait until eight."

"You're very gracious," John said.

"No. I, too, am blunt. If you'll excuse me while I finish preparing the progress of beauty. I promise not to be too long." She was halfway up the grand staircase by the time she finished speaking.

John sat on a straight-backed chair in the foyer, grinning at his good fortune. Then he remembered how foolish Veronica Godwin had made him look the previous fall, and his happy expression slipped. He told himself that this was just a dinner out with an attractive woman and that his objective was to charm her into releasing a few of her secrets.

Apparently annoyed that no food had been left out for it, the tabby returned to the foyer. It sat on its haunches and stared at John. John stared back. His preference for dogs redoubled.

Because of its size, the house seemed all the more empty and quiet. Nothing moved. The noise of the street carried faintly to his ears, but Whimsy House was like a tomb. The living room and library bracketed the foyer with darkness. John felt as if he were sitting in the vestibule of a mausoleum. He twiddled his thumbs out of desperation. After what seemed like twenty minutes but which was only seven by his watch, Lordis returned. She had applied lipstick, and now she wore a matching jacket to the skirt. Although she was not petite, she glided gracefully down the staircase and approached John with her elbow raised. He hooked his arm to hers.

"Do you have a cab engaged?" she asked.

He started at the question. "No. Is it difficult to find one at this hour?"

"Not at all. I'd get Mr. Hastings to chauffeur us, but he's off with Mr. Pinckney. Where are we going?"

"I had thought to the Hotel Savoy. I have an unlimited charge account. However, if you'd—"

"No, indeed! They have an excellent chef. It's only a few blocks. Shall we promenade?"

"I would like that," John said truthfully.

While they strolled southward on Fifth Avenue, John reviewed aloud what little progress he, O'Leary, and Tidewell had made that day. Lordis was encouraging. They spoke of heritage and the southern mania for family history. John commented on his quest for learning about his family background, how he had purchased several books in France on the Le Brun and du Bignon families and was working his way through the French. Lordis was attentive and contributory. As they walked, several women said hello and several men tipped their hats. John's heart felt young. He realized how empty the crook of his arm had been.

"Is there nothing you miss of the South except its men?" John asked.

"Oh, some of its foods. I suppose the cleaner air and verdure. Every now and then, when all the brownstone and cobblestone become too much, I ferry across the Hudson and catch a train up to Bear Mountain. They have wonderful hiking trails there. Excellent vistas. But it's not the same as the low country. Not the same profligate scents of flowers, of the marshes, the tides. No cry of the mockingbird."

They entered the Savoy dining room, where John had a reservation. Once they had analyzed the menu and ordered, John said, "Don't you sometimes long for simplicity?"

Lordis paused from rearranging the buds in the vase between them. "Simplicity?"

"Yes. It must become tedious caring for such a monstrous house year after year."

"But it's what I do. What I do well."

"I'm sure you can do many things well. For example, you are not only the house's chatelaine and shopper, but you are surely its secretary."

"Yes, I do much of the bookkeeping and correspondence."

"More than that," John said. "I am speakin' in the original meanin' of the word. You are the house's keeper of secrets. Such as the one you would not share with me this mornin'."

Lordis regarded her companion at an angle. "You are far too observant a man for me to insult with denial. I have not been totally open with you. However, it is not to prevent you from solving this murder. Far from it."

"But it has to do with the murder nonetheless."

"Yes. I have made a solemn promise I cannot break."

"To whom?"

"I cannot say."

"To Miniver Pinckney."

Lordis smiled with difficulty. "I cannot say," she repeated. "But I am sanguine that my silence will not prevent you from learning this secret on your own. Actually, I do not know how the secret *can* be long kept."

"This is not what is ordinarily meant by 'a woman of mystery,' " John observed.

Lordis answered with a nonreply, still fiddling with the flowers. "I can't stay out late tonight, on account of the funeral tomorrow. But perhaps we can dine again, and then I shall take you on a little tour of the city."

John set the vase to the side of the table. "So that's the end of the discussion about the murder."

"You really do look like my old swain," Lordis replied, returning the vase to its original place.

J OHN AWOKE AT TEN minutes after three to relieve his bladder. Generally, his habit placed the visit closer to 4:00 A.M., but he had drunk too much 1900 Moët Brut Imperial in his vain effort to loosen his guest's tongue. He began thinking about Lordis Goode. To his annoyance, she so occupied his thinking that he exercised his brain past the point where he could fall back to sleep with no problem. He reviewed their conversations of the day, particularly those at the restaurant. After the incident with the flowers, they had approached their dialogue as would two grand master chess players who had never met, sallying slowly and carefully. It had been Lordis on the steady offensive, however, keeping John so busy telling her about London and its environs, about Paris, Normandy, and Brittany that he had not been able to direct more than two questions together at her before he was back to answering hers. None of his subtle stratagems had extracted her secret. He wondered if she had lied and had been the paramour of Edmund or was currently the lover of Miniver. Miniver of the peppermint breath.

John sat up in the hotel bed. Although his good eye could see little in the darkness, his mind's eye saw much. Facts fell into place as swiftly as chess moves against an overmatched opponent. He smiled broadly at his revelation. When he lay back, he was able to regain sleep within seconds.

THE PINCKNEY VIEWING was scheduled to begin at eleven in the morning. John made sure he was knocking on Whimsy House's front door at ten-twenty. He recognized the timid maid from the previous day. He announced himself to her and was let in with no hesitation. Before the maid could retreat up the stairs, Lordis leaned over the upper railing.

"Thank you, Minna. You are unfashionably early, John," she called down.

"I wanted to be here before anyone else, so I could watch them all as they came in," he answered.

"Then you've gotten your wish. I'll be down in five minutes."

"Take your time," John said, noting the fresh bouquet of roses among the several photos of Edmund Pinckney on the lowboy table. He also noted the mirror above it draped in black crepe. The moment he was alone, he hastened into the living room, closed the doors, and locked them. The intermingled odors of a dozen-odd floral tributes invaded his nostrils. He tossed his hat down on one of the many folding chairs whose rows he moved between. As quickly as he could, he locked the matching set of doors on the opposite side of the bar. Only then did he turn and focus on the corpse lying in its coffin in front of the fireplace.

John noted that the corpse's resemblance to the surviving brother was uncanny, down to the streaks of gray at the temples and the sunken cheeks. It had been dressed with a high starched collar and wide cravat, to disguise the deep cut across its throat. John regarded the face for another second, then moved to the bottom of the black lacquered coffin and flipped the half lid back. He scowled at the pair of trousers and the shoes confronting him. He knew that, often as not, when the bottom lid was closed for a viewing, morticians took dressing shortcuts. Not so here. John studied the table on which the coffin lay. It was wide and sturdy enough for his need. When he held his breath and dragged the body over the edge and onto the floor, he didn't want the coffin to follow.

John reached into the casket. He found the body and the silk liner quite cold; at least a cellar and perhaps ice had been employed to retard decay in the summer warmth. He dug his hands under the torso, counted to three, tightened his stomach and back muscles, and heaved the corpse up and out. He had been lifting corpses since his teenage years in the Civil War, and he knew well what the term "dead weight" truly meant. Exhaling loudly, he let it down to the floor with less than respectful ceremony. He straightened up and took stock of himself, determining with relief that he had not pulled any muscles. Then he went down on one knee and straightened the head, which had lolled to the side that had not been cut by the knife.

Undressing a corpse was not the labor that dressing it was, but still John had his share of trouble yanking off the shoes and socks, undoing the belt buckle, and skinning down the trousers. Fortunately, the funeral dresser had used a scissors on the backs of the trouser legs. Underwear had been omitted, to John's great relief. The body had not been embalmed, so that the blood had pooled in the backs of the legs and buttocks. John studied the marble white anterior side and found nothing more than an ancient and small scar on the right kneecap.

As he was rolling the corpse over to examine its purple-red posterior, the doors to the foyer rattled. A moment later, they rattled more loudly. John kept his head down.

"John?" Lordis said through the door. "Are you in there?"

"Yes, I am."

"Unlock the door, please."

"In a few minutes. I'm busy."

"What are you doing?"

"I'm workin' on your secret."

To John's surprise, the housekeeper made no more entreaties or demands. He continued by drawing up the jacket and dress shirt, which had both been slit fairly high in the back. He exclaimed with pleasure when he saw a brown, kidney-shaped birthmark in the small of the corpse's back.

A key was inserted into one of the doors leading to the dining room. An instant later, Lordis burst into the room.

"My God, what are you doing?"

John looked up at her with absolute calm. "I already told you." He stood. "I have found a distinguishin' mark to prove who this really is. Now, if you will confirm it is not Edmund Pinckney, I can desist from this desecration."

"You already know who it is," Lordis said in a small voice.

"Confirm it."

"Miniver Pinckney."

"Thank you."

At that moment, Edmund Pinckney appeared from behind his housekeeper. "What in God's name . . . ?"

"Could you give me a hand in putting Miniver back together, Mr. Pinckney?" John asked.

The man's mouth worked for a moment, and he squinted as if facing a sudden, harsh light. Then he moved beside Le Brun and began the process of redressing his brother. Lordis retreated to the far end of the room.

"When did you know?" Edmund asked.

John expelled an exasperated breath. "Surprisingly late. I must have entered my dotage without noticin'."

"But you never met Miniver, and you only met me briefly yesterday. *How* did you know?" Edmund asked.

"How could I *not* know?" John countered. "Let's see. First, the members of the Metropolitan Club said that Edmund Pinckney was not behavin' in his usual manner. Much more aggressive and rude. Then I came here and met you. Your teeth are too white for those of an habitual smoker." John tugged at the trousers as Edmund lifted the legs. "Was Miniver also in the habit of sucking on peppermint?"

"No. He must have thought it would hide the smell of cigarette smoke from his breath when he was at the club."

"I thought as much." John went to work fastening the belt. "And you, because you *don't* smoke, also decided to use peppermint candy."

"That's right. My teeth," Edmund chided himself, wincing at his mental lapse. "I worked so hard on dressing, walking, and talking like him. Goes to show you how desperate I am; I should have known I couldn't get away with this masquerade."

"You did well enough."

"What were you doing here?"

"I read a medical text once that said that even identical twins can almost always be distinguished by maturity. If there is not some difference at birth . . . such as a mole or nevus . . . one often appears with age. And then the wounds of happenstance produce distinctive scars. Failing that, there are sometimes healed broken bones which can be detected by X ray. You don't have the same birthmark in the small of your back as your brother, do you?"

"No."

"And, of course, his wife would be able to identify it if I made a fuss."

"You aren't going to expose me?" Edmund asked.

"What would be my advantage in that?" John asked. "No, you are welcome to continue with your charade for a time. Keep quiet and keep your distance from the other mourners. Let grief be your excuse. Everyone will accept that. Let's lift him into the coffin," John directed. "It'll be easier to get his shoes on up higher." After they had redeposited the body, he said, "It was a great deal more than your teeth. You must put on your brother's personality as well as his clothes. You failed to laugh when I said I was gonna make J. P. Morgan pay through the nose. Miniver, bein' a Democrat and havin' a wicked sense of humor, would have at least smiled at that, even given the solemnity of the day. You also went to that bar over there for water. From what I hear, Miniver would have enjoyed a few fingers of somethin' a lot harder."

"Yes, yes. All true," Edmund lamented.

John looked around and found that Lordis had slipped silently out of the room. From the foyer came the sounds of voices.

"Saints in heaven!" Edmund expelled. "People are arriving!"

"We'll have him lookin' presentable in a minute," John said in a steady voice as he widened laces and worked the second shoe back on. "At least as presentable as a corpse can look. The doors are locked; we have a minute or two. I take it you had somethin' special to do this past Wednesday night."

"Yes."

"Would you mind sharin' it?"

"I'm sorry. It's very private."

"May I remind you that someone recently tried to kill you? 'Very private' matters are often the precise kind that prompt murder."

Edmund swallowed the admonition as if it were glass. "Nevertheless, I cannot reveal it."

"And yet your brother learned about it."

"In a fashion."

John tucked Edmund's careful reply into his mental clue compartment. "So he decided to pull one of his famous pranks and use your campaignin' for a new club to get you in Dutch with Metropolitan Club members."

"I can't think of any other reason for him to have gone there," Edmund said. "He even borrowed one of my suits."

"And, by his horrible misfortune, he got in the way of someone lookin' to kill."

Edmund brushed his brother's hair back gently and looked sadly at the image of his own face. "Looking to kill *me*. What else could it be?"

John closed the lower lid. "It could be that the *second* man masqueradin' that night . . . the one pretendin' to be Witherspoon King . . . was there only to kill a member of the club. Not any particular member."

"I can't believe that's true," Edmund said, "although I also can't understand who would want me dead. Especially to go through all that trouble."

New voices echoed from the foyer. The doors were tried.

"We have to let them in." Pinckney's hands were shaking.

"I shall do that," John volunteered. "You slip out those other doors and make yourself scarce. When I see Miss Goode, I shall recommend that she say you are quite overcome with grief. Only after the minister arrives and everyone is seated should you enter. Then take a seat in the front row. Talk in a whisper, and don't show your teeth. If you can find any cigarettes, I would smoke one or two before comin' down."

John dashed to the bar. "What was his favorite liquor?"

"Jack Daniel's."

John grabbed a bottle of Old No. 7, opened it, poured a bit into his left palm, and dabbed it on Edmund's cheeks as if it were cologne. "There. Now make yourself scarce. We'll talk after the burial."

Edmund nodded. "Thank you." He took a last look at his brother, then bolted from the living room.

John strode to the front doors, unlocked them, and threw them back. He found Lordis standing in front, blocking the way of anyone who might be bold enough to try to venture in.

"Everythin' is in order, Miss Goode," John said.

Lordis turned and offered him a baleful look. Then she reapplied her stolid countenance and turned toward the group that had gathered. "You are welcome to pay your respects now," she said.

John stepped back and eyed the mourners as they drifted into the living room. In the moments when the doorway was empty, Lordis would take a step back and, in a lowered voice, announce those who had just entered.

The first to pay his respects was William Hastings, the handyman cum chauffeur. He was a burly man, with ears that stuck almost straight out from his head. He had ruddy cheeks, droopy eyelids, and a shock of hair that looked like dried hay. His heritage was clearly English but not from one of the more delicate strains. He held his cap in his thick-fingered hands. He walked up to the coffin, bowed his head for half a minute, then took a seat near one of the windows that faced Central Park. For the rest of the viewing, he gazed out at the vista.

"I thought he was married," John said after Lordis had announced him.

"He is. With one child. His wife is governess to a family that lives three blocks from here. They're up at their Bar Harbor summer residence, and Mrs. Hastings is obliged to go with them. Takes her son as well."

John nodded at the intelligence.

In the next twenty minutes, thirty-nine other people entered the room. Half again that number of chairs had been set out. John reflected on his own inevitable end and figured that even he, hard-edged curmudgeon that he was, would turn out a better crowd than had come for wealthy and prominent Edmund Pinckney, on an island with more than two million inhabitants. He wondered how the real Edmund Pinckney would react to seeing how few respected him. *It has to be insult to injury,* John thought. Lordis's descriptions detailed six business associates, eleven club members, two she didn't know and whom she suspected to be crashers interested in having a free lunch, the maid, Mrs. Lassiter the cook, the minister who had been bribed to say the service since Edmund was not a member of any church, two men from the cemetery, three tradespeople, Detective Kevin O'Leary, six neighbors, Miniver's former wife Agatha, his sister Sarah, her husband Ben Topley, and their two children, Ben Jr. who was ten, and Leslie Lordis, who was eight. The surviving Pinckney brother entered from the dining room just as house clocks chimed out the hour. He stood for about half a minute eyeing the gathering, nodding every so often as his gaze met one person or another. Then he sat.

John had put himself down alongside one of those whom Lordis suspected of being a crasher. He was a man in his late forties or early fifties, wearing a well-worn suit.

" 'Mornin'," John whispered.

"Good morning to you," the man said. His eyelids were rimmed in red, as if he had been crying. John thought he knew better, from the faint smell of bourbon on his breath.

"How did you know the deceased?" John asked.

"Oh, we met over in the park from time to time. We used to walk the same paths. Feed the birds together. I live just around the corner."

"Nice of you to attend the service."

The man shrugged. "I would have been walking otherwise."

"My name's John Le Brun." He held out his hand.

The man accepted the handshake. "Alexander Byrum."

John observed the man's frayed shirt cuff. "I'm a cousin, up from Georgia. Edmund may have mentioned me?"

"Sorry. Can't say as he did."

"Did he ever mention a fear that he might be murdered?" John asked.

"No. But I believe it was foreign communists."

"And why is that?"

"Well, he was a capitalist, wasn't he? They have to start with someone."

"I see. I'm in insurance, just like my cousin," John lied. "What do you do?"

"Me? Oh, I'm at leisure."

At two minutes after eleven, the minister placed himself in front of the coffin. He thanked everyone for attending and mentioned that there would be a luncheon in the house for all, followed by a procession out to Greenwood Cemetery in Brooklyn for those who wished to attend the burial as well. He read several biblical passages about the promise of the Resurrection, then wove a skillful homily that might have fooled the unsuspecting into believing he had actually known Edmund Pinckney. He invited the gathering to follow him in the singing of "I Know That My Redeemer Liveth!" From the lack of participation, John assumed he stood among few churchgoing regulars.

Lordis sat in the left front row, with Leslie Lordis Topley and Ben Topley, Jr., to her immediate right. John observed the loving exchanges between the woman and children. Edmund sat on the end of the row, to Lordis's left, so that no one else could speak with him. The moment the service ended, he retreated through the dining-room door.

As the mourners made a last pass by the coffin and moved slowly into the dining room, John overheard one of the women remark to her male companion, "Well, at least Miniver seems to have gotten rid of the awful cold that was plaguing him."

"Yes, that cough was fearful," the man agreed.

John made a note to find Edmund and remind him of his brother's recent chest complaint. In trying to insinuate himself through the crowd to reach Lordis, John found himself among the Topleys and Miniver's former wife. He figured that a decade earlier Agatha must have been a stunning woman, turning heads everywhere she went. Now, as Pulitzer had stated, she looked as if she had lived hard, fast, and loose. Her makeup was well applied but could not hide the wrinkles in the corners of her eyes and mouth or the bags forming under her eyes. *Ridden hard and put away wet,* John thought to himself.

"Now it's just Miniver in this monstrosity," Agatha commented to Sarah Pinckney Topley.

"Better him than me," Sarah replied.

"Wrong brother died, if you ask me. Well, he'll probably sell it right away," Agatha speculated after taking a deep drag of the cigarette she held. "You know, with his financial predicaments and all. Your father's will did say the survivor could sell, right?"

Sarah stared at John with curiosity. He redirected his attention to an oil landscape hanging on the wall.

"Yes, it did," Sarah confirmed.

Agatha snatched up her ex-sister-in-law's hand and squeezed it. "But the important thing is: How are you holding up?"

"Tolerably well."

The former showgirl blew out a cloud of smoke and nodded. "That's good. Of course, you have your family to support you."

While John listened to the last exchange, he stole several glances at Benjamin Topley. He was a tall, good-looking man with curly dark brown hair starting to go thin, liquid brown eyes, and a hook nose. His stance was rather regal, with his hands clasped in front of him. In those hands he held a walking stick with a brass jackal-head handle. John had noted when he entered the room that he had walked with the cane under his arm and did not need it to support his weight. John supposed it was simply a theatrical affectation, like the large and flamboyant hats and capes that some impresarios wore. In staring at the cane, John noted that the man sported two other affectations: On his left pinkie, he wore a gold ring with the comedy persona mask of classic Greek theater. His right pinkie displayed a matching ring with the mask of tragedy.

Topley had fixed his attention on the same landscape painting John had been pretending to study. Le Brun noted that, unlike himself, the man was truly observing. His gaze moved slowly around the room and seemed to be taking in the furnishings with a secondhand-furniture buyer's eye. John suspected it was because Topley had always been unwelcome in the house and had probably never seen its insides.

Sarah Pinckney Topley looked so much like her brothers that John would have been able to pick her out from among a crowd of women. The features she shared were somewhat mannish, although her hair and dress were quite feminine. She carried herself in a shy and nervous manner and seemed ill at ease receiving condolences from those around her. John wondered if she was like several women he had met who had pursued acting so that, for a few hours at least, they could shed their brown feathers and pretend to be peacocks.

John abandoned catching Lordis for the moment. As he came closer to the dining-room doors he edged over to the bar, where the cheekier men were pouring themselves liberal drinks. Among them stood Detective O'Leary.

"So," O'Leary said under his breath, "which one is the murderer?"

John jerked his head toward the north end of the living room, at a place far from where anyone stood. The two men retreated to one of its windows.

"It ain't Miniver," John revealed.

"And how can ya be so sure?" asked the city detective.

"Because he's the one lyin' in the coffin."

"The devil you say!"

"I'm not jokin'. Edmund had some business other than supper at the club Wednesday night. Miniver knew it and decided to play a prank there. He died for it."

"And why has Edmund assumed his identity?"

"He says he's done it to keep himself safe."

"Merde!" exclaimed O'Leary. "Pardon my French."

"I promised him we'd keep his secret for a while."

O'Leary thought for a moment. "Well, not forever, but I suppose no harm can be done for a day or so, long as *we* know what's going on. This seems ta kill the easy solution ta the crime."

"Deader than old Miniver over there," John agreed.

"What else have you found out since last I saw ya?"

"A whole mess o' nothin'."

O'Leary scratched his nose thoughtfully. "I tell ya what: Let's split up. You hang around here with the stragglers, and I'll go out to the boneyard with the rest. Maybe someone new will show up there."

"Still workin' on your pyromaniac-at-the-fire theory?"

"I am. Often as not when we checked back, premeditated murderers attended their victims' funerals."

"That's because most premeditated murders are committed by people close to the victim," John countered. "Who else gains from them, hates them for such intimate reasons, is jealous of them?"

"All I know is: It works," said O'Leary. "Can ya get a list of everyone who came this mornin'?"

"I'm sure I can."

"Good. Let's get together tonight and compare notes. I'll look ya up."

The detective and the ex-lawman separated, O'Leary back to the bar and John to the dining room, where a generous and varied luncheon had been set out. Try as he might, John could not get Lordis alone to warn her about Miniver's cough. He surreptitiously presented his back to several gatherings, straining his ears to hear their remarks. The noise, befitting the occasion, never rose above a mild buzz. He heard nothing damning for his troubles.

At ten minutes before noon, one of the cemetery men announced that the hearse had been loaded and the procession was about to begin. He advised that the hearse was motorized. Several men moved toward the foyer, to fetch or summon automobiles.

John sauntered outside among several women. He stayed on the mansion's stoop and watched most of the mourners walk east or west on the pavement. Only five cars pulled up behind the hearse. The first belonged to the Pinckneys and was driven by William Hastings. Lordis, Edmund, and the minister climbed inside. The Topley family followed, in a rented machine. Miniver's former wife brazenly hitched a ride with Detective O'Leary, after she handed John an empty whiskey glass without thanks. The fourth vehicle held a neighborhood family, and the last was chauffeured and took two club members.

John watched the procession pull away from the curb and head east. He turned and realized he stood alone on the stoop. He banged on the doors. It took a full minute for the maid to answer. She looked at Le Brun with alarm.

"Yes?" she said.

"I'm glad you answered the door, miss," John said. "It's you I wish to speak with."

The maid's eyes grew even wider. "Sorry. I speak the English not so goot."

John stepped forward into the house, forcing the young woman to retreat. "But you understand English all right, don't you?"

"Yes."

John closed the door behind him.

"I haf already say to the police what I know," she protested.

"But you must also speak to me. Miss Goode explained this?"

"Yes."

"You are Miss Minna Gottfried."

"I am."

John gestured to a nearby chair. "Sit, please."

Minna dropped to the seat gratefully. Her fingers tightened around the upholstery as if she expected momentarily to be blown away. John came up closer to her than either Hamburg or Manhattan custom allowed. He bent slightly, putting his face only a foot from hers. "Whom are they about to bury in Greenwood Cemetery this afternoon?"

"Mr. Pinckney."

"*Which* Mr. Pinckney?"

A tiny sheen of perspiration had appeared as if by magic on the maid's forehead. "Mr. Miniver Pinckney."

"That's right," John said, raising his face and taking a step backward. "How do you know that?"

Minna's eyes unfocused and swept back and forth, searching to assemble thoughts. "I haf been here since eight month. I see how each brother walk, how fast, how he goes up and down stairs. I hear that this one has no cough. I smell no cigarette. He sleep in Mr. Miniver's room and wear his clothes, but he is not Mr. Miniver."

John wondered if the action of the maid's eyes betrayed a search for English words or excuses that would cover something else. He maintained his stern expression and pointed his finger.

"There's more to it than that. You knew it wasn't Miniver because Miniver was your lover."

A blush swept across the young woman's face even more swiftly than the perspiration had appeared. "No."

"You're lyin'. I shall have to bring Detective O'Leary here to speak with you. You could very well be sent back to Germany for lyin'."

Minna gasped. Her hands flew to her lips. She sucked in a quick breath to calm herself. Then she lowered her eyes and gave her head an affirmative shake. "He . . . Sometime, he come to where I live, and he pay me to make the love. I . . . haf not tell anyone in the house when I apply for work that I am married. Often, they do not like such. But when Mr. Miniver want to make love wis me, I tell him. He does not care. He knows I need money to bring my husband to America from Hamburg, and he promises to give me so much as I need in a few months. I . . . I am sorry. I know it is Mr. Miniver dead from what I haf say first. Aber also because he not touch me or talk wis me. I think if it was Edmund dead, Mr. Miniver would haf come to me."

"How many other lovers do you have, Miss Gottfried?"

The maid's head came up. Her eyes blazed, and her jaw was set. "No one. I am a goot woman! I only haf the sex wis Mr. Miniver so I not lose my job. Und because I bring my husband here sooner, so I can leave dis place." Suddenly, the anger vanished from her face, replaced by a pleading expression. A single tear escaped her eye. "Can you not tell anyone this?"

"Whom have you told about Mr. Miniver?"

"No one! I swear this."

"Why didn't you tell this to the police?"

The maid flinched. "Mr. Edmund and Miss Lordis both pretend that Mr. Miniver is alive, so I know they not want me to tell anyone."

John's intuition told him the woman's story was genuine. "I will keep your secret for as long as I can," he promised. "Perhaps I will never have to tell anyone. What else can you tell me to help find the murderer?"

"Nothing." She shook her head vigorously. "I am so frightened. For myself and for Mr. Edmund."

"You never saw a letter from anyone when you were cleanin' Mr. Edmund's room that was angry toward him?"

Minna drew herself up indignantly. "I do not read the letters of others!"

"I see. Mr. Miniver never spoke of wanting Mr. Edmund dead?"

"No!"

"Mr. Miniver's cough was bad?"

"Ja. And he never get rid of it. But he said it was nothing. Only a cold. I was afraid I catch it, but I never did."

"All right," John relented. He looked around and up to the second story, to be sure no one listened. Then he made a shooing gesture. "Get along and help Mrs. Lassiter clean up."

The maid sidled off the chair, as if afraid to turn her back on Le Brun. "Thank you much." When she was several steps distant from him, she dashed into the dining room.

John stood in thought for several moments. Then he took out the blank notepad he always kept with him. He wrote a message asking Lordis Goode to detail for Detective O'Leary the visitors to the morning's ceremony and left it on the lowboy. He exited the house, went to the corner, and turned south on Fifth Avenue. As he walked, he convinced himself fully that the maid's story was just an ugly and unrelated incident. Miniver Pinckney's death seemed less and less a tragedy. She had, however, confirmed to Le Brun that Edmund's disguise as his own brother was fooling fewer people than he intended. John wondered if anyone had walked away from the service newly knowing the truth.

By foot memory, John found himself in front of the Hotel Savoy. He secured a telephone to call Joseph Pulitzer's house. Within a minute, he was speaking with Arthur Billing.

"Yes, Mr. Le Brun. Mr. Pulitzer would rather not make the trip to the telephone if I can act as your go-between."

"That's fine," John said. "I was wonderin' if he has dug up any more information that might be of value in the Metropolitan Club murder."

"He has, in fact. He said that the information is in the hands of his managing editor, Mr. Frank Cobb. He also gave me Mr. Cobb's itinerary today."

"What if I wanted to meet with him as soon as possible?"

"Then he would be at the Manhattan Club. From one o'clock until about three. Do you require directions?"

John dug out his pocket watch and consulted it. "No. I'm sure I can get myself there. I thank you kindly."

JOHN TOOK A CAB to Park Avenue and Twenty-sixth Street. The Manhattan Club was located in a fair part of the city, with ancient-tree-studded Madison Square immediately to its southwest. The building was tall and impressive but by no means on the scale of the Metropolitan Club. It was dwarfed by a structure immediately to its north across East Twenty-sixth Street. This building stretched the entire length and width of its block. It looked to John like a gigantic version of the Moorish Alhambra in Spain. He stepped to the curb to get a better view of its tower, which he could tell rose more than three hundred feet. This looked to him like the bell tower of the great cathedral in Florence, Italy. When he saw Augustus Saint-Gaudens's thirteen-foot-high figure of the goddess Diana atop the tower, he realized he was looking at Madison Square Garden, the largest exhibition structure in the country.

"Going out, sweetie?"

John turned and redirected his gaze to the woman who had addressed him. He judged that she could not have been older than twenty. Her eyes, however, were ancient. She looked clean on the surface but seemed to have a deep-down griminess about her. Her clothing was cheap and flashy. She stood appraising John, with one hand upon her hip.

"Excuse me?" John said as a reflex action, before he had registered that she was a prostitute.

"Going out? Want a little fun?"

John didn't know whether to frown or smile. He thought of the word "meretricious." "Aren't you plyin' your trade a bit early in the day?"

"I work the tourists," she said, taking a step closer. "They're ready for what they can't get in the sticks any time of day, and I'm ready to supply it." She hooked her arm familiarly inside the crook of John's elbow. "That's why I'm called Morning Mary."

"Well, I'm called Detective John Le Brun."

The young woman's arm fell. "Get off!"

"And you can spend the mornin', afternoon, and night in jail if *you* don't get off this street, Miss Mary."

The prostitute took a step back to size up Le Brun and decided that even if he was putting her on he wouldn't patronize her. She turned and sashayed away with hips that swung out a message that he had missed a great time.

John shook his head at the encounter. If nothing else, it had reminded him that he had not yet earned his right to be a tourist. He entered the Manhattan Club and handed his calling card to the front-desk watchdog. A second man retreated into the club to fetch the object of John's visit. Two minutes later, a tall man with the face and form of a gymnasium prizefighter appeared. He was clean-shaven, which made him appear even younger than his thirty-six years.

"Mr. Le Brun, a pleasure," the man said, giving John's hand a firm shake. "I'm Frank Cobb."

"Well, you look surprisingly integrated, Mr. Cobb," John observed, "given that you are responsible for Mr. Pulitzer's beloved newspaper."

"He and I have our moments," Cobb replied through a lopsided smile. He started up the stairs, with Le Brun beside him. "*Many* moments each day, in fact. We're very keen on being the newspaper that breaks this murder. Hearst's *Journal* scooped us on a lurid murder recently, and the boss is rabid to turn the tables. It would seem that Mr. Pulitzer *and* the Metropolitan Club are both pinning their hopes on you." He stopped in front of a man wearing the club's livery, a blue dress suit with gilded buttons. "John Le Brun, this is Mr. Alfred Comyns, our headwaiter."

Greetings were exchanged.

"Would you care for lunch?" Cobb asked. "Our kitchen rivals that of Delmonico's."

"Actually, they had an excellent spread for Mr. Pinckney's send-off this late mornin'. But if you'd like to dine."

"Perhaps we can both eat later. The Manhattan Club has the city's best clam chowder. Thanks, Alfred." Cobb changed direction. "Ordinarily, we are only allowed to entertain guests in the dining room, but I believe that you constitute an understandable exception. Let's chance moving to the library."

"Your club is not as grand as the Metropolitan, but I like it more," John judged.

"Thank you. The Metropolitan, of course, is the bastion of wealthy Republicans. We call ourselves 'Democratic in politics, aristocratic in clientele.' Heavily weighted toward judges, politicians, and the press. Mr. Pulitzer, myself, and Louis Seibold from the *World* are members. There's also Caleb Hamm from the *Journal* and Edward Riggs from the *Sun.*"

"How many members do you have?" John asked.

"At this moment, about a thousand."

"And that supports such an enterprise nicely, does it?"

Cobb laughed. "It does, barely. This club used to rent the A. T. Stewart mansion from his heirs. He was pretty much the inventor of the department store and made his fortune down on Broadway and Chambers. His house on Fifth Avenue and Thirty-fourth was *the* great mansion of the city for many years. I believe the first done in marble. It's still called the Marble Mausoleum or the White Sepulchre. Anyway, the rent was too rich for our blood. Do you know a good club that doesn't have financial problems?"

"I'm not much on clubs," John replied.

"The problem is the exclusiveness issue. Amazingly, the middle class won't be taxed for the benefit of those allowed to join," Cobb said, with a twinkle in his bright eyes.

They entered the library together. John noted that despite being degrees less grand in design and decor than the Metropolitan Club, the Manhattan Club possessed a much finer and more extensive book collection. Cobb noted John's intense delight at all the titles. He stepped back and allowed his guest to tread the hardwood floor along the line of bookcases. The ex-sheriff paused in front of the many anthologies and then again before the encyclopedias.

"Now if your club were in my part of the country, this would convince me to join," John shared.

"I'm glad you're impressed." Cobb crossed to one of the three French doors that faced Madison Square Park. He opened it and leaned out. "It's a beautiful afternoon. Shall we sit on the balcony?"

"By all means." John followed his host to a pair of wrought-iron chairs and put himself down, regarding with a left-to-right sweep of his good eye Madison Square Presbyterian Church, the Metropolitan Life Building, the Hotel Bartholdi, a vista of fashionable stores stretching south to Union Square, the "Flat Iron" Building, Scribner's, the Fifth Avenue Hotel, Lincoln Trust, the Albemarle Hotel, the Brunswick Building, and the headquarters of the SPCA.

"Tell me about Miniver Pinckney and the Manhattan Club," John said.

"I barely know him," Cobb revealed, "but I checked around. He isn't universally liked. We have several clubs within the club. He's a member of one made up of those in the raw-materials and manufacturing sectors. They tend to have a cruder sense of humor. Miniver, however, stands an entire class above in his pranks and practical jokes. Mean-spirited is what I gather them to be. And then again, he's not popular as a party Democrat either. Seems to be one in name only."

"He sounds like he would have had more enemies than his brother," John probed.

"True. Are you getting at something?" the newsman asked.

Despite his pledge to Pulitzer to share the case's progress with the *World,* John was yet not about to reveal the fact that Miniver and not Edmund had been murdered in the Metropolitan Club.

"No. I merely figure that, since Mr. Pulitzer's money is on Miniver as the murderer, he's had you diggin' dirt in that direction."

"He has indeed. From what we've been able to pick up, he could live the rest of his life on what he got from selling off his interests. *If* he lived frugally. Perhaps he doesn't want to live frugally. Perhaps he doesn't want to live in that monstrosity of a mansion."

"Have you been inside it?" John asked.

"No."

"It's grander inside."

"It's something of a folly," Cobb said. "Did you know that?"

"No."

"Mr. Pulitzer said you had asked why it was named Whimsy House. We tracked down the answer: Its builder, Miniver's father, apparently had secret passages and hiding places built into it. He used to tell friends, and I quote: 'Hawthorne's house had seven gables; mine has seven secrets.' "

"But this has nothin' to do with the murder?" John asked.

Cobb shrugged. "I'm sure it doesn't. It merely suggests genteel insanity in the family."

"Yes, we southerners are notorious for our genteel insanity."

Cobb touched Le Brun's sleeve. "I meant no offense."

"Only a bit taken."

Cobb relaxed back into his seat and extracted a slip of note-covered paper from his inner jacket pocket. "Let me continue to fill you in on Miniver's finances and movements in the past few days."

John listened to Cobb's recitation with polite but detached interest. While the crime's guilty party might be linked closely to Whimsy House, it was certainly not Miniver Pinckney. Nor could John suspect Edmund, who had been shaken to his boots by the event. Once again, it seemed just as likely that the motive for murder was some action on Edmund's part rather than the Pinckney money and real estate. He and Kevin O'Leary were still stuck at A and would never get to C unless they could uncover the invisible B. The prospect that he could not solve this crime twisted at John's gut. Failure in crime solving had been rare to him, and with Morgan and Pulitzer expecting his success, he was doubly determined to triumph. He found himself hoping that Warfield had been able to uncover the elusive B fact.

"I must be more boring than I thought," Cobb remarked.

"Excuse me?" John said.

"You're paying more attention to the street than to me."

John had been distracted by the image of the same young prostitute who had accosted him standing on the corner and importuning another man of about John's age. "Sorry. I—"

Cobb looked down. "Ah. Right. Morning Mary."

"You know her name?" John asked with surprise.

"How can a man not who walks in this area? Persistent creature. She's one among two dozen girls working Madison Square. All the hotels and the Garden being here, you see. She's pays the police for protection."

"It's a very sad affair."

"Absolutely. But what are these uneducated women to do? They either find a faithful and sober man or else they're left to their own devices. That usually means the sweated shops. Sixteen hours a day locked in a large room with fifty other women, cutting and sewing clothing. Beading or whatever. Given the choice, I might work on my back as well."

"It all comes down to education and opportunity," John observed.

"So true. And Mr. Pulitzer is one of their most ardent and vociferous champions. It's not just on the streets, either. Down in the Wall Street district they have the flower girls. Some as young as fourteen. They go from office to office carrying bouquets of paper flowers. They go into the top men's offices for half an hour or so and come out with the same number of flowers. Of course, they've lost their own 'flowers' and their innocence long before."

"Humans are cruel animals," John said, watching the prostitute walking down the street with her arm hooked in the man's. "They prey upon their own."

"In so many ways." Cobb slapped his hands upon his knees. "Perhaps we should turn from the sad sights of the street. That's about all I have to report to you."

"You've been quite helpful."

"I hope so. May I again invite you to dine?"

"That's very kind of you," John said, pushing himself up from his chair, "but I really should be gettin' back to the Metropolitan Club."

At the Manhattan Club's front doors, Cobb needlessly forwarded the admonition that John was expected to pass along news to the *World* as soon as he uncovered it. As he shook Cobb's hand, John worried that Detective O'Leary would publicly release the truth about Miniver's death before he warned Le Brun. The case was becoming messier and more annoying by the moment.

T HOSE POLICE PHOTOGRAPHS were useless. Europa Wines and Spirits and all the other liquor stores came up dry. I uncovered just one good fact for the whole day's work," Warfield told his friend.

They had once more been relegated to the Strangers' Waiting Room of the Metropolitan Club, which sorely annoyed John. Warfield looked as if he had put in a long day. His tie hung loosely around his thickly muscled neck.

"It turns out there are a number of motorized cabs that frequent this club for fares," Warfield went on. "One of those drivers actually remembered the murderer when I described him."

"Why hadn't he gone to the police with the information?"

"He doesn't read newspapers. He hadn't heard of the murder."

John shook his head in disbelief. "Not even by word of mouth? And how many fares had he picked up at the Metropolitan Club between the murder and the time you spoke with him?"

"He said he had taken Thursday off. Yesterday and today, apparently no one mentioned the murder in his cab."

"Bad luck. You got his name and address."

"Of course. And his license information."

"Did he recall where he delivered the man?"

"Yes. Times Square. He said one reason he remembered him was because when he got into the cab he just asked to be driven south. It wasn't until a full minute later that he specified Times Square."

"Interestin'."

"But not very illuminating," Warfield replied. "After all, it's the crossroads of the city. From there, he could have gone anywhere. He probably picked it precisely so his final destination couldn't be traced."

"Not a lot of houses or apartments there?"

"Heavens, no! The real estate is too dear. Trolley routes, the new subway under the *New York Times*. Restaurants, shops, theaters, a score of hotels."

"I see. Well, you were still useful in preserving me from all those dead ends," Le Brun said. "Time for you to return to Brunswick."

"Unless I want Aurelia to hand my head to me. I thank you again for the opportunity to explore that automobile-agency deal."

John rose from his seat. "I shouldn't have done it. When the folk in Brunswick learn about it, they'll declare me a traitor for deprivin' them of a good sheriff. I'll have to bring you back the hundred dollars Morgan owes you. Let me walk you down to the Hotel Savoy." He reached into a side jacket pocket. "Oh, and would you deliver this to your wife and my niece?" He held out a beautifully printed silk scarf he had purchased in Madison Square. "I want at least one woman in this world to think well of me."

J OHN ARRIVED AT THE PINCKNEY mansion a bit before five o'clock. Lordis answered the front door and seemed pleased to see him.

"We thought you'd return before this," she said as she ushered John into the living room. "In fact, we had hoped it."

The rented chairs had been removed and the room restored to its normal arrangement. The flowers were gone as well, but their fragrances lingered. Edmund Pinckney sat close to one of the Fifth Avenue–facing windows and was reading a newspaper. He stood when John entered the room.

"How was your afternoon?" John asked.

"Bizarre," Pinckney said. "Not only was I pretending to be my brother, but I was also burying myself. Have you come any closer to solving this thing?"

"Not close enough," John answered. He lowered himself into the plush armchair opposite Edmund. He looked over his shoulder and saw Lordis lingering in the archway.

Lordis said, "I found your note. I've written up the list of this morning's visitors."

"Wonderful. Come in, please, and close the doors behind you."

Both Lordis and Edmund still wore their mourning clothes. Her long black dress was extremely elegant. Instead of imparting the intended somber aspect, John thought, it made her look seductive. It was cut tight to her voluptuous figure, and its length caused her to move slowly. After delivering the list, she chose to move past the men and to lean against the wall beside the window. As she did, her charm bracelet tinkled softly. It was the only piece of jewelry she wore.

"We're alone in the house," Lordis imparted. "I've given the cook and maid the rest of the weekend off."

"That's good. Was anyone at the cemetery who was not at the service?" John asked.

Lordis shook her head.

"So much for Detective O'Leary's hope," John muttered. He looked at Edmund. "Tell me how you first heard about your death."

"I told him," said Lordis. "On Wednesday night, about quarter to ten, two detectives came here. Neither of them Mr. O'Leary. Their purpose was to announce Edmund's death to Miniver."

"But my brother and I were both out," Edmund said, "as you know."

Lordis put her right hand to her bosom, as if the memory were affecting her heart. "I took the news with great agitation, of course, and assumed it was true. They asked a barrage of questions. Few of them could I answer. I had no idea where Miniver was. I'm usually alone here at night. I'm not either brother's keeper. As soon as they left, I telephoned Sarah, their sister. She could barely find her words. She wanted to come over, but Ben is at his theater every night, and there was no one to look after her children."

Lordis moved to the window's broad sill and rested her posterior lightly on it. Her shadow fell across the surviving Pinckney brother. "A few minutes later, Edmund came walking through the front door. I've lived here so long that it took me but an instant to realize it was he."

"How?" John asked.

"He was wearing a brown suit. Miniver wouldn't be caught . . . He would never wear brown. Miniver also has more nervous energy late at night. And then there's his breath and his habitual inebriation at that hour. And the reek of smoke in his clothing. I nearly fainted from the shock."

"It's true," Edmund corroborated. "I had to help her to one of the chairs in the foyer. We quickly concluded that Miniver had been playing one of his nasty pranks and got himself killed over it."

"And then the vultures from the press descended," Lordis added. "Would you believe that they have no qualms about banging on the door at midnight?"

"Yes, I would," John replied, remembering his problems with reporters in London. He recrossed his legs and looked at Edmund. "Who suggested you assume Miniver's identity?"

"I did," Edmund said. "I also swore Miss Goode to secrecy. I'm afraid it put her in a poor light with you."

John waved away the apology. "How well do you think you carried off your ruse today?"

"Quite well, thanks to you. I tried to nod as much as possible. I took a couple of puffs from a cigarette out at the cemetery. I also affected some of his unique mannerisms." His eyebrows elevated. "Oh, and I coughed quite a bit."

"I was hopin' to get that bit of intelligence to you," John said. "I'm glad you remembered it. Did Miniver have a bad cold?"

"He said that's what it was. It had gone on for months."

"He's always had a smoker's cough in the morning," Lordis interjected, "but this began around January and never left."

"He thought the spring warmth would cure him," Miniver said, "but it wasn't seeming to do much good."

"Had he gone to a doctor for it?" John asked.

"Yes. About six weeks ago. The doctor said he was fine except for the cold and that there was nothing the art of medicine could do for him. Miniver said the doctor told him it would help to stop smoking. He apparently laughed in the man's face."

In remembering the people at the viewing who had mentioned the cough, John suddenly recalled the man he had sat beside. "You don't know an Alexander Byrum, do you?"

"Alex? I certainly do. We feed the pigeons together in the park."

"He says he lives just around the corner," John said in a dubious voice.

"He does. He has plenty of money. Don't let the shabby clothing fool you. He's just eccentric."

"Crazy," John corrected.

Lordis shook her head. "I don't know about Brunswick, Mr. Le Brun, but up here when a man has plenty of money, if he's daft he's called eccentric. Sorry I gave you bad information. He's never come to the house, and he didn't introduce himself to me."

"Can Mr. Hastin's tell you and your brother apart from just lookin'?" John asked.

"Not if he expected me to be Miniver," Edmund said. "He's always taken some time to sort us out. Usually waits for us to get right up close."

"What about Mrs. Lassiter and Minna Gottfried?"

"I think they've expected to see Miniver, and so they have," Edmund said with some confidence.

Knowing that the maid could indeed distinguish, John felt little confidence in Edmund's masquerade. He looked at Lordis. "I wonder if you could make me some hot tea?"

Lordis glanced at Edmund, then back at John. "Certainly. The water should still be hot."

The two men let the housekeeper pass through the doors before resuming their conversation. "Was anyone in this house today a big loser from your insurance firm's collapse?" John asked.

"No."

John leaned forward. "All right. Time for real candor. If you want me to keep you alive, you must confide your deepest secrets with me. J. P. Morgan brought me up here as much for my tight-lipped nature as for my crime-solvin' abilities."

"I understand."

"Have you any business dealin's other than Western Horizon that might create enemies?"

"Well, I recently contributed five thousand dollars toward bribes to facilitate the building of the canal in Panama. You know, against preferred stock. But I don't see how that would put me in danger except from some foreigners at a great distance."

In a little more than twenty-four hours, John had heard of three nefarious dealings from wealthy New Yorkers he or Warfield had interviewed. He had experienced the grimy dirt unique to other large cities, but that physical filth felt so much cleaner to John than the dirty dealings that were part and parcel of privileged New York. He was sure the admissions were three among hundreds of plots and cabals hatched by the men of the Metropolitan Club. He longed to return to Georgia, to dig his hands in the honest dirt of his backyard garden.

"That doesn't sound germane," John agreed. "Unless there's more to it."

"No."

"What about Wednesday night? Where were you?"

Edmund sighed. "I've been thinking about this morning . . . when you first posed this question. I realize now that I must trust you with this. I am not the seducer of women that Miniver was. Please believe that. However, I am also not immune to Cupid's arrows. I have fallen in love with the wife of a wealthy man. Do you know the name Van Leyden?"

"No."

"There's no reason you should. It's a family that came to Manhattan Island two hundred years ago. They were smart enough to buy up as much of the land as they could. They're not the Rhinelanders, but they are rich. Maurice Van Leyden is a descendant. He's sixty-two. He was very taken by the daughter of a French art dealer in the city. She was twenty when he met her. He was able to bring many patrons to the dealer, so the man ransomed off his daughter's happiness in exchange for his own success."

"What's her name?"

"Marie. She's nearly thirty now."

"How long have you two been havin' an affair?"

"Four months. Our trysts are unfortunately few and far between. Van Leyden is an inveterate clubber, but he has servants who go back decades. They watch her like a hawk. Last Wednesday, she visited a charity quilting exhibit for fifteen minutes, then rushed to the St. Regis Hotel. We managed two hours together. We planned to have her divorce him when I regained financial liquidity." Edmund studied his fingernails. "Now suddenly I'm rich again, but with terrible complications. I wonder if her husband suspected and had us followed recently. He probably knows I dine at the Metropolitan Club every Wednesday; he's a member himself. Perhaps he paid the man to kill me."

"It sounds like as good a motive as I've heard to date," John said.

"Van Leyden has actually been a member of the club longer than I have," Edmund added. "He introduced me to his wife in front of the ladies' restaurant. It would be ironic that his wife's infidelity should condemn me *and* save me."

"This is a very delicate situation," John acknowledged.

Edmund looked up. "Truly. Because if Maurice Van Leyden knows nothing, approaching him will bring unnecessary disgrace upon both Marie and me. If, on the other hand, you find the murderer is someone else and have gone nowhere near Van Leyden, Marie can sue for divorce and come to me with no blemish. You understand that any public fall from grace kills you permanently in New York society, Mr. Le Brun."

"I do. The bigger the city, the bigger the hypocrisy." He thought about all the well-off people who could turn blind eyes and deaf ears to the city's prostitutes day after day while enthusiastically filling those days actively ostracizing society women for their sexual dalliances. "Perhaps if you two took a step back from that precipice . . . ," John dangled.

"You're right. We really shouldn't see each other. After we wed, we would both like to stay in New York City if we could."

"It sounds like *you* should be havin' *Mr. Van Leyden* investigated," John said.

"How could I do that without admitting my relationship with his wife?"

"A very delicate situation indeed," John echoed. "When I said this mornin' that Miniver obviously knew you had a special appointment Wednesday night, you said he knew 'in a fashion.' What did you mean by that?"

"I meant that he had asked me to dine with him and skip my normal Metropolitan Club supper. But I told him I had a private appointment."

"He didn't push you on it?"

"No."

"Might that have been because your brother already knew the answer? He knew of your affair?"

The look on Edmund's face showed that he had not considered the possibility.

"Did he perhaps know of your intended assignation that evenin' and was teasin' you?" John continued.

"I don't think so."

"Think harder. Could he have followed you on a previous occasion? Could he have even alerted Mr. Van Leyden?"

"Why would he do that?"

"To gain his inheritance. To get someone else to kill you for him."

"Monstrous!" Edmund exclaimed. "He was ruthless in business, but he loved me as I loved him."

"Did he?"

Edmund bristled. "Well, we didn't *like* each other much, but the love remained. We were the same flesh, after all is said and done."

"They say blood is thicker than water, but gold is thicker than blood.

He was becomin' poorer by the day. How desperate do you feel about *your* financial future?"

Edmund brushed his forefinger across his lips. "You think he was pretending to be me to get someone to kill me over my campaigning for a new club? His two plots crossed, to his misfortune?"

"Absent better clues, we should pursue this line of thinkin'," John replied. "It's somethin' I shall sleep on."

Edmund reached out. "I'm wondering if you shouldn't do that sleeping here in Whimsy House. I would like to repeat the offer I made yesterday. I could see in your expression that you aren't convinced I fooled everyone today."

"That is true."

"Then, unless my brother was killed purely because he was taken to be a random member of the Metropolitan Club, someone still wants me dead."

"But the chances that they would come after you in your own house are minuscule."

All drapings of Pinckney's usual mild manner vanished in the fervor of his argument. "So were the chances they'd come after me in a fortress of a men's club. You are a man familiar with the criminal mind and violence. You also want to solve this crime. Does it not make sense to keep yourself around me as much as possible?"

"You do present an interestin' argument," John allowed.

"I'm in this house half the time. Even more right now. And I would pay you ten dollars a night," Edmund offered.

John reflected briefly. Pinckney's thoughts had merit. Moreover, it would place him so much closer to the attractive Lordis Goode, and for so many more hours.

"I would keep my room at the Savoy," John decided, "if only to run up the bill on J. P. Morgan."

Edmund leaned far forward and offered his hand. "Splendid! You don't even need to return to your hotel unless you want. We have nightgowns, tooth powder. I'm sure we have a spare toothbrush somewhere."

"No. I would need to return to the Savoy," John said.

"Fair enough." Edmund sprang from his stuffed chair with an energy John had never witnessed. "Well, let me get your room ready at least."

"What's this?" Lordis asked, entering the room with a tea tray.

"Mr. Le Brun has agreed to stay the night! I'll just go and get towels and so forth."

As Edmund hurried past her, Lordis said, "That's what you pay *me* to do, Edmund."

Pinckney's pace did not slow. "I'm not helpless. You entertain Mr. Le Brun."

John was pleased to see that Lordis had brought two teacups and saucers. "We never did get to drink tea together yesterday. Will you keep me company while the master is on safari?"

"I would be delighted." Lordis snatched up a tea table with her free hand as she approached the chairs. John noted the ease with which she moved the table and how steady the tray was in her grasp. Although she was clearly in her forties, she was no wilting flower.

Lordis set down the tray and looked at the vacated chair with some concern. She turned her face to John. "Although you've said you're not married, I'm sure such a charmer as you has been intimate with at least one woman in your days. It won't embarrass you if I hitch up my skirt to sit, will it?"

"No, ma'am."

Lordis grabbed the dress at knee level and drew it up to the point where the tops of her ankles showed. They were encased in black stockings. She sat carefully.

"Heavens, this feels good!" she exclaimed. "The first time since dressing that I've been able to really sit."

"Allow me to pour," John offered.

"Tell me about your intimacy with women, John," Lordis bade, arching one eyebrow.

"You are direct."

"I'm too old to be otherwise. It took all my restraint to avoid the subject last night. Tonight, we're better friends. And with Edmund's secret out, no more need to seek out foibles with verbal fencing."

"Well put. I was married many years ago, to a wonderful woman. A woman much nicer than I. She tamed me. I was a wild, embittered young man."

"Why embittered?"

"Because I was meant for somethin' different than cotton farmin'."

"For pursuits of the mind."

"Yes. My family intended me to attend university. But then the War of the Secession broke out and the South was ruined."

"Yes, of course," Lordis said in a sympathetic voice. "And how did she tame you?"

"Patience, good example, lots of listenin', sharin' my dreams, encouragement."

"Love."

"In a word. But she died of yellow fever. So did our unborn child."

"Oh, John! How terrible! That must have been some time back."

"The early eighties."

"And since then?"

"I've had a number of ladies care for me, off and on. Sort of like your feedin' the neighborhood stray from time to time." John had put one spoonful of sugar into each cup and then portioned out just a spot of cream into Lordis's.

"How clever to have observed my habit," Lordis registered as John began to pour. "I'm sure these ladies benefited as much as you have."

"I don't know about that." While the woman's intimate questions aroused him, John was at the same time somewhat embarrassed by the unaccustomed directness. In Brunswick, even the most bold of women would not have broached such subjects. They made their interest in him known in subtle, indirect ways. The only reason John was not blushing and perspiring was that he had faced an even bolder woman in London the previous fall. He suspected that social mores changed most rapidly in the biggest cities, and that he and Brunswick were relics of a past century, clinging to codes of behavior that the modern life would eventually kill. To regain his equilibrium, he said, "Tell me about Whimsy House's seven secrets."

Lordis's eyes went wide. "My, you do have a way of finding out things! Yes, Chriswell was one of those eccentrics we spoke of. There's a hidden closet under the staircase. There's also a secret passage connecting the brothers' bedrooms. The family safe is inside one of the foyer closets. And, finally, there are unmarked doors to access the two turrets on the top floor. But those five are all that have ever been found. You know, Miniver got his wicked sense of humor from his father. We all figured there were only five secrets, but Chriswell made out that there were seven to drive us all crazy looking."

"Have *you* looked?"

Lordis laughed. "Off and on."

"With Mr. Hastin's or by yourself?"

"Both. I mean, with such a story and living in this house for so long, you can't help but test a wall every now and then. But we don't see how there can be anything else. Mr. Hastings has had to make repairs in virtually every room, and he's never found anything."

At that moment, Edmund reappeared in the living-room archway. John noted that he held a Colt Single Action Army revolver in his right hand. His left fist was wrapped around something unseen. "Your room is ready. It's my brother's room. Closest one to mine." He cracked open the gun.

"I hope you know how to use that," John said. "It could do you more harm than good."

"Oh, I've shot it before," Edmund assured. The objects in his left hand were bullets, which he began to feed into the weapon's cylinder. "When will you leave to fetch your belongings?"

"I had thought rather soon," John replied. "Perhaps we might all go out. Miss Goode has given the cook the night off."

"That's true," Edmund said, "but I'm frankly afraid of being gunned down in public. There's plenty of food from the viewing in the icebox. I'll take some up to my room and barricade myself in." He snapped the cylinder shut, raised the revolver, and pointed it at an imaginary assailant. "I'm not really afraid as long as I have this and am awake. You two go out for a couple of hours and have a good time."

Lordis's face lit up as she looked directly at John. "I could really use a bit of lightness. And I must atone for both my disingenuous behavior and for hurrying our dinner last night. Can you wait until I change?"

"Certainly," John allowed.

Lordis took a sip of her tea and worked her way decorously up from the chair. "I won't be but a few minutes."

The two men watched the housekeeper's departure with male appreciation.

"I know the maid and cook are gone," said John to his host, "but is Mr. Hastin's about?"

Edmund pointed the weapon toward the fireplace. "I think so. He's leaving for a fishing trip momentarily."

John stood. "Is he?"

"Yes. One he's been counting on for weeks."

"Then I had better speak with him right away. I should return by the time Miss Goode is ready. Please be careful with that gun, sir."

"I shall."

John felt under his jacket tail to reassure himself that the little holster and double-barreled derringer were still on his belt. He found his way across the foyer and the library and through the pantry to the house's back door. He made sure it locked behind him. He noted that although the daylight still filtered strongly through the mansion's small garden and driveway, a light shone in the carriage-house apartment. John climbed the stairs and knocked on the door. William Hastings appeared, wearing a buff-colored work shirt, khaki pants, and work boots.

"Yes, sir?"

"You know who I am?"

"Yes. Mr. Le Brun, investigating on behalf of the Metropolitan Club."

"That's right."

"Come in, please."

John entered the home. It was intimate, with a patent woman's touch in the decoration. They stood in the parlor. John saw a small dining area beyond, as well as part of the kitchen. He assumed that the bedrooms lay even farther back, as the entire carriage house had an upper story. Arrayed on the sofa were a surf fishing pole, a reel, a creel, a blanket and pillow, and a large suitcase.

"On your way to some fishin'," John noted.

"I am. Taking advantage of a day off and my wife and son gone up to Maine."

"Where do you fish?"

"This time it's down on the Jersey shore. Another caretaker who lives nearby has access to a bungalow. We'll meet two pals there."

"Sounds like fun. Been long in the plannin'?"

"About a month. Would you care to sit?"

John rocked back and forth on his heels. "I don't think I'll be that long. Don't want to keep you. I'm sure you can't think of anythin' valuable in the investigation. Otherwise, you'd have shared it with Detective O'Leary."

"I wish I did know something," Hastings said, ponderously nodding his large head. "It's truly terrible. Probably end up costing me my live-lihood."

"I'm sorry to hear that. Tell me about the seven secrets of Whimsy House."

Hastings smiled. "Five secrets. If there are seven, I'd be astonished."

"You've looked, eh?"

"I won't say that I haven't."

"What were the other two secrets supposed to be?"

Hastings shrugged. Only a hint of his smile remained. "The old man would never say."

"When was the house converted to electricity?"

"The kitchen and basement early. The rest quite recently."

"You were in their employ when it took place?"

"I was. I've been here more than fifteen years."

"And no extra secrets were uncovered when the baseboards were removed and so forth?"

The smile disappeared altogether. "No."

"Who did the wirin'?"

"A local company for Westinghouse. I might be able to find the name when I get back from my trip."

"If you could."

"What would this have to do with Mr. Pinckney's murder?"

John shrugged his shoulders. Images of priceless necklaces and bracelets sparkled in his mind's eye. "Nothin'. I'm just curious. I'm also idly curious about Miniver Pinckney's cough. He should see a doctor."

"He already has."

"Really? And what is the name of the quack who's letting him walk around with such an affliction?"

"I don't know. One day about six weeks ago, he asked me to drive him up to St. Luke's Hospital. We stopped a block away. He walked into one of the houses there. The whole row had doctors' offices in them."

"You didn't see a name?"

"No. Why not talk to him about this?"

"I shall. Did this doctor pronounce him fit?"

"He did. Said he was hale enough and simply had to tough it out. That the summer would probably clear it up. To take long walks and stop smoking, is what Mr. Miniver told me. You seem quite concerned for a stranger."

"A friend of mine had a cough just like that," John lied, "and ended up in the cemetery. One dead brother this year is enough, don't you think?"

"Certainly. But nobody tells Miniver Pinckney what to do."

"Both brothers went out last Wednesday. Did you drive one or both?"

"Neither."

John stopped rocking. "Now, that seems curious. Why have a car and a chauffeur if you're not about to use them?"

Hastings folded his arms across his chest. "Mr. Edmund only had me drive him to the Metropolitan Club if the weather was inclement. It's but a few blocks south. As to where Mr. Miniver went and why he didn't use me, you need only ask him."

"Yes, I shall. Anythin' else you'd like to share with me, Mr. Hastin's?"

"Nothing I can think of."

"Very well. I wish you good fishin'."

"Thank you, sir." Hastings moved with speed to open the door for Le Brun. As John passed, he gave the man a last look. His intuition was telling him nothing.

T HE MANSION'S LOCKED back door made it necessary for John to walk around to the front doors. Once again, he knocked with one of the large brass rappers. Edmund appeared and put his eye to a clear space in the frosted glass before opening.

"Excellent way to get yourself shot, puttin' your face up to the window like that," John remarked.

"I suppose you're right." Edmund still held the revolver.

"Let Miss Goode answer the door."

"I shall."

"And when we're gone, don't answer the door at all."

"Very well. Anything revealing from Hastings?"

"Nothin'. You sure you won't reconsider and come out with us?"

"Not on your life . . . or mine."

John looked past Edmund's shoulder to the grand staircase. Lordis was descending. She wore a pale plum outfit decorated with white stitched helixes. The floor-length dress flared slightly in the back, a nod to the age of bustles. Its overjacket was cut to reveal the woman's décolletage and to accentuate her rather narrow waist. John observed as she came down that her shoes of brushed suede perfectly matched the outfit's color. Her feather-trimmed and broad-brimmed hat matched as well. Clearly, this was a tailor-made costume that cost several weeks' salary.

"And aren't you the lucky one?" Edmund remarked to John, turning to see what had so captivated his guest.

"I am indeed," John said.

Lordis glided across the foyer floor and offered her arm. John observed that she now wore golden earrings and a gold lapel pin, but that the unfashionable charm bracelet was still around her wrist.

"Hastings can delay his vacation for a few minutes. Why don't you have him drive you?" Edmund suggested.

"It's a beautiful night, in spite of our horrible day," Lordis replied. "We can again promenade the few blocks."

Edmund stepped back two paces to admire. "You make a handsome couple. Just be sure not to paint the town too red. Please be back here by ten."

"Yes, Father," Lordis said as she encouraged John toward the doors.

I THOUGHT YOU HAD ABANDONED ME," Lordis said through a pout as John approached the Hotel Savoy pouf upon which she sat, reading a copy of *The Century* magazine.

"I'm dreadfully sorry," John said, laboring to catch his breath. "I hurried my packin' and changin', but then as I was leavin', I noticed somethin' peculiar about the door. My room had been set up for robbery tonight." He put down his suitcase.

"Gracious! How did you know?"

"Someone had drilled a small hole through the door so that a wire could be passed through and the safety chain slipped off. They fill the hole with a putty that matches the color of the door. They work in pairs. When you're sure to be asleep, one stands lookout and the other enters the room. It's incredible how quietly they can go through everythin' you own. It's a trick I've had to deal with down in Brunswick.

It's a resort town, y'know, and people arrive with great deals of cash. Sorry about the delay." John neglected to mention that he had taken some time to shower, shave, and apply cologne.

"Don't mention it!" Lordis said, rising from the circular seat. "I imagine the hotel is quite grateful."

"They are. Offered to knock last night's stay off the bill, but I wouldn't hear of it. They're storin' the rest of my belongin's. Shall we go?"

"You look especially dashing," Lordis admired, looking up and down the formal clothes John had acquired the previous fall in London. It was only at the last second that he had thought to grab the tails before rushing for the train in Brunswick.

"Thank you," John said, glowing from the feel of the desirable woman on his arm. He noted with pleasure the approving glances of two businessmen just entering the hotel.

"You must have a very sharp eye to detect such a small hole," Lordis said. "And that would have to be your left eye."

They passed out of the lobby doors and under a building-long balcony topped by ornate lamps that had just been illuminated.

"Your vision is sharp as well," John returned. "I can usually fool most people into thinkin' I have the sight of both eyes."

Lordis squeezed John's arm. "But you turn your head farther to the right than the ordinary man. And I caught your surprise at the viewing when someone came up to you from your right shoulder. It must be a recent loss."

"It is. Happened last year."

"I'm sorry."

"Well, you get to keep nothin' forever. I'm glad I've still got one."

The doorman ushered them toward a motorized cab parked at the curb, but Lordis said, "We'd rather take that hansom, if you please." When they got into the horse-drawn cab, she turned and called up to the driver, "To Washington Square in no hurry, and then back up to Fifth and Forty-fourth!" When she turned back, her charm bracelet tinkled.

"Do you ever take that off?" John asked.

Lordis held it up for John to admire. "Only when I bathe and sleep. I know it doesn't go with the outfit, but it's from my godchildren. See, here's a figure of a girl. Here's the boy. This is the Eiffel Tower and the Leaning Tower of Pisa, when they took their trip to Europe last year. And this heart is for me."

"A treasure," John said. "You must be quite close to the Topleys."

"I am. I'm sure I told you that from the first day of my employment at Whimsy House, Chriswell Pinckney encouraged me to nurture my friendship with Sarah. The hardheaded monster would never reconcile with her, so he needed me to carry messages back and forth and to gather intelligence for him on her welfare, her family. It's always been a pleasurable task. We're as close as any sisters."

"They must be quite well off to go to Europe."

"Ben had a hit on his hands two years ago. They used some of that money."

"But you weren't invited along?"

"I wasn't allowed six weeks' leave. I suppose if I had ranted and threatened I could have gone. But I didn't want to be a financial drain, and I'm not a great one for prolonged travel. You, however, seem to enjoy it. I am upset that this murder is consuming so much of your visit. Let's tuck your investigation away for a few hours, shall we?"

John agreed with enthusiasm. On the unhurried route south they ran the gauntlet of palaces and mansions to pass St. Thomas Episcopal, St. Patrick's Cathedral, St. Nicholas Collegiate Church, and Brick Presbyterian, all of which promised forgiveness of sins for those so perpetually in need. They passed the venerable Union and Union League Clubs, which predated the Metropolitan and Manhattan. Lordis pointed out the colossal, seven-level New York Public Library and Bryant Park behind it, which had recently replaced the Egyptian-style reservoir that had served the city in times of smaller population and lesser mechanical wonders. Between Forty-first and Thirtieth, they looked upon the largest or best jewelry, art, silversmith, motoring-apparel, haberdasher, furniture, fine-linen, and music shops in the world. They viewed the hotels and banks of Madison Square, continued on to the eastern verge of the common man's shopping district and down to the older homes of the rich. At Seventh, they turned west and circumvolved Washington Square Park, with its august monument to the hero of the Revolutionary War and first president. As they traveled back north, the sky turned violet and then indigo. As if to compensate for hiding the stars, a galaxy of artificial light softened Fifth Avenue until it became a twentieth-century fairyland.

In a sudden rush, John realized why Lordis's voice so soothed him. It was the same range and timbre as his mother's. Memory of his father's voice was endless alternations between stern chastisement and stony silence, but his mother's voice was always calm, an anchor for the most troubled familial seas. He winced at not having thought of her for so long, the first woman who had encouraged the flexing of his intellectual muscles. The first important woman whom he had loved and the first he had lost. Listening to the tinkling of the charm bracelet, John finally understood how important the few women in his life had been. Their influence was far out of proportion to the time he had spent with them. He was ready for the other bookend, the closing arabesque to counter his mother and be with him until the end of his days. He looked at Lordis Goode and wondered.

As they clip-clopped along the verge of Madison Square, Lordis pointed out the spire of the Madison Square Garden tower peeking above the trees.

"I admired it earlier today," John revealed. "I was across the street at the Manhattan Club."

Lordis adjusted herself and ended up with her length pressed against John's arm. "You do get around. Miniver left behind two tickets to a new production that's opening on the roof garden Monday night. I have no one to share them with, and it would be a terrible waste not to use them. Promise me, no matter what's happening with the investigation, that you will be my escort."

"If it's within my power, I would be delighted," John responded.

When they again passed the library, Lordis said, "I put in reservations at both Louis Sherry's and John Delmonico's. You tell me which you prefer."

"What do they cost, if I may be so crass?"

"More or less the same. If we really do it up well, about ten dollars."

"Which is precisely what I am bein' paid to guard Whimsy House," John remarked, glad to earn the unexpected money. Even in London and Paris, restaurants were not so dear. He registered that Lordis liked to live high. He wondered how often she got to fulfill her tastes given her salary, wondered if there were other men who indulged her.

"If it's all the same to you, I've had several Delmonico's meals down at the Jekyl Island Club," he told her. "They provide the caterin' during the winter season."

"Then Sherry's it is."

They dined from Consommé Balzac to Romanoff Pudding, with Cases of Squabs and Partridges Braised à la Molière and several vegetable dishes in between, washed down with Johannisberger Gold Seal. In between courses, they cleansed their palates with various ices and sherbets. To end the feast, they drank Heidsieck Brut champagne.

They spoke of literature, chess, Harry Pillsbury, and theater. John found that Lordis could talk a blue streak, but she had interesting things to say, and he was by nature more inclined to listen than speak. He appreciated, however, that she was quite interested in his knowledge and opinions and took the trouble to draw him out. They expressed a mutual admiration for the extent of their largely self-taught knowledge. They agreed upon America's expanding influence in the world, a belief in God, the mixed blessings of organized religions, of the need for more hours and years of public education, of the right for women to vote but, at the same time, a minimal standard of knowledge for both men and women, to earn the right. They spent a good deal of time smiling at the joy of finding a kindred soul. Only their promise of returning to the Pinckney mansion by ten prevented them from lingering at Sherry's until midnight.

O N T H E W A Y N O R T H, John and Lordis detoured to the police station so he could deliver the list of funeral service attendees to Kevin O'Leary's makeshift office. O'Leary had gone home some time earlier but had left word that he would visit the station for a time on Sunday.

When they entered Whimsy House, they found half the electric lights blazing but the downstairs deserted. Together, they climbed the stairs and moved to Edmund's room, which, with its private bathroom, occupied the northern half of the Fifth Avenue side of the house. Lordis knocked and called out the surviving brother's name.

"I'm here," Edmund called back from his room. "Safe and sound."

Lordis tried the door and found it locked.

"I told you I was safe and sound," the voice from the other side of the door proclaimed.

John heard a few muffled noises from inside the room, then saw a key appear from under the door.

"I locked Miniver's door from the inside as well and came through the passage. There it is."

"Do you need anything?" Lordis asked.

"Other than for Mr. Le Brun to solve the murder? No, thanks."

John took his small suitcase to the other door on the same hallway wall, unlocked it, and deposited his belongings inside Miniver's bedroom. When he emerged, he found Lordis waiting for him with arms folded across her chest.

"Now, what is your pleasure?" she asked.

John suspected the question was every bit as provocative as it sounded. "I'd like you to lead me on a stem-to-stern tour of the house. Durin' my sheriff days, I had a man slip into a wealthy house durin' a garden party and stay hidden until the night. He was able to clean out the place and leave, lockin' the door behind him, without anyone sleepin' there havin' the slightest awareness. I wasted days suspectin' members of the family and their help."

"Are you saying that one of the mourners might still be in here?" Lordis asked, her eyes perceptibly rounder.

"Did you count 'em as they left?"

"No."

"I glanced at your list. You had written '1 unknown man.' Did you see him leave?"

"I did not."

"Is there another gun in this house?"

"Yes. In the hiding place under this stairs. There's a gun rack with several shotguns and rifles."

John nodded. He saw that he had the chatelaine's full attention. "Why don't I hang up my belongin's, then go downstairs and fetch a weapon while you change into somethin' . . . more comfortable." *Two can play at the verbal-innuendo game,* he thought.

"Very well," Lordis said. She started toward her room with strides as long as her elegant costume would allow.

John had purposely not asked for the secret to the hidden staircase room. He found it in short order, by pressing in on one of the carved daisies decorating the woodwork. Inside, he found high-quality Daly Hammerless and W. W. Greener Ejector 12-gauge shotguns. He also found a Winchester Model 1894 repeating rifle and two old Merwin Hulbert & Company Junior Target Rifles that had probably been gifts to the teenage brothers. He took the Greener and loaded two shells into it. When he emerged from the space, he found Lordis wearing a nightgown and overdress that looked home-made and yet alluring. She had let her hair down so that it cascaded over her shoulders and onto her back.

"Top down or bottom up?" she asked

"Bottom up," John replied. "If someone is in here, I want to keep them trapped."

T HE BASEMENT CONSISTED OF A KITCHEN, laundry, larder, and storage room on the east side, a furnace and boiler room on the west side, directly under the fireplace end of the living room; and a yawning space running the middle of the house, punctuated only by two rows of four thick columns running north to south. Lordis called the space "the gaming room." It contained a billiard table, a pool table, a shuffleboard court, and twin dartboards. All the games looked undersized within the great open space. Directly under the foyer was a table that might have sat twelve, had there been any chairs around it.

"That came from some boardroom," Lordis explained. "Chriswell bought it to hold the model for Whimsy House. He had it built to one-twelfth scale, to be sure it was as grand and functional as he had envisioned before spending an actual cent."

"Except that the model must have cost a fortune," John noted.

"He said it was about four hundred dollars. It's sixty-six inches long, forty-eight inches wide, and fifty-four inches high."

"You said 'is,' " John registered. "Where is it now?"

"That's a long story."

"Why don't you tell me while we walk?" John suggested, checking the first of four basement windows that faced East Sixty-second Street, each of which he found locked and with encased iron bars just beyond the glass.

"All right. It was built in 1879. Sally immediately wanted to commandeer it for a doll house, even though she was almost a full-grown woman. Chriswell, however, would not have it touched. She used to leave one-twelfth-scale dolls she had fashioned inside the rooms just to spite him.

"After the real house was built, Chriswell deeded it to her, in lieu of a twenty-first birthday present. It had been brought down here on the day the house was first occupied. For a time, Sally lavished her time and a good part of her allowance on it, furnishing and decorating each room." Lordis made a little noise in her throat. "I believe it was her substitute for having her own home and family. When she got into acting and then met Ben Topley, she abandoned it."

"So where is it now?"

"Crated up, in a warehouse. I'm a member of a council of citizens who are trying to raise money to create the Museum of the City of New York. One of the permanent displays we decided on is doll houses from famous families and of historic city styles. Since Whimsy House was the first mansion on this part of the Upper East Side, the council voted to take it as a contribution."

"And when did it go to them?"

"Shortly after Chriswell died. I made the suggestion to Sally, and she was delighted to oblige. It's in good company. There's Ann Anthony's Pavilion from 1769, the Shelton-Taylor house from 1835, Brett House from 1838, Goelet's from 1845, Elder House from the time of the Civil War, and Altadena's from about ten years ago. Why are you so interested in it?"

"Because if it's accurate to the smallest detail, then the other two secrets should be in it."

Lordis smiled and shook her head. "Chriswell evidently figured people would examine the model for the house's secrets. The space under the staircase exists, of course, but there's no door to enter it. The empty space between the brothers' bathrooms is also there, but without access. Sally thought of it, and years later so did I."

"Too bad."

"I believe that model was explored as fully as the actual house."

"Then it's fine in its crate," John said. He pushed up the last of the basement windows and tugged on each of the iron bars. "No way in or out through these," he declared.

Large double-doored storage closets lined the southern wall. Lordis opened each while John trained the shotgun. They proved too full of the accumulation of privileged lives to hold so much as a child.

U SING ROOM KEYS, John and Lordis worked their way methodically around the first floor, locking as they went. They moved counterclockwise from the preparation pantry, into the library, to the east foyer closet, through the foyer, checking the hidden staircase room, to the west foyer closet, where Lordis showed John the concealed safe, into the living room, and around the dining room. John paused to admire a grand and very colorful oil painting of the Battery in Charleston.

"At least there's one nod to their heritage in the house," he remarked.

"That's mine," Lordis said. "I bought that with money left to me by a great-aunt. It's too large for my room, so Chriswell let me hang it here."

"It brightens the room considerably," John admired.

They examined the lavatory that served the first floor and continued out to the pantry. Before agreeing that the floor was secure, they checked both front and back doors.

On the second level they began with Edmund, reassuring themselves that he was still awake and hale. They explored Miniver's room and bath, and Lordis showed John the spring-loaded, knobless door that opened to the secret passage between the brothers' bedrooms. John locked the room and pocketed the key, and they moved on to the room that had once belonged to Sarah Pinckney. In the modern fashion, this room had a built-in closet, but it stood all but empty. The room had two doors, so that its occupant could choose to descend by either the east or west wing of the staircase. Just beyond the east door lay the entrance to Lordis's room. This was by far the smallest bedroom, but it had a spacious closet that Lordis had crammed with the acquisitions of a lifetime. John noted that she had all but exhausted her collection of summer gowns. Her bathroom, accessible only via the hall, had once been shared with Sarah.

The last remaining rooms on the second floor were the master bedroom and its bath. A small built-in cedar closet stood in the far northwest corner of the room. The room was spacious enough to hold its own fireplace, with plenty of footage for an enormous bed, night tables, a rocking chair, two armoires, and a tea table with two cane-backed chairs. The room was immaculate and dust-free.

"Why don't you move yourself to this bedroom?" John asked.

Lordis shook her head. "Chriswell wouldn't like it."

John laughed and then saw that Lordis was serious.

"This was an unhappy room," she said. "I'm fine where I am. Anyway, Miniver entertained in here, to impress his women." Lordis relocked the room.

T HIS WAS THE BALLROOM in name only," Lordis shared as they entered the top floor. "As you can see, the mansard roof and the turrets shrink it dreadfully. The ceiling's too low for chandeliers. Not impressive at all. And the climb is not for anyone over fifty. When I come up here directly from the basement, it takes me two minutes to catch my breath."

"Was it ever used for balls?"

"Twice, I am told. The first time when the house was opened. The second to celebrate Miniver's wedding."

In spite of its relative smallness for a ballroom, John observed that a significant amount of money had been poured into its construction. The parquet floor gleamed. The walls were covered with the finest French paper. Ornate gilt sconces lit the room between every one of the ten gabled windows.

"Show me the accesses to the turrets," John invited.

The room was wainscoted, and every few feet the walls were boxed with woodwork. Lordis moved to one of the sections and pushed hard. It moved slowly but silently. John found himself looking out the turret windows to the housetops across the street.

"Chriswell evidently cleaned the windows himself, when no one was around," Lordis said. "Edmund was the first one to stumble upon the secret. He drove Miniver crazy when they played hide-and-seek."

"And there is a twin access door to the other turret."

"Secret Number Five."

"Let's open it," John said.

As it was the last possible place an intruder could hide, John lifted the shotgun and gestured for Lordis to push the wall aside. The space was exposed. No one hid within.

"We are now officially secure," Lordis pronounced through a sigh. She allowed the wall to swing back in place. "All alone, except for the mice." Her eyebrows raised in anticipation.

"And Edmund Pinckney," John reminded her.

Lordis offered him an amused look. "He'd have to be blasted out of his room with a cannon." She stood so her length curved in a provocative *contrapposto,* her arms clasped behind her, accentuating her bosom. She looked barely more than thirty from the play of light on her face.

"I'm not satisfied," John said.

Lordis abandoned her pose. "Why not?"

"Because, as I indicated tonight at the Hotel Savoy, no door is safe from professional criminals. They can bore through a door in ten minutes and not be heard from twenty feet away. Windows are even easier, usin' a diamond-tipped stylus and a suction cup."

"Are you going to sleep in the foyer?"

"No indeed." John started for the stairs and gestured for Lordis to follow. "I saw little Christmas bells in one of the basement storage closets. While I fetch them, would you round up some sewin' thread and a scissors? Light brown thread if you can find it. Meet me in the foyer."

WHEN LORDIS ENTERED the foyer with the thread, she found that all lights on the first floor except for the central chandelier and two wall sconces had been extinguished. John sat on the grand staircase's third step with five round bells in his hand.

"Do you have any other business down here?" he asked.

"I do not."

"Then sit beside me. Pay out about eight feet of thread, cut it, then pass it through this bell's thingamabob." One after the next, they strung four of the bells together. When they were finished John connected the ends of the thread tightly to opposing balusters, with two bells each near the knots.

"But they're so small. How will we hear them all the way upstairs in our rooms?" Lordis argued.

"I thought you might ask that," John said. He tossed the remaining bell up the stairs and let it tumble back down. The sound of metal and clapper against oak was surprisingly loud.

"What was that?" came Edmund's distant voice from inside his room.

"Just an alarm for your further safety," John shouted back.

"Thank you!" descended the voice.

Lordis stood and surveyed the job. "I can see them without much trouble."

"That's because you're lookin' for them," John countered. "And because you haven't turned off the chandelier yet."

Once the two dozen star-shaped chandelier lamps were extinguished, the trip-alarm was indeed all but invisible.

"I am yet again impressed by you," Lordis praised, stepping carefully over the thread.

John, too, arose. He stretched his arms. "I should retire."

"Are you tired?" she asked.

"Actually, I'm not. Champagne makes it difficult for me to sleep."

"Me, too. How about that game of chess?"

"I was supposed to solve the murder first."

"I have infinite confidence in you. We can play on account."

"I think we should leave the library dark," John said.

Lordis started up the stairs. "I have my own board and pieces. In my room." She did not look back.

John followed.

JOHN LOOKED at the alarm clock on top of Lordis's nightstand. "It's almost midnight."

"Oh, no you don't!" Lordis exclaimed. "I'm only down one pawn. I can still win this game."

"I'm willin' to call it a draw," John said. Respectful of each other, they had progressed through turns slowly. Often, more than a minute ticked by without a move being made. He had had enough of staring impotently at the beguiling woman from across the scant distance of a game table. Her scent was all over the room. The gentle rising and falling of her chest accentuated her breasts. Her fingers lingered on and caressed her smooth ivory men. He had all he could do not to upset the board and take her in his arms.

Lordis shook her head, her eyes roving the board for a winning combination of moves. "What truly galls me is that you're beating me in a formal suit. You haven't even . . ." She half rose, reached across the table, and yanked on his bow tie. "There! What are you waiting for? Permission to get comfortable?"

John stood and slipped out of his jacket. He unbuttoned his white vest. "Now are you satisfied?"

Lordis stood as well and moved around the table. "Not yet," she said in a low voice. "I'm willing to call it a draw if you can think of a different game."

They kissed for the better part of a minute, before Lordis walked him backward to her bed.

SUNDAY

JUNE 24, 1906

THE GUNSHOT ECHOED through Whimsy House at precisely 4:14 A.M. John sat upright as if propelled. He had barely fallen back asleep from his routine midsleep visit to the bathroom when the sharp report pierced the door to Lordis's bedchamber. John swung from the bed, grabbed the shotgun, and had left the room before Lordis could find her voice.

Le Brun raced down the half flight of steps to the center landing of the staircase. The barrel of his weapon led his survey of the house. He found no movement in the foyer, on the balconies, or on the staircases that led up to the ballroom.

"Edmund Pinckney!" he called out as he climbed the opposite stairs and moved warily toward the man's bedroom door. As he tried the knob and found the door still locked, Lordis spoke from behind him.

"I have your clothes, John. Edmund!"

The lack of response from Edmund's bedroom was ominous.

John retreated to the top of the stairs, elevating the business end of the weapon. "Can you fire this if you need to?"

Lordis held out a steady hand. "I can."

He exchanged the shotgun for his clothing and pulled on his trousers over his undershorts. From the holster attached to the belt he extracted his double-barreled derringer. He put his arms into his shirt, then took his vest and fished out the door key to Miniver's room. When he reached the door, he stood well to the side while he inserted the key, not wanting to take a blast in the torso or head.

The key turned with no problem. John grabbed the knob and pushed the door inward with a gliding movement. He dropped to one knee and peered around the door with his gun hand extended. The room was too dark to survey. He ducked back for a moment, stood, and reached in quickly to punch the electric light button.

Light washed across the bedroom. John dashed to the opposite side of the door, drinking in as much of the image as he could in a moment. He caught his breath and rushed inside, gun thrust before him. He checked in order the built-in closet, the bathroom, and the space under the bed.

"Are you all right?" he shouted out to Lordis.

"Yes. Are you?"

"Yes. I'm goin' through the passageway."

John repeated his careful entrance into the secret passage, first pushing it open from the side, then peering in from one knee, crossing to the opposite side as he checked the space, then moving forward. The passage had no light of its own. He felt up and down both sides of the far end until he found the little button that served as door handle. He pulled it back and stepped inside.

The acrid smell of gunpowder was the first sensation that came to Le Brun. Then he spotted Edmund Pinckney on his bed. His body lay under a light sheet. The left extreme of the sheet, the bottom sheet, and the spare pillow on the left side of the double bed were liberally sprayed with blood. Pinckney's arms were thrust out in the attitude of a supine crucifixion victim. On the carpet below his right hand lay a Colt revolver.

John dropped again to his knee and peered under the high bed, assuring himself no one hid there. The only other possible hiding place in the room was behind a door in the far northeast corner. When John opened it, he found the mirror image of the cedar closet he had seen in the master bedroom. After looking in vain for a pair of feet, he pushed aside the suits and trousers that hung from rods on either side of the closet. He found no one.

"John, may I come in?" Lordis's voice filtered in from the hallway.

"I don't think that would be a good idea," he answered. "Edmund is dead."

"I want to see."

"No, you don't." John had closed the closet door and was staring at the black wound in Edmund's right temple, then looking at his wide, unblinking eyes, their pupils enormous in death.

"What happened?"

"I don't know. Fetch my suit jacket and find Detective O'Leary's card. His home telephone number is on the back. Call him and tell him the second brother is dead in his bedroom, with the door locked. Ask how long he'll take to get here."

"Very well."

John looked around the room. It was the only one in the house he had never seen. All the bedrooms except Lordis's were overlarge. The bed had a night table on either side. There was a towering and over-wide armoire just to the right of the secret passage. A large desk occupied the northwest corner of the room, with a bookcase on either side. A Morris chair and a small table dominated the remaining area.

At variance with the rest of the neat room, the desk was in disarray. Two stacks of papers leaned against one another on the upper surface, and the top center drawer lay half opened. John crossed to it and scanned the documents without touching them. He saw that two were wills, surrounded by various bond and stock certificates and what looked to be receipts. Among them was a sales slip for a Colt revolver, dated July 9, 1901.

John reminded himself that he was merely a consulting detective. He moved his feet cautiously, making sure he would neither disturb nor destroy any evidence left on the floor. He saw nothing to avoid. He moved to each of the room's four windows and examined them. All had been left open about a foot, to provide circulation on a sultry summer evening. John noted that the outside ledges were wide enough for a nimble man to have rappelled down from above and gained entrance. At the moment, it seemed the only possibility short of the unthinkable.

The door rattled softly from gentle rapping.

"It's me again. Mr. O'Leary is on his way. He said he would telephone the station. May I come in?"

"I wish you wouldn't," John replied. "In fact, I'm gonna exit the way I entered. I'll see you in a minute."

Le Brun retraced his path through the passage and Miniver's room and regained the upper hallway. He found Lordis sitting on the stairs just above the intact trip thread, her elbow on one knee and her fist supporting her chin. She had donned her nightgown but had left her overdress behind. Her hair was wildly tangled. Her face, without makeup and drawn with care and sorrow, looked several years older than when she had retired. John noted, however, that she was still an attractive woman. He was sure that the tender treatment she had given him between midnight and one had also colored his perception of her.

"So, what happened?" she asked, continuing to look straight ahead at the front doors. Her toe gently nudged the thread, causing the bells to tinkle.

John sat beside her. "At the moment I have no idea. There's only so much snoopin' I'm allowed to do."

"I understand."

"Are you gonna be all right?" he asked.

Lordis laughed ruefully. "How do you mean 'all right'? Mentally? Physically? Spiritually? Financially?"

"All of the above." John plucked the thread forcefully upward. It snapped. He let it go. The four bells rolled and clattered for several seconds.

"I'll survive. I'll take one day at a time."

John took Lordis's free hand in his and squeezed. "I'll help in any way I can."

"You're not beholden to me, John." She took the thread from his hand. "There were no strings attached to last night."

"Nevertheless," he said. He groaned as he pushed himself up from the landing. "I had better make myself presentable."

"I as well," Lordis said as he again offered his hand to help her up.

T HE FRONT-DOOR KNOCKER sounded just as John was descending the staircase. He had washed and shaved and changed to one of his everyday suits. He had looked alert enough when examining himself in the bathroom mirror, but his brain ached dully just above and behind his eyes from lack of sleep. He noted as he approached the doors that dawn was creeping pinkly upon the city.

Kevin O'Leary stood alone on the door stoop, wearing no collar or tie under his jacket and a shirt he must have rescued from the hamper. "I won't say 'Top of the mornin' ' ta ya. I waited ta call the station until I got ta Columbus Circle. Wanted ta see this with just you and me before the bulls in blue descend. What do you know?"

John led the way up the staircase. "Nothin' except the fact of my ignorance."

"Then you're in good company. I believe the first one who said that was Diogenes," O'Leary observed.

"Yes. Although he was less cynical than I. This case will either kill us or make us famous. I'll wait to have *you* tell *me* what happened. This way."

John led the city detective through Miniver's bedroom and the secret passage into the death chamber.

"This is something out of Edgar Allan Poe," O'Leary pronounced as he traversed the dark passage.

"It's only the beginnin'. Brace yourself." Le Brun stood close to the wall so that his companion could take in the entire bedroom unhindered. "I will tell you that Miss Goode and I patrolled the house from bottom to top, from a bit past ten until a bit before eleven. Every nook and cranny. As to someone gettin' in from the outside, it was shut down tighter than a drum. I even booby-trapped the stairs. Edmund had locked and bolted himself in his room. I had the key to the bedroom we came through in my possession."

"You were here t'rough the night?"

"I was."

"But ya didn't sleep in that other bedroom."

"Don't ask," John said, lowering his chin, raising one eyebrow, and daring the Irishman to pass a crude observation. "I was hired by Mr. Pinckney."

O'Leary grinned. "Oh. A private house dick, is it?"

John ignored the barb. "I was up seconds after hearin' a single gunshot. The time was four-fourteen. I was half awake already. It sounded just like the report made by a forty-five revolver."

"So, you're saying that no one could have been in this room at the time except the deceased here?" asked O'Leary, observing the carpet in front of his feet as he moved slowly toward the body.

"If I said that, I'd be admittin' that he committed suicide."

"Well? Isn't that what ya have been saying all along?" O'Leary asked, raising his arms and letting them fall in a gesture that begged the ready evidence.

The door echoed with Lordis's tapping. "*Now* may I come in?"

John nodded toward the door. "I didn't want to touch it until you'd examined it."

O'Leary crossed to the door and made a minute examination of the knob and bolt. "Everything looks sound and undisturbed." He took out his pocket handkerchief, wrapped it around his hand, and turned the dead bolt. "Where's the key?"

"On that nightstand," John replied.

"Fetch it for me, will ya?"

Several moments later, the door stood open. Lordis ventured into the room like someone crossing thin ice.

"Miss Goode," John said to the bulging-eyed housekeeper.

Lordis tore her eyes from the gruesome scene.

"Detective O'Leary wants to know why . . . despite the evidence . . . this is not suicide."

She expelled a sound of disagreement. "Impossible!" Lordis exclaimed. Not knowing what Le Brun had already imparted, she proceeded to tell O'Leary how the man in the bed was actually Edmund, and why and how that had come to be. She emphasized that he had insisted on the masquerade specifically out of fear of losing his life. She attested, while inviting John to support her, that Edmund's every word and gesture the previous night had indicated his desire to stay alive.

"Merde!" O'Leary exclaimed, turning a full circle in his frustration. "I won't even ask ya to pardon my French this time. It's deserved."

"It is," John agreed. "I wonder aloud, before your brother officers arrive, if there's any reason now to complicate the issue by tellin' them who died first."

"Who knows at this point? I'll have to share it with my superior," O'Leary said. Then his face took on a quizzical expression. "Are ya still asking me to keep that information under my hat?"

"I would appreciate it. At least for a few hours."

"Why?"

"Because I'm usin' Joseph Pulitzer and his army of reporters to do legwork for us, and his payback is first rights to break the story."

O'Leary nodded grimly. "I *knew* you knew how to play the game. All right. But if all hell breaks loose for some reason, I'm telling everybody that you withheld the information from me."

"Fair enough. Do me one more favor."

"Now what?" O'Leary exclaimed in exasperation.

"Please make sure the body is turned over and the small of the back is examined. There had better not be a kidney-shaped birthmark there."

"Why's that?"

"Then this body would be Miniver's. Again."

O'Leary did another full-pivot turn. "Jesus Christ! You're sayin' somebody dug up the body I saw put inta the ground yesterday afternoon and brung it back inta this house?"

"Humor me," John said. "The impossible has already happened in havin' a dead body in here; Perhaps merely checking for a repaired throat will suffice."

"Consider it done."

The front doors sounded so smartly that John assumed a patrolman was banging on it with his nightstick.

"I'll let them in," Lordis said. She had turned so pale that John was glad to have her leaving the bedroom.

O'Leary raised a forefinger at her retreating back. "But don't let them upstairs! Tell them Mr. Le Brun and I are scrutinizing the scene and don't want lots of hands and feet mucking it up."

"Shall I use those words?" Lordis asked.

"Those very words. Then they'll know 'tis me."

"That desk might have been rifled through," John pointed out.

O'Leary crossed to it. "That's a weak point. It just looks like he had a lot of business to care for, what with his brother's death."

"Why would he take out the revolver purchase slip?" John asked.

"It was probably in the same box as the revolver," posited the city detective.

"What box?"

"Have you seen a box?"

"*You're* the one talkin' about a box, Detective. There may not be one. He could just as well have kept the gun in one of the drawers."

"And he kept the sales receipt with the revolver, either way." O'Leary whirled around and regarded the windows. "What about those? Open when you came in?"

"Just as they are."

"Could someone—"

"Have rappelled down from the roof onto one of the ledges and climbed back up?" John supplied. "I'd check it out if I were you."

"But wouldn't that be a brassy thing to do, what with Fifth Avenue fronting two windows and Sixty-second Street the other two?"

"You mean 'brassy' as in bluffin' your way into the Metropolitan Club, changin' disguises, and committin' murder in a hallway?"

O'Leary nodded his understanding. He shoved up one of the windows. John observed that, between the frame's age and the humidity of the summer, the wood and glass moved with some scraping and rattling. In his estimation, it would have been enough to awaken a skittish man. The city detective leaned out and looked down, then up. He whistled at the proposition of entry from the roof. "Not for me, brother! That's asking ta have yourself splattered all over the pavement."

"But what's the alternative?" John asked.

"Suicide," said O'Leary with conviction. He walked to the bed and bent close to Edmund's head. "There are powder burns around the entry hole. Someone would have ta have gotten right up beside him."

"He was fast asleep," John noted.

"More likely he was wide awake and put the gun to his own head," O'Leary said.

"I don't believe it," Lordis repeated. She had returned to the doorway.

O'Leary's hand swept over the bed. "Look at the evidence!"

"There is hard evidence to the contrary," John said.

"And it is . . . ?" O'Leary invited.

"That's not his revolver."

Lordis took several steps into the room and studied the weapon. She looked up at Le Brun with a pained expression. "I think you're wrong, John. He was loading that gun right in front of us only a few hours ago."

Le Brun shook his head. "He was loadin' a Colt Single Action Army revolver all right, but not that one. That's a Model 1850. You see how long the barrel is? It's five and one-half inches. The weapon we saw Edmund load was a Model *1840,* with a four-and-three-quarter-inch barrel."

[125]

"Other than the barrel length," O'Leary said, "they are virtually indistinguishable. And we are only talking three-quarters of an inch. It's not a Buntline Special."

"I know my handguns," John insisted softly. "Tellin' me that was the weapon he was loadin' is like tellin' a banker that a nickel is a quarter."

O'Leary straightened up and crossed to the desk. "Wait a minute! This slip says that the revolver is an 1850."

"But it doesn't say to whom that revolver was sold," John pointed out.

"Ah, Joseph, Mary, and the kid!" O'Leary threw himself onto the Morris chair. "My cabbage is killing me. You're saying whoever slipped in here shot Mr. Pinckney with the 1850, stole the 1840 from his dead hand, and deposited that receipt there just to confuse us."

"He had an 1840 before he locked himself in here," John insisted. "That's an 1850."

O'Leary pinched the bridge of his nose, then rubbed vigorously. "You've been at this business longer than me, and you've got a sterling reputation. So let's stay on your path for a while. The killer was friendly enough with Mr. Pinckney to know that he had a Colt Army, but not well enough to know the model?"

John had taken out his pocket handkerchief. He blew his nose before replying, "It's just as likely that the murderer knew nothin' of the other Colt. That's why he brought along the sales slip; he wanted proof left in the room that Mr. Pinckney owned the weapon. So you could assume suicide."

O'Leary shook his head. "But *two* Colt Single Action Army revolvers?"

"The Peacemaker is the most popular handgun in the country," John stated evenly, using the Colt Single Action Army's popular nickname. "How many have you found on criminals, Detective?"

O'Leary tipped his imaginary hat. "One point for you."

"Was Edmund a sound sleeper?" John asked Lordis.

"I would have no idea concerning the middle of the night," she answered. "Occasionally, when I had to arouse him for an early appointment, he was difficult to awaken. I'd have to bang on his door."

Le Brun said, "He hadn't slept much the previous two nights, worryin'. Once I was in the house, he seemed to relax a great deal, wouldn't you say?"

"A great deal," Lordis agreed.

"And I failed him. One minute he's sleepin' the sleep of the dead; the next minute he *is* dead. What about his desk?" John asked. "Would he leave it like that?"

Lordis regarded the document-strewn writing surface and open drawer. "Ordinarily, no. He was a fastidious man. Check his closet if you want some idea. But, then again, he was greatly distracted." She hunched up her shoulders as sign of her uncertainty.

John gave the cranky window another glance, trying to calculate the likelihood that it had been used.

O'Leary pushed himself up from the chair, stooped, and retrieved the revolver by hooking his pinkie finger around the trigger guard. Using his handkerchief, he cracked open the cylinder and slowly spun the chambers. "One shot fired." He set the gun back down, precisely where it had been. "Precious little to go on," he judged. "I guess I'll have the boys in now, unless there's something else."

"I think it best if we remove the wills and other documents," John suggested.

O'Leary hitched up his trousers, which had neither belt nor braces to hold them. "That's fine. Why don't you take 'em, Miss Goode?"

"We'll be downstairs," John said. "I'm anxious to hear about the roof."

"I hope one of the boys used ta be a steeplejack," O'Leary said.

JOHN FOLLOWED LORDIS down to the pantry, where she dropped the stack of documents on the table. She sat, and John followed suit. For a few moments, Lordis just stared at the manila envelopes that contained the trifolded wills.

"Both brothers said they had mentioned me. I hope they didn't leave me too much. It's enough to bear these tragedies without being suspected myself."

"Open them and find out," John prompted.

Lordis first selected Miniver's last will and testament. She pulled it from its envelope, smoothed it out on the table, and read it aloud. It left the sum of one dollar to his ex-wife, so that she could not contest on the basis of his having overlooked her. After debts and expenses, it left the balance to his brother, mentioning the terms of Chriswell's will concerning the lapsing of the house. In the event of Edmund's predeceasing him, he left the bulk of his estate to his sister. Lordis was to receive the sum of three thousand dollars. She seemed genuinely touched.

"That's two years of my salary. At least I won't have to worry about being out on the street for a while."

"I'm sure Mrs. Topley would never let that happen," John said.

Lordis pointed to the two witness signatures. One was that of the lawyer's clerk. The other belonged to William Hastings.

"I wonder that he didn't leave Mr. Hastings anything," Lordis remarked. "He's served the family longer than I have. And he has such a nice family."

"Open Edmund's," John directed.

The second will was much like the first. In fact, the same attorney had drafted both. Edmund had no ex-wife to worry about, but he stipulated that if he had any future heirs, the estate after expenses should be divided equally among them. He bequeathed two thousand dollars to the Metropolitan Club. Again, Lordis was left the sum of three thousand dollars. The rest went to Miniver as survivor and Sarah if Miniver should predecease. Again, William Hastings was one of the witnesses. The wills had been made within weeks of each other, in March of 1904.

"Looks like the brothers talked this out between them," said John.

"And came to a mutual estimation of their affection toward me," Lordis added.

"Six thousand's nothin' to sneeze at," John declared. "Are you acceptin' proposals of marriage?"

Lordis smiled. "No. I'm far too preoccupied worrying that the money will put me on the list of suspects."

John scowled at the suggestion. "The one who now heads the list is your sister-in-spirit, Mrs. Topley."

"That's absurd!" Lordis returned, her face fierce in support of Sarah. "They are doing very well. And money has always been of secondary importance to her and Ben. Ben's very smart. If he had wanted to be rich, he wouldn't have managed a theater. In this city, with his brains—"

John laughed. "All right, all right, Barrister! You've made your point."

"Ridiculous!" Lordis exclaimed, still winding down. "I'd rather believe someone *flew* through one of those windows before I suspected Sarah or Ben." Her eyes went wide. "We've missed something!"

"What?"

Lordis leaned far across the table toward John, as if afraid he might not get her words. "The killer entered *Edmund's* bedroom, not Miniver's! That means that Edmund was the target after all! It also means that somebody saw through his ruse to assume his brother's identity. So the killer was somebody Edmund was close to on Friday or yesterday."

"Good observation, but faulty extrapolation," John said, touching Lordis lightly on the nose. "Miniver's bedroom windows were closed tight. The killer could merely have observed from the street that the way into the house was through Edmund's bedroom. Once inside, he found his victim sooner than he expected. Since there was only one brother left, Miniver could just as easily have been the target. Or the remainin' heir, if we suspect the Topleys."

"I forbid it!" Lordis said.

"Then help me find the real killer."

"How?"

"We must locate a copy of the house blueprints. Comin' into that room by rappellin' from the roof is somethin' out of a Sherlock Holmes story."

"And getting to Edmund any other way would have to be done by Kellar or Malini."

"You mean Harry Kellar, the magician?"

"Right."

"I don't know the name Malini."

"Oh, I suppose he's a local phenomenon. He came to this country when he was young and was raised on the Bowery. He's a constant hit at the Waldorf-Astoria and other large hotels. I've seen him actually take a man's hat off while they're seated at a table, set it down for a time, then lift it up and produce two pounds of ice underneath."

"You understand it was a trick," John said, knowing that Lordis was searching for upbeat conversation but determined to keep on the track. "If Edmund didn't kill himself and I'm wrong about the gun, this murder was similarly a trick. It's up to me to figure out how it was done."

"Up to *us*," Lordis affirmed.

"Very well."

Lordis rapped on the tabletop. "The killer can't have gained entry from inside the house. The ceilings of both Edmund's and Miniver's rooms are solid, with the open ballroom above. The floors are directly over the open living room . . . not to mention mostly covered by carpeting. Two of their walls are outside ones. The third ones are bathrooms and connecting passage, with the open living room below and open ballroom above. The fourth walls are shared with the hallway. No breaks in them like those secret doors in the ballroom."

John merely stared at his companion. Every word she said was true. He had waited for her to consider a second key to the empty bedroom, but the idea evidently had not occurred to her. The possibility had come to John more than an hour earlier. He could not, however, reconcile the timing. He was out into the hallway before a murderer could have dropped the revolver, taken Edmund's revolver, placed the sales receipt, slipped through the secret passage, gone out the other bedroom door and locked it.

"Here you two are!" Detective O'Leary walked into the pantry from the library. "You'll be greatly relieved to know that the body has *not* had its t'roat slit and sewn up."

"That's a mercy," John exhaled.

"One of the boys scampered out on the roof and said there are plenty of places where a rope could be belayed, but he saw no evidence."

"Do you think the shop that sold that Colt would have a record of whom it was sold to?" John asked.

"They might. It's on my list to check. But I wouldn't be too hopeful. The sale was made five years ago."

John glanced at Lordis, then back at the detective. "I need to share with you a possible suspect." He proceeded to relate the story of Edmund's married lover, Marie Van Leyden. "I don't know how you'll handle it," he concluded, "but it's gonna be a trick maintainin' the woman's reputation while investigatin' her husband."

"The woman be damned!" O'Leary exclaimed. "She's an adulteress and deserves whatever befalls her!" The flames of Catholic damnation smoldered in the Irishman's eyes.

"For pity's sake," Lordis said, "put yourself in the young woman's place, Mr. O'Leary. She was bartered off for her father's benefit. What would you do in a loveless marriage?"

"Drink and stay outta the house. It's what I do in *my* loveless marriage." He did not pronounce his words through a smile.

"I think there's a way to get what we want and still keep the peace with the Van Leydens if they're innocent," John said. "Would you let me have a stagger at it?"

"All right," O'Leary relented. "Ya have until noon tomorrow. I'll be damned if I fail ta pursue a lead to its conclusion. Not with this blessed mystery of a case." He glanced around the room. "The simplest explanation is most often the right one. I'll report what I've seen and your objections to havin' it declared a suicide, but my superiors may want it 'solved' . . . if ya know what I mean."

"And you?" John asked, to be sure.

"I won't rest until I have a long conversation with the man who played Witherspoon King on Wednesday night."

Le Brun nodded with satisfaction. "How long until you're finished here?"

"Another hour maybe." The detective looked at Lordis. "It being Sunday and all, I suppose you'd like us ta deliver the body ta the morgue."

"Please."

"And as ta cleanin' the room?"

"I'll do it," Lordis said.

"But . . ." O'Leary face pinched. "It's more than blood."

"I'll do it," Lordis repeated.

Y ET AGAIN, JOHN FOUND HIMSELF relegated to the Metropolitan Club's Strangers' Waiting Room. He took advantage of the three Sunday newspapers that had been delivered to the room. Among their pages, he found news of the opening of the New York Yacht Club's "Great Regatta." *Commodore Morgan is sure to be in his glory today,* John thought. Queen Maud and King Haakon of Norway were in attendance. He read of the effects of the eruption of Mt. Vesuvius six weeks earlier and of Teddy Roosevelt's bears. He also read of Roosevelt's impending visit to Panama, the first such visit of a president to a New World country. *Edmund Pinckney's money at work,* John thought. A body had been found floating in the East River. That bit of news had merited only four lines on page 5.

"Well, Mr. Le Brun!" Charles Lanier had entered the room at full speed. He had a white carnation stuck in his lapel buttonhole. "I'm so glad I happened to visit the club on the way back from church. How is it going?"

"Not well," Le Brun said. "Both Pinckney men are now dead."

"Good God! How?"

"Again murder. Right inside their house this time."

"Astounding."

"It is. Mr. Maurice Van Leyden is a member of this club."

"He is."

"Have you ever heard rumors of dalliances between his young wife and other men?"

"I have not. Should I have?"

"I can't answer that. I'm sure you will keep this between us. Is Mr. Van Leyden a regular attendee of this club?"

"He belongs to several clubs, including the Union, so he spreads himself around. If I'm not mistaken, he's here mostly on Fridays. He plays whist at another club. It's a passion with him. I can't recall the name of that club, though."

"You had a book in this room that listed the various clubs."

"So we do! *Rossiter's.* Now where . . . ?" He opened a cabinet door. "Here it is. Let's see. Van Brock. Van Buren. Van Dyck. Van Hise. Van Leyden. Yes. The Knickerbocker Club."

"Is there an address for the club there?"

Lanier riffled through the book and located John's need. Le Brun extracted his notebook to copy down the street and number. The photographs of Edmund Pinckney and Witherspoon King dropped onto the floor. He picked them up and tucked them more securely into the notebook's back pages.

"And Mr. Van Leyden's home address?"

"I'll get it for you. You think he's tied to these murders?"

"He has recently entered the list of suspects."

"Was his wife involved with Edmund Pinckney?"

"This is the kind of information I wouldn't want to know if I were in your position," John suggested.

"Yes," Charles Lanier relented. "You're right." He gave Le Brun a sideways look. "Are you starting to regret getting involved?"

"On the contrary; I am more determined than ever to solve it. I find that crimes of the simple mind are simple, done because of rage, drunkenness, laziness, and the like. It takes the truly clever to provide a cunnin' challenge. Since their brains generally earn them more than their fellow man, the motivation is often fear of loss. But whatever the motive, they *plan*. It's the difference between playin' tick-tac-toe and chess."

Lanier erected a knowing smile. "And you are the chess player. I'll get you Mr. Van Leyden's address."

THE VAN LEYDENS lived a block north of Washington Square, among the old money that had declined to emigrate to the northern wilds of Manhattan Island. Le Brun arrived at twenty minutes past eleven. He was shown into the large and stately brownstone town house by a stout woman in servant's dress. He presented his business card and his letter of introduction from the Metropolitan Club. While he waited in the parlor, John noted that Maurice Van Leyden had indeed bought a great deal of European art. Oil paintings filled the ten-foot-high walls, with barely any room between their gilt frames. Marie had not come cheaply.

The first to greet him was a beautiful woman with enormous brown eyes and an elegantly long neck. She had a fetching smile and deep dimples, but there was no mistaking that she had endured stress in the past few days. She had entered the room in a rush.

"Mr. Le Brun? I am Marie Van Leyden." She extended her right hand.

John clasped her hand in his. His left hand pressed another of his business cards firmly into her palm, just as her husband entered the room. The woman was sharp enough not to look down at the card. John watched her move it up into the tight sleeve of her gray silk dress.

"Mr. Van Leyden," John said, moving past the wife. The husband was short, rotund, and appearing every one of his sixty-two years. His rugose nose and mouth seemed childlike, below his large spectacles and surrounded by a wealth of bristly white mustache and beard. "I sincerely apologize for invadin' your house on a Sunday mornin'."

"Not at all," the real estate mogul insisted, returning the letter of introduction. "Please, have a seat."

"I thank you."

Van Leyden grabbed his wife's hand just as it retreated from her sleeve and pulled her to the sofa, where they sat side by side. "I asked Mrs. Van Leyden to meet you as well because she also knew Mr. Pinckney."

"Do tell!"

"She took the news very hard," Van Leyden stated, staring at his wife. "Harder than I would have expected."

John tried not to look fully at the woman, but he saw out of the periphery of his vision that she was looking down at her clasped hands. "Why do you say that?"

"Well, they didn't know each other very well. I introduced them about six months ago at the Metropolitan Club. Actually, outside the ladies' restaurant."

"Women are not allowed inside the club," Marie said.

Maurice rolled his eyes. "That's *why* I introduced them. Marie espouses suffrage and other rights for women. I knew that Edmund had a vague notion to form a more *sexually* equal club. I suppose it's an idea whose time has come, what with the new century and everything. At any rate, *he* had been pitching it full tilt for the past month or so."

"I grieve for a man who had such forward-thinking and generous views," Marie said softly.

"This is precisely what I came to ask you about," John said. "We have exhausted leads among those at the club Wednesday night. You were not there."

"No. I'm a whist enthusiast. There was a three-day tournament at the Knickerbocker Club Tuesday through Thursday." He beamed. "I took second place."

"Congratulations. I need to know if you believe Edmund could actually have been murdered for his new club campaign."

Van Leyden scrunched up his moon face. "I wouldn't think so. To tell you the truth, the club talk about him was more of derision than anger." He looked at his wife. "You know that it's true, Marie. If such a club is to come into being, it won't get much support from the Metropolitan. Nor from the Union, the Union League, or the Knickerbocker for that matter."

John took out his notebook, extracted the photograph of Witherspoon King, and held it up for view. "Do you know him?"

"I do now. That's Mr. King."

"Is it true that you have in your employ a man who closely resembles King?" John watched the man carefully for a reaction to a scenario the investigator alone had concocted. Van Leyden showed none at all. Rather, he was the most relaxed person Le Brun had interrogated for the case.

"No indeed! I have seven men working for me, and four typewriter girls." He laughed and held up the photograph for his wife to look at. "Actually, Matilda looks more like him than any of the men. Am I right?"

Mrs. Van Leyden nodded without smiling.

"Who told you I employed such a person?" Van Leyden asked.

John shrugged and offered his lie in a casual tone. "Someone at the Metropolitan Club. He was clearly mistaken."

"I should say so! I'm not an idiot. Whoever it was insinuated that I was behind the murder." He gave out a small harrumph. "I think I know who it was. Not below causing me trouble, that little weasel."

"Do either of you have *any* idea why Mr. Pinckney would be murdered?"

The pair shook their heads in tandem. Marie sat bolt erect on her seat, so that she was half a head taller than her husband. John had all he could do to keep his disapproval of the marriage off his expressive face. Marie looked too young to be his daughter, much less his wife.

John retrieved the newspaper scrap. "Unfortunately, you will be readin' in tomorrow's paper that Mr. Pinckney's twin has also died."

The couple started visibly at the news and exchanged astonished remarks.

"I am not at liberty to reveal any details," John said, closing discussion. "As one of the city's most prominent real estate persons, might you have any delicate information to share with me about the Pinckney family?"

"Chriswell, the father, was known for his eccentricity," Maurice said without hesitation. "And you know what they say: The nuts don't fall far from the tree." He gave his wife's hand a good squeeze. "They evidently got themselves in trouble with someone powerful."

"If you'll excuse me," Marie said. "I want to go to twelve o'clock

Mass early and pray for both men." Her hand was released by her husband as she rose from the sofa.

"Will you be goin' as well, Mr. Van Leyden?" John asked.

"No indeed. I'm Dutch Reformed. My wife is the papist in the family."

"I wonder, then, if you'd allow me to ride with Mrs. Van Leyden," John said. "I'd like to attend Mass myself."

"By all means. Anything more I can answer?"

"Not at the moment, sir."

Van Leyden grunted as he pushed himself up from the sofa. "I'll have the carriage pulled around front. It was a pleasure meeting you."

M RS. VAN LEYDEN had already disappeared from the room. Left to his own devices, John let himself out the front door. The sidewalk and street were fairly abustle with groups of people in fine clothing heading by foot and carriage to their places of worship. A minute later, Marie appeared with a Belgian lace shawl around her shoulders. A handsome landau pulled by a proud pair of horses exited from the Van Leyden driveway into the street. *No modern horseless machines for the old money,* John thought. He opened the carriage door and allowed the woman to enter first. With the Van Leydens' driver just behind and above his left shoulder, John kept up a steady stream of bland tourist questions which she answered during the few minutes it took to reach their destination. While he spoke, she swiftly pressed the business card he had given her back into his hand. He glanced at his note. His scrawled message about needing to speak with her alone and the telephone number of the Hotel Savoy had had no reply jotted down.

St. Francis Xavier Church was crammed between residences on West Sixteenth Street. John guessed that in such a dynamic city, the Romanesque structure would be gone within twenty years. It was a dinosaur from a less affluent era, beggared by the uptown Gothic St. Patrick's Cathedral, which was supported by those of old money who had moved north and the nouveaux riches of the Upper East Side. John led the way into the dark sanctuary but allowed Marie to select their seats. He was relieved when she chose the next-to-last pew, far from any of the early-arriving parishioners. They genuflected, sat, and bowed their heads.

"How much do you want?" Marie asked.

"What?" John replied. He had been about to question the woman when she had surprised him and turned the tables.

"I have heard from other women in society that *Town Topics* will pay up to four hundred dollars for news of marital infidelity. I can offer you five hundred dollars."

"I want none of your money, madam," John whispered with emphasis. "I am a southern gentleman."

Marie Van Leyden looked John Le Brun hard in the eyes and saw the truth. A great weight seemed to rise from her shoulders. He tried to put himself in her place, to imagine hearing of the death of Edmund Pinckney and knowing the man had been in her arms at the time. Puzzling out the fact of who had died in Edmund's place. Wondering what it all meant and if it could have anything to do with her and their secret. Then, just minutes before, hearing that the real Edmund, her lover, was now dead in truth.

John said, "Edmund confessed everythin' to me because he trusted me."

"When did he do that?"

"Just yesterday. I hope you will confide in me as well. Does your husband know about you and him?"

"I didn't think so, until Wednesday night," she answered. "I'm so confused, and I've had no word. Edmund was with me. Who was killed that night?"

"His brother. And now Edmund's dead, too. Murdered inside his home. The most likely reason is that the murderer learned that Miniver Pinckney was the one at Edmund's club Wednesday."

"Which means that Edmund *was* the original target."

"It would seem that way."

"Why was Miniver there?"

"Pardon me, Mrs. Van Leyden," John said, raising his hands to his lips in an attitude of prayer. "Precious time is flyin', and it's more important for me to get answers right now than for you. I noted several occasions durin' my interview with your husband that he made remarks that sounded like he was torturin' you."

"The 'sexual' remark."

"And belittlin' Edmund with that remark about nuts. He also made a point to drag you into the room when I had only asked to see him. Has his nature changed in the past few weeks? Overly sweet or sarcastic?"

"No. Just preoccupied by his whist tournament."

"Has he ever revenged himself on someone, say over money that wasn't paid?"

Marie's head was bowed so low that her chin nearly touched her chest. "He has tenants thrown out on the street for not paying their rent. But that's always done for him by lawyers and the police."

"The Pinckney brothers were certainly murdered by proxy. Does he have a temper?"

"He doesn't get mad, Mr. Le Brun; he gets even."

"Just as bad. Have you told anyone at all about yourself and Edmund?"

"Only Mrs. Alice Ainsworth. She's my best friend."

"Has she provided excuses for your trysts?"

"Yes. I needed an understanding confidante who could pretend to have been with me. She was married to the third earl of Devon. Years ago, her newly rich father sold her in marriage so he could become the father-in-law to an English title. The earl died last year. Alice is free to help me."

"Does she dislike your husband?"

"Intensely."

"You'll pardon me for this observation, but he seems easy to dislike."

"He's good to clients, friends, and trusted servants."

The wife's reply spoke volumes. John put it on the top of his mental file. "You may need to use Mrs. Ainsworth more in the comin' days. Your husband mentioned that you visit his place of business."

"Yes."

"I doubt highly that he would leave incriminatin' evidence about killin' Edmund for you to find at home. You need to play detective, Mrs. Van Leyden."

"Am I in danger?"

"I don't think so," John said, more to put the woman at ease than out of a firm conviction. He added an outright lie he hoped she would believe. "Husbands generally take their anger out on the other man.

Look for business cards that make no sense. See if he has withdrawn large sums of money for no stated purpose."

Mrs. Van Leyden took in a large breath. John watched her neck and jaw working with emotion. "I believe I may be in the family way, Mr. Le Brun."

John took a moment to absorb the news.

"I am quite regular in my months," she went on. "I am overdue by two days."

"Perhaps it's caused by the shock of the news."

"I hope so."

"Are you and your husband intimate?"

"Less and less. The last time was around Easter. He would know this is not his child."

The church organ had begun to boom out during Marie's last words. John used the sounds as an opportunity to look around, as if seeking out the pipes. When he had surveyed the entire sanctuary, he again lowered his head.

"Is your chauffeur Catholic?"

"No."

"Does he usually stand in the back of the church and wait for you to finish?"

"No."

"Don't raise your head. He's standin' six feet behind us. You can always leave a message for me at the Hotel Savoy."

The old chauffeur's presence compelled John to remain in the pew for the entire mass. He said prayers for himself and those he loved. The rest of the time, he mumbled through the responses from memory and concentrated his mind on all that he had gathered concerning the murders in the previous days. He no longer felt at sea; he had two focuses. Moreover, he had two plans of attack.

WHEN THE MASS ENDED, John bade Mrs. Van Leyden goodbye and chose to walk east rather than accept another carriage ride. He caught a northbound trolley and rode it up to Seventy-third Street. He hurried to Joseph Pulitzer's house and was admitted by a man named Pollard whom John recognized as one of Pulitzer's battalion of secretaries.

"Mr. Pulitzer is about to take a carriage ride in Central Park," Pollard informed. "He would no doubt enjoy your company."

"I would be delighted," Le Brun said.

John fought the temptation to wander into the parlor and pick out a tune on the grand piano. He would not be the cause of a Pulitzer tirade. Five minutes later, John climbed into his second landau of the day. Already seated were Pulitzer and his faithful driver. The editor wore full morning clothes and a top hat. He had a pink tea rose pinned to his lapel, and a pair of vases on either side of the landau were filled to overflowing with the same flowers.

"A good Sunday to you, Mr. Le Brun! I trust you remember Mr. Eugene Stewart," Pulitzer said of his coachman.

"I do indeed. Mr. Stewart." The gentlemen tipped their hats to each other.

They crossed Fifth Avenue and took the entrance to Central Park that lay almost directly opposite, heading toward the lake. All manner of New Yorkers were making use of the sidewalks and meadows, pushing perambulators, walking, picnicking, coaxing along hoops with sticks, "scorching" by on safety bicycles, flying kites, buying food from the cart vendors, admiring the works of artists, browsing boxes of secondhand books. Those not engaged in vigorous activities were invariably dressed in their Sunday finery, adding to the beauty of the park in its summer best before the drying days of July and August stole its vibrant colors.

"You know, I have never asked your age," said Pulitzer.

"Fifty-nine."

"Exactly my age! No wonder we see the world in the same light."

"And *don't* see the world in the same light," John added.

Pulitzer laughed. "How far have you gotten in the investigation?"

As they rode, John went into considerable detail concerning the events of the past forty-eight hours. Pulitzer listened with rapt attention, speaking only to ask insightful questions. He refrained from exclamations or judgments when John spoke about himself rising from Lordis Goode's bed or when he passed along Marie Van Leyden's fear that she was pregnant with Edmund Pinckney's child. In spite of the fact that he was a newspaperman, Pulitzer had earned Le Brun's respect for circumspection on Jekyl Island years before. He was not surprised, therefore, when Pulitzer said, "I can't print much of this yet. Not until you have the culprit in your sights. Otherwise, he could see how far you've come and slip away. Besides, with Van Leyden entering the list of suspects, the chase is now divided. I will not have my paper printing anything that can later be refuted."

"What about Miniver bein' killed in Edmund's place?" John asked.

Pulitzer shook his head vigorously. "We'll sell an extra fifty thousand copies when we shout that we've solved the crime. What can I do to hasten that day?"

"I must prevent the police from declarin' the second murder a suicide and pinnin' the first one's death on his brother. I'm workin' alone up here. I cannot let them close this case by declarin' it what it isn't. I need to be able to call upon their resources at any moment."

"Of course you do," Pulitzer agreed. "So you need to know how someone got into that bedroom and shot Edmund."

"I do. Whimsy House's blueprints might could unlock the puzzle."

"What year was it built?"

"In 1881."

"That's why I don't recall anything about it," Pulitzer said. "I didn't move to New York until 1883. But I bet I know someone who can locate those blueprints: Stanford White."

"Can I speak with him today?"

"We'll give him a call when we finish this ride. Eugene, why are we moving so slowly?"

"The traffic is terrible, sir," the coachman called back.

The number of landaus, hansoms, hacks, four-in-hand coaches, sulkies, barouches, gigs, cabriolets, coupés, victorias, stanhopes, phaetons, and tallyhos was frankly amazing to Le Brun. Central Park's lanes were choked with horses and carriages. He had been informed by his friend Geoffrey Moore when in London that the protocol was to tip one's hat the first time another carriage was passed but that a mere nod was deemed appropriate for subsequent meetings. The huge four-in-hands, which harkened back to the days before the railroads, when four horses pulled stagecoach-sized conveyances across the countryside, caused great confusion by their sheer dimensions. When Pulitzer's landau approached the Metropolitan Museum of Art, they were passed at breakneck speed by two coaches racing west through the center of the park, sending up clouds of dust.

"Goddamn four-in-hand imbeciles, racing up to the Westchester

Country Club," Pulitzer declared. "I hope they drown in the Spuyten Duyvil."

John assumed the all-but-blind man had identified the coach types by the tattoo of hoofbeats. Amazingly, he had also heard the greetings of no fewer than fifty other carriage riders and had been able to call back the names of half of them.

"According to what you have related," Pulitzer said, "the Benjamin Topleys and Maurice Van Leyden top the list of suspects."

"That is correct," John replied.

"And despite Van Leyden's words and behavior this morning, Topley would seem the more likely," Pulitzer declared.

Despite Pulitzer's reputation for irascibility and a wicked tongue, John enjoyed the newspaperman's company. There was no question in the country's mind that Joseph Pulitzer was a genius. This same genius treated John as an equal. Where others struggled to keep up on their mental walks with the blind man, John was perpetually either at his side or ahead. At this moment, they were hurtling at top speed on parallel tracks. For a man whom fortune had kept in Brunswick, Georgia, the validation was invigorating.

John concurred with Pulitzer. "Because a man who could look *and behave* so like Witherspoon King would most logically be an actor."

"Just so. Benjamin Topley is an impresario."

"Which brings me to my second need from you. This is one of the greatest cities in the world concernin' entertainment. Hundreds of actors must live here."

"Thousands. New York has actors like Kansas City has steaks."

"Is there any single place where I might gain information on all of them?"

"All? No. But on a significant number of them there is," said Pulitzer. "It's yet another club. The Players Club. Considering the low esteem with which actors are generally held, it has a venerable reputation. That's because it was created by the great Edwin Booth."

"I never saw him act," John said, "to my everlastin' regret."

"No surprise there. Despite being born south of the Mason-Dixon line, he stayed out of the South after his brother shot President Lincoln. Nearly ruined his career. Deprived us of perhaps his best years as Hamlet, Brutus, and Romeo."

"The Players Club, you say?"

"Correct. It's in Gramercy Square. I don't have any truck with the group, but you know who does? Morgan!"

"*J. P.* Morgan?"

"The Corsair himself. He wouldn't know good acting if it fell on him, but he holds the theater in high esteem. He knows it's one of the pillars of modern civilization, and consequently he supports it. I'll make a call to him as well when we get back. The Players Club will do backbends to please him. You'll also be needing photographs of Witherspoon King to distribute. I'll have Frank Cobb deliver copies of the *World* edition with the photo to the club. What else can I do?"

"Do you think you could part the Hudson River?" John asked. To his relief, Pulitzer chuckled.

A LATE LUNCHEON was the price for Pulitzer's telephone calls. The food was excellent, the screaming was endurable, and John for the first time met Kate Pulitzer, the mistress of the house. The woman, a distant cousin of Jefferson Davis, was so ordinary looking that John could have sworn he had seen her face drawn hundreds of times in catalogues. While Pulitzer fawned over her as if she were Athena and Aphrodite combined, Le Brun found nothing special about her. He supposed her unique quality was that she loved the tyrannical, hypochondriacal, mercurial man in spite of himself. He wondered just how unqualified this love was when he realized that the reason for her appearance was to wheedle more out of Pulitzer than her allotted eight thousand dollars per month for running the household. He ranted half-heartedly and lectured her, and she waited patiently for the typhoon to expend itself, clearly knowing that she would have her way. John felt modified compassion for most of Joseph Pulitzer's many complaints about his life, but for having a wife who did not scruple to use a guest as part of her tactics for winning money he sympathized fully.

B Y THE TIME John emerged from 7–15 East Seventy-third Street, he had two appointments. The first was for the evening, at the Players Club. The second was to meet with Stanford White, one of the nation's foremost architects, on the morrow. Pulitzer had related White's tale of Whimsy House after hanging up the phone. It seemed the house had been designed by Auguste Pelletier et Cie. The firm went out of business shortly after Pelletier lost his balance and fell to his death down an elevator shaft. All firm records had been sold to McKim, Mead, and White, then a rising star in the architectural firmament but not long afterward the very North Star. The problem, Stanford White had told Pulitzer, was that the Whimsy House blueprints were stored in a building near the Hudson. They would have to be retrieved Monday afternoon. White was taking Monday off, since his son had come down from Harvard during session break. The architect had rattled off his intended itinerary. When John had heard that his last stop was to be the opening of the new show at Madison Square Roof Garden, he proposed to meet White there. That way, he could take Lordis to the musical using Miniver Pinckney's tickets with no guilt. It vexed the Georgia ex-lawman that an entire day would be lost before getting the blueprints, but he told himself that he was lucky enough to receive that rapid a degree of attention in the country's biggest city.

"I AM SO GLAD you're back!" Lordis exclaimed as she let John through Whimsy House's front doors. Neko San, her white Persian, stood beside her. She wore a simple housedress covered by a large apron. The charm bracelet tinkled as she touched her hair self-consciously. She had it pulled back and tied with a calico ribbon. "This house has been an insane asylum."

"More reporters?" he asked.

"And gawkers. And more police, and even a funeral director trying to drum up business."

John noted a redness and puffiness around the woman's eyes. "I see you finally let your emotions out."

"Oh," Lordis said, touching a lower lid. "Do I look a fright?"

"No, you look fine."

"It was Sally who got me crying. We were reminiscing about her brothers. She was trying to think of one really nice thing either one had done for her. She couldn't. Isn't that awful?"

"It is."

"I was actually crying for her. I had long harbored a premonition that one or both of the Pinckney men would end badly. Of course, not *this* badly. And now Sally has to tidy up this mess. With me at her side, of course."

"How long was Mrs. Topley here?"

"Not very. She came to fetch all the legal documents, but I said they should remain here until the police gave us permission to move them."

John followed Lordis toward the library. "That was the thing to say. If the Topleys want copies of the wills and other legal papers, they should go to the lawyer who has the originals."

"Of course, this being Sunday, those offices won't be open until tomorrow. So we looked at everything together on the pantry table. I pretended not to have read the wills. She's stopping here tomorrow morning with Ben. He was holding auditions this afternoon."

"I can come by then," John said.

Lordis stopped walking. "Come by? Aren't you staying here tonight?"

"I don't think I should. You and me alone? What would that look like?"

Lordis shook her head in a frustrated manner. "Look like? First of all, who would know? Second, we *have* slept together, so why be hypocritical?"

"All right," John relented. "Speakin' of comin' by . . . has Mr. Hastin's returned?"

"I don't know. I haven't checked." Lordis walked to one of the windows and looked across the driveway up to the carriage house. "I can't tell."

"I'll check," John said. He moved through the library and pantry and out the house's back door.

"H OW WAS THE FISHIN'?" John asked when Hastings opened his door.

"Come in and find out," the handyman invited. He was in the process of applying fresh ice to half a dozen cleaned striped bass. "I was about to put these in the cellar," he said. "Mrs. Lassiter will have a smaller grocery bill."

"The other Mr. Pinckney is dead," John said, watching the man carefully. Surprise came onto his face, but John could not tell if it was genuine.

"Good Lord! How?"

As briefly as possible, Le Brun reviewed the early-morning murder and investigation. Hastings sat after a few seconds. He shook his head through most of the recounting. When it was finished, he said, "This is truly frightening. I feel so terrible for the brothers . . . and for their sister. But I also feel sorry for myself. Now me and my family are out on the street for sure."

"Why's that?"

"Because Mrs. Topley will inherit the place, and I'm sure Mr. Topley won't want it."

"How do you know Mrs. Topley is inheritin'?" John asked, drawing in a deep breath and getting a good whiff of fish and seaweed.

Hastings started. This reaction John was sure was genuine. "Well, doesn't she?"

"Unless a more recent will turns up. At least you don't have to worry about becomin' a suspect with all these fresh fish," John said. He took the notepad from his pocket. "Why don't you give me the names and addresses of the men you were fishin' with last night. And the place where you stayed. You know, anythin' that will corroborate your story."

"Let me have that," Hastings said, taking the notepad. He took a pencil from his kitchen table and printed two pages of notes in a fastidious hand while John observed the sand on the creel and the seaweed on the rubber boots. "Anything else?"

"While you're at it," John obliged, "please write down where you were on Wednesday night. I know you said that neither Miniver nor Edmund asked you to drive them anywhere."

"That's right. I was at my church, matter of fact, helping them paint the narthex. I'll write down the church name and the minister who was there. Anything *else*?"

"Have you thought more about the address of that doctor you delivered Miniver to?"

"I have. All I can tell you is the block. I'll write that down here too. Am I being considered some kind of accessory?"

"Not that I know of," John replied, rocking back and forth on his heels as he waited for the return of his notebook. "Of course, I am conductin' a private investigation for the Metropolitan Club. The police are pursuin' the case on their own track."

"But you consult with each other."

"That we do."

"I really know nothing."

"Then you are an innocent victim," John pronounced. "I shall say a prayer for you and your family. You witnessed wills for both brothers that were drawn a few years ago."

"I did."

"I take it from your uncertainty over Mrs. Topley inheritin' that you didn't actually read the wills."

"No. Evidently, that isn't a requirement. I merely signed them in the presence of the lawyer and the respective brothers."

"Did you know that a witness cannot be mentioned in a will?"

"I did not."

"Is this news to you now?"

Hastings paused for a moment. "Yes. Well, you're confirming something I had heard someone in my church pass as a remark several years back. At a funeral, I believe it was. I never planned to inherit anything from anyone, Mr. Le Brun, so I never confirmed the point."

"I see. You've worked for the Pinckneys one more year than Miss Goode."

"That's correct."

John narrowed his eyes and tilted his head slightly. "And yet she inherited a tidy sum from each brother and you inherited nothin'. Why is that?"

Hastings blinked several times. "Possibly because she's related. Why don't you ask her that? Life isn't fair, Mr. Le Brun. Surely you know that."

"If these wills hold up, and you inherit nothin' and she thousands, won't you be angry?"

"I'll be disappointed. Saying less wouldn't be honest. But if you're trying to implicate me, you're way off the mark. After I was asked to serve as witness to both wills and heard the remark in my church, my primary task became keeping those men safe and healthy. I figured the only money I'd get out of them was my salary while they were breathing."

"Right. Now that you know the second Mr. Pinckney committed suicide inside his locked bedroom, why would you say he did it?"

Hastings looked up at the ceiling. "I'd say that he might have had his brother killed because he was in deep financial trouble. When he felt he hadn't gotten away with it, he killed himself. Prison is not a place for those who have known nothing but the soft life."

"That's pretty much how it looked," John said.

Hastings folded his arms across his chest. "Since we both agree, perhaps I can ask you to help me carry this trough down to the cellar. Then you can let me get to sleep. I was up till all hours last night carousing."

"Makin' the best of days without wife and child, eh?" John said, plastering on a smile that exposed his molars.

"Absolutely. Come, grab an end!" Hastings said.

H ASTINGS LEFT LE BRUN in the pantry. In the dimness, John almost tripped over the stray neighborhood cat, Waif. He swore under his breath and gave the hissing creature a wide berth.

John had held on to the key to Miniver's bedroom door. He removed it from his vest pocket, went upstairs, and entered the room. He wondered where Lordis had gone, but he was just as glad he had not encountered her. He turned on the electric ceiling fixture and crossed to a French rococo writing desk. It had a solitary center drawer, but there was also a miniature rolltop "garage" of mahogany sitting on the back right corner of the writing surface. Le Brun went to his suitcase and took out his lock-picking tools.

In exchange for sixty days of better food, a second-story-burglar guest of the Brunswick jail had long ago given John invaluable lessons on the fine art of simple and combination lock picking. John had kept the tools by which he learned and had personally paid the train ticket to get the thief as far as Atlanta. The rococo desk's two locks took all of seventy seconds to open.

John had been hoping against hope to find either a business card of the doctor Miniver had visited or else the physician's bill. Instead, he found an unopened envelope that contained Miniver's cashed checks from the last two weeks of April and the first two weeks of May. Two of the checks, written eight days apart, were made out to a Dr. Jeffrey Stundel.

A tapping on the bedroom door caused John to drop the checks into the drawer and ease it closed.

"John? Are you in here?"

"I am."

The door opened. Lordis had taken off her apron and brushed out her hair. He saw that she had also applied makeup.

"Was Hastings in?"

"Yes."

"Do you think he's involved in the murders?"

"I don't know," John said. "Come on in."

"If you're as tired as I am, you must be exhausted," Lordis said through a weary smile. She sat on the edge of the bed.

"I am."

"Then I'll fix us something light to eat, and we can just rest."

John made a regretful expression. He slipped his lock-picking tools into one of his jacket pockets as surreptitiously as he could. "Unfortunately, there is no rest for the wicked. I have to pick up some information on the false Witherspoon King that Mr. Pulitzer is providin' for me."

"May I come along?"

"No. It's at a club."

Lordis nodded. The fact of female exclusion was implicit. "What happened with Maurice Van Leyden?"

"He managed to make himself a prime suspect," John replied.

Lordis sat up straighter. "Oh, really? How?"

In a few sentences, John repeated his interview with Mr. and Mrs. Van Leyden. He omitted Marie's personal news delivered in the church. He watched Whimsy House's "keeper of secrets" carefully as he spoke. The hunt had come closer and closer to Sarah Pinckney Topley, and John could trust Lordis neither as a willing nor unwitting accomplice to her "sister." He had great respect for clever men as criminal adversaries, but his respect for clever women was on an entirely higher level. Men used brains and muscle to struggle through life; women had only their brains. The extra exercise made them that much more formidable.

"I'd better get movin' if I want a good night's sleep," John said, rising.

"You will come back *here*?" Lordis worried. "I really don't want to spend tonight alone."

A question that had been pestering John for two days resurfaced with her words. "I've been meanin' to ask you, Lordis. You obviously know the city's restaurants, museums, and theaters. Who accompanies you when you go out?"

"Sally, of course. She has an understanding with Ben that, for her sanity's sake, she has to get out at least once a week. They arrange for the children to be watched, and she and I go out." She smirked. "Did you think it was some young and handsome man?"

"It should be," John replied. "You deserve a line of them, brawlin' for your attention."

Lordis stood as well, closed the distance between them, and kissed him gently on the lips. "I do so miss the flattery of southern gentlemen. Hurry back, John."

Reinvigorated by his words, Lordis sashayed from the room. John fetched his hat and hunted up a sharp pencil to replace the dull one in his pocket. By the time he exited the bedroom, Lordis had disappeared.

T HE PLAYERS CLUB was located on the south side of Gramercy Park, across the street from old elms and willows that grew behind the protection of an encircling iron fence. It was a tall brownstone building with a wide front balcony. The ironwork and overlarge gas lanterns were unique and fanciful. The traditional tragic and comic masks of acting looked down on the Georgia native, making John think of the twin pinkie rings that Benjamin Topley sported. The entrance design made it necessary to descend from the sidewalk before climbing the white marble front steps. A doorman allowed John to enter with no question, but he was immediately confronted by the club's major-domo with a smile and an outstretched hand that barred as well as greeted.

John announced himself.

"Mr. Le Brun! You are most welcome to the Players Club. I am Walter Oettel. Let me get Mr. Drew for you." He hurried up the steps immediately beside his post, turned to his right, and disappeared. John took the time to peek down the stairs that descended to his right. He heard raucous laughter and saw several men playing billiards. From somewhere above drifted down the strains of "Camptown Races," played upon the piano. As soon as it ended, the pianist struck up "I Dream of Jeannie with the Light Brown Hair."

"So, this is the celebrated John Le Brun of Georgia!" said the man walking down the stairs toward John with a very erect posture. He was a thin, impeccably dressed gentleman and appeared to be about fifty. He wore a supercilious look of worldliness. Part of his look came from highly arched eyebrows and heavily lidded eyes. He sported a mustache which curled up at either end and which imparted something of a sneer despite his broad grin.

"I am John Drew, president of the Players Club," he said, offering his hand, "and we are quite pleased to have you visit." He shook his head at the racket that reverberated from the lower level. "We don't play only billiards and poker. We also have a chess group and a periodic golf outing."

"Chess, eh?" John exclaimed. He felt immediately more comfortable.

Drew nodded. He leaned over the rail and called down to the billiard players in the cellar, "He's here!" Then, to John, "Allow me to give you a brief tour."

John grew more alert at the unusual activity on his behalf, but there was nothing he could do except follow his host upstairs, into a large room that contained a huge fireplace, a long sofa, half a dozen chairs, a grandfather clock, many pictures and paintings, and a bust of the founder, Edwin Booth, as Hamlet. At the archway between this room and a dining area stood a Steinway piano, upon which a young and very good-looking man was playing. Drew continued in a clockwise direction, through another archway that led into the club reading room. Here were a near-life-size painting of Edwin Booth above a small fireplace, chairs, sofa, and a long reading table with three lamps. From the walls hung memorabilia from the careers of the two generations of Booth actors. Around the next corner and up several steps was a cozy sitting area that led to the balcony. The windows above the French doors were leaded and dedicated to de Vega, Alfieri, Molière, and Goethe.

"What a wonderfully comfortable place this is," John said honestly.

"We think so. A wonderful dream, actually. Edwin Booth conceived of it after he visited the Garrick Club in London. But his concept went even farther. He wrote that its aim was to be 'the promotion of social intercourse between the representative members of the dramatic profession and the kindred professions of literature, painting, sculpture, music, and the patrons of the arts.' He purchased it. It was his home until his death. We preserve his rooms on the third floor exactly as they were."

"Might I be allowed to see them?"

"Certainly!"

They ascended the stairs. John was led into a large room that ran the length of the front of the building. It was not at all grand, as he had imagined, but rather homely and unprepossessing. The walls were filled with miniature portraits in frames. An old mirror topped a large fireplace. The wallpaper, upholstered chairs, and carpet were all of complementary floral patterns. A bust of Shakespeare perched above the writing desk. The center of the sitting area was dominated by a table and four chairs, as if waiting for a foursome of card players. In one corner sat a glassed-in cabinet filled with books. On a smaller table sat Booth's collections of pipes. At the opposite end of the long room were the actor's simple brass bed and, close by the window that looked out upon Gramercy Park, the chaise longue upon which he rested during the day. In short, the room looked very much as did John Le Brun's rooms in his home.

Drew picked up a human skull minus the jawbone, which sat next to a pewter mug. "The skull of Poor Yorick, used by both Edwin and his father. Not a man given to ostentation and vanity," the president commented, as if reading John's mind.

"Not at all."

Drew turned the skull around in his hands and appeared to be studying it, but John saw that his eyes were unfocused in memory. "There are many whose pleasing form and voice, whose ability to memorize a script and to prance upon a stage with confidence win them acclaim from the common audience. There are few whose nobility of soul shines through to illuminate the characters they play. This rarer class wins the hearts and minds of both the common playgoer and the cognoscenti. Edwin Booth was such a man.

"He loved to hear the members singing downstairs. Loved Stephen Foster particularly well, in fact. For years, we offered a full-course meal for fifty cents. When inflation threatened to make that impossible, he ordered us to hold the charge and bill him the shortfall. He liked old clothes and old friends." A tiny tear formed in the corner of Drew's eye. "I tell you this not as the club president or historian but rather as his friend."

By the time the president brought John back down to the piano, the number of converging members had grown to thirty. So many names were hurled at him that he could not absorb them all. He did, however, register five names he already knew. They were Charles Dana Gibson, the illustrator of the famous Gibson Girls who helped define the era; Augustus Saint-Gaudens, the creator of many monumental American statues; Richard Watson Gilder, the editor of *The Century* magazine; Childe Hassam, the American impressionist painter; and William Gillette, the actor whose incarnation of Sherlock Holmes forever after would define the role. The company impressed John far more than those of any other club, in London, Georgia, or New York, ever had.

"We've already shown around the photograph of Witherspoon King that was delivered from the *World*," Drew told John. "And we have decided that two New York actors could pass as Mr. King with little makeup. However, if you want this information, you shall have to earn it." Drew's smile was devilish. Several men laughed.

"And how might I do that?" John asked.

"Every few weeks, we declare a Pipe Night. That's when we haul down the churchwarden pipes, break out a keg of beer, and do a bit of performing. Not just the actors, mind you, but everyone in the club. Now, no less a patron of the arts and stalwart supporter of the Players Club than Mr. J. P. Morgan has informed us that you are an accomplished actor."

John shrank in his suit. "I am nothin' of the sort."

Drew took a backward step and lifted his hands in mock shock. "Then you have accused no fewer than ten members of the Jekyl Island Club of being gross liars. It seems that they traveled over choppy waters to Brunswick for some high-class entertainment last February and caught you in a production of *Macbeth*."

He was trapped. John was a frequenter of all sorts of productions at the L'Arioso Opera House in Brunswick. Over the years, he had come to know some of the men in the Dixie Shakespeare Company out of Atlanta. Consequently, when one of their number lost his voice hours before a mounting of *Macbeth* in John's hometown, the director and producer hunted John down and prevailed upon his "impressive presence and famous memory." Guilt was added to the plea, along with the old adage of "The show must go on." Secretly, John had enjoyed being asked. He was, eight months into his retirement, bored to distraction and searching for new outlets. Only the fear of embarrassing himself prevented him from accepting outright. When the producer promised to come out in front of the curtain before the production and present John's laundry list of hesitations for the audience, Le Brun at last acceded.

In true Shakespearean troupe fashion, the company had only eighteen players, many of whom doubled, trebled, and even quadrupled the tragedy's more than fifty parts. John played three small roles, furiously repeating his lines in the wings between entrances. By the time Macbeth's bloody head had been beheld, he knew that he had delivered passable performances. He had been allowed his own bow, and the applause had been tumultuous. When the actor's voice had still not returned the following night, John was again treading the boards, this time using his hands as well as his voice. The word of his first-night triumph had reverberated through Brunswick and across the waters to Jekyl Island. The second-night house was filled to overflowing, and a large party had come over from the ultraexclusive club. On the third night, he was sorry to relinquish the parts.

"The Bloody Sergeant!" William Gillette called out. "Set the stage for us, Mr. Le Brun!"

John exhaled forcefully. He was nervous but excited. Precisely this sort of high creative experience was what he fantasized about in little Brunswick. He told himself that he had no choice in the matter, but another part of him thrilled at the opportunity.

"You expect a simple ex-sheriff to remember a speech he memorized in February for two performances?" he asked.

"Enough cadging," Drew said with a stern tone in his mellifluous voice. "Mr. Morgan assured us that your memory is one of the marvels of the modern world."

"You tell 'em, Uncle Jack!" said one of the actors.

John cleared his throat. "Very well."

"Give the man room!" Childe Hassam cried out. "Back, ruffians, back!" He held a filled beer mug in his hand, obviously not the first one of the night.

John closed his eyes for a moment, then opened them and began to breathe in a labored manner, as if fresh from battle. He leaned forward and supported himself by clasping one knee. Without hesitation and with feeling, he recited the seventeen lines that depicted Macbeth's martial triumph over Macdonwald.

John had determined to stop at that point, but Gillette quickly supplied two of Duncan's interjections, compelling him to remember the eighteen other lines that completed the speech. When he had finished faultlessly, a cheer went up from the crowd. Hands slapped John on the back, and smiling mouths spoke high praise. A filled beer mug was pressed into his hand.

"Nobly done," Drew said once the noise had died down, "although the sergeant must have hailed from the *south* of Scotland."

The room erupted with laughter.

"Come, let's move out to the veranda," Drew said to Le Brun. The others left them to the more serious business of the night while Pipe Night rollicked on.

Beyond the Grill Room and its long dining tables lay a three-sided glassed-in veranda that overlooked a town-house garden with a single tree in its center. Drew gestured for Le Brun to sit at one of the tables.

"Considerin' it was originally a town house, the residence has been well adapted to a club," John observed.

"Thanks to Stanford White."

"Stanford White yet again!" John marveled. "Everywhere I go. The Metropolitan Club, the Players Club, Joseph Pulitzer's house, Madison Square Garden. Is he designin' the entire city himself?"

"It would seem that way. He lives just across the park. He's every actor's dream of a patron. Attends virtually every first night in New York. He charged nothing for all his work on this club."

"I'm meetin' him tomorrow night at Madison Square Garden," John let on. "He shall have my high praise."

"But you came about an entirely different matter," Drew said. "We have indeed thought of two actors who could easily pull off this infamous act. Both, however, have impeccable reputations. What's more, one is starring in a road production that was in Chicago last Wednesday."

"And the other man?"

Drew sighed. "We learned that he died last month. Went to his daughter's house in Teaneck and never told anyone how sick he was." The president brightened quickly. "Our club catalogue of actors has revealed no dead ringers for the culprit. But don't despair. The acting profession is quite tight. We've got the photograph circulating among more than a dozen producers and impresarios so far. By tomorrow, a score of candidates will have been suggested."

"But will you be able to track down their whereabouts?"

"Most certainly," Drew replied. "Actors want to work, so they're constantly pestering producers, directors, and even other actors about opportunities. They make sure, no matter how often they change addresses, that people in the profession know where they are."

"That's a mercy. Have you gotten the photograph to Benjamin Topley?" John asked.

"Topley? No. Of the twenty-three theaters operating full-time, half are music halls and vaudevilles. That's what Ben Topley mostly deals in . . . the quasi-legitimate fare."

"But the man we're seekin' would probably be on the less legitimate side of performin'," John said.

"Good point. We'll consider the music-hall performers as well."

"I was told you keep a repository of all the theater playbills here."

"We try to."

"You would have Topley's?"

"We might. But—"

"How many would that be within the last, say, six years?"

"He mounts four productions a year, on average."

"So someone could take the casts from those twenty-four productions and see if anyone in them resembled Mr. King?"

"We could try that," Drew allowed.

"And you should definitely distribute the photo of King to men like Topley."

"I understand."

"But *not* Topley," John emphasized.

"This I *do not* understand."

"He's the brother-in-law to the murdered men."

"You said *men?*" Drew uttered, with palpable surprise.

"Yes. Both brothers are now dead. And Mr. Topley's wife, their sister, stands to inherit what is left of their fortunes and their father's mansion."

"The plot thickens," said 'Uncle Jack' Drew.

"It does indeed."

"Not everyone needs to know this, clearly," the elegant president said. "I will tell all that I am personally delivering a copy of the photograph to Mr. Topley."

"Thank you very much."

Drew rearranged the utensils on his side of the table. "Speaking of things thickening, did you know that we make the most celebrated stew in all the city?"

"I did not."

"It's called Gramercy Stew. Two pounds of cold lamb and beef, flour, stock, two carrots, two turnips, four onions, two stalks of celery, salt, pepper, bay leaves, mushroom, ketchup, and chili pepper. It will sustain a thespian even through *Hamlet*."

"Sounds wonderful," John said.

"And our brandied peaches are the envy of restaurants throughout the city. Won't you stay to dinner?"

"I would like that," John allowed as yet another Stephen Foster tune wafted from the Steinway piano.

P ART OF THE REASON why John did not hurry back to Whimsy House was that he had been working nonstop for days in the most diverting city in North America. He told himself that he was owed the time. Moreover, he suspected that his opportunity to rub shoulders with some of the most famous and accomplished artists in the country would be a once-in-a-lifetime experience. To a man, they were gracious and welcoming, apparently fascinated by his line of work. Moreover, the longer he stayed, the more chance there was that other luminary members such as Mark Twain or Booth Tarkington might walk through the front doors. Another reason he lingered was that he did not want to spend hours hashing and rehashing his Sunday activities with Lordis Goode. While he fervently hoped against it, for all he knew she was the inside person working for the Topleys in securing the Pinckney fortunes before they totally evaporated.

John arrived at Whimsy House at half past ten. Lordis had clearly been waiting downstairs, because she answered the door within seconds.

"I was worried about you," she said, her eyebrows knit. "The streets can be deadly late at night."

"The clubs and houses can be just as deadly," he said. "I'm sorry if I kept you up."

"I catnapped for a while, but I couldn't sleep," she replied. "Now I can."

John yawned. "I think I'll sleep in Chriswell's bed."

"Really?"

"Yes indeed. I'm trustin' that any intruder will not expect to find someone there."

Lordis secured the front-door bolts. "Do you truly expect another intruder?"

"I have come to expect anythin' from this case," John said, climbing the stairs. He went to Miniver's room, slipped out of his clothes, sponge-bathed and brushed his teeth in the private bathroom, then changed into his nightshirt. In his haste to leave Brunswick on Wednesday, he had neglected to pack slippers. He fetched his derringer, walking across the carpeting in his bare feet. He exited the bedroom and checked the sleeping quarters of the Pinckney brothers and sister. When he came to the hall landing and looked down into the massive foyer, he saw that Lordis had extinguished all but two wall sconces. The darkness of the center of the house was thick and eerie. He descended and picked up the pace of his patrol, flicking lights on and off, throwing open doors and shutting them almost as quickly. No matter how quiet the house was, no matter how secure the locks or how empty the rooms, he could not relax. Someone knew secrets about the house that made it more shooting gallery than castle. Inevitably, finding nothing again, he was forced to end his watch.

John entered the master bedroom, poked around it for a few moments, then climbed into the bed, laughing softly at the luxurious feel of the cool, crisp sheets. He was about to slip his derringer under his pillow when he heard a noise in the master bath. He whirled around.

Lordis entered from the bath wearing a diaphanous nightgown.

"I took this from my trousseau this afternoon and aired it out," she said. "If I'm aging as badly as it is, you should send me away."

With those words said, there was no refusing the woman his bed. Nor did he wish to do so. He was certain that talk would be a secondary activity.

MONDAY

JUNE 25, 1906

THE DIFFERENCE BETWEEN FORTY-FIVE and fifty-nine was made quite clear in Chriswell Pinckney's bedroom. The sheer excitement of a beautiful woman's sexual attention had John's boiler glowing until midnight, when the last reserves of energy ran out. He could tell from the brightness in Lordis's eyes, however, that she who had "catnapped for a while" could have gone on for some time. After returning from the bathroom, he begged a few minutes to catch his second wind. The next thing he knew, full sunlight was streaming through the eastern windows onto his face. When he found his pocket watch, he was amazed to see that the time was ten minutes to nine. Lordis was so long gone that the smell of her had almost vanished from the bedclothes.

When John descended into the mansion's foyer fully washed, shaven, and dressed, he heard the sound of several voices. He followed them into the living room.

"Damned inconvenient," he heard a male voice complain. When he passed through the archway, he saw Ben Topley. The man was pacing in front of his wife and Lordis. He held a clipboard and a fountain pen. His suit was dark, with a band of black cloth around the left arm. Sarah Topley also wore black. A demure hat with a black veil lay on the coffee table in front of her. Lordis wore her wraparound housekeeper's dress and an apron. All three looked at him and waited for his voice.

"I apologize for interruptin'," John said.

"Quite all right," Topley allowed.

"I tried to speak with you and Mrs. Topley at the viewin' Saturday, but there were so many around you."

"How are you, Mr. Le Brun?" Sarah Topley asked.

"Fine. Run a bit ragged with this investigation and more than a little confused by it."

"As are we," she responded.

"My condolences. Has Lordis told you about the mix-up between Edmund and Miniver?"

"She has," Ben answered.

Lordis shot John a look that asked him if she had made a mistake to do so. He smiled in answer.

"Just the damnedest thing, isn't it?" Ben remarked.

"Damnedest infernal thing," John amplified. "And what do you two believe about Edmund's death in the bedroom?" John asked.

"Lordis has told us how agitated he was the night before," Ben said, again answering for his wife, "and what you thought you saw with the revolver. But what else can it be but suicide?"

"You think he went insane?" John asked.

"Something like that. For all we know, Edmund was so inwardly panicked about the collapse of his insurance firm and owing so much money that he might have been desperate enough to have his brother murdered. Naturally, if he had it staged inside the Metropolitan Club, no one would suspect him."

"But how could he have guessed that Miniver would masquerade as him?" John asked.

Topley shrugged casually. "That is the big question. Perhaps Miniver had already performed the same masquerade on a previous week. As an identical twin, I'm sure Edmund had special knowledge of his brother's thoughts."

"Put that aside," John said. "You would still be left with the question of whether or not Edmund intended to live the rest of his life as Miniver."

Topley threw out his hands. The gesture belonged on a stage. "Per haps he planned to leave New York and start a new life somewhere else. I truly have no idea. What sane man can think like an insane one? Apparently, *you* showed him how impossible his impersonation was. In a particularly black moment, he turned his weapon on himself. What other possibility can there be?"

"Do you know of a man named Maurice Van Leyden?" John asked.

Topley's pace had already slowed and now came to a stop. "The name sounds familiar."

"He's a real estate mogul," John informed.

"Ah, yes! Small man. Looks like Father Christmas."

"Precisely. Well, Edmund admitted to havin' an affair with his wife."

Lordis confirmed the information with a nod. The Topleys' focuses swung from her to each other.

The ex-lawman waited until both Topleys were gazing at him, shook his head, and offered a look that mixed calculated proportions of apology and sadness. Although he had had only eight years of formal education, John Le Brun had invested a lifetime observing the human character. He knew that while a big lie was often not believed, the stretched truth seldom failed. "Yesterday, in church of all places, Mrs. Van Leyden admitted to me the same thing. She also confided that she is one month pregnant."

"Pregnant! You didn't mention that yesterday, John!" Lordis blurted out.

"I probably shouldn't have mentioned it *today,* either," he answered. "As you can imagine, it was spoken in the utmost confidence. The female of the triangle may be the next person to meet an untimely death. Such a scandal might ruin the Van Leyden name in this city."

"He won't do his wife harm after you showed on his doorstep," Ben Topley affirmed. "But he could divorce her."

Lordis's hand flew to her mouth. "Ben! That child would be Edmund's heir."

John swung his good eye directly at Topley, glowing inwardly at his success.

"Lordis is right, Ben," Sarah said. "Remember, I told you about the clause he put in for heirs?"

John nodded soberly. "If Mrs. Van Leyden is suddenly separated from her source of money, she very well may come after the Pinckney estate. As guardian of her child, of course. I wonder if Edmund told her about that clause in his will."

Benjamin Topley looked like he had taken a shotgun blast to the chest. He swayed backward for a moment, then regained his equilibrium. "She may lose the child. Or, for all we know, Van Leyden might be happy to have it, to show he's still virile. Even so, he could still have arranged to have Edmund killed. Perhaps to guarantee he wouldn't lose his wife and the child."

"A great deal of speculation that merits investigation," John said. "In the meantime, you're saddled with the estate, whether you're managin' it for yourselves or an unborn heir."

"There's nothing else to be done for the moment," said Topley, again surveying the room. "The stocks, bonds, and money are no problem. And with the real estate market as hot as it is, we should be able to unload this white elephant inside a month. That's what we're discussing right now."

John remembered Topley on the morning of the funeral, carefully appraising the wall hangings. "You haven't spent much time in the house, have you?"

"My father referred to Ben as 'that Jew gypsy,' " Sarah replied coolly. "I think you can understand his aversion to Whimsy House."

"Certainly."

Sarah turned to Lordis. "Did Edmund's will say 'legitimate heirs' or just 'heirs'?"

"I think the latter," Lordis replied.

Sarah's eyes flashed. "Wouldn't it just be the final kick in my teeth from one of the Pinckney men to give everything away to the issue of his love sport?" She looked at the group. "Can an unborn child inherit an estate?"

"Ask the lawyer when you see him," John counseled.

"If you'll excuse me," Ben said. "My time is overtaxed today. I must complete an inventory this morning."

"Certainly," John allowed.

Topley walked into the dining room.

John said to Sarah, "I take it from certain things Lordis has said and from your 'kick in the teeth' remark that you have been treated shabbily by all the men in your family."

"I won't deny it," she replied, trembling with anger and gripping

Lordis's hand for comfort. "This would just be the last of many straws. My father was not particularly nice to anyone, but he was bad to my mother and awful to me. My brothers watched him and learned."

"I have heard about your engagement to Mr. Topley and your father's intolerant anger."

"Are you trying to develop a motive for *me* having my brothers killed?" Sarah asked, setting her chin in a defiant attitude.

John registered the uncontrolled emotions pouring out of the woman. "Not at all. I merely find your story sad. I can hardly imagine a father treatin' a daughter so badly. Especially this business with your mother's jewels."

"You don't know the half of it," Sarah shot back. Her voice had risen several decibels. "In fact, the whole tale is so terrible that I've never told anyone. Not even my husband or Lordis. You've heard that he told the police all my jewels had been robbed?"

"I have."

"Well, when he had his first heart attack, he finally asked me to come visit. I did. I sat with him alone in his bedroom. He swore to me, on a Bible no less, that the jewels had not been stolen after all!" Lordis opened her mouth, but Sarah touched her fingers to her best friend's lips. "Let me finish! They were hidden inside the house, he said. All I had to do was stay with him until he got better. Like the old days. Abandon my family for a month or two. If I did, he would tell me where the jewels were."

"Sally!" Lordis exclaimed, pushing the fingers aside. "Why did you never tell me?"

"Would you have stayed with him if I had?"

Lordis nodded her understanding. "No. I couldn't have."

"There you are. Someone had to stay with the bastard. You were the only woman he halfway respected. You actually seemed to like it here. I didn't want to drive you away."

"He was an even greater monster than I knew," Lordis said.

"Yes, he was. So, when he delivered this last ultimatum, I told him that he had manipulated me for the final time," Sarah went on. "That even if I believed him—which I didn't—I would rather lose the jewels than spend another night under his roof."

John felt a presence to his left. He turned and saw Benjamin Topley standing on the far side of the foyer archway, all but hidden from view.

He was scribbling onto his clipboard. When the conversation in the living room paused, he looked up with a quizzical stare.

"Was someone talking to me?" he asked.

"No, dear," Sarah replied.

"Fine. I could really use your help, Lordis," Topley said, crooking his forefinger.

Lordis rose from the sofa. "Certainly. Please see that Sally doesn't blow a gasket, Mr. Le Brun."

"I will try my best."

John watched the housekeeper and the impresario move together toward the central staircase.

"I don't know what I would do without either of them," Sarah declared.

"Once you get through these hard days," John rejoined, "life should be easier for all of you. Certainly, the money will help."

"If it turns out to be ours, I want to give some of it to charities," Sarah declared.

"And what does your husband think of that idea?"

"Oh, Ben agrees wholeheartedly. My father had a stipulation in his will to help rehabilitate fallen women if Edmund and Miniver fell out with one another. I believe he meant it as a cruel joke, but I would like to carry it out."

"Very noble of you."

Sarah picked up her hat and played with the veil. "And then there's my husband's lifelong dream."

"What is that?"

"You know that he owns a music hall."

"I do."

"But what he longs for is to produce more legitimate theater. Like David Belasco or the Schuberts. Every few years, he finds a dark house and—"

"Dark house?"

"I'm sorry. Actors' jargon. A theater not being used. He rents it and quickly assembles a revival of Shakespeare, Jonson, or one of the old French *comique* writers. There are some very avant-garde works coming out of Russia and the Scandinavian countries that he'd like to champion here as well. The sale of this house will allow him to realize that dream."

John watched the woman's sad eyes kindle with excitement. "How long has he had his dream?"

"Years. Since before he met me. Now, before he's too old, he can offer the quality of theater he was born to produce."

"That's a noble aspiration."

"If you stay in town, Ben and I would love to give you complimentary tickets to his music hall. The Hyperion . . . on West Forty-seventh. You could take Lordis." The woman's face momentarily transformed to that of a teenager. "She likes you very much."

"The feelin' is mutual. I'm sure I would enjoy the performance."

"You still don't believe Edmund committed suicide?" Sarah asked.

"I am dubious, Mrs. Topley, but I may have to bow to circumstantial evidence."

"I understand."

"And *you* still don't believe those jewels are in this house?" John asked.

Sarah offered a gentle smile. "Not I. They're long gone. The gems were knocked out of their mounts, and the silver and gold were melted down. My father's gambling habit had all but ruined him during that period."

John pushed himself up from the sofa. "A shame."

"They were just objects. I have my treasures in my husband, my children, and Lordis," Sarah proclaimed. "That, a roof over my head, and health. Who needs more?"

John noted the sizable diamond engagement ring on Sarah Topley's wedding finger, her golden earrings, and the obvious quality of her clothing, but he chose to say nothing.

"I must be on my way to confer with Detective O'Leary, ma'am."

"Ah, yes. Now *there* is a character out of an Abbey Theatre production."

"I agree. Will you be all right?"

Mrs. Topley set her hands primly in her lap, as if to signal her regained composure. "Right as rain, thank you."

"Then I shall say good mornin' to you."

John backed out of the room into the foyer. Lordis and Ben had moved to another part of the mansion. If Mrs. Lassiter, Mr. Hastings, and Minna Gottfried were about, they had also made themselves scarce.

John took the opportunity to escape from Whimsy House into the warm and slightly breezy Monday morning.

A S JOHN WAS CLOSING the front door to the mansion behind him, he noticed something that had escaped him when he had previously stood in the alcove. A huge capital letter W had been formed in bas-relief in the brownstone that formed the alcove wall to his left. He turned his head sharply to compensate for his blind right eye and saw that the surfaces of the stones on the right collectively formed a matching capital H. He rolled his eyes at the level of whimsy that Chriswell Pinckney had indeed built into the structure.

John turned to his right after descending the mansion stoop. Within a few steps, he was in view of its driveway, garden, and carriage house. He found William Hastings on the brick drive, speaking with a man who was scribbling onto a notepad. When Hastings spotted Le Brun, he turned the other man south and walked him around the house's corner. John had no doubt how the New York newspapers were getting such accurate information on Whimsy House and its inhabitants. The man who had been forgotten in two wills and who had several times complained about the turn of events depriving him of his livelihood was making a few extra dollars while he could.

Le Brun hailed a cab on Park Avenue and directed the driver to St. Luke's Hospital, far uptown on the west side, overlooking Morningside Park and the Hudson River. After he decabbed, it took him more than an hour of wandering the neighboring streets to locate the office of the physician to whom Miniver Pinckney had written his checks.

Dr. Jeffrey Stundel was a pulmonary and thoracic specialist, associated with St. Luke's. He had five people in his waiting room, three of whom coughed almost continually. Out of pure fear of contagion, John flashed his business card and his letter from the Metropolitan Club and would have flashed his derringer had the receptionist not immediately shoehorned him into the doctor's schedule.

Dr. Stundel was a small man with a large voice. From a remark the physician passed to his assistant as he handed over his smock, Le Brun ascertained that he had just returned from a surgery that had gone well. Stundel's mood was patently good, which delighted the ex-lawman.

"How can I help you, sir?" he asked Le Brun as they entered his office together.

John handed over his letter of introduction. Stundel fitted spectacles over his ears. It took him less than ten seconds to get the gist. He returned it.

"You are here about the late Miniver Pinckney."

"That's correct." It was clear that the doctor had had time before his surgery to read one of the morning newspapers.

"But you are not the police."

"I am workin' directly with Detective Kevin O'Leary of the New York Police Department." John produced the detective's card. "You can insist that he come up here and listen to whatever you can tell me. Or you can save a second interruption of your day and speak with me now."

The physician saw that, unlike with his patients and the hospital staff, he was not lord of the situation. He nodded his acceptance.

"Mr. Pinckney was dying of lung cancer."

"When did you make that diagnosis?"

"I'll consult his file if you insist, but I would estimate not more than two months back. We took a tissue sample under local anesthesia over at the hospital. The cancer was confirmed to him shortly after that."

"How long did he have to live?"

"One would never predict these things to the patient, but I would have been surprised if he lasted until Thanksgiving."

"And how did he take the news?" John asked.

"He laughed. And then he asked me if I smoked. I told him I did not. He took a machine-rolled cigarette out and lit it in front of me. I personally believe that cigarettes and cigars are injurious to the lungs, so I asked him to stop. He told me to go to hell. He wrote out his check and left."

"Two visits?"

"Two visits to the office and one to the hospital." Stundel glanced at the clock hanging on his wall.

"Did you notify anyone in his family?"

The doctor scowled. "Of course not. He was a mature, independent man. He came in by himself. Such a man would take care of that in his own time."

"The Pinckney family name is rather well known in this town," John said.

"I have had more than a dozen patients better known than he. What are you driving at?"

"Who else did you mention his condition to?"

Stundel rose from his desk and slapped it at the same time. "This interview is over, sir. I am a professional. I discuss my patients with *no one*. Do you think I need to puff myself up by gossiping about wealthy and famous patients? I see now that I should have refused to speak with you as well."

"I do apologize," John said, rising from his chair. "I will tell you, however, that *someone* learned of Mr. Pinckney's condition. I am convinced that is the fact that set a chain of deadly events in motion."

"Then *he* told that someone. I have one man who files my records, and I trust my career to his honesty and discretion," Stundel asserted.

"Very well," John said, plucking his hat from the corner of the doctor's desk. "Let me ask you one final question, and then I will leave you to your busy day: Did you deliver your diagnosis to Mr. Pinckney in writin' as well as in spoken word?"

"I did not."

"Very well. Thank you, Doctor. Good day."

Stundel waggled his finger. "If I see my name in any newspaper in this regard, I will sue you, Mr. . . . ." His angry expression slipped.

"Poe," John said from the door. "Edgar Allan Poe."

WITH CHARM, perseverance, and a ten-dollar bill, Le Brun advanced his luck at St. Luke's Hospital. The investment of another hour brought him to the administrator who answered the telephone concerning test results for the hospital. According to Miniver Pinckney's file, a man claiming to be his brother had called three days after the test. The caller had been able to reassure the administrator of his authenticity and had been delivered the news of advanced lung cancer. Le Brun left the facility whistling a sprightly ragtime tune.

WHEN JOHN VISITED the police station to find Kevin O'Leary, he was told that the detective had gone to Whimsy House. He found the man sitting in the warming kitchen, consuming a good deal of the last of Saturday's funeral spread. John had been let in by Minna Gottfried, who balanced a pile of old bed linens on one arm. She had recently been crying and turned from the door as quickly as she could.

"Ah! The peripatetic John Le Brun returns ta Bleak House. Miss Goode and Mrs. Lassiter are shopping," O'Leary informed John as he reached for a pickle. "They left not five minutes ago."

"I'm just as glad. It's you I need to speak with. You have mustard on your cheek," Le Brun pointed out. "What's upset the maid?"

"The apparent new owners, Mr. and Mrs. Topley, gave the staff their notice. They will be paid for two weeks and given next week off to look for other jobs."

"I assume that's normal procedure up here, isn't it?" John asked.

"Normal under normal situations," O'Leary returned, suppressing a belch. "I t'ink it's a bit hard-hearted, considering the circumstances. But, then again, you have to consider the new owner is a Jew. They're tight."

Le Brun held his tongue. He knew the ice of Old World bigotry was often thick enough to resist the American melting pot. *The Irishman's words are kindness in comparison to what Chriswell Pinckney's must have been,* John reflected. If he were Benjamin Topley, he might have been tempted to burn the place to the ground and go after the insurance money instead.

John pulled out a chair and sat. "I've got a passel of interestin' news." He proceeded to tell the city detective about his visits to Dr. Stundel's office and to St. Luke's. Before O'Leary could take off like an Irish Sweepstakes horse with the information, he immediately added the facts concerning the Van Leydens, his expectation through Pulitzer and Stanford White of receiving Whimsy House's blueprints, and his enlistment of the Players Club in finding the duplicate Witherspoon King.

"Now that's what I call a busy twenty-four hours," O'Leary remarked. He had set down his sandwich and begun working his brain instead of his jaw. John was relieved to see that he was not doing a jig on the kitchen linoleum; the detective was too smart to believe the case was completely solved. "I'm sure God will forgive ya for working so hard on His day of rest. But this morning's news is the best. So, Edmund telephoned and found out about his brother's impending death."

"The administrator only said the man identified himself as Miniver's brother," John pointed out.

"But you said the caller provided all the information demanded and even offered to have the administrator make a return call to Whimsy House as verification."

"True," John said.

"Then let's accept this as the most likely occurrence. Neither brother can sell the home until the other dies. Both are in financial straits, relative to their former positions. Edmund finds an appointment card or whatever concerning Miniver's surreptitious visits to the physician and the hospital. Possibly, Miniver even shares the fact of the visits with him. Edmund is secretly overjoyed to learn of his brother's terrible news. He begins to formulate a plan to get back into the money. He won't sell this house but rather rent it. What are there no fewer than ten of on this avenue?"

"Hotels, restaurants, churches," John teased with a straight face, knowing full well what O'Leary meant.

"No! Clubhouses! And most of 'em rented, not owned. Edmund had been espousing the idea of an 'abstemious club' for well over a year, but you and I have both heard how he radically stepped up his campaigning about six weeks ago. Six weeks! Isn't that curious? The same time he learned of Miniver's impending end. Whimsy House would become the Twentieth-Century Club."

"And how does that relate to Miniver's murder?" John asked. "What you have just proven is that Edmund would be the *last person* to try to murder his brother. He knew he would be dead within weeks or months at the latest."

O'Leary waggled his forefinger. "And isn't that a lovely t'ing to know? Not only isn't Edmund a prime suspect, but he has no reason to commit suicide. His behavior on the night of his death, as you described it, is perfectly believable now. Blue ribbons for your observation about the revolver."

"Then who is the likely murderer?" John asked.

"*Murderers*," O'Leary corrected. "Benjamin and Sarah Topley. If Miniver will die naturally by T'anksgiving and they see to it that Edmund is murdered before then, suspicion will be off them. Sarah inherits as sole heir. Further, if they have Edmund murdered in his club, where he is trying to seduce members away ta his *new* club, they can redirect suspicion all the more. Topley uses magicians in his music hall. He has no doubt learned about misdirection from them. He is also the most likely among our suspects ta be able ta recruit an actor who looks like a member of the Metropolitan Club."

John thought briefly of Lordis's mention of magicians, of the one named Malini producing a block of ice from under a top hat or derby, but he pushed it back into his memory to address more pressing issues. "There are several problems to your theory. Shall I state them, or have you already considered what they are?"

"Let me see." O'Leary rested his chin on the points of his tented fingers. "You're just giving me all this news, remember. I haven't had time ta consider it from all angles." Suddenly, his head reared back. He snapped his fingers. "How would they learn about Miniver's impending death? Well, he must have told them."

John shook his head slowly. "I don't think he told anyone. He was a scalawag through and through. Not the kind to tip his hand and show his cards. And he wouldn't have given his brother the satisfaction."

"Well, the Topleys wouldn't have learned from Edmund, would they?" O'Leary asked.

"No. Edmund wouldn't have told anyone either."

"Then the answer lies with Miss Goode. She has always been their conduit ta information of the goings-on inside Whimsy House."

"But which male did she learn the news from?" John persisted. "Remember that it was a man who called the hospital for the diagnosis. A male willin' to take a call from inside this house." Since O'Leary failed to provide a ready reply, he added, "The other question is: How would they be able to get to Edmund to kill him in his bedroom?"

"The second answer is again Lordis Goode," O'Leary replied. "She must know more secrets to Whimsy House then she lets on. Chriswell told her."

"Who else has been associated with the house as long as Lordis Goode?" John asked. "Longer, in fact."

O'Leary's eyes narrowed. "William Hastings."

"The same faithful Mr. Hastin's who was left out of both brothers' wills. A male who had access to the house's telephone when the brothers were gone for the day and Mrs. Lassiter and Miss Goode were out shoppin'. The same man who has much latitude of action with his wife and child away for the summer. A man who made damned sure to have ironclad alibis durin' both murders. The man who drove Miniver Pinckney to Dr. Stundel's office."

O'Leary pushed the plate and half-eaten sandwich away, more hungry now for truth than food. "You t'ink he sold the information ta Ben Topley?"

"I saw him this mornin' conferrin' with a man who was surely a reporter. I think, since his loyalty was not valued in their wills, Mr. Hastin's loyalty has been to his own pockets for some time. I wouldn't be surprised if he wasn't on Mr. Topley's payroll for years."

"Lay it all out as you see it, then," O'Leary invited.

Le Brun folded his arms across his chest and settled into a more comfortable position. "Benjamin Topley married Sarah Pinckney with the long-term expectation that she would eventually reap some benefit from the Pinckney family fortune. Either Chriswell would soften as they had grandchildren, or else her brothers would find a way to include her in the largesse.

"Neither came to be. Sarah herself freely provided me his motivation for murder this mornin'... which is why I believe she is an innocent in this affair. Mr. Topley has always aspired to be a legitimate producer. To buy an upscale theater and pay the best dramatic actors. He has been trapped into producin' low comedy and musical revues. But after his marriage failed to yield money, he more or less gave up. That is until William Hastin's carried to him the news of Miniver Pinckney's impendin' death. This, however, would only half solve the problem. Edmund needed to die. As you stated, it would be much preferable to have him precede his brother in death, to allay suspicion.

"Edmund had created a motive for his murder... albeit a flimsy one in my opinion... in his campaign for an 'abstemious club.' The one thing workin' in his favor was that *all* these clubs are apparently operatin' on a shoestring and just squeezin' through. There *is* a perpetual panic over the prospect of their failure.

"Benjamin does his research on various club members and manages to align a desperate actor with the likeness of a Metropolitan Club member. He knows from Hastin's that Edmund always dines at the club on Wednesday night. He sends the actor out, armed with cases of champagne, a change of costume, and a knife."

"But why choose an actor who looked like a man with an ironclad alibi?" O'Leary asked.

"Do you recall me askin' my associate, Mr. Tidewell, to check all the newspapers concerning Mr. King's honorin' at the banquet?"

"I do."

"He was only able to find one little article out of all the papers."

"Truly?"

"After all, Mr. King is from Philadelphia," John said, "so that hardly rates as news in New York City."

"Fair enough. So Topley just has bad luck, selecting a club member who happens ta come ta town *and* have a perfect alibi."

"Bad luck indeed. But he's about to have even worse luck. In the meantime, Miniver has found out that Edmund has a different agenda on this particular night. He has no doubt learned from acquaintances about Edmund's stepped-up campaign for his new club. He is determined to play an elegant prank and ruin his brother's plans. He dons Edmund's suit, strolls into the club, and affects his manners. He sucks on peppermint to disguise his cigarette breath. However, in his eagerness to get his brother truly hated for his cause, he overdoes his pitchin' to the point of obnoxiousness. He dies as Edmund, gladly followin' the false Witherspoon King upstairs to discuss the new club."

"Then Topley goes ta the viewing and sees that Miniver is actually Edmund," O'Leary broke in.

"I think it's more likely that Hastin's told him earlier," John contradicted. "At the viewin' and the burial, Edmund was very careful about his performance. So much so that he fooled his own sister."

"Unless she hid her surprise. Remember, she's a trained actress," O'Leary warned.

"Very good. But concentrate on Ben for the moment and assume that Sarah was also fooled. Remember that Ben Topley had had no more dealin' with the brothers than the minister who led the service."

"Right. Hastings is a likely source. But don't forget the Topleys' bosom buddy, Miss Goode." O'Leary nodded his head several times in a knowing manner. "Your opinion of her has been clouded, but mine has not."

"Mr. Hastin's is the more likely to know the secrets of Whimsy House," Le Brun went on, ignoring O'Leary's last words. "For example, he supervised the house's conversion to electricity. We may know much more tonight, after I secure the blueprints from Stanford White. If Mr.

Hastin's fingerprints are inside an unknown secret passage, you can sweat him to implicate Mr. Topley."

"I have the feeling you rarely waited for clues ta appear during your career," O'Leary observed. "You're the type who likes ta put the red and black ants in the jar together and see what happens."

"I have a different analogy," Le Brun said. "I'm a chess player. You can hold your own with defensive play, but sooner or later you have to go on the offensive to win. These blueprints may do that for us."

O'Leary waited for more from his companion, but Le Brun had said his piece. "The revolver receipt won't provide the big break. I came here direct from the store that sold the Colt. They had no record. You t'ink it was Topley's gun?"

John shrugged. "It might have been purchased for a theatrical production. But I wouldn't go askin' his staff about it right now."

"No. So, once Topley knows the wrong man was killed, he's forced to do in the healthy one as well. And his best option is to make it look like suicide."

John nodded. "Which is why his informant *isn't* Lordis Goode. She would have told him about me stayin' in the house *and* about Edmund's anxiety to live *and* about his Colt revolver."

"I suppose." O'Leary straightened up on his chair. "So, now what?"

"We wait. For the blueprints and for the Players Club to find any actors who look like Witherspoon King. Topley's not goin' anywhere. He thinks he has us bamboozled."

"And you're getting those blueprints at Madison Square Garden tonight?"

"Barrin' unforeseen circumstances."

Le Brun lifted his hand. "In spite of the scenario we just concocted, there is still the possibility that Maurice Van Leyden is the real one behind these murders. The man who killed Miniver in the club didn't *have* to be an actor, you know."

O'Leary indicated his disdain for the suggestion by blowing a rude noise through his lips.

"The man sounded more guilty than anyone else I interviewed," John persisted. "Mrs. Van Leyden is doing some detective work of her own. We shouldn't let that thread drop completely."

The detective stood. "Fine. You hold on to all the t'reads you want.

I am going home and invite Morpheus ta pay a visit. 'Twill be a long night after you get those blueprints."

"Can we not wait until mornin'?" John asked.

"No, indeed. I want the guilty ones in cuffs by daybreak. The next time I want to see Chinatown is when I have a yen for sour pork."

B EFORE LORDIS could return to Whimsy House John departed, leaving her a note saying that he would pick her up at six-thirty for their night at Madison Square Roof Garden. Then he packed his belongings and caught a cab back to the Hotel Savoy. With the hunt pointing to the Topley family, he could no longer afford to linger in the arms of their best friend. When he checked in at the hotel, he learned from an effusively grateful manager that a pair of hotel thieves had been caught trying to enter his former room. As thanks for his alertness and warning, the ex-lawman was given a top-floor corner suite with a view facing Fifth Avenue and the bottom edge of Central Park.

Le Brun washed the grime of the city off his face and hands, stripped down to his underwear, and crawled into bed. Detective O'Leary was not willing to defer investigation of Whimsy House until the next morning. John figured that he and Lordis would return to the mansion with the blueprints no later than midnight. Depending on what they showed, however, he and a platoon of police might be tromping around until dawn. John set his mental clock for six and pulled down the window shades. He fell into a profound but confused sleep, where he was Hamlet, Lordis was Ophelia, and Ben and Sarah Topley were Lord and Lady Macbeth, thrown into a single, shadowy tale. Whimsy House was alternately Dunsinane and Elsinore, and the language shifted back and forth between Shakespearean and American English. He was vastly relieved when six o'clock arrived before the fall of the final bizarre dream curtain.

W HEN THE MOTORIZED CAB reached Madison Square and turned east, John felt as if he were coming home. All told, he had passed the same area four times in as many days. He wondered if, with the proper change in attitude, New York City might not after all be the place to end his days. He had liked the Manhattan and Players Clubs very much. He already had high-placed friends in the city. The mighty cityscape by day and its myriad fairy lights by night were seductive. And then there was the woman at his side.

This Charleston lady has accommodated well to New York, John reflected. *Perhaps I should follow her lead.* If, as he expected, Lordis was innocent of collusion in the murders, he wanted the opportunity to know her better. He knew that she would leave the city with great difficulty. Whimsy House was being sold out from under her, but she still had the bond of the Topley family.

On the opposite hand, the Topley cornerstone might soon be rocked from its foundation, giving Lordis little to hold on to. If their relationship continued to grow at its present rate, she might be convinced of a life change. Sarah Pinckney was also rooted in the South. If it turned out that Ben alone was guilty and went to prison, his wife might well want to flee the city. Perhaps he could convince both women to make a new home in Brunswick. After so many years of loneliness, having women and children around him was not at all an unwelcome prospect. Either scenario held promise in John's eyes. In order to see which should be played out, however, he had to solve the crime. He felt like a racehorse in the starting stall. He knew he would have to force himself to relax in order to enjoy the evening.

In the summertime, New York City sweltered. Tenement dwellers and those with mansions alike found themselves escaping to their rooftops on the hottest nights. Patrons attended the theater to get their minds off their work and the heat, but auditoriums with a thousand exhaling, perspiring bodies produced the opposite effect. Which was why roof-garden entertainment had become the summer vogue. While Madison Square Roof Garden was the most famous, there were also Aerial Gardens and Hammerstein's Paradise Roof.

The crowd converging on Madison Square Garden amazed Le Brun. He and Lordis waited for more than five minutes to cram themselves into one of the elevators that climbed to the roof. They passed through a lobby and handed over their tickets. John had a silver dollar in his palm when they reached the maître d'.

"We are expectin' to meet Stanford White tonight," John told the man, pressing the coin into his hand.

"I was not informed of guests at his table," the table manager said.

"We are meetin' to do a bit of business. I simply want a table near his," John countered.

The maître d'led the way across the brick floor, toward the small raised thrust stage with its roof painted and decorated like the top of a carousel. The night was clear, so all canopies had been removed. The clever ironwork made to hold the canopies curved gracefully over the audience, each one holding three downward-turned, glazed, capsule-shaped lamps. The center poles were each capped with four more identical lamps. Bentwood chairs surrounded the dozens of tables, arranged so tightly that maneuvering was a torturous adventure. The maître d' glided with practiced precision among the straw skimmers and flowered bonnets to a place on the Twenty-sixth Street side of the building, eight table rows from the orchestra.

"And which is Mr. White's table?" John asked.

The man pointed three rows ahead.

John dug into his trouser pocket. "Can you get us closer for additional 'thanks'?"

"Those tables are reserved for regulars . . . not for people from foreign parts," the waiter said, lifting his chin. He pulled out one of the chairs. "Madam."

"Cretin," Lordis replied, through a broad smile. The maître d's shoulders tensed, but he did not slow his retreat.

"There's nothin' like havin' a brave woman defend you," John remarked. "A brave, *beautiful* woman."

Lordis wore a white summer-weight gown that showed off her shoulders. John could have sworn he had not seen the dress two nights before, when he had looked in her closet. He decided she had either bought it especially for the occasion or had borrowed it.

A temperate breeze blew across the rooftop, making the night quite pleasant. After admiring the space and studying the other patrons, the couple concentrated on the menu. The fare was similar to that of a beer garden, with sandwiches, salads, beer, iced tea, and lemonade. Among the desserts were ices and large hot pretzels. The crowd was raucous to the point that conversation with Lordis was difficult. It was clear that several large groups had been booked for the musical's opening night. People wandered from table to table, chatting and laughing, changing places.

John noted among the patrons one particular man. He was dressed in evening clothes as so many others were, but he stood out for two reasons. The first was that his movements were agitated and erratic. He kept popping up from his seat and looking in Le Brun's general direction. Every few minutes, he would pace along the rail that separated the orchestra from the audience. The second reason he stood out was that he had a white muffler wrapped around his chin and mouth. Nothing about the weather recommended such apparel. From the darkness of his hair and the agility of his movements, John judged him to be relatively young. His table was in a little niche down beside the orchestra. Also at that table sat several women. Among them was a young woman with one of the most beautiful faces John had ever gazed upon. He craned his neck for a better look at her.

"I should be jealous," Lordis said as she followed his stare.

John stammered out the beginning of an apology.

Lordis laughed. "Don't be absurd. You saw the giant statue on the Garden's tower when we came in?"

"Yes."

"She was the model for it. That's Evelyn Nesbit."

"I don't know her name."

"You would if you lived in New York. She was one of six women in the chorus of a show over at the Casino a few years back. *Floradora*. The show had a song addressed to them." Lordis sang softly, in a pleasant alto voice: " 'Tell me pretty maiden / Are there any more at home like you?' And then the girls sang: 'There are a few, kind sir / But simple girls and proper, too.' Let me tell you: None of the six was proper. Between their looks and their behavior, every one married a millionaire. I believe the fellow who's pacing is her husband, Harry Thaw."

"Should I know *his* name?"

"He's one of the spoiled children of the rich. His father was William Thaw, vice president of the Pennsylvania Railroad. His sister is the countess of Yarmouth."

John continued to watch the former showgirl and her friends. Their pale hands fluttered above their table like alarmed doves, and they all seemed to be talking without listening to each other. "Another of those weddin's of convenience to gain a title?"

"Exactly. According to the gossip columns, the family was livid when Harry began cohabiting with Evelyn. They ran off to Europe together, I think, and were supposed to have married there. But the family raised such a stink that they later denied it. His allowance was cut off for a time."

"How did they come to be married again?"

"Harry was going to get his inheritance on his thirtieth birthday anyway—three million dollars—so the family caved in."

"Ah, the joys of bein' in high society."

Lordis touched John's arm. "Knowing that every time you break wind, it will be in tomorrow's paper."

"He seems to be waitin' for someone too," John observed. "From the look of his eyes and his movements, I'm not sure I'd want to be that person."

Time swept along, and the orchestra began filing onto their chairs. The conductor appeared to applause. The overture to *Mamzelle Champagne* struck up. Like its name, the musical was bubbly and giddy, with hardly a serious moment. John had trouble concentrating on its inane excuse for a plot. His gaze kept slipping over to Stanford White's empty table.

Intermission came and went, and still the architect failed to appear. John worried that perhaps the blueprints had disappeared, and White was too embarrassed to tell them so in person. His pocket watch indicated ten minutes to eleven. On the stage, two of the male leads were trading snappy words and insults. Immediately afterward, six chorines came on and accompanied one of the men, singing "I challenge you / To a duel, to a d-u-e-l." During the song, Stanford White at last appeared. Lordis pointed him out the instant he came into view. He was a tall man with close-cropped red hair going to white. He looked distracted. He carried under his arm the sort of tube used by architects to transport blueprints. John sighed with relief.

"How long will this go on?" John complained, wishing he had gotten a playbill.

"Not much longer," Lordis promised.

A bit more monologue from a comedian with the predictably ridiculous stage name of Fuller Spice was followed by a song entitled "I Could Love a Million Girls," accompanied by the same six winsome chorines. As John was yet again consulting his watch and seeing that the time was 11:05, the man in the white muffler stood up. Since his table was right beside the stage, his movement was hard to miss. He said a few words to Evelyn Nesbit Thaw, then advanced on Stanford White's table.

John did not like the man's movements. His lawman's instincts told him that some violence was imminent. He angled in his chair to reach the derringer holster hidden in the small of his back. He found himself hemmed in by the knees of the woman behind him. He inched his chair forward.

Harry Thaw was now at White's table. The architect, resting his chin on his right hand, surely must have seen the man, but he chose to keep his attention fixed on the stage. John heard Thaw cry out, "You'll never go out with my woman again!" As he spoke, he pulled a pistol from his breast pocket and aimed it point blank at White's temple. The architect flinched away, and then the gun blasted. White rebounded against the back of his chair. Thaw fired two more shots in quick succession and stepped back.

White pitched over headfirst onto the round table. His forehead struck its corner. It tipped over noisily, taking with it a glass and silverware.

John had brought the derringer to his side, but he saw Thaw raise his weapon above his head and let it dangle, to show that he meant no harm to anyone else.

Onstage, several of the actors had focused on the disturbance. The comedian and two of the women stopped singing. Several members of the orchestra faltered.

A man in the front row of tables called out, "Go on. Go on! What's the matter then?"

John realized that the dialogue and song about dueling had convinced many in the audience that the gunshots were merely part of the madcap show. He himself had attended productions where the actors had broken the "fourth wall" of the front of the stage and had conducted wildness among the patrons.

The suspension of disbelief held for only a few moments. More and more of the orchestra hitched their playing. A woman at the table beside White's rose in slow motion and then began shrieking. Her noise set off a chain reaction. Pandemonium set in.

At the gun's report, Evelyn Nesbit Thaw had also arisen. She rushed through the tables to her husband's side. Between the screams, John heard her exclaim, "My God, Harry, you've killed him!"

In answer, Thaw gathered his wife into his arms, embraced and then kissed her. Two of her table companions had been only steps behind her. They pulled her away toward one of the exits. The murderer, again raising the gun with barrel pointed down, rushed toward the main exit. Panicked patrons parted for him like the Red Sea for Moses.

"Aren't you going to stop him?" Lordis asked John.

"I'm just a citizen," John reminded. "Besides, he's done all the killin' he's gonna do. The policemen downstairs must have heard those shots. We have needs for our own murders. We can't lose those blueprints."

Lordis nodded. Before John could suggest a plan, she had dashed into the space created by the patrons shrinking from the dead man. She knelt beside White and put her fingers to his neck. When she stood, she had the blueprint tube in her hand. She retreated toward Le Brun.

From the stage, the manager was crying out, "Don't panic, people! There has been a terrible accident, but you are all safe. Please move toward the exits in an orderly fashion."

"Let's follow his suggestion," John said.

"He's definitely dead," Lordis reported.

Movement was retarded by the alarmed audience pressing through the close-set tables toward the few exits. As the patrons inched urgently forward, John watched several of the waiters pushing tables away from the body. Two moved White's arms and legs together, and a third provided a linen tablecloth to cover him. Rarely had John seen so much blood pour out of a human being.

"You show remarkable coolness under stress," John observed to Lordis.

"Blood has never bothered me," she came back. She pressed the tube into his hands. "If I'd been born twenty years earlier, I would have made a good battlefield nurse. Would you lend me your handkerchief?"

John pulled the material from his pocket and handed it over. Lordis cleaned her hand. "Wouldn't do to get blood on a new dress. I'll wash this and get it back to you."

John now had his question answered concerning the white dress. He was greatly flattered. His joy was balanced by a frightening realization: Lordis embodied the French expression of *sangfroid*, literally "cold blood."

"Well, this will bury the Pinckney murders in quick fashion," Lordis remarked in a composed voice, as if to validate Le Brun's observation.

"Which may be advantageous," he replied. He realized that witnessing Stanford White's murder from thirty feet had not appreciably quickened his heartbeat. The difference between himself and Lordis Goode, however, was that he had experienced violent death on a regular basis since his teenage years. He wondered not idly of what the woman was made.

A REN'T YOU GOING to look at the blueprints?" Lordis asked, not a minute after they had climbed into a northbound cab.

Le Brun had been lost in thought about the murder of Stanford White. He remembered what Joseph Pulitzer had said about White's fascination with beautiful women and his immoral attitudes. *All his chickens have come home to roost, as my father used to say,* John thought. He wondered how the newspapers would treat White's darker past and what Pulitzer would reveal to him that could not go into newsprint. Lordis's question returned him to task.

"Let's hope they're the right ones," he said as he twisted off the metal top. In all, there were eight pages of blueprints. Almost immediately, he saw the name "Whimsy House" on the corner of the top one. It was of the first floor.

"There's the secret room under the staircase," Lordis pointed out. "And what's that?"

John made an angry noise in his throat. "Of course. I should have paid more attention to the thickness of the archways between the livin' room and the dinin' room and foyer. The front space is the closet that has the hidden safe. Here's the safe, indicated by little dashes. The middle space contains the bar. But the back space is totally boxed in. Look here: There appears to be a trapdoor in the floor inside. And this tiny print says 'ladder.' "

"But how does one get into it?" Lordis asked.

"From the trapdoor."

"And then what?"

"We'll have to see."

"So, that's Secret Six," Lordis said. She pointed to the fireplace in the living room. "And this rectangle made of dots looks to be Secret Seven. Another safe?"

"Perhaps." John rolled the paper closed and looked at the one below.

It was of the footprint and selected elevations of the first floor of the carriage house. The plan revealed no special markings. He became aware of Lordis's chin on his shoulder. He looked at her from a space so close that it was difficult to focus on her face.

"Detective O'Leary and a few other police will be waitin' for us," he said. "Either Mr. Hastin's will be drawn from his apartment by their presence or else I will see that he accompanies us. No matter what happens, I want you to keep silent concernin' what Miss Sally said about the jewels."

"You mean being hidden inside the house?" Lordis asked.

"That's correct."

"Why?"

John smiled. "You had your secret about Edmund that you kept from me. I need to keep this secret for another day. Promise me you won't say anythin'. If you do—even behind my back—I shall ultimately know it."

"No need for threats, John. You can trust me." Lordis's face tightened into a convincing hurt look. John chose not to apologize.

Neither John nor Lordis expected the attic blueprint to hold any surprises. Both were stunned to find dotted squares in the little turret rooms behind the hidden doors.

"More trapdoors?" Lordis asked.

"I believe so."

"The way into Edmund's room?"

"I wouldn't be shocked. Evidently, Secrets Four and Five contained more parts than you or the brothers knew."

On the second-floor plan, they found a space between Sarah's and Miniver's bedrooms. This was where the ladder indicated on the first-floor blueprint led.

The last plan was of the basement. It was the most revealing. A legend actually read "Secret entrance." The words were connected by a line and arrow to the storm drain in the alley behind the mansion. Dashed lines indicated a short tunnel leading into the basement. The other end of the tunnel emptied into a long space formed by a false front running the entire length of the gaming room. It was narrow enough that the human eye would not miss the few feet that had been stolen.

"This is incredible. More parts of Secret Number Six. To live in a house for so many years and not know all of its secrets. No question of suicide anymore," Lordis pronounced.

"Let us see."

Lordis squeezed John's upper arm. "Does Brunswick know what a treasure they have in you?"

John rubbed the back of her hand in thanks. "From time to time." The truth was that whenever a baffling crime was committed, he became the darling of the town fathers. On most occasions, he was regarded as the "arrogant old monster who prowls the Oglethorpe," as the mayor's secretary had once said. The remark had hurt when it was gleefully carried back to him. A day later, John was able to shrug it off. The next time someone dredged the words up, he replied, "The good silver is just a pain to polish until a big occasion. Then it's paraded out with pride."

"I'm very glad you decided to come to New York," Lordis confided.

John returned his companion's smile, but he remembered his dream of himself as Hamlet and felt no less conflicted.

As SOON AS THE CAB that had carried Lordis and John pulled away from Whimsy House, four men stepped from the black automobile parked on the Park Avenue end of the block.

"I need to go inside and change my outfit if we're traipsing through drains," Lordis said, leaving John standing on the pavement, waiting for the men.

Kevin O'Leary led the pack of policemen. All wore dark suits, fedoras, and thin kidskin gloves, as much uniforms as if they had been wearing blue serge with brass buttons and silver badges. Two carried black satchels and two had unlit electric lanterns. Le Brun was introduced to Officers Ricciardi, Levine, and Heinze. The diversity among the group pleased John; he wondered where else on earth four lawmen might hail from so many backgrounds.

"Stanford White come t'rough with the blueprints, then," O'Leary said, pointing.

"His last act," John replied. He took a minute to relate the murder at Madison Square Garden. His audience responded with little more than raised eyebrows. They asked a few terse questions, with the dispassion of surgeons reviewing an operation. Then they were back to the task at hand.

"We need to go down into a sewer drain," John told them.

O'Leary rolled his eyes. "We'll get some larger tools from the caretaker. Unless you t'ink we shouldn't involve him."

"Oh, no. We must definitely involve Mr. Hastin's," John countered.

O'Leary glanced up at the appearance of lights inside the mansion. "What about Miss Goode?"

"The whole cast of characters," John said, leading the way around to the carriage house with the blueprint tube in his hand. He climbed the stairs alone and knocked on the caretaker's door. The carriage house was dark. He waited for a minute and was about to knock again when William Hastings appeared. He wore what looked to John to be silk pajamas, which was not at all in keeping with the man's appearance, his station in life, or his salary. John wondered if they might not have recently belonged to either Edmund or Miniver. John quickly delivered the news of securing the blueprints and asked for Mr. Hastings's help. Hastings replied with a nod and disappeared to the back of the apartment.

Ten minutes later, six men and a dressed-down Lordis Goode moved out of the carriage house, carrying a wealth of tools and instruments for illumination. Hastings led the parade to the storm drain. John realized after a few moments without the omnipresent soft tinkling accompaniment that Lordis had taken off her charm bracelet.

"Have you ever been down there, sir?" O'Leary asked the handyman.

"I have. A number of times. To clean out the leaves that build up. But I never saw an entrance."

"To your knowledge, has this drain ever backed up?" Le Brun asked.

Hastings shook his large head. "Not this high on the island. They musta made the storm sewers large, because I've never seen water cover the lower grate."

The drain was covered by a heavy iron grate. The light of two electric torches playing through it revealed a second, mesh cover about six feet below. The drain's northern wall had three grab-iron steps attached to it. Everything was bone-dry from a summer week without rain. Officers Heinze and Ricciardi wrestled the top cover off, and

O'Leary clambered down. He played his lantern back and forth.

"No bolts or openings here," he reported. "And this mesh I'm standing on . . . its bolts are rusted in place."

"Try pullin' the wall with the grab irons toward you," John directed. "If that doesn't work, push on it hard."

Neither attempt produced a result.

"Maybe it was on the blueprint, but Pinckney decided to abandon the idea," O'Leary mused.

"Grab two of the bars and try slidin' the wall left or right," John persisted.

The Irishman shot him an exasperated glance but wrapped his powerful gloved hands around the iron. When he tugged to his left, three feet of wall moved perceptibly. Another half dozen pulls exposed a dark opening big enough for a man to wriggle through. O'Leary thrust his lantern inside it.

"Son of a bitch!" he exclaimed. He looked up. "Sorry, ma'am. You were right, John. It's here."

"Keep your gloves on," John called down while keeping his eye on Hastings. "Let's try to find some usable fingerprints."

The caretaker's eyebrows knit at the instruction. John wondered if the man knew anything about the recently adopted technique of using fingerprints in criminal investigations. His expression was not out of keeping with that of an innocent man's.

"No use all of us tryin' to enter this way," John told the group. "Miss Goode, why don't you take Mr. Hastin's and Officers Heinze and Levine inside and go down to the cellar. You may be able to give us some help from that side."

The group retreated, trailing a pair of excited conversations. John got himself down the iron steps with Ricciardi's help, clutching the blueprint tube under one arm. While he was passed down the specialist's fingerprinting satchel, O'Leary ventured into the tunnel. John took a moment to observe the cunning fashioning of the false iron wall. It rolled along a pair of tracks, the lower of which was lined with ball bearings. Time alone had made the wall difficult to move, as rust had accumulated. *When this was new*, he thought, *it must have moved quite easily*.

The tunnel was a mere six feet in length. It ended at a door that looked like it belonged in a subriver caisson. An iron wheel served as handle and needed to be spun counterclockwise several times before the door would open. It smelled of a petroleum lubricant which had certainly been applied within the past few years. Directly beyond this point, three steps led down into a passage that ran at right angles to the tunnel. At the end of this short passage was another door. This had a lever that also swung counterclockwise, about thirty degrees.

"I'll be damned!" O'Leary exclaimed. "I'm in the back of some kind of closet."

"Let me see," said Le Brun. "Yes. I recognize it. It's one of the closets built into the south wall. Just duck under the shelves and push your hands out. The closet doors should open easily."

Inside of twenty seconds, O'Leary and Le Brun were standing in front of the four people who had separated to enter the cellar. Officer Ricciardi remained in the tunnel, using his dusting equipment.

"So, the man who killed Mr. Pinckney in his bedroom came in t'rough the game room and kitchen," the city detective said.

John ducked back into the closet. "I don't think so."

"Where are you going?" O'Leary called to him.

"Up."

"What?"

"Give me that lantern, Mr. O'Leary. Miss Goode!" John said loudly, turning. "Please bring everyone up to the dinin' room."

"Very well."

John reentered the narrow passageway and took the few steps back to the airtight door. He continued beyond it to a dark wall. When he put his hand against it, it swung to the left, revealing itself as spring-loaded. He was not surprised to find a ladder just beyond, attached to the outside wall. Juggling the blueprints and lantern, he worked his way carefully up the ladder. At its top, he found a trapdoor with large hinges secured to its bottom and one of the side walls. He shoved it up with the crown of his head and bulled through the opening he made.

When John came up to shoulder height into the level above, he brought up the tube and the lantern and set them on the floor. He wriggled up through the trapdoor opening, came to his knees, and stood. He lowered the door, tested, and found that he could stand on it. He knew from having studied the blueprint of the first floor that he stood in a space about two and a half feet wide which lay between the dining and living rooms. He noted the ladder secured to the southern wall, looked up, and saw another trapdoor. The studs framing the other three walls were so close together that he knew there was no access to the living and dining rooms. He heard voices from the room to his left.

"Hello!" he cried.

"Where are you?" O'Leary asked.

John rapped on the wall lathing. "Behind this wall. Go upstairs and listen for me in the back bedroom."

"Sarah's bedroom?" he heard Lordis say.

"Yes."

Close spaces were not a favorite of the ex-sheriff. He drew in a few slow breaths of stale air and counseled himself to stay calm. He picked up the tube and lantern and climbed. Again using the top of his head, he moved the trapdoor aside, and again he smelled lubricating oil. When he finally stood inside the second-story passage, he was relieved to find a spring mechanism that ran across the space, indicating a door. He also found a pair of latches in the wall to his left and three hinges at the angle of the south and east walls. Careful to touch them only on their edges, he spun the latch tongues from their locks until he could push the wall out. It swung without noise. Light burst into the space.

Four wide-eyed faces greeted Le Brun as he emerged. He handed over the blueprints and lantern and dusted himself off.

"Would someone kindly hand me that jewelry box on the dresser?" John asked through the babble of his companions.

"Pardon me if I offend, miss," Officer Heinze said, "but the man who built this had a couple of screws loose. I've heard of peepholes cut from closets, so's people could watch others in their bedrooms, but why did he need to do all of this?"

"He never said," Lordis replied.

"He did it because he had the money to do it," John answered as he wedged the jewelry box between door and wall. "If you saw the vacation houses they've built down where I live, just so they can use them for a month or less, you wouldn't ask. And to top it off, they call twelve-room homes cottages!"

"At least he named it proper," Detective O'Leary stated. "Whimsy indeed."

While everyone else speculated, William Hastings stood quietly near the bedroom's west door, his hands folded in front of him.

"This is still a long way from the inside of Edmund Pinckney's bedroom," observed O'Leary.

Le Brun headed toward the door not obstructed by the handyman. "True enough. Let's leave this for Officer Ricciardi's work and continue upstairs."

O NCE THE GROUP was assembled in the house's ballroom, John demonstrated the moving wall that led to the western turret. Everyone filed inside, and the policemen gravitated to the view from the turret windows. John, meantime, moved to the opposite end of the space and went down on one knee. From his pocket, he extracted his folding knife. His fingers moved over the six-inch-wide floor planking, pushing, probing. Finally, he found what he sought and inserted the blade of the knife into a space between two boards. He twisted it a bit and caused the board to rise up.

"What is it?" Hastings asked, from just behind him.

"A way down into Mr. Pinckney's closet. Hold this!" Once the first board was lifted, the other seven were easy to remove. "I should have noted the shortness of these several planks the first time I was in here," John said, after making a throaty noise of self-criticism. "And the fact that there are only two lengths, so that each is interchangeable with three others." When he had finished removing the last board, he stood so that everyone in the group could see the trapdoor below with its inset lift ring. "Tarnation!" he suddenly exclaimed, lapsing the others into silence. He looked at Lordis. "Do you ever go into the brothers' closets?"

"Rarely. Only when I've brushed down a suit for them or returned them from the dry cleaners."

"Do you recall the shelves across the back wall in Edmund's room?"

"Yes."

"Solid cedar and, I would bet, firmly secured in place."

"Like steps," William Hastings broke in.

John pointed a congratulatory finger at him. "Precisely. No ladder needed."

"And the older Mr. Pinckney specified that the electric light be mounted on the wall and not the ceiling," Hastings revealed. "Couldn't hang it there because of this door."

John offered Lordis a grim look. "Do you know what this means? You and I had the killer trapped up here. All we had to do was tell Detective O'Leary about the hidden doors when he arrived, and he and his men would have found the person."

A frisson shook the housekeeper. "Here all that time. When did he leave?"

"Who knows?" John bit on the inside of his lip to hold back an oath that no lady should hear. He again used his handkerchief to haul the trapdoor up. The blackness below might as well have been the bottom of a mine shaft.

"But the killer did have to move in the open between the back bedroom and the ballroom," O'Leary puzzled out loud.

"It certainly seems so," said Le Brun. "Both comin' and goin'. A quick dash by way of the stairs to and from Miss Sarah's bedroom."

"You said you were in the hallway not twenty seconds after you heard the revolver go off."

"That's right."

"Then the killer *must* have remained hidden in this room for some time."

"I can see no other way."

O'Leary gritted his teeth and shook his head forcefully at the reply. "Rotten luck. Miss Goode, would you be kind enough to take us down to the room below?"

"Certainly."

The chatelaine and the policemen left the hidden alcove. William Hastings stayed behind with Le Brun.

"Well, the old coot wasn't lying," Hastings said, moving to the turret windows. "There were seven secrets."

"If you count this trapdoor and the one leading down to his closet as parts of Secrets Four and Five."

Hastings turned. "What do you mean?"

John nodded at the blueprint tube. "Hand me that, would you please?" When he had the tube, he pulled out the eight blueprints and found the one that covered the first floor. Hastings put the toe of his shoe on the far end of the curling sheet to keep it open. "Much obliged." John pointed to the giant fireplace in the living room. "The drain entrance is Number Six. If you squat down for a moment, you can see that there are dotted lines inside the fireplace. I would imagine you don't work on the fireplace yourself, do you?"

"No. We have chimney sweeps in every other year."

"But you do clean the ashes."

"There's a trapdoor on the floor. A chute drops down directly to the furnace room."

"The fireplace is large enough that you can stand up straight inside it."

"Not quite, but almost."

"According to this drawin', Secret Seven lies inside. Not that it has much to do with someone gettin' into Mr. Pinckney's bedroom, but I'm sure you're as curious as I am what's there."

"I must admit I am."

"Who could possibly know the secret of the drain door if you didn't, Mr. Hastin's?" John asked.

Hastings shook his large head ponderously. "I think Edmund and Miniver must have known. Their father would have confided in them as the heirs to the house. One of them told somebody in confidence. I been thinking about it ever since you went down into the drain. I believe Miniver must have bragged to one of his lady friends about it. He was always showing them the house, giving the grand tour and showing off the other secrets to impress them. Let them have the false hope they might one day be its mistress, y'know?"

"I understand."

"He jilted half a dozen women after his divorce. Any one of them might have wanted him dead for seducing them. I only wish I could remember their names."

The inky hole in the floor took on definition from a soft light below it. An instant later, when the closet fixture was turned on, it glowed brightly, exposing the top shelf and the rows of suits and trousers.

"Drop that door for a moment so we can have a look at its underside," O'Leary called up.

John obliged, then pulled it back up.

"Perfect fit. Right over the ceiling molding. There's no way anybody could have suspected it. Damned good thing I had my superiors hold the suicide determination."

"We're comin' down," John said. He again lowered the door and let the ring grip fall into its recess.

"I'm very sorry Mr. Edmund and Mr. Miniver have died," Hastings said, sliding his foot over the boards, "but I must say I'm relieved to finally know the last of this house's secrets."

"Let's see about that last secret," John invited.

A S THE GROUP TROOPED DOWN Whimsy House's center staircase, they met a yawning Officer Ricciardi ascending with his fingerprint satchel.

"Not a print anywhere on the outer door, the tunnel, or the inner doors," the dusting specialist reported.

"I'll show him to the other places," Officer Heinze volunteered.

O'Leary, Levine, Hastings, and Goode followed Le Brun into the living room. When John came to the fireplace, he handed over the tube filled with blueprints to Detective O'Leary. "Evidence. And now for a bit of fun as a reward for our dusty night's work: Whimsy House's final secret. Would you do the honors, Mr. Hastin's?"

"Where exactly do I look?" he asked.

"If the blueprint is accurate, it would be in the wall on the room side, perhaps goin' into the mantelpiece face."

While Lordis's cat wound itself around her legs and meowed for attention, Hastings ducked into the fireplace and twisted around. "Might I borrow your jackknife, Mr. Le Brun?"

John handed over his knife handle-end first. The group waited in expectant silence, listening to the scraping of steel on brick. From time to time, Hastings would grunt as he accommodated himself to the tight fit. Finally, he exclaimed in a happy tone.

"A loose brick. Another."

In all, four soot-blackened bricks came out of the inner chimney, to be set on the log cradle.

"I feel a handle."

"Pull on it!" John directed.

A more hollow, resonant metal now scraped against brick. Hastings emerged into the living room holding a metal container about the size of a cigar box. He carried it to the bar, set it down, and stepped back.

"Would you do the honors, Miss Goode?" John asked.

Lordis approached the box as if it were a holy relic. She lifted the lid slowly and gazed inside. She reached in, extracted several papers, and opened each in turn.

"Bills of sale for Mrs. Pinckney's jewels," she reported.

"So, they weren't stolen after all," Hastings exclaimed. "He sold them!"

"No," Lordis replied. "These are the original bills of sale. Sales *to* the Pinckneys. This one dates back to 1868."

"Sort of anticlimactic," O'Leary judged. "Well, that was fun, but not so much fun as figurin' out how Edmund Pinckney was killed inside a locked room. I t'ank you so much, Mr. Le Brun. Now, if you will only supply the killer, I will be eternally in your debt."

"I'm workin' on it."

"How much longer will you be investigating in the house?" Lordis asked the city detective.

"No telling, ma'am."

"Then I shall say good night unless I am required further," she said.

"You just go about your business, ma'am."

"May I go?" Hastings asked.

"Certainly."

"And I shall retire to my hotel as well," John allowed. He had gotten as much out of the night as he had expected. He wanted to be as fresh as possible the next day, when he intended to deliver over the killer, just as Kevin O'Leary had asked.

TUESDAY

JUNE 26, 1906

A S JOHN HAD EXPECTED, there was little else in the front of the New York newspapers other than the Stanford White murder. The first six pages of the *New York Times* were devoted to the incident. Not enough time had elapsed for the in-depth, behind-the-scenes reporting. What had been gathered in the few hours between the murder and press time, however, seemed to the southerner nothing short of miraculous. He registered several interesting facts that had been gathered. By coincidence, both the Thaws and White had dined at the Café Martin before the show, but neither was aware of the other's presence. White was entertaining his son, Lawrence, and the son's college friend. White had also stopped in at the Manhattan Club, just across the street from Madison Square Garden, before attending the musical's opening performance. Harry Thaw was reported to be "about thirty years old" and was all but called an insane playboy.

It was reported that White "was a persistent first-nighter and liked pretty girls." He had shown a very personal interest in Miss Florence Evelyn Nesbit since her first arrival in New York City at the age of fifteen. She had posed nude for him as a model, and he had introduced her to theatrical managers. After she became celebrated in *Floradora*, "White remained her very good friend and she in turn was grateful to him." One of the theatrical managers was quoted as saying "She is of frivolous disposition and no doubt refused to break off her friendship for him after marrying young Thaw, who is a cigarette fiend."

John noted also that an unnamed woman in white had been seen kneeling beside White's body. No mention of her taking away a metal tube had been made.

Le Brun sat in the dining room of the Hotel Savoy. He folded the newspaper as his breakfast of scrambled eggs and toast was delivered. *That's how passions of the heart turn into murder,* he reflected. *Not by hired actors entering exclusive men's clubs or finding their ways into locked bedrooms.* William Hastings had had his jilted-lover theory ready and seemed eager to deliver it the previous night, despite its absurdity. The handyman was a relatively cool character, John judged, but he figured this was because he had been well prepared. *Well rehearsed, by a professional theatrical director?* John wondered.

As John was enjoying his second cup of coffee, Kevin O'Leary entered the hotel dining room. He walked as stiffly as if he had been horseback riding for hours. Dark crescents underlay his eyes. John noted that he wore the same dark suit he had worn the previous night and that it was badly wrinkled.

"Have you gotten any sleep at all?" John asked.

"T'ree precious hours. Not a single damned fingerprint anywhere," he said as he plopped himself down on one of the chairs uninvited. "I went over to the station and fell asleep on one of the couches."

"Why not go home and catch a few winks?" John asked.

"Because the whole case now relies on finding that hired murderer. Let's go down ta the Players Club."

"They said they would contact me here," John told the detective.

"I mean ta push 'em. Make a useless profession useful for once. Saints alive, but that coffee smells good!"

John shoved his cup across the table. With no embarrassment, O'Leary lifted it to his lips and drank it down in a single gulp. "If me wife could brew coffee like that, I'd eat at home."

As they walked through the lobby, John held up his hand to pause O'Leary and went up to the front desk.

"Any messages for John Le Brun?"

The clerk smiled. "One just came in. From a Mr. John Drew."

Le Brun turned to his companion with a grin. "No wonder he's the president of the Players Club: Perfect timin'." He took the message and read it. "They've found an actor who fits the bill. His name is Joseph Ogden. He's been sendin' a new address to bookin' agents around the city: A boardinghouse at 435 West Thirty-eighth Street."

O'Leary flashed his badge at the clerk. "Get me to a telephone! I've got an important call ta make."

A S SOON AS HE SAW the uniformed officer step into place at the far end of Thirty-eighth Street, O'Leary patted the shoulder of the policeman by his side and gestured for John to follow him up the sidewalk. Two plainclothesmen had earlier approached Joseph Ogden's boardinghouse from a back alley off Thirty-seventh, sealing the rear escape route.

"Time to get this t'ing solved," O'Leary said to Le Brun.

Three boys who looked to be between twelve and fourteen were playing stickball in the middle of the street. The pitcher and the outfielder stopped their motions and stared at the men like deer sizing up approaching hunters. Their expressions signaled the batter, who turned for his own look.

O'Leary crooked his index finger at the kid holding the broomstick handle, a dark-haired urchin with filthy face and arms. "You! Come here!"

"Blow it out yer ass!" the kid yelled back.

O'Leary took off like a Fourth of July rocket. John was astonished at his speed until he remembered that the man had earned his passage to America as a professional runner. The boy scampered about twenty paces, realized he was outclassed, and tried to duck, jink, and double back. The Irishman caught him by the scruff of the neck and banged him into a trash wagon.

"Who runs that apartment house over there?" O'Leary demanded of the boy.

"Mrs. Tindale."

"You go to school, tough guy?"

"School's out for the summer."

"You go to school when it's not out?"

"Sure."

"Next time yer in school, ask 'em to teach you some manners. Now get moving." He gave the lad a soft kick in the rear. The boy ran to his friends, who then moved as a pack to the far end of the block. By the time they gave O'Leary a unison raspberry from a safer distance, he and Le Brun were entering the tenement building.

They found Mr. Tindale, a ferret of a man wearing a pince-nez, in the first-floor apartment on the left. O'Leary flashed his badge.

"You own this building?" he asked.

"The bank owns it, but we're halfway there."

"How many renters?"

"Seven."

O'Leary turned to John. "Show him your picture."

John produced the newspaper photograph of Witherspoon King.

"You have an actor who looks like this living here," O'Leary stated.

"That's right. Mr. Joseph Ogden."

"Lives by himself?"

"He does. Been here less than three weeks. Has one of the efficiencies on the top floor. What's he done?"

"Good question. Is he usually in at this hour?"

"I've never seen him up before noon. What's he done?" Tindale repeated.

"Why don't you show us which room, and maybe we'll all find out."

The trio climbed the creaking stairs to the third floor. Mr. Tindale knocked on the door of the rearmost apartment. There was no reply. He tried again, with the same result.

"He might be a murderer," O'Leary let the landlord know. "You don't want that class of renter, do you?"

Tindale bridled. "Certainly not!"

"Then why don't you let us in?"

"Can I do that?" Tindale asked.

"It's almost your building," O'Leary said.

"I've never been in trouble with the law."

"Why start now?" O'Leary dipped his head toward the lock.

The landlord fished into his trousers for his keys. He isolated one, fitted it into the lock, and opened the door.

"Mr. Ogden?" Tindale called softly, halfway inside. Then he gasped and retreated just beyond the door tread.

Kevin O'Leary guided the landlord back and entered the flat. John waited two beats and followed. The room was uncomfortably warm, even though the outside temperature was only in the mid-seventies. A dead man rested on a small dining chair, with his head lying on the table directly in front of him. The bluish white face was turned slightly toward the door, so that his half-opened left eye stared down onto the checkered cloth that covered the table. To the side of his head was an empty champagne bottle and an equally empty drinking glass.

"Did you see enough to identify Mr. Ogden, Mr. Tindale?" O'Leary called into the hall, shooing a fly that had ascended out of the corpse's upturned ear.

"Yes. That's him."

"When did you last see him alive?"

"Saturday afternoon it was. He came in with his shopping pail loaded."

"Did you speak with him?"

"Just to say hello."

O'Leary saw that Tindale was more afraid of death than curious about it. He returned to the doorway. "Did you see anyone come ta visit him in the past week or so?"

"Nobody. He's been a very private lodger."

The detective turned to Le Brun. "Why don't you stay with the body while I fetch Duffy and Hassler from the back. They can interview the neighbors while we search the place."

John merely nodded. He listened to O'Leary and the landlord trudging down the stairs, the detective soothing and counseling as they went. John took out his pocket handkerchief, wrapped his hand with it, pulled back the chair opposite the body, made sure it was free of clues, and sat. He leaned forward and sniffed at the champagne bottle. He put his nose close to the corpse's lips and inhaled deeply. He studied the ashtray on the table, the six cigarette butts in it and the one that seemed to have been allowed to burn into a long ash without having been puffed. Then he eased back on the chair and took a leisurely inventory of the small living quarters.

Of his free will, John owned few possessions. All he had in abundance was books. His home consisted of two bedrooms, a bathroom, a small kitchen, an equally small dining room, and a parlor. A central hallway ran through the one-story bungalow and provided air circulation. Most of the furniture he had acquired from his relatives or as bequests. He had no fancy jewelry or silverware, no porcelain from the Orient, no European lace or linens. And yet, looking at what was most probably the sum total of Joseph Ogden's lifetime accumulation, he felt like a rich man. The man's chosen profession had not been good to him. *Perhaps,* John mused, *he was a poor performer who deluded himself as to his talent. Or perhaps he was a good actor but fortune had not been kind.*

His observation notwithstanding, the apartment flat was not in the bottom-of-the-barrel category. The mattress and bedclothes looked clean and in good shape; the walls had recently been repaired and painted; the fixtures were of average quality. Likewise, the hallway had been clean and well lit. It took more than begging money to live in this building.

Wiping the perspiration from his brow with his handkerchief, John rose from the chair and made a slow circle around the body and table. On the far side of the room was a single unmade bed in an alcove. Two pillows lay at the head, the top one in a pillowcase, the other, which appeared spanking new, uncovered. A rod above and in front of it held a curtain of heavy cloth. From the wall over the bed were pinned several playbills. The inner side of the alcove was formed by a small room that contained toilet, sink, and medicine cabinet. Against the hallway wall stood a painted dresser with a built-in mirror. Atop the dresser sat a large metal box. Next to it, according to its title, lay a pocket daybook with a fountain pen attached. The wall opposite the bed held a small clothes closet, in line with a sink, a counter with a few drawers, a small icebox, and a pair of cabinets attached to the wall. Creating warm meals was not possible in the flat. A single window bisected the length of the outer wall, looking out on an alleyway. A low table beneath it held several newspapers. John riffled through the rather thick pile. The topmost were the Sunday editions of the *World* and the *New York Times.* The window was closed.

"Had a good look-see?" Detective O'Leary asked, coming back into the room.

"Just a first pass," Le Brun said as the Irishman walked over to the window, unlocked it, and raised it as far as it would go. A breeze immediately began pushing the room's hot air out to the hallway. "You do the touchin'."

"Good enough."

While O'Leary pulled on a set of kidskin gloves, John said, "Start at the back wall over the bed."

"T'ree playbills." O'Leary unpinned them from the wall and laid them on the table next to the corpse's head. He opened one after the other. "He's in the cast in each of 'em. Pretty far down the list. Not a headliner was Mr. Ogden. And these two shows go back four or five years if memory serves."

"Interestin' that not one of those shows was at Mr. Topley's theater . . . the Hyperion."

"That's true. Do you imagine something was in the champagne?"

"I do. Somethin' to stop his heart. How old do you think Mr. Ogden was?"

"Not younger than fifty. Not older than sixty."

"And about thirty pounds overweight. People assume that actors have bad livin', eatin', and medical habits. I am sure the hope was that he'd be found by the landlord or a friend and that the regular police would be summoned. The locked room would show no violence nor evidence of a visit by anyone else, and he'd be carted off to a local hospital at city expense, where a cursory autopsy would be done. Official cause of death: heart failure. No connection at all to the Metropolitan Club murder."

"That's exactly what would have happened."

Le Brun had not turned from the bed area. "When the coroner performs the autopsy, make sure he doesn't quit if he finds no common poison in the system. For example, he should consider nicotine. May I open Mr. Ogden's mouth?"

"Be my guest."

John thumbed the lips apart with some difficulty, exposing yellowed teeth. He tugged the corpse's right hand up and noted the stains on the fingers. "The ashtray was not put there as a prop; he was a longtime smoker. It would be excusable if an unenlightened coroner found a good deal of nicotine in his blood and assumed it had come in through the lungs only."

"Nicotine ya say. A chemical in tobacco?" O'Leary asked.

"Indeed. A very deadly one. I own several books on poisons. I read of a tobacco processor from Höfen, Germany, who died of nicotine poisonin' a few hours after he gashed himself on a tobacco cutter."

"Amazing."

"Yes, it got my attention."

"I meant *you* are amazing, Mr. Le Brun. No wonder J. P. Morgan respects you so much."

"Thank you. Would you look through the bedclothes for us?" John asked, trying to keep the detective methodically focused.

The bedclothing revealed nothing. Neither did the two suitcases stored under the bed. The medicine cabinet and the toiletry kit in the tiny lavatory likewise held nothing out of the ordinary. The front door had the type of mechanism that locked automatically whenever it was closed. The dresser held several packages of factory-rolled cigarettes and boxes of safety matches. Among the clothing in the dresser and the closet were several new items.

"Looks like he come inta some money recently," O'Leary proclaimed, holding up a new pair of trousers and a new dress shirt.

"Anythin' that looks like the suit everyone described on the false Witherspoon King?" John inquired.

"No."

O'Leary moved on to the kitchen area. It was extremely tidy. Inside one of the wall cabinets stood a drinking glass identical to the one on the dining table. It had been carefully washed and showed no sign of fingerprints. O'Leary glanced at the newspapers and did not find them interesting. He looked out the window for a moment, then turned back to the dresser. He grabbed the metal box and the daybook and carried them to the table. He sat and opened the metal box. It contained the tools of the actor's trade: greasepaint, cream, rouge, sponges, liner pencils, a few wigs and mustaches, spirit gum, stage jewelry, and a knife whose blade disappeared into the handle when pressure was put upon its point. Absent was any hair that approached the shade of Witherspoon King's. In the box's lower bay was twenty-five dollars in paper and coin.

The daybook was filled with neatly printed, minuscule notes. O'Leary began with the current date, which was empty, and read backward.

"Here's an interesting notation," he said. " 'Pick up form from printers.' Eight days back. Could be the duplicate of the delivery form from Europa Wines and Spirits." He licked his forefinger and flipped back another page. "Mother of God!"

"What is it?" John asked.

" 'Meet Maurice Van Leyden.' "

"What date?"

"June eleventh."

"May I see?"

The printing looked the same as that around it. Further, it was written in the same ink. John uncapped the fountain pen and made a few strokes on a blank page toward the back of the book. It seemed to be the ink that had created all the entries for the past month.

"Didn't I say Van Leyden couldn't allow himself to be embarrassed?" O'Leary asked, abandoning Ben Topley as suspect with alarming alacrity.

Before Le Brun could respond, a soft rapping on the flat's door frame drew the two investigators from the book. The plainclothesman previously introduced to Le Brun as Fred Hassler stood beside a petite woman with straw-colored hair, a homemade flower-print dress, and a flour-splotched apron.

"Excuse me, gentlemen," Hassler said. "This is Mrs. McMahon. She lives on the floor below. She saw a man come down from this floor yesterday afternoon."

"I did," the woman verified. Her button eyes shone with excitement at being a witness for a police investigation. "I was coming back from baking for the Hibernian Society. Had me key in my door when a man comes around the bend in the stairs from above. We spotted each other, and for a second he looked like he was about to turn around and march back up. Kinda took a hitch in his step, if ya know what I mean." She smiled at each of the men in turn, then looked behind her, where the landlord stood trying to remain unobtrusive.

"Go on," O'Leary encouraged.

"He looked like the newspaper drawings of Santa Claus," she said.

O'Leary gave John a knowing look.

"Did he have a white beard and mustache and a red nose?" John asked.

"That he did. And little spectacles."

"A heavyset man?"

"Exactly."

"Maurice Van Leyden," O'Leary proclaimed to Le Brun. "A notebook entry *and* a verifying witness."

John refused any look or word of confirmation. The description was precisely that of the cuckolded real estate mogul, but more needed to be asked. "And short?" he asked Mrs. McMahon.

"Short? No. Rather tall," the woman attested.

"You're certain?"

The little woman drew herself up in high dudgeon. "I am. He walked right past me. He was about this high." She raised her hand five inches over the crown of her head. "Perhaps an inch shorter or longer, but no more than that."

"How did he walk?" John asked.

"Like a heavy man does," Mrs. McMahon replied. "Wheezing as he passed. Like so." She demonstrated. Then she snapped her fingers. "And there was something else that reminded me of Santa Claus. You know how the drawings show him holding his big belly?"

"Yes."

"Well, this man was doing that. Holding his belly, like it weighed too much to hold itself up."

"Thank you very much, Mrs. McMahon. You have excellent powers of observation." John focused past the beaming woman on the plain-clothesman. "You should take down the lady's testimony very carefully."

Hassler looked to O'Leary, who nodded his agreement.

"Let's go back to your apartment, ma'am," Hassler said. A few moments later, the hallway was empty.

"Was it Van Leyden or wasn't it?" O'Leary asked Le Brun.

"It was not."

"You're sure?"

"Close the door," John said. "Yet again, we are bein' confronted with appearances that are not what they seem to be. How do I know this?"

"That's what I'm asking."

"There are a couple things you may have overlooked," John said, not being able to couch the accusation any more gently.

"Pray, enlighten me."

"Check Ogden's pockets first. That should exhaust the possible clues here."

O'Leary's inspection yielded a cheap pocket watch and a folding knife, the key to the flat, two pennies, a billfold containing identification and a five-dollar bill, and a well-used handkerchief. Le Brun manipulated the corpse's elbow and wrist as O'Leary worked, judging the degree of rigor mortis.

"Physical evidence of time of death jibes with the lady's testimony," John observed. "He's just beginning to loosen up. He died less than twenty-four hours ago but more than twenty, based on a closed flat and recent temperatures."

"He's wearing a suit!" O'Leary exclaimed, rolling his eyes as if in apology for his oversight.

"True enough. Looks like he might have been preparin' to go out. I don't know about you, but I don't leave on my suit jacket when I drink alone."

"And you probably don't drink champagne alone either."

Le Brun smiled. "Never. Champagne to the common man is either to impress a woman or to celebrate a special occasion or victory."

"Which would be carrying off two murders."

"Spot on, as our British friends say."

"He arrived here less than t'ree weeks ago. Which suggests the person who hired him wanted him hard to find. But that doesn't get us closer, does it?"

"I don't think so."

O'Leary's eyes narrowed. "All of that could still point to Van Leyden just as easily as to Topley. What else did I miss?"

Le Brun rocked back and forth on his heels. "Wasn't it interestin' that the three playbills were arranged on the wall in a wide V."

"I'd put 'em up in a row. Why did he do a V?"

"He didn't," Le Brun answered. "If you'll look very carefully at the wall, there are four tack holes. In a diamond pattern."

O'Leary hurried to the bed, kneeled on it, and inspected the back wall. "Blessed saints! You're right."

"And wouldn't it be interestin' if Mr. Ogden had been in a Benjamin Topley production in the past few years?"

"So it was Topley and not Van Leyden?" O'Leary asked.

"I believe so. First of all, whoever it was wanted the police who found the body to believe this was a natural death. The door was locked. With that kind of mechanism, simply a matter of closin' the door . . . from either side. The window was locked as well, preventin' anyone from enterin' or exitin' by the fire escape. On a warm summer day, however, that should raise as many questions as it supplies answers."

"A smart man but not a brilliant one, then. Wouldn't that describe both Topley and Van Leyden?" O'Leary argued.

"True. But would Van Leyden be as methodical? Perhaps. All I can say is I've observed Topley making careful notes. Our murderer did not hurry about in here," Le Brun stated. "Did you notice the new pillow under the old, covered one?"

"Yes. Another recent purchase."

"But by whom? I believe the murderer entered this buildin' in disguise, with that pillow under his shirt and trouser top, actin' as a pretend belly."

O'Leary's eyes riveted on the pillow. "But Mrs. McMahon said he left with a big belly, actually holding it up. He carried away *something else* in the pillow's place. Inside its pillowcase."

"What?" John asked.

O'Leary snapped his fingers. "Ogden had not discarded all the evidence. I'll bet he ditched the false beard and mustache, but he was unwilling ta part with the suit. Finest t'reads he'd ever worn."

"I believe you're right. Perhaps new shoes as well. The murderer intended to arrive and depart with the pillow, but he had to leave it behind when he found the incriminatin' clothin'."

"Topley's a tall man," O'Leary recalled.

"Perhaps five inches taller than Van Leyden. An actor can don a white beard and mustache and rouge up his nose. He can put on spectacles and stuff up his suit and walk like a heavyset man and huff and puff. But he can't make himself shorter."

"But we haven't found any hard evidence that it was Topley," O'Leary noted.

"Absolutely correct. We are standin' together in a set designed by a consummate stage director. He is a man whose job demands vigilant attention to detail. He hopes there will be no link to the Pinckney murders when this man is found, but he leaves nothin' to chance in case the police are not fools. We can only construct a reasonable scenario from a succession of facts."

O'Leary moved the small table from under the window and plopped his posterior on the sill. "Do me a favor and review those facts."

John repeated a slow circling of the table and corpse. "Topley learns of Miniver Pinckney's impendin' death from lung cancer. He wants to kill Edmund Pinckney long before that happens. He knows an actor whom he believes capable of murder for money. He does his research on members of the Metropolitan Club and comes up with a match in Witherspoon King and Joseph Ogden. He gives Ogden enough cash advance for him to move to a decent flat here. Ogden performs the role of his career; he does a perfect job of the murder . . . except that he has killed the wrong brother through no fault of his own. He meets with Topley in some clandestine place on Friday or Saturday night . . . dependin' upon when Topley learned the truth . . . and is told the unhappy truth."

Le Brun had come up close to O'Leary. He paused his perambulation for a moment. "Topley knows about Secret Number Six of Whimsy House from the handyman, Hastin's. He now has a choice: Either he kills the real Edmund himself or else sends Ogden in. I believe he would send this man and have his alibi solid for that entire night. Ogden is not so old or heavy that he can't accomplish the job."

"He was actually pretty sprightly if he hoofed on the stage," O'Leary surmised.

"Once again, Mr. Ogden is successful in his bloody task. No doubt, Mr. Topley would not hurry to meet up with him for fear of bein' followed by you or your minions. Ogden has clearly been instructed to lie low. But you and I keep sniffin' around. Topley knows that every minute his actor is allowed to live means a greater chance of bein' caught. What convinces him not to wait any longer to dispose of him is somethin' he heard from my lips yesterday mornin'."

"The story about Edmund and Mrs. Van Leyden."

"Exactly. Benjamin Topley has learned from me an excellent candidate for wantin' Edmund Pinckney murdered. Someone who would continue that pursuit if he found that Miniver had been killed first by mistake."

O'Leary drew in a deep breath, to finish the race. "So Topley quickly digs up a photograph of Van Leyden."

"Or else relies on his memory. He admitted he knew what the man looks like. He creates his disguise, completed with a newly purchased pillow. He arrives with a celebratory bottle of laced champagne, and—"

"Wait a bit. The champagne was tampered with. Wouldn't Ogden become suspicious when the cork failed to pop?"

"Not if Topley injected the poison through the cork with a hypodermic needle. Topley also told me he had a very busy day. This was no doubt true, considerin' he had to assemble a disguise, purchase champagne, get a wad of cash to convince Ogden he was home free, find his poison and a needle, and buy a pillow to create his belly."

"So, he arrives unheralded and finds Ogden holed up as ordered," O'Leary said, snatching the baton. "He hands over the cash and the champagne and disarms the actor with a fusillade of praise. He chews the fat with Ogden until the man becomes unconscious. Then he pours the rest of the champagne down the drain."

"Have somebody carefully open the sink trap with a pan under it," Le Brun said. "If he washed the glasses first and emptied the bottle last, there may still be some of the adulterated champagne in the trap."

"Brilliant!" O'Leary exclaimed.

"Now *I* would have brought a hip flask with unlaced champagne in it and refilled the bottle," John said, "just in case the contents were checked."

"Stay on our side of the law, Mr. Le Brun."

"I shall."

"Then Topley reclaims most of the cash, but he leaves enough in the metal box and the dead man's trousers to make it seem reasonable he could afford ta stay here. He finds the diary book and decides to use it to his advantage. Fortunately for him, Ogden prints his notes. Printing is much easier to duplicate than a cursive scrawl."

"He probably saw that the note on pickin' up the form was in the book," John added, "but it is not specific. The benefit of leaving the book behind outweighs the risk."

O'Leary nodded. "And he has ta leave the new pillow behind in order ta sneak out the incriminating suit and perhaps shoes. But he takes the playbill linking Ogden with his theater."

John pointed toward the moved table and its pile of newspapers. "Ogden was readin' the papers on a daily basis, both out of boredom and to see what was bein' written about the Pinckney murders. Topley probably removed yesterday mornin's papers, hopin' the body would be found far enough in the future that the papers might have suggested the man died on Sunday."

"If he's that careful, we've got a real problem," O'Leary said.

"We do indeed," Le Brun agreed. "I've seen nothin' here that would convict him beyond the shadow of a doubt."

O'Leary swore under his breath, scratched his head, and stood. "Ogden t'ought nothing of Topley arrivin' in disguise?"

"I'm sure not. He knew that Topley would do whatever he could to keep himself a league away from the murders. I'm sure Ogden had no idea that Topley had disguised himself as an actual person. He no doubt thought the man had used white hair and the big belly purely to conceal his true looks."

O'Leary shook his head at the corpse, then stared at John. "If we can't prove it's Topley, then why not Van Leyden?"

"Other than the missin' playbill? What did Mrs. McMahon say?"

O'Leary picked up the apartment key. "She said four or five t'ings that described Van Leyden and only one that contradicted them. Only the pope is infallible."

John walked out into the hallway. "I'd match Mrs. McMahon with the pope any day. When I reach her door, you stop a couple steps above me." He walked down to the second floor and found the apartment door open. Hassler took notes as the woman parceled out her words one by one.

"Mrs. McMahon," John interrupted, putting on his most ingratiating smile. "I want to congratulate you again on your powers of observation."

"T'anks," she said.

"The man standin' next to me upstairs . . . what color are his eyes?"

"Blue."

"His hair?"

"Dusty brown."

"And is he taller or shorter than me?"

"Taller. A bit more than an inch."

"You ought to consider detective work, ma'am. Thank you."

O'Leary shambled down the steps with a scowl. He gave Mrs. McMahon a perfunctory nod as he passed her door.

WHEN O'LEARY AND Le Brun stood outside on the apartment house's front stoop, the city detective said, "I can tell she's not long off the boat from Cork. I shoulda known she'd have such a good eye. My wife does too, along with a memory that's catalogued every one of my sins and errors since I met her. It's the way with Irish women."

"It's the way with all women," John observed. "Fortunately for us men they forgive most of our faults. If I didn't know you for a jokester, I'd believe you didn't have a happy marriage."

O'Leary stood stock-still and fixed John's eyes with his. There was no trace of humor in his expression. "Believe it. You're a bachelor, aren't ya?"

"I am."

"You're lonely a great deal of the time, right?"

"Right again."

"There's worse loneliness than yours, John Le Brun. Try bein' in a marriage that you can't get out of because your religion forbids it. Comin' home to a person who loathes you as much as you do her. When all you have in common anymore is the kids and a bottle of whiskey."

John kept his mouth shut. He could think of no sentence that would improve O'Leary's black outlook. The detective saved him from the embarrassment of a deepening silence.

"And then, on top of it all, to spend my days in Chinatown. I need this crime solved to everybody's satisfaction, and that's the truth of it. All right, then. I'm convinced Ogden did at least the first Pinckney murder. But the evidence is circumstantial. I'm also convinced that Topley hired him. Even less evidence. The actor won't tell us anyt'ing more. The only other link between Topley and the murders seems to be William Hastings. I'm ready ta sweat him."

John inhaled the street's smells. A pungent scent of tomato sauce intermingled with the aroma of freshly baked bread wafted by. "I think that's a mistake. He's been too well tutored. 'Directed' is probably the better word in this case. If I were Benjamin Topley, I'd have told Hastin's that any attempt to sweat him means we don't have hard evidence."

O'Leary shoved his hands hard into his pockets. "John, I cannot just sit by and hope somet'ing breaks."

"I understand. You know how you said I like to put red and black ants together in the jar and see what happens?"

"Yes?"

Le Brun put his hand lightly on the city detective's shoulder and guided him down the stoop steps. "I wonder if you'd let me shake the jar now."

WILLIAM HASTINGS WAS halfway through cleaning and re-gapping the Pinckney automobile spark plugs when Lordis Goode appeared in the carriage house. He wiped his hands on a rag and rolled down his sleeves as they exchanged greetings.

The housekeeper held a small plate of cookies. She extended it toward the handyman. "Have you started to look for another position?"

Hastings shook his head at the offer of food and indicated his dirty hands. "I have. Put the word out around the block. And at my church. Nothing solid yet."

Lordis smiled weakly. "At least people won't question why we're looking, once they hear we come from Whimsy House."

"True. Very nice of you to tell Mrs. Lassiter and the maid that they had been left some money in the wills. That all came out of your pocket, didn't it?"

"I would have told you the same, except that you know from signing the wills that you got nothing. After I blew half of old Mr. Pinckney's bequest to me on clothing, I put the rest in the bank. Between that and what Edmund and Miniver left me, I didn't see how I couldn't share some of it. Everyone in the house shared the tragedy; some of us must continue to live after it."

"Well said."

"Won't you accept a few hundred dollars?" Lordis asked.

"That's all right. I've been putting aside. But thanks." Hastings cleared his throat. "No more information from the cops?"

"No. They look like children who've had their balloons pricked. They were evidently pinning a great deal of hope on the last secrets of the house."

"The whole thing has been creepy," Hastings said, giving his hands a more diligent cleaning with the cloth.

"I agree. But it will all be behind you and me soon, one way or the other. I intend to avoid this street entirely once I'm gone. Probably the next time I see Whimsy House will be in a new museum."

"What do you mean?" William asked

"You remember Sarah's doll house? That jumbo model of—"

"Right."

"Shall I leave these?" Lordis asked of the cookies.

"Please do."

She set the plate down on the garage's workbench and turned to leave.

William dropped a spark plug into a tin can half filled with kerosene. "Will you be staying with the Topley family once the house is shut down?"

"For a time." Lordis smiled. She looked over her shoulder at Whimsy House. "Perhaps the new owners will want a handyman who already knows the house."

"Perhaps."

"Good afternoon, Mr. Hastings."

"Good afternoon, Miss Goode."

The handyman stood unmoving until the housekeeper had returned to the house.

T EN MINUTES LATER, Lordis exited Whimsy House via the front doors and headed west, across Fifth Avenue and into Central Park. A hundred paces in, she came to a bench. John Le Brun sat on it, reading a newspaper.

"I did what you asked," Lordis reported as she sat down beside him. "Just touched on the subject, as you asked."

"He didn't dwell on it?" John asked.

"No. He was focused on his future. Where he's going to work and live."

A pair of pigeons fluttered down from the trees to the sidewalk in front of the couple, parading back and forth, hoping for a handout.

"What about *your* future?" John asked. "This would be the perfect time to widen your choices. Think seriously about southern cookin' and verdure."

Lordis sighed. "I've grown so used to this city."

"People accommodate themselves to diseases as well."

Lordis slapped him gently on the knee. "New York is *not* a disease."

"It's dirty and dangerous."

"It's like any great city. It has the best and the worst. One simply has to know how to avoid the worst."

"Brunswick isn't so very small," John fished.

"Compared to Savannah perhaps. But to New York City? It's not even as large as this park."

"Come south when I return," John invited. "We can take the slow boat. Not to China but at least as far as Philadelphia."

"You only get the use of Mr. Morgan's yacht if you solve the case," she reminded him.

John didn't bother to discuss the possibility of failure. "Then the train down to Washington. From there, we could go to Charleston. Drop in on some of the relatives."

"*My* relatives? That would be a hoot. The prodigal daughter returns."

"Then Savannah. Finally Brunswick. Give yourself a month or so to get all this out of your system. Breathe fresh air. Eat fresh food. Give yourself the perspective of distance."

"What about my cat?"

"Let Sally mind it."

Lordis shifted herself so that she looked at John more directly. "And why don't *you* consider moving to New York? You seem to have accommodated yourself much more quickly than I did."

John nodded his head very slowly. "Maybe."

His companion gasped and put her hand to her chest. "What? The country sheriff would actually tolerate the noise and the grime?"

"And the crime. I'd consider it. But only if you come south with me first."

Lordis extended her right hand. "Deal!"

For a moment John just stared at the proffered hand. He had stopped believing that Lordis would agree. He had believed instead that he would leave another piece of his admittedly atrophied heart behind in New York, as he had the previous year in London.

Lordis laughed at the realization that she had surprised her admirer so profoundly. She lifted her hand and rubbed her fingertips affectionately across his cheek.

"Not for you, of course," she joked. "Who could pass up sailing to Philadelphia on J. P. Morgan's yacht?" She rose from the bench. "I must go. So much to do."

"I won't see you until tomorrow," John said.

"All right. Still busy catching the murderer?"

"Very much so."

Lordis bent and placed a light kiss on John's forehead. The brim of her hat pushed his derby back as she did. She walked briskly toward Fifth Avenue.

John remained on the bench. The newspaper stayed where he had set it down. He contented himself with drinking in the green trees, blue sky, and white clouds, the passing parade of people, the semitamed animal life. He found himself humming one of the more catchy tunes from *Mamzelle Champagne*.

Kevin O'Leary emerged from among the plantings. He put himself down on the bench where Lordis Goode had sat three minutes earlier.

"Your girlfriend just hailed a hansom cab and headed south. I have a carriage following her. I'd bet my badge she isn't headed for the Van Leyden residence."

Sitting quietly on park benches during investigations was ordinarily something John Le Brun would not do. He was calm at the moment because he had gotten complete agreement on a plan of action from O'Leary an hour before. With the probable killer of the Pinckney brothers dead and no telltale clues left behind in Whimsy House, Le Brun had devised a set of chesslike moves based around what William Hastings and Benjamin Topley separately knew or thought they knew. As in chess, Le Brun could not force his opponents to make most moves, but he could coerce them in self-destructive directions.

"You didn't mention Ogden's name or profession to her." O'Leary wanted to be sure.

"I did not. I merely said that the police had been called to pick up the corpse of a man who had a strong resemblance to Witherspoon King. I mentioned the book entries about him pickin' up a form and meetin' Maurice Van Leyden. I told her that there had to be an informant and helper within Whimsy House, and that our suspicion focused on Mr. Hastin's. Then I recruited her. All exactly as we had agreed."

O'Leary alternated twiddling his thumbs and tapping them together. His agitation had increased inversely as Le Brun's had decreased.

"But she's no fool. She knows that we still suspect the Topleys. She fulfilled her promise ta you, and now she's running downtown to warn them. Smart enough not ta trust the telephone. Well, I have somebody watchin' the Topley residence already, even if her cab loses the tail."

"She also knows that you still suspect her as well," John remarked.

"She has to consider that you might be followin' her. I admire her loyalty to her adopted family. She's riskin' her own safety if she goes to them."

"Why should she? If they're innocent, she doesn't need to warn them about anything. If they're guilty, she'll get herself locked up as an accessory."

"I'm hopin' she's just runnin' errands, as she intimated."

"Oh, sure." O'Leary finally noticed the frantic speed with which his thumbs circled each other. He separated them and stuck his hands into his trouser pockets. "You own a Colt Single Action Army."

"Among other weapons."

"Can you hit a tin can from a hundred feet with it?"

"I haven't tried recently. I used to could."

O'Leary got up from the bench and looked down on the out-of-town ex-lawman. "Well, let's hope you're still able ta make long shots. 'Cause that's exactly what this business with William Hastings is."

THE WAREHOUSE LAY within the shadow of the Brooklyn Bridge, on the Brooklyn side of the East River. It had been built during the Civil War and had long since seen its glory days of handling America's exports. Now it held only long-term storage, of commodities uninteresting to the normal thief. Consequently, its protection against theft was minimal. There were no night guards, no alarms, no steel doors. Which was a perfect invitation to William Hastings.

Le Brun sat with his back against a wooden crate, a quilted moving blanket tucked behind and under him. Next to him sat Kevin O'Leary, twiddling his thumbs.

"Don't ya hate long watches?" O'Leary asked his companion.

"I'm retired now, remember," John answered. "But when I was a sheriff, I didn't mind the ones where I'd set somethin' up. Like this."

"But the ones where a warehouse had been hit twice in a month, and you figured t'ree was the charm?" O'Leary persisted.

John laughed lightly. "I had several of those. My hometown is a seaport, with quite a few warehouses. Yes, it was tedious."

"I'm using the last hole on this old belt since I stopped walking a beat. Two extra inches around the middle. Not good. I blame all the sedentary watches."

You should lay off the whiskey and take your wife out for a stroll and a conversation, John thought, but he kept his mouth shut. He fetched his pocket watch and struggled to catch the time by the last light of day filtering through the Manhattan skyline to the immediate west. He extended his hand so that it came into a weak patch of steel blue falling through one of the building's numerous skylights. When the warehouse was built forty-odd years before, electric lighting was unknown. Natural work light was much preferable to flame, with so much constant movement of goods and men.

John saw that it was ten minutes before ten. They had not expected Hastings to show, if indeed he would show on this night, before ten-thirty. However, O'Leary had decided to move his team into place at eight. John had been allowed to tag along purely out of O'Leary's gratitude. The careful detective had made his companion sign a note absolving the police department if he was injured or killed during the operation. When Le Brun had made the suggestion of the trap, the New York detective had grabbed at it like a drowning man a rope. Once it became a police operation, however, he was determined to make it fully his and to take maximum credit.

Although the sun had set, the accumulated heat of the day lingered inside the warehouse. John mopped his brow with his handkerchief. The silence in the large space was eerie. He supposed that was what caused O'Leary to make a comment every few minutes. He himself was content to stay quiet, watch, and listen. And to think about Lordis Goode. According to O'Leary, the tail on her from Central Park had indeed revealed that she had gone directly to the Topleys' brownstone house. Two minutes after she had arrived, Sarah Topley had exited. John had suggested to the detective that Lordis had come to act as baby-sitter. Surely, Sarah and her husband had a hundred chores thrust upon them from the deaths of the Pinckney brothers. O'Leary pictured more nefarious schemes and would not entertain the idea. Privately, John wondered.

The giant crate containing the model of Whimsy House had been relegated to a spot toward the middle of the warehouse where many objects for the intended Museum of the City of New York were stored. Because of its great size, it had been put on the bottom of a three-layer stack. Officer Hassler had suggested that they move it, to make it more obvious and easy to open, but John had commented that the years of dust would be disturbed. William Hastings was clearly a careful and an alerted man. O'Leary had sided with the Georgian. Fortunately, it sat in a place where it could be observed well from hiding. Even two rows away, as Le Brun and O'Leary were, they could see the crate by shifting their heads a bit and peering between stacks of crates.

The warehouse became uncomfortably dark. John estimated that half an hour had passed since he was last able to see his watch face. He was adjusting his cramping back muscles when he heard a noise on the warehouse roof. O'Leary looked up at the same time.

For a time, all that could be discerned was a soft crunching of gravel from the roof, twenty feet above them. Then the glass of one of the skylights became darker. The metallic sound of tools being set down echoed off the roof. Seconds later, ancient nails began to complain as they were pried out. John listened to the sounds of scoring as the skylight frame was worked loose from its flashing. The intruder was not content to smash and enter; his purpose was clearly to come and go with no one being the wiser, at least until the next hard rain.

The roof work went on for almost fifteen minutes. Then the skylight was hauled aside. Through the newly made entrance fell a rope. It was of a good diameter and more than thick enough to bear the weight of a full-grown man. Every foot or so, it had been knotted, to give the user better purchase. So much rope snaked down that the last five feet coiled on the floor.

An electric torchlight knifed through the blackness from the roof opening and played around the warehouse. Le Brun and O'Leary ducked down and froze in place. Presently, the light went out. A large but indistinct figure clambered over the edge of the hole and came down the rope. It dropped the last few feet to the wooden floor, so that the landing reverberated through the center of the warehouse.

The torchlight came on again. Its holder began to walk up and down the aisles. The skylight had been situated toward the opposite end of the building from where John sat. He watched the intruder move in a methodical pattern, up one aisle and down the next. At last, he came to the crate that held the model of Whimsy House. He set the light on a box directly across the aisle. As he worked to remove the higher crates, John observed that the figure was indeed William Hastings.

Hastings made good use of his size and strength. He had the crate fully exposed within two minutes. He paused to catch his breath and listen to his surroundings. Then he reached for a rucksack that he had laid down next to his light, which John had not seen before that moment. From the backpack, he pulled a claw hammer and a cat's-paw pry bar. He went to work on the crate, trying to ease it open rather than brutalize it. Little by little, the top yielded. He set the wood aside and began gently tapping the pry bar into the front, widening it from each side until he could extract the nails that held it. Now he had the entire front and roof of the house exposed.

O'Leary had seen enough. He took from his inside jacket pocket a police whistle, put it to his lips, and blew with all his might. The shrill sound filled the warehouse.

Hastings jumped half a foot off the floor.

"William Hastings, this is Detective Kevin O'Leary. You are surrounded. There is no point in resistance." Before he could call out his last sentence, a light shone down from the skylight opening. The sound of doors being unlocked came from the front of the building.

John watched Hastings's shoulders slump. He turned and leaned against a pile of crates.

"That was easy," O'Leary said, standing, his revolver in his hand. He offered his free hand to John. As he pulled his companion up, he said, "My eternal t'anks ta ya. Now let's see if this goes as you've hoped."

The two men hopped down from the crates and worked their way to the aisle where Hastings stood. John winced mentally when he saw the handyman's body language. He stood with his arms folded across his chest and one foot crossed over the other, his back resting against a tall wooden box.

"You are officially under arrest," Detective O'Leary told the man.

"For breaking and entering," Hastings said calmly. "I didn't even take anything."

"Oh, you're under arrest for a lot more than that, boyo!" O'Leary exclaimed. "This is the final proof that you are a willing accomplice in the deaths of Miniver and Edmund Pinckney."

One after the other, three banks of overhead electric lights came on. John observed in the increasing illumination that the muscles of Hastings's face tensed a bit, even as he affected a smile. "That's crazy!"

"Is it?" asked O'Leary as Officers Levine and Hassler approached the aisle from two different directions, weapons in hand. "You are here looking for the Pinckney jewels. You have said over and over that you were sure they were sold. That is what the world assumed. However, Benjamin and Sarah Topley knew different. When Mr. Le Brun here supplied the blueprints to the real Whimsy House, you yourself opened the last of its seven secrets. It had held the jewels, but it no longer did. Therefore, the only Whimsy House that could still hold the jewels was this one."

"So, I'm looking for jewels," Hastings said. He maintained his casual attitude, but the tips of his fingers had begun to quiver. "I figured it out myself. I didn't need the Topleys to tell me anything."

O'Leary placed himself directly opposite Hastings. He leaned back against a pile of crates in a precise mirror image of Hastings. "Well, that might have held some water a week ago. But t'ree men are dead now."

Hastings's eyebrows furrowed at the words.

"Right," said O'Leary. "T'ree, not two. This is going down in one of two ways, boyo. Either it was Benjamin Topley as the mastermind and you feeding him inside information, or it was you as the mastermind. I figure it was Topley, sour as could be after all those years of him and his wife being treated like dirt by the Pinckney men. He paid you a few dollars every month ta report news. Maybe you were working with them exploring the house for the jewels. They promised you a sizable cut. Maybe not. Anyway, this part we know for fact: About six weeks ago, you tell him about Miniver's trips ta the doctor's and the hospital. You even called for old Ben from Whimsy House and asked the hospital for Miniver's diagnosis."

John noted the movement of Hastings's throat as he swallowed.

"Topley wants Whimsy House, and he offers ta cut you in big-time. But Edmund has to die before Sarah gets her inheritance. You've seen it's the truth, as you signed the wills that you had been left out of. So Ben hires an actor to kill Edmund at the Metropolitan Club. But it goes terribly wrong. That nasty Miniver up to his old tricks. You, of course, made sure to be at yer church that evening. And Ben had his alibi. But you see t'rough Edmund's masquerade as his brother, and it's back to square one.

"Saturday night, you're off to the Jersey shore with another alibi. This time Edmund is killed. T'anks to you havin' found that trapdoor sometime in the past. The actor does his dirty work again. And then, guess what? He's found dead!"

Hastings had begun to draw deep breaths, but his jaw remained rigidly set.

"Joseph Ogden," O'Leary said. "Second-rate actor but first-rate killer. Was in one of Mr. Topley's vaudevilles t'ree years back. We just got that news this afternoon. That's one of the reasons why we t'ink he and you were Ben Topley's pawns." The detective affixed his brightest smile. "Or else you done it all yourself. Hired Ogden precisely because he knew Topley. 'Twould be clever. And wouldn't ya know that Joseph Ogden kept a daybook with little neat notes?" He dropped his left hand from his chest and left his right over his heart. "I swear ta God as a faithful Cat'olic, and may I rot in hell if I'm lyin'." He reached into his side jacket pocket and pulled out Ogden's daybook and waved it in front of Hastings's nose. "And you'll never guess whose name was put inta that book? I'm no handwriting expert, but I'd say Ben Topley done it, ta t'row the blame off himself."

John kept his face neutral. O'Leary had warned him he would try the ploy. Based on what he had said, he was indeed not lying. Topley was no doubt the one who had penned in a name. That the name was 'Maurice Van Leyden' and not 'William Hastings' was left unspoken.

The handyman's eyes darted back and forth between Le Brun and O'Leary. "I didn't murder anyone. I didn't *plan* to murder anyone," he said with vehemence. "You can't prove anything like that."

"Have you ever heard of 'the overwhelming body of evidence'?" O'Leary asked him. "You don't have ta be holding the smoking gun, boyo. Don't your being here tonight speak volumes of your interest in the Pinckney estate? Someone *will* get the electric chair for this. Make sure it's not you."

Hastings nodded his large head slowly. His arms dropped to their sides. "I *was* paid by Benjamin Topley from time to time, whenever I reported something interesting that went on in the house. That's all I ever did."

The Irishman sucked in his cheeks and nodded solemnly. "Did you suggest the spying, or did he?"

"I went to him, after I learned I wasn't getting anything in either brother's will."

"Good. Go on."

"And then, like you said, Miniver went to the doctor's. I reported his cough and that the doctor was a specialist. Topley had me call for the diagnosis. I told him Miniver was dying of cancer. The next thing I knew, he warned me to be someplace last Wednesday night that was an ironclad alibi. He promised me ten thousand dollars by the end of the year if I just turned a blind eye."

"You're not a dumb man; you knew what that meant," O'Leary said.

"He never specifically mentioned murder."

The detective brayed like a jackass at the words. "Ah, get off the pulpit! You could have prevented Edmund from being murdered."

Hastings's eyes flashed. "He was a bastard. Him *and* his brother. They treated me like dirt. They both treated women the same. And their clients like dirt too. Just like their old man."

"But that doesn't mean you had the right ta let him die," the detective said. "In fact, you had a second chance to redeem yourself. Instead, you went off ta the Jersey shore." O'Leary sighed deeply. "You're in trouble deep, my friend, and on many planes. You're a churchgoing man who supposedly believes in the Ten Commandments. In my church, they say confession is good for the soul. In your case, it might save you from the flames of eternal perdition."

"I knew nothing about the actor," Hastings insisted. "I never heard his name before tonight. Of course, when I read in the newspapers how the man entered the Metropolitan Club pretending to be a delivery man and then smoothly shifted to playing a member, I had my suspicions."

"He carried out his roles ta perfection," O'Leary stated, "and look how Benjamin Topley rewarded him. What do *you* t'ink you'd have gotten from him as *your* reward? Certainly not ten t'ousand at the end of the year. No, sir."

Le Brun could see that the idea of being double-crossed had already entered William Hastings's mind.

"If I do confess," Hastings said, "what can I expect?"

"You'll get several years in prison, but you won't die. It depends on just how t'oroughly you cooperate. And how many names you name."

For a moment, Hastings looked confused. Then he shook his head. "No, no. If you want me to implicate Mrs. Topley, I can't do it. I'm sure she had nothing to do with this. Nothing at—"

"Forget Mrs. Topley," O'Leary said. "What part did Lordis Goode play?"

Hastings's eyes grew wide. He shrank back a step from the accuser. "Absolutely none! Miss Goode is completely innocent. She's one of the most kindly and honest women I've ever met. And generous. I won't buy bits of freedom by falsely accusing her."

John stepped across the aisle and patted the handyman on the shoulder. "Good for you. Thank you."

O'Leary gave Le Brun an annoyed glance. Then he produced a pair of handcuffs.

"Oh, not just yet," John said. "The man has paid a great price by comin' here tonight. Let him at least complete what he came to do." O'Leary lowered the cuffs. John turned to Hastings. "Lordis told me she believed the model house had been examined as thoroughly as the real one."

"Exactly," Hastings replied. "But in both, the living-room chimney was not looked at carefully enough. Before I brought this here, I removed the library chimney completely and found it a solid piece of carved pine. I . . . and I suppose everyone else . . . assumed that the living-room chimney was the same."

O'Leary gestured toward the model. "Be my guest."

Hastings stretched his right arm the full length of the living room and reached up into the chimney, which had a hearth opening about four inches wide. His fingers curved up, exploring. He felt in all directions. Then he came back out, shaking his head.

"Nothing."

O'Leary lifted the handcuffs again. "I hope yer happy. *Now*—"

"One more minute," John interrupted again. "We've all come so far. Let's really be thorough. Help me slide the model out of the crate, Mr. Hastin's."

O'Leary muttered under his breath and retreated several paces. "May I remind you that we have other places to be, Mr. Le Brun."

"We'll be quick."

Together, the two men wrestled the sometime doll house halfway out of its crate. When it got stuck, O'Leary signaled for Officer Hassler to give a hand, and he provided the fourth lifter. In rapid order, they had the monstrous model sitting in the middle of the aisle.

"Our sensory organs of sight, hearin', taste, and smell are all oriented to our front," John lectured. "So we pay attention to what's before us but tend to overlook what's behind. Likewise, this model was built as what doll house makers call a 'front opener.' We pay great attention to the front and what's inside, but we don't think about the back."

"There's nothing back there," Hastings declared. "The designer of the real house knew that another mansion would be built close along the back side someday, so it's almost all solid wall."

"Almost all solid wall," John echoed. He stepped around to the back of the model. "Except for that part of the chimney that sticks out."

"I tried to pull it off years ago," Hastings said. "It was solidly anchored. If anyone hid something behind it, they'd have to have wrecked the house to get at it again."

John turned to the Irish detective. "That secret entrance from the drain . . ."

"Yes?"

"It didn't move when you yanked it back or pushed it forward."

"True enough."

"But it did move when you worked it to the side."

John saw that he had the rapt attention of every man standing in the aisle. He approached the model's living-room chimney stack and pulled upward. For a moment, it resisted his effort. Then it came loose from a layer of putty hidden in a small well at its bottom. After that, it came up with great ease. The group saw that the wooden chimney stack had been fitted into an inner metal track.

John handed the long stack over to Hastings. He stuck his middle and index fingers down into a small, dark opening below where the stack had been and came back, after considerable wriggling, with a black velvet bag. The bulging bag was not much larger than those used by children to hold marbles. John widened the bag's throat, which was secured by a bit of golden braid. One by one, he produced and laid out against the black of the model's roof a diamond necklace, a pearl necklace, a diamond bracelet, a bracelet of diamonds and rubies, two sets of diamond earrings and a set of pearl earrings, a crescent-shaped brooch with diamonds and a large sapphire, a diamond solitaire lace pin, two European cameos, and three gold rings, one holding a single enormous yellow diamond, one set with diamond clusters and a ruby, and the last holding a large emerald. Not one piece in the collection was less than magnificent.

"Holy mother of God!" O'Leary exhaled when the last piece was exposed. "And all of that fit into one little bag."

John looked at Hastings. "Life just ain't fair, is it? If you'd only known, you coulda stopped somewhere on the way to this warehouse years ago. A few months later, you coulda quietly retired to Europe and bought an old castle."

Hastings replied with a baleful look.

"You can repeat that speech again to Benjamin Topley before this night is over," Kevin O'Leary said.

O NCE LE BRUN HAD SUCCEEDED so brilliantly with his warehouse stratagem, it was impossible for Kevin O'Leary to turn down his second request. Just before leaving for the stakeout, John had telephoned Frank Cobb at the *World* and asked him to be ready to witness the tie-up of the Pinckney brother murders. The chief editor had promised to keep himself available inside the newspaper building.

The Manhattan police had taken three horse-drawn vehicles over to Brooklyn. A paddy wagon holding William Hastings peeled off from the two sedans shortly after crossing Brooklyn Bridge, headed for the city prison. Located on the edge of Greenwich Village, it was called the Tombs, and it looked like a cross between a French chateau and a French Gothic cathedral. The remaining carriages took a two-block detour to the headquarters of the *World*.

"Cobb is not to leave the carriage," O'Leary fumed from the backseat of the brougham. It went against his grain to be so accommodating to any member of the press.

"Whatever you say," John replied. He was mightily pleased to be able to repay Joseph Pulitzer with such a scoop and happy to make small concessions. He glanced at his watch. Only thirty minutes remained until midnight. From the amount of information gathered on Harry Thaw and Evelyn Nesbit after the 11:05 P.M. murder of Stanford White the previous night, he figured the city newspapers could not "go to bed" any earlier than 2:00 A.M. If the story failed to get into the morning edition of the *World*, there would be no scoop.

"And he's not to say anywhere in his article that he hitched a ride with us," O'Leary added.

"You tell him what you want," John said as the brougham stopped in front of the towering structure. He stepped outside before O'Leary could think of another caveat. Despite the hour, the newspaper's front doors were still open, and a man sat at the reception desk. John announced himself. The receptionist sent a runner up in one of the elevators, and four minutes later, Frank Cobb appeared, notepad in hand.

"Andes will be so pleased," Cobb said, using Pulitzer's newspaper code name, after shaking Le Brun's hand.

John gestured to the pair of carriages waiting outside the building. "I hope so. If you'd do me a favor, remember that I'm retired. I don't need any credit in this affair. But Detective O'Leary is very intent on advancement."

"Say no more," Cobb replied. He crossed the sidewalk with long strides, grabbed the handle of the lead vehicle's door, and opened it. Ducking inside, he put on his best smile. "Ah, Detective O'Leary, we meet again."

"Get in, ink slinger," O'Leary said, in a somber voice.

John followed. He sat beside the detective while the reporter sat directly across.

"Where to?" Cobb asked.

"Ben Topley's house," O'Leary replied. Officer Hassler, who was driving, knew to head for an address on West Twenty-sixth Street, just south of Chelsea Park. "His show ends at about five to eleven," he told Cobb. "He's been getting home at about eleven-t'irty."

"How long have you been watching him?" Cobb asked.

"That's not news," responded the detective.

John elbowed the policeman. O'Leary sighed. After that, he relaxed and provided Cobb with the goings-on of the past two days. Questions and answers flew back and forth nonstop until the pair of carriages came within a block of the Topley residence.

"You two wait here," O'Leary instructed as he and Hassler left their carriage and headed for the house's front door. The two other detectives in the rear conveyance hastened up an alley to cover the house's rear.

John watched O'Leary and Hassler waiting at the residence door for some time. "Quite a week for murder, eh?" he commented to Cobb.

"It is," the editor agreed. "And then next week it'll be a political scandal, or a major boiler explosion. In a city this size, we rarely lack for something to print."

At last, Sarah Topley came to the door. She wore a nightgown with a wrap over it. A few sets of words were exchanged, and then she stepped aside and allowed the detectives to enter.

"Tell me the truth, Mr. Le Brun," Cobb said. "Who really solved this crime?"

"Does it matter?"

"The pieces that O'Leary describes sound like the sort of things Mr. Pulitzer says you normally assemble. And the trap in the warehouse reeks of you."

"What a pleasant image."

"Sorry. I do manage to keep offending you."

"Quite all right." John leaned out of the carriage window and looked up and down the block. "It's enough for me that you get the scoop, O'Leary gets the collar, and Mr. Morgan gets to keep his precious Metropolitan Club unblemished."

"And do you get the girl?" Cobb asked, through a knowing smile.

John wondered, a bit irked, exactly how reporters got all their information without benefit of badge or official letter. He wondered if the man he had seen Hastings talking with in the Whimsy House driveway had been one of Pulitzer's minions. "That depends on her." To avoid Cobb's stare, he leaned out the window again and concentrated on the Topley residence. Lights had appeared in the windows on both floors.

"He's not in there," John stated flatly.

"Where would he be at this hour?" Cobb asked.

"He's a clever one. If he suspected we were closin' in, he could be halfway to Boston or Washington by now."

The two men sat in silence for another minute. Just when Cobb began to say something else, Hassler and O'Leary barreled out of the house's front door and came running toward the carriage. One of the other detectives was not far behind them. John assumed the other had stayed behind to watch Sarah Topley. Hassler swung athletically up into the driver's seat, and O'Leary came headlong through the passenger door.

"What's happening?" the editor inquired.

"He never came home," O'Leary replied. "We checked the house top to bottom."

"Then why the rush?" John asked.

"He just telephoned from his t'eater. We had Mrs. Topley answer, and I shared the earpiece. He told her not to ask any questions, to pack a few suitcases, rouse their kids, and meet him up at his t'eater."

"Did Mrs. Topley warn him in any way?" John asked.

"Not with words. But her voice was edgy. I'm hoping he assumed it was because of what he was asking her ta do." He rapped on the front of the carriage. "Whip 'em, Fred! We have a good shot at capturing him if we hurry."

WEDNESDAY

JUNE 27, 1906

BROADWAY WAS THE PULSING ARTERY that fed Times
Square, the heart of New York City. Just past midnight down
in Brunswick, John was sure that only dogs and a few drunks
wandered the streets. He could not believe how much life he was witnessing on the Crossroads of the World at that hour. It was not simply
trucks and vans resupplying the shops and restaurants; pedestrians
moved as if they had no plan on ever sleeping. They chattered and
laughed as they entered and exited bars, clubs, and hotels. Vendors
were still selling flowers, candy, magazines, and newspapers. Panhan-
dlers staggered up to passersby or lay propped against buildings like
living bags of rags. Morning Mary's midnight counterparts plied their
trade under lights that blazed as if electricity cost nothing. In comparison, London and Paris after midnight were sleepy burgs.

As the police carriage's horses trotted briskly north on the thoroughfare, John noted the theaters. First came the Casino on East
Thirty-ninth, then the Broadway between Forty-first and Forty-second
and Hammerstein's Victoria & Paradise on Forty-third. Then they were
in glittering Times Square itself, with the brand-new twenty-three-story
Times building sitting dead center on the south triangle. The Belasco,
Lyric, Gaiety, New Amsterdam, Aerial Gardens, Astor, and Hudson

Theatres stood practically shoulder to shoulder. Above Forty-fourth, the entertainment palaces began to thin out, with the New York and Lyceum on Forty-fifth and the Globe on Forty-sixth. Benjamin Topley's Hyperion Theatre stood all by itself on Forty-seventh, between Sixth and Seventh, as if a pariah. Some of the theater marquees had continued to blaze, despite the fact that their productions were finished for that night. Many stood dark. The Hyperion's front lights were all lit, and yet it seemed to John the most somber of all the theaters he had seen. He wondered if it was the unglamorous street or the building itself. *Or, possibly,* he thought, *my opinion of its owner has colored my perception.*

"Impossible! Not a policeman in sight the last four blocks," O'Leary fumed. "Somebody's goddamned head's gonna roll for that! Pull over, Fred!"

The carriage came to a stop a hundred feet past the Hyperion's front doors. O'Leary peered up and down the block.

"Joseph, Mary, and the kid! Where's a cop when ya need one?"

The second carriage came up to the pavement and stopped. Officer Levine tied the reins to a post and closed in on the other two policemen. O'Leary looked at Hassler and Levine.

"Either of you fine officers know how this t'eater is laid out?"

Both shook their heads.

"There's got to be an entrance to load in the flats and drops," John said.

"The what?"

"The scenery. An alley, runnin' parallel with the back or with one side of the theater," John explained.

O'Leary nodded forcefully. "T'anks. We got precious few t'eaters down in Chinatown. I need more than t'ree men to make sure he doesn't slip away. Hassler, you run back to Seventh. Levine, you take Sixth. Collect whoever you can find in the next five minutes."

The officers went off with loping strides.

"That leaves us," O'Leary said, looking quite unhappy.

"It's not as bad as it seems, Kevin," John said, using the man's given name for the first time, in an effort to break his mood and get his attention. "I see a fair-sized alley on the side of the buildin'. That means the load-in doors and the stage door are probably both on that side. You can cover that until your men return." He reached behind himself, to the small of his back, and took out his derringer. "And I'm not without firepower." He nodded at another alley across Forty-seventh Street, where a ladder dangled tantalizingly, ten feet above an iron fire escape. "Mr. Cobb can look for somethin' to stand on and perhaps get up on that fire escape. From there, he can shout out if he sees Mr. Topley escapin' via the rooftops."

"Good plan," Cobb enthused. He pushed his notebook into his jacket pocket and trotted across the street.

"I didn't say it *was* the plan!" O'Leary called out.

"Is it?" John asked.

O'Leary rolled his eyes and nodded. He pulled the revolver from his shoulder holster and trudged heavily toward the Hyperion's alley.

John approached the theater's front doors. There were four in all, side by side. He tried each in turn and was not surprised to find them locked. He stepped into the street and looked up at the dark marquee. The show was called Comme ça. It was a phrase often used by his relatives, meaning "Like so." Across the marquee in red ran the bold-lettered exhortation: COME SEE COMME ÇA, which was a wordplay on the French phrase meaning "Like this, like that." John appreciated the multilingual pun and wondered if Topley had been its creator. At the same time, he wondered what all those who did not speak French thought of it. He walked up to one of the glassed-in display cases on the theater's front wall and studied the promotional materials. Around a stylized drawing of the Eiffel Tower was the cast list. More than half the names were French. John suspected that Topley, ever determined to rise above normal music hall fare, had imported a Parisian farce.

Other than himself pacing back and forth in front of the four doors, Forty-seventh Street was devoid of humanity. John watched a piece of white paper cavorting along the gutter, coaxed by a gentle night breeze.

When the five minutes had elapsed, Hassler and Levine returned. Hassler had one beat patrolman in tow; Levine had found no one. O'Leary went through his litany of curses again. He positioned the beat cop at the front doors and instructed Levine to find his way up to the roof.

"You were right," Detective O'Leary told Le Brun after he checked the far side of the theater. "There's no other doors except out here and in the alley. Do I dare ask you ta stand guard outside the stage door?"

John wanted to argue himself inside, but he knew the detective would not allow a civilian to come in harm's way. It was the sort of mistake that would lose a cop his badge.

"I'll do it," John said, sorely disappointed that he who had led the chase all the way could not witness the fox being captured in his den.

O'Leary drew his gun. "Let's go, Fred." The two men approached the stage door with revolvers raised. O'Leary tried the door and found it open. He nodded for Detective Hassler to take the lead. He took a breath and entered a moment later.

Five seconds after Fred Hassler passed through the door, a large-caliber weapon boomed out.

John pulled back the door and peeked inside. There was a naked lightbulb hanging on a cord from the ceiling just inside the door. It backlit the policemen perfectly. John saw Hassler half lying, half sitting on the entrance floor and O'Leary pressing himself against one wall, trying to become one with the paint.

"Police!" O'Leary shouted. "You are surrounded. Give—"

A second bullet tore down the hallway and ricocheted off the bottom of the steel door, caroming into the alley. The gunman was aiming to finish off the man on the floor. He was evidently at a fair distance, however, and using a handgun. John jumped up and knocked out the lightbulb with the nose of his derringer. Then he fired one barrel into the absolute darkness at the far end of the hallway.

"Get out!" he shouted to the lawmen. He fired his second and last bullet.

O'Leary tossed Le Brun his revolver. While John methodically emptied it in a fan pattern, the Irish cop grabbed his partner under the armpits and dragged him outside. The wounded man still held his revolver.

John closed the door.

"Kill the bastard!" Hassler wailed. "He shot me in the leg."

John kneeled on the gritty pavement. "Let's see." He fetched his pocketknife from his pocket, flipped it open, and cut the man's trousers around the wound.

"Oh, Jesus!" Hassler cried out when he saw the wound. The hole in the flesh five inches above his right knee was large. In the dim alley, the blood looked almost black as it welled rather than spurted out.

"Missed your bone. It hasn't hit anythin' vital," John confirmed with relief, putting his face down near the pavement. "And it went clean through. You're lucky."

"Lucky? Hell I am!"

"If you can yell that loud, you'll be fine," John admonished. He pulled out his handkerchief. "Give me your nose rag if it's clean," he instructed O'Leary. Quickly and expertly, he knotted the two pieces of cloth together and tied a tourniquet above the wound.

Frank Cobb ran into the alley and skittered to a halt when he saw the wounded policeman. "Oh, brother! What can I do?"

"Find a telephone. Call for an ambulance," O'Leary commanded. "Warn the officer on the sidewalk to be alert for Topley to make a break out the front doors. Then call for a platoon of cops. This son of a bitch wants a battle."

Cobb nodded and tore out of the alley.

Levine appeared on the roof edge of the building that formed the other side of the alley. He looked down.

"Should I stay up here?"

"Yes," O'Leary shouted. "Is there a door to the roof up there?"

"Sure is. The roof rises real high in the back third of the building."

"That's the fly space," John said. "Where they pull up the backdrops. They usually have catwalks runnin' over the stage. Doors to the lower roof are common. There's at least one ladder down to the stage."

"And where do you know all this from?" O'Leary asked.

"I read a book on auditorium architecture once," John replied.

O'Leary merely shook his head in wonderment. Then he looked up at the fire-escape mechanism directly above them.

"You said Topley was a careful person," O'Leary said to Le Brun. "He wasn't assuming his wife could be the only one ta walk t'rough that door."

John, too, studied the fire escape. "I want to know real bad what tipped him off. This man is very smart and methodical. He wouldn't have asked his wife to meet him inside the theater if he didn't have a way out. If we don't act in the next few minutes, he might very well disappear."

"I agree," said O'Leary. He cracked open his revolver's cylinder and dumped out the spent shell casings.

John measured the alley width with his eye. "I've seen you run, and you're still damned fast. Do you think you could clear this alleyway from the buildin' Officer Levine's on?"

O'Leary looked up again. "Piece o' cake."

"Make your leap directly over the fire escape. That way, if you slip, you'll only fall fifteen feet or so. I'll find a way to get up the escape; you take the roof door. He can't watch every entrance."

"Deal! You gonna be okay, Fred?"

"Sure," the wounded man said through gritted teeth. He had one hand holding the tourniquet and the other holding himself erect. "Sorry I was such a baby for a moment."

O'Leary tousled his hair. He pointed to the oozing wound. "Baby? With a canyon in yer leg? That's a promotion for sure and t'ree months off, ya lucky bastard." He bent down, collected Hassler's revolver, and handed it to Le Brun. John, in turn, reloaded his derringer and gave it to Hassler, whom they lifted together and propped directly opposite the stage door.

"Drive him out here," Hassler said. "I'll give him a grand finale."

While O'Leary reloaded, he got from Levine the directions for reaching the roof. He was off in a sprint as John pushed a garbage can up to the edge of the theater wall, gingerly mounted it, and hauled down the escape ladder. He swung onto it and used his weight to drag it down. Then he began climbing. He felt every one of his fifty-nine years as he worked himself onto the iron landing. Out of the corner of his good eye, he caught the sight of O'Leary sailing across the open space of the alley, well above wires that supplied electricity to the theater. He landed hard enough that John could hear the air whooshing out of his lungs.

"You okay?" John called.

"Yeah. I shoulda taken up broad jumping instead of sprinting," O'Leary gasped.

John came to the escape door. It had no handle on the outside but merely a hook that could hold the door open to provide air circulation on hot nights. John could see from the door's strike plate, however, where the lock tongue lay. The door opened outward; there was no point in trying to kick it down. He put the nose of the revolver close to where he knew the locking mechanism to be, stepped to the side, and fired.

On the roof, a similar explosion cut through the night.

John tried the door and found it still secure. He pulled out his knife, inserted the tip of the blade in the hole the bullet had made, and picked back the remaining mechanism. The door swung open.

From the safety of the side of the wall, John strained to see into the theater. He saw a good-sized aisle with rows of cushioned seats above and below it. He knew he was looking at the balcony seating. He counted to three mentally and crawled into the darkness, keeping his head lower than the line of seats closer to the stage. From high in the stage rafters, the clanging of metal proved that Kevin O'Leary had also effected entry.

"I have an audience," Benjamin Topley's voice sounded from below. "Tickets, please." He laughed at his own joke.

John refused to speak and hoped the detective would as well.

"Were you listening in on my home telephone line?" the impresario's voice asked. "Isn't that an invasion of privacy? Don't we have laws against that sort of thing?"

John crawled on hands and knees along the length of the curving aisle. His plan was to rise only after he had moved as far away from the fire-escape door as he could.

"I heard your voice, Mr. Le Brun," Topley called out. "Why the hell didn't you stay in Georgia? What a royal pain in the ass you are."

John dared a peek over the tops of the seat backs. There were three rows of seats below and three above him. The stairs down lay just ahead. A single red bulb shone above the fire-escape door and at the top of the stairs. It was only enough light to delineate crude shapes within its tight circle. He was counting on it not being enough for Topley to spot him from his place below.

"Come out, come out, wherever you are," Topley's voice chanted.

John could tell that his quarry was either in the orchestra pit or on the stage. He put himself against the wall and inched forward until he could peer down over the balcony rail. It was bad enough that he could see nothing from his right eye; his good eye was collecting precious little for him to assess. There were two emergency doors that opened into the alley, and over them also glimmered red bulbs. By their faint light, he could see that Topley was not hiding in the stage-right orchestra seats of the first ten rows. The light revealed nothing more. He decided to descend and work his way toward the stage along the outside end of the orchestra seats. His heart threatened to burst through his ribs, but he was elated that Topley was still inside the theater.

"Scary up there, isn't it?" Topley asked O'Leary. "One misstep, and it's curtains." He laughed again.

Then there was a silence so long that John worried Topley had fled. He was putting his foot on the bottom step of the balcony stairs when he again heard the theater owner.

" 'Light seeking light doth light of light beguile'!" Topley quoted.

Suddenly, the stage area was flooded with illumination. Topley was nowhere to be seen. But John knew where he must be. The question was: in which wing? He rushed down the aisle that ran along the stage-left wall in a semi-crouch, revolver pointed at the stage.

The main curtain had been pulled up, and a frothy pastel-colored set of several levels occupied a rough semicircle around the limits of the stage floor. John guessed that the show's final number had involved many singers and dancers, demanding that the center of the stage be empty. Encircling the set were the teasers, tormentors, and legs, the heavy black curtains that masked the sides and top of the stage from audience view. They also masked Benjamin Topley's presence. But, John knew, they also limited the impresario's ability to watch his advance.

A shot rang out. The bullet echoed off iron. Two shots were returned from above.

" 'Out, out brief candle!' " Topley recited. The theater again plunged into darkness. "I want you to know that my wife and Lordis Goode are completely innocent of this business," he yelled. "It was me alone, taking back what was Sarah's from those soulless brothers of hers. And that monster of a father."

Another bullet tore down from the stage catwalks. Kevin O'Leary had used Topley's voice to fix the man's location and had tried a blind shot. In answer, the lights winked on. Topley's gun sounded. The lights went back out. John knew that he was working a master switch from a lighting cage. Such cages were invariably located on the downstage edge of either the left or right wing, close by the stage manager who "called the show." John guessed that this cage was on the side nearer the alley, to make the connection to the street wires simpler. Acting on that assumption, he continued down the stage-left aisle, guiding himself by the wall, duckwalking.

From outside the theater came clanging alarms. It sounded as if every police vehicle and fire wagon on the island had answered Frank Cobb's call.

"I'll be meeting Chriswell in hell soon enough," Topley called out, "because I won't be taken alive."

John maintained his silence. He continued his advance and came suddenly and unexpectedly to the lower corner of the auditorium where the orchestra pit met the proscenium wall that separated audience from performers. His eye had adjusted enough to the darkness so that he could see the apron of the stage. It rose about four feet higher than the auditorium floor. John leaned his elbows on the stage and aimed between two of the footlights, in the general direction where he supposed the lighting cage must be.

" 'Long is the way / And hard, that out of hell leads up to light,' " Topley proclaimed.

On the last word, the stage lights again came on. This time, however, they rose to only half intensity. It was enough, however, for John to spot the man's back, beyond the thick wire mesh of the cage. Without hesitation, he fired his weapon. An instant later, Ben Topley dashed across the opening between proscenium wall and masking leg and exited the cage. As he moved, he snapped off two shots in John's direction. One hit the scallop-shelled footlight just to John's right and burst the bulb inside it. The resulting sparks temporarily blinded Le Brun. By the time he recovered, Topley had long since disappeared.

John decided to change his position. He vaulted over the orchestra rail and dropped the four feet into the pit. Then he worked his way through the chairs and music stands to the conductor's podium. As he ascended the steps, he spotted Topley through a thin break in the rear of the set. He was moving in a stage-left direction, away from the stage door and alley. John instantaneously calculated the man's speed of movement and fired through the set wall. He heard an exclamation of pain.

"O'Leary!" John shouted.

"Yeah?"

"He's moved to the back corner of the buildin'."

"I'm almost down on the floor!" O'Leary called back.

"Don't go onto the stage! I have that covered. He's gone backstage. Go toward the alley and make sure he doesn't circle around behind the set."

"Right."

John jumped off the podium and moved down to the orchestra-pit door. It had been locked from the other side. He swore and danced back through the musicians' chairs to the stage-left corner of the pit. From there, he snaked his way under the brass rail and the black masking skirt back onto the auditorium floor.

Behind him, in the lobby, men were laboring to break down one of the main doors. John considered for all of an instant waiting for reinforcements, then ran to the side of the stage and leapt up onto it. To wait thirty seconds might mean allowing Topley to escape.

Drawing in a deep breath, John swung around the proscenium wall and onto the stage proper. In the half light, he was able to see well enough to be sure Topley was not waiting for him in the stage-left wings. Nevertheless, he did not stand flat-footed in place. Instead, he ran for the protection of a collection of flats that had "SCENE X" stenciled on them. He went down on one knee and risked peeking past the flats. The rest of the wing space was visible from where he looked, and it provided no place for ambush. At the far end of the wing area was a fire door. It stood slightly open.

John advanced cautiously on the door, looking onto the stage and up into the theater fly. Out in the lobby, the police had finally broken through. A small army came pouring into the theater.

"Officers are on the stage and in the back of the theater," John called out. "Hold your fire!" Having protected his rear, he dared opening the door.

Beyond the door was a hallway that ran not more than ten feet before making a left turn. John moved into it and came to the corner. He could see that the area held the dressing, makeup, costume, and other backstage rooms. As he leaned cautiously out to take a good look down the length of the next hallway, Benjamin Topley dashed from one of the rooms. He held a metal can in one hand and a revolver in the other. He spotted Le Brun and snapped off a hip shot.

John ducked behind the protection of the wall as the bullet tore out a chunk of its corner.

"He's back here!" he yelled, to no one in particular.

"So am I!" Kevin O'Leary shouted. By the hollow echo, John figured the detective stood somewhere past the opposite end of the hallway. "We've got him trapped."

A noise of sloshing came to John's ears. He feared sticking his face around the corner lest Topley be aiming for him. While he pondered what to do next, two uniformed policemen came up behind him, their guns drawn. They said nothing, as if awaiting orders. He figured they were assuming him a plainclothes detective, and he did nothing to disabuse them.

Just as John heard the clanging of an empty metal can hitting concrete, he inhaled the first smell of the fluid it had held.

"Kerosene!" O'Leary shouted from his end of the hall.

A door slammed shut.

"Step well back!" John called. He turned to his support force. "We will all move into that hallway at the same time. You on the left, me in the center, you on the right. Have your weapon cocked and ready to fire." The men nodded. "On the count of three."

John said the words. The three men leapt into the open area and found themselves confronting a long, empty hallway. A large pool of liquid covered the concrete floor halfway down its length. John signaled for the men to hold their place. He had seen roughly where Topley had gone. As he came to the center of the hallway, he read the gold lettering on the thick oak door: "Benj. Topley."

O'Leary appeared in the hallway from the opposite end. He pointed to the floor. "He's soaked the place in kerosene."

A bullet thundered from the opposite side of the oak door. It managed to create a small, splinter-filled bulge in the wood.

"You will not take me alive," Topley called through the door, his voice filled with bravado.

"You're a coward, Topley!" O'Leary challenged.

"And you're an idiot, O'Leary. I could have fooled you. It's your pal Le Brun who beat me."

"Who tipped you off that we were onto you?" John asked.

"I heard you found Joseph Ogden."

"Heard from whom?" John persisted.

"You're the great detective; you figure it out. I'll give you two clues: It wasn't Sally or Lordis."

John put his ear against the wall. He heard Topley scurrying around. It sounded as if he was moving furniture, barricading himself in. Then he heard the click of a revolver hammer falling. There was no explosion. Something hard banged against the door.

"Give yourself up," O'Leary demanded. "It's the only way you can be sure to protect your family."

"Go to hell! In fact, if you don't clear out in the next few seconds, you'll be coming to hell with me."

O'Leary backed to the opposite side of the hallway, then threw his weight against the door. It held firm.

From inside Topley's office came the *whoomph* of kerosene catching flame.

"Jesus, he's done it!" O'Leary said to Le Brun. "We gotta get out of here." He snapped his fingers at the two waiting policemen. "Get the firemen back here in a hurry!"

John lingered in the hallway until the smoke began pouring out from under the oak door. As he was exiting, the kerosene on the hallway floor caught and burst into a waist-high wall of flame. He shook his head and retreated toward the alley.

G IVEN THE DISASTER that might have occurred, the fire was well contained. John marveled at the skills and daring of the New York City firefighters. The entire back of the theater had caught fire, but no walls had collapsed. John looked for Frank Cobb among the throngs on Forty-seventh Street, to thank him for his foresight in calling the fire department as well as the police, but the editor had left to write up his story before the press deadline.

When O'Leary was finally given the okay to enter the charred building, it was almost nine o'clock in the morning. He invited John to accompany him. Together, with rags clasped to their noses and mouths against the choking particles in the air, they followed the fire chief back into the hallway. The oak door, well charred, had been chopped apart and its pieces laid against the hallway wall.

The inside of Benjamin Topley's office was a study in charcoal. Not a bit of the room had been unburned. Topley's badly charred body sat behind his ruin of a desk, on the frame of his once expensive chair. His hair had been singed entirely away. His eyeballs had melted in the heat, as had most of the skin of his face. His teeth were exposed in a lingering grin.

O'Leary said, "The chief told me it would have been a lot worse, except for the t'ick walls and the restricted flow of air back here."

John shook his head. "Well, this room was completely closed in, and look at the damage."

"I have to hand it to the bastard," O'Leary said through the rag that covered his mouth. "He certainly had a flair for the dramatic."

"He had nerve," John agreed. "I sure as hell couldn't sit calmly at my desk as flames licked around me."

O'Leary made a gagging noise and bent over.

"Never seen a charred corpse?" John asked.

"Once before," the detective said, spitting out. "Good t'ing I ate nothin' since six last night. It ain't the sight of him that gets me; 'tis the smell."

John turned to regard the hallway wall of the office. In so doing, his foot happened upon something on the floor. He looked down. Then he squatted. He reached into his pocket and took out a pencil. With the pencil, he picked the object up by its guard.

"Colt Single Action Army. Model 1840."

"Edmund Pinckney's weapon?"

"I wouldn't be surprised."

"He looks like he was conducting an interview," O'Leary remarked. "Maybe he wanted to look formal for the coroner's photos."

The corpse's two arms were extended atop the desk, with his hands palms down.

John leaned close to the hands. He touched one of the little fingers tentatively, to be sure its heat had dissipated. When he was certain he wouldn't be burned, he rubbed the soot off the gold pinkie ring. The metal mask of tragedy scowled up at him.

FRIDAY

JUNE 29, 1906

JOHN FOLDED BACK the page of the *World* and continued to read. It was the Thursday edition. He had been too busy riding around Brooklyn the previous day and going to his first professional baseball game. The Brooklyn team had beaten Boston 2–0. He noted that the Stanford White–Harry Thaw murder, then three days old, still took precedence over the Pinckney murders. *It's because a beautiful woman wasn't involved in our affair,* John thought, with no rancor. The edition had particulars on the Thaw wedding and a lengthy list of the buildings Stanford White had designed. Harry Thaw's lawyers were preparing an insanity defense, even though police interrogators had judged him highly rational.

In other news, Deputy Police Commissioner Rhinelander Waldo had almost been knocked out of his limousine by a thrown raw potato as he was returning from bowling on 172nd Street. Near Yonkers, an Italian man had been hacked to death. He had been found near Old Jerome Avenue with a hatchet buried in his skull. The rings left on his body and the $2.50 found in his trousers suggested that the murder was not a robbery. A Mr. James McKeon, coachman for broker Frank L. Graves, had been found the previous afternoon with the top of his head blown off. The place of the murder was his room above the Graves stable. There had been a fatal stabbing at the Mulbery Park concert. The victim had knocked the child of his assailant out of the father's arms in pushing through the crowd. An Edward Tietsen of Fort Hamilton was dying of a bullet wound in the head. His companion hadn't liked a remark that Tietsen had passed about his girlfriend. Celebrated street tough "Lefty" Boyle had been shot at 1:30 A.M. on the corner of Twenty-eighth Street and Seventh Avenue. He refused to tell the police who had wielded the gun, "as he is no squealer," but he vowed that if he lived he would "kill the guy."

John closed the *World*. *Solving the Pinckney murders was like spitting in the ocean,* he reflected. He supposed if he divided the population of Greater New York by the population of Brunswick, the mayhem might have been in proportion, but it was overwhelming to read about in one newspaper. He admired the Central Park meadow for another minute, then rose and deposited his reading material in a nearby trash basket. He was expected in five minutes at Joseph Pulitzer's home.

JOHN FOUND HIMSELF not in Joseph Pulitzer's work chamber but in the formal dining room. He was at the genius's right hand, with the *World*'s chief editor, Frank Cobb, seated directly across. The other fifteen chairs around the mahogany table were unoccupied. Pulitzer wore a natural-colored linen suit. John expected to see the jacket looking like an artist's palette by the end of the lunch.

From the nearby music room, someone produced dulcet plucking and arpeggiation upon a harp. The melodies were classical, but John was not well versed enough to recognize the composer. At least a hundred blooms constituted the floral arrangement in the center of the table. Two servants stood waiting for plates to become half empty, at which point they would move forward to refill them.

At the moment, the three men were dining on oyster soup with raviolis. Pulitzer had promised roast stuffed chicken with tomato sauce as the entrée, creamed fritters and lima beans, and almond ice cream for dessert. John planned to eat lightly in the evening. And alone.

"It's such a shame that Miss Goode could not join us," Pulitzer lamented.

"She must be incredibly occupied," Cobb replied. "If, as she told John, she considers herself Sarah Topley's sister, then she must be holding the poor woman together. Can you think of any other incident when a woman lost her two brothers and her husband in one week?"

"And found that her husband was the one who killed her brothers," Pulitzer remarked. His voice held none of the sympathy that his editor's had.

John took a deep draft of his ice water. The servant on his side of the table hurried forward to refill his glass. "She's promised to contact me when she can," he said. "I may have to wait some time."

Pulitzer set down his spoon and pushed his soup bowl away. "That was splendid!" He had used the word three times since John had arrived. The perpetual termagant was in the best mood the Georgian had ever witnessed. "Have you gotten any word back from our spies at just how livid Ochs and Hearst are over our Pinckney murder scoop?" He spoke of the men in charge of the *New York Times* and the *Herald*.

"Like Carrara marble," Cobb jested.

Pulitzer laughed. His spidery fingers crept over the tablecloth, searching out his knife and fork. As they did, a servant replaced his soup bowl with the entrée plate.

"I'm pleased with myself for having you as a friend," Pulitzer revealed to John. "I can only imagine how pleased you are with yourself for solving this bizarre series of murders."

"I am more relieved than pleased," John confessed. "I would feel a great deal better if I only knew how Topley learned we were closin' in."

"It had to be one of the other impresarios," said Cobb with confidence. "The Players Club had the word out all over Broadway. He had to know they were looking for an actor who had played Witherspoon King. Topley's big mistake was using an actor to play a member of the Metropolitan Club. How long did you consider that motive of killing Pinckney because of his proposed new club, John?"

"Not long at all."

"You see? Topley should have paid some street thug to rob him and gun him down."

"He should have paid one of those four-in-hand drivers who barrel through Central Park on Sunday to *run* him down," Pulitzer interjected, stabbing his fork several times onto the plate until he found a piece of chicken. He began to cut it. "Eh, Mr. Le Brun?"

"Nothin' works like simplicity."

Pulitzer's smile slipped like a painting falling from a wall. The next instant, he was frowning in Cobb's direction. "Speaking of simplicity . . . Why the hell did you have to print that Benjamin Topley's real last name was Horhovitz?"

Cobb swallowed his first taste of chicken before it was well chewed. "*You* gave me that fact."

"But I didn't want you to use it in the paper. Why bother even printing Horho-goddamned-vitz? Why not just write: 'And he was another duplicitous and murderous Jew'? Don't the Jews get enough bad press without us contributing gratuitously?"

"You're right," Cobb acknowledged.

John was sure the chief editor knew as well as John did that Pulitzer was half Jewish, even though he denied it. He was nominally an Episcopalian, although he never attended services. Behind his back, the low-class rich called him Jewseph Pulitzer.

Pulitzer lifted a piece of chicken to his lips. Then he set it back down and swung his blind eyes toward John. "Did you know we sold thirty-seven thousand more papers on Wednesday? And thirty-one thousand more yesterday. Some from the White murder, but more from your work."

"I'm gratified," John allowed. He liked to keep his sentences simple when around Pulitzer.

"I helped you greatly with the Jekyl Island Club murders."

"You did."

"I can't say we did much this time, though. However, I will make it up to you for your service. I have a few surprises for you today." Pulitzer rubbed his hands together. "First, I have learned from a reliable source in Jupiter Morgan's office that you are to be made an honorary member of the Players Club."

"How wonderful!" John responded, feeling truly elated.

"Make like you don't know when they contact you," Pulitzer advised. "Second, I have submitted your name for nomination to the Manhattan Club."

"How kind."

Spidery fingers waved through the air. "Think nothing of it. We need brain power like yours in the club. We say the club is 'Democratic in politics, aristocratic in clientele.' That describes you nicely."

John swallowed. "I am mightily flattered."

"Anyway, when I make a nomination . . . which I rarely do . . . membership is virtually assured. And I insist on paying for your first year's dues."

"Very kind," John said. "I very much like both clubs. Frankly, I never thought I'd hear myself say that about one gentlemen's club, much less two."

"Well, your antipathy toward the Jekyl Island Club is understandable. But then the only reason I dare to nominate you is that I had heard you had accepted an honorary membership to the Sceptred Isle Club in London."

"I did like their manager. Unfortunately, I shall never be able to use any of the privileges to which the honor inures, or however the document reads."

Pulitzer set down the fork and its captive morsel of food. "I can understand that about London. But why can't you enjoy the Players Club and the Manhattan Club? I've been thinking about you for some time today. Brunswick is not a bad place to live in the tourist season. Interesting visitors. Good imported entertainment. Excellent weather. But from May until Thanksgiving, it's dead. And torrid. Am I not right?"

"You are."

"Then why not establish two residences?" Pulitzer asked. "The one you already own in Georgia, and a flat here in New York City?"

"Because multiple residences are a luxury of the rich."

Pulitzer shook his head vigorously. "What did you earn for solving the Manhattan Island Club case?"

"One hundred dollars per day. A total of seven hundred dollars."

Pulitzer beamed and threw his hands out wide. His right hand just missed his water tumbler. "You see? On this island, the average worker earns forty cents an hour and survives. Our detectives are pitiful. Trust me. We deal with them constantly at the paper. Am I right, Frank?"

Cobb was caught again in midchew. "He's right," he managed.

"They're only good for finding lost dogs. You'd have all the work you could handle. More! You could pick and choose what you wanted to pursue. While you're up here, you could live comfortably off of three weeks' earnings. Or you do the thinking and hire somebody else to do the legwork. Then you could work a few hours a week. Perhaps hire Kevin O'Leary if the business takes off."

John offered no rebuttal. To his great surprise, the notion did not sound ridiculous.

Pulitzer picked up his fork, then set it back down. "By the way, O'Leary's been released from the purgatory of Chinatown. He's been transferred up here."

"Good for him," John said. "He's a competent and honest man."

"Please consider spending time each year in New York," Pulitzer said, using his most cloying voice. "Such a cultured and clever southern gentleman as yourself would be a great asset to this tired old Knickerbocker town."

Despite his hardened and suspicious nature, a thrill shot through John Le Brun's being. One of the most respected and accomplished men of the world, much less New York City, had paid him the compliment he had waited his entire life to hear.

"I thank you deeply, sir," John said in an uncharacteristically soft voice. "I shall give the matter my serious consideration."

"Good! Good."

In the music room, the harpist had stopped playing.

"Hey! Where's the goddamned soothing music!" Pulitzer yelled.

A moment later, a tune from *Carmen* wafted into the room.

"That's better," Pulitzer said. "You *can* change, Mr. Le Brun. Look, if I'm down here in the dining room, anyone can change." At last, he put the piece of chicken in his mouth. His face screwed up. "Jesus Christ in holy heaven! Why is my food never warm?"

MONDAY

JULY 2, 1906

E VERY DEFENSE WORK of the Metropolitan Club was lowered for their victorious knight. When John climbed the steps and looked at the small window to his left, the staff member on duty waved to him. He was fairly mobbed in the lobby, with staff and members alike clapping him familiarly on the back, shaking his hands, and offering congratulations. One of the men who had given him an icy stare when he had sat with Witherspoon King two Fridays before was particularly effusive in his praise. Before he could remember to introduce himself, he was inviting John to dine with him and his friends.

"That's very kind of you, sir," John replied, "but I just stopped in to use your necessary. I'm meetin' someone for lunch in the Ladies Restaurant."

After blinking and recovering from John's first sentence, the member repeated his offer for a later date. He pressed into John's hand his business card. John thanked him and made a mental note to reserve a cold day in hell.

Le Brun took his time moving through the club entrance and main halls. To each person who approached him he asked directions to the lavatory. When he was finished relieving his bladder, he made sure to visit the West and the South Lounging Rooms before exiting the men's portion of the club and crossing the turnaround driveway to stand in front of the Ladies Restaurant door.

Five minutes later, Marie Van Leyden arrived in a horseless carriage. As she stepped down and paid the driver, John noted the tranquillity on her face. She was heartbreakingly beautiful, wearing a cream chiffon day dress with shawl print borders and machine Alençon lace details. The chiffon rustled and swayed with her graceful movements as she stepped onto the brick walkway and paid her fare.

John removed his derby and approached her as she turned toward the restaurant entrance. He took her right hand and kissed it lightly.

"I expect that you have good news," he said, having first checked to see that no one stood within earshot.

"I do," Marie replied. "You were right. My lateness was due to my extreme state of emotions."

"It's kind of you to come all this distance to tell me." John expected more. The appointment had been made by Marie's confidante, Alice Ainsworth, by calling the Hotel Savoy. John had confirmed the meeting to the friend's home.

"Shall we venture inside for tea?" Marie suggested. It was eleven in the morning.

"That would be delightful." John offered his arm, and they entered.

Unlike in the men's clubs, the presence of a member of the opposite sex caused no stir. Mrs. Van Leyden selected a table for two next to one of the windows that looked out upon the driveway and the club entry arch.

After they had ordered, Marie said, "I took your advice and did some investigating. It wasn't easy."

"I would imagine."

"Maurice keeps no key to his office at home. Aside from those held by the two office managers, the only key remains on his person at all times."

"Except when he sleeps," John remarked, wanting to see if he could guess what the wife would say.

"Exactly. For all his importance and all the properties he owns, he has only four keys on his ring."

John nodded. He had developed an observation into a saying some years back: Poor men carry little cash; middle-class men carry much cash; rich men carry little cash. Poor men have few keys; middle-class men have many keys; rich men have few keys.

"One key was to the front door of our town home," Marie went on. "The second I recognized as the front door of our cottage in Newport. While he slept, I pressed the other two keys into the wax our cook uses to seal cans of fruit." She looked patently pleased with herself. "Alice told me how to do it. I put the brick of wax in very warm water. Then I pressed both sides of the keys into the wax while it was still warm. Finally, I cleaned the keys carefully."

John smiled and nodded. Marie Van Leyden had been honing her skills as an adulteress; now she was gleefully becoming a lock cracker.

"I gave the impressions to Alice, and she knew someone who turned them into duplicate keys."

John nodded again. He deposited in his memory that if he actually did move up to New York City part-time and open a detective agency, Alice Ainsworth might prove a brilliant female associate. If he added the acutely observant Mrs. McMahon from the boardinghouse, he might have an unstoppable team.

"I learned that I wasn't in the family way only a few hours after leaving you at church," Marie said, "but I waited to contact you because I wanted to have gotten into Maurice's offices first. We did yesterday."

"We?"

"Alice and I. No one goes down there on Sundays. Not even the cleaning crew. Well, the office key didn't work right away, but Alice had brought along a little file. After about five minutes, it did. While she looked through the bookkeeper's office, I went into my husband's. I found that the smaller key fit into his desk drawer. There, I found a book with checks. They were from a different bank than the business uses."

The waiter arrived with the tea tray and a half dozen petits fours. When he had departed and while John poured, Marie said, "Maurice had indeed hired a detective agency!"

John stopped in midpour. "Really? When?"

In answer, Marie reached into her clutch bag and took out a piece of typing paper, folded in four. She opened it and smoothed it upon the table, then turned it to face Le Brun. He saw no fewer than thirty lines of writing. She pointed to the next-to-last line.

"I made a copy of every check notation for the past twelve months. I knew about not one of these expenses."

"I am sure," John replied. "This is his private spendin'." He looked at the notation. It read "Thos. Janney Detective Agency." It was dated "6/15/06." John did a quick calculation. The day was the Friday before Miniver Pinckney had been mistaken for his brother Edmund and murdered in the Metropolitan Club.

"Could Maurice not have had Edmund killed, despite what the papers wrote up?" Marie asked.

"Impossible," John said. "The man behind the murders was Benjamin Topley."

"Truly?"

"I am certain. But I am quite relieved for you that the notation was not for several weeks earlier. Had it been, your husband might have had your lover killed."

Marie's expression remained calm. John wondered if she was contemplating his scenario and regretting that it had not happened that way.

"How long before your last tryst with Edmund Pinckney had you met alone?" John asked.

"Twelve days."

"That was probably the meetin' that made your husband suspicious. Unless someone like Miniver Pinckney had tipped him off. In any case, this check was made out for fifty dollars. I would guess that amount to be a retainer fee. You cannot remember seein' anyone follow you on that Friday or any day after?"

"No."

John shrugged. "That means that either Thomas Janney was good at his job or else he had not yet begun to follow you. If he had, the most he would have been able to report was your one tryst with Edmund. And on that night, Edmund was supposed to be dead. There was no subsequent entry for Mr. Janney in the checkbook that you failed to note here?"

"No."

"Then we can assume one of two things: The more likely is that he was dismissed by your husband as no longer necessary. The other is that he was hired for an entirely different matter than to watch you."

"Maurice has hired detectives from time to time," Marie reported. "But those fees he always took care of in the company books."

John nodded. "How has your husband acted this past week?"

"Quite merry. And pleased with himself."

"Then if he did suspect, he is happy with the turn of events. The threat of losin' you has passed." John pushed the paper toward the woman.

Marie pushed it back.

"I actually asked to meet with you because of these other entries," she said. "If you will notice, there are eight. Each is made out to Cash for exactly one hundred dollars. There is one for December first of last year, and for December twenty-ninth. This year, for January twenty-sixth, February twenty-third, March thirtieth, April twenty-seventh, May twenty-eighth, and June twenty-ninth."

John had always surprised even himself with his mathematical abilities. He knew almost without willing it what the dates indicated.

"Except for December first, the last Friday of each month."

"That's right."

"What does he do on the last Friday of every month?" John asked.

"He leaves the office at noon. When I asked him years ago what he did, he said he was playing poker with a notorious group of men whose positions in life forbid such crass pastimes. Therefore, they played on Friday afternoons, in secret."

"Just the last Friday of the month?"

"No, every Friday. However, the one-hundred-dollar entries began only eight months ago. What would you say of this, Mr. Le Brun?"

"It's more important what you think, Mrs. Van Leyden," he countered.

The woman's facial muscles tightened. "Perhaps he once used every Friday afternoon for poker. Perhaps he alternated poker with women of easy virtue. But now, I believe he has a mistress. You know, among the many properties his family owns are more than one hundred apartment houses and boardinghouses, with almost a thousand individual residences. He could put a woman up in one of them, and I'd never know it. I would say that this is her monthly cash for living."

John wanted to laugh. There was a good chance she was right in the suspicion that her husband had been doing more effectively to her what she had been doing to him.

"You told me in church that his attentions toward you had been flaggin'. How long ago did that begin?"

"Eight months."

"Ah. And what would you like to do about this?"

"I wish to find out for certain if he is philandering."

John nodded slowly. If he wanted, his New York office had its first case. "I tell you what I will do. A certain gentleman with power owes me a favor. I will have him lean his weight upon Mr. Thomas Janney and learn why he was hired by your husband." Kevin O'Leary had made it clear to John that he owed him much in the Metropolitan Club murder case. "When this gentleman learns the truth, he will write a note and send it to Mrs. Ainsworth."

Marie smiled and touched John's hand. "Thank you! But what about the eight checks?"

"Before you do anythin' else, you must ask yourself: If your husband is cheatin' on you, do you want to divorce him?"

Mrs. Van Leyden stared at her tea companion for several seconds. "I'm not sure."

John had expected the answer. Two weeks earlier, with another man begging her to marry him, she would have leapt at the opportunity to have caught her husband in flagrante delicto and sued for divorce. Without someone to run to, the situation had changed. When she was twenty, she was the daughter of an art dealer. Beautiful, but with no significant dowry and evidently no prospects for a well-off, handsome young husband. John did not doubt that, as had been reported to him, her father had put considerable pressure on the woman. But she could have said no. He doubted the father would have thrown her into the street. Marie wanted the fifteen-room town house and the six servants, and the summer cottage in Newport, Rhode Island. And the balls, and the theater, and the clothes, and the fancy restaurants, and the rich friends. What would she get by divorcing herself from her husband? New York City was, as Edmund Pinckney had astutely noted, an unforgiving town for scandal. In his experience, outrageously unfair as it was, the men were forgiven for their sins; the women were not.

"Divorce does not have quite the stigma it had in my youth," John said, "but neither has it become fashionable. Unless you are compelled to get free, you might not want to know the truth. Then again, if you believe your husband knows about Edmund, you might want him to know that you are aware of his infidelity. In that case, you might ask around for the most circumspect detective agency in the city."

"I thought you might be in town for several more weeks," Marie hoped.

"I will not," John said.

She swallowed and averted her eyes. She looked out the window. She took a sip of tea. All in silence. Then she reached into her bag and produced a silver dollar, which she laid upon the table. She smiled at last.

"Thank you for your help, Mr. Le Brun. You are indeed a gentleman. Can I offer you monetary thanks as well?"

"No, ma'am."

She rose, and John came out of his seat quickly to help her from the table. They left the restaurant together, talking of the weather and the city in order to avoid slipping back into serious subjects. The club doorman whistled for a carriage to pull inside the archway. John helped her up and offered a courtly bow. The open-topped carriage pulled away. Marie Van Leyden turned to wave.

When the carriage cleared the arch, John found himself looking at Lordis Goode. An arch was in her eyebrow. She walked slowly toward John.

"Two-timing me, are you?" she asked. He could not tell if she was playing or serious.

"That was Mrs. Van Leyden. Edmund's girlfriend."

"Ah! No wonder he was so smitten. A great beauty."

"As far down as the skin."

Lordis hooked her arm under John's elbow. "A wise response, whether it's true or not."

"I am powerful glad to see you," John said, intent on turning the subject. "And a bit surprised."

"No more surprised than I. I know you understand that Sally and the children are my first priority."

"Indeed. How are they?"

"The children are desolate. I'm just so grateful it's the summer, and they don't have to face their classmates. Children can be so cruel."

"And Sally?"

"Stoic. She shows almost no emotion. Just says she must keep on. Not only tending to the Pinckney business but burying her husband

and dealing with the theater and its personnel. I believe she's working day and night so she doesn't have to think about the horrors of the past two weeks."

"Probably."

"Can we walk?" Lordis asked. She wore a simple but fetching shirt-waist and skirt, and a parasol to fend off the summer sun's rays. The skirt was short enough not to drag on the ground, revealing high-button shoes.

"Of course. Which way?"

"North." They started off. Lordis said, "I keep waiting for Sally to dissolve in a puddle or to begin ranting and have to be carted off to an insane asylum. That's what I'd be like."

"She may yet unravel," John said.

"That's why I've been as close to her as scent on a rose. This morning, she got tired of it. Forbade me to follow her around. 'Go visit with your friend Mr. Le Brun,' she told me. 'He's going home soon, and then you'll hate me for taking you from him.' "

"Very sensible woman."

"Too sensible. Of course, she didn't publicly announce her husband's burial yesterday. She knew his friends and employees wouldn't come, and the rest would only have been gawkers."

They rounded the corner of the Metropolitan Club and started north up Fifth Avenue. John invited Lordis to review the past three days. She did so in excruciating detail. She only paused briefly when they walked past Whimsy House. As they did, she stared at it in silence. John picked up the conversation by telling about his trip to Brooklyn, his lunch with Pulitzer, and his daylong tour of the great Museum of Natural History.

"Have you been to the Metropolitan Museum of Art?" Lordis asked.

"I have not."

"It's just ahead, across from Eighty-second Street. Are you of a mood to walk there?"

"If you are."

They ambled on, arm in arm, and John felt fine. He could only guess how angry Sarah Topley must have been with him for having been the cause of not only her husband's unmasking but also his death. He had been relieved to hear that the woman forgave him enough to push him and her best friend back together. But he was most grateful that Lordis apparently harbored no ill will against him. Again and again, her words returned to Sally and the children.

By the time they reached the museum, the noon hour had arrived. The museum was open on Sunday afternoons, and no fees were charged. They entered the succession of gargantuan buildings by the formidable front steps. Lordis had clearly visited many times. She led him with assurance through the Hall of Statues, the East Asian exhibit, and the Egyptian collection. Toward two o'clock, they paused in the cafeteria for cucumber-and-dill sandwiches and mineral water.

"You know who the president of this museum is, don't you?" Lordis asked.

"Not J. P. Morgan."

"Exactly."

"He does so appreciate the arts. And did Stanford White design it?"

"I don't think so."

"Its collection underscores how little I know of our planet," John confessed. "And how little I've traveled."

"You've traveled more than I have," Lordis said.

"We can remedy that right away. I've already asked you to come down to Brunswick and visit with me. Wouldn't it be a smart thing if Sally and the children came with you? There is only embarrassment and snubbin' for them up here."

"Sally has too much to do."

"Does she? Or is she, as you say, keepin' herself busy on purpose? Certainly, in another week or so, her task sheet will have dwindled. Then lawyers and estate agents must take over. I can ask Mr. Pulitzer or Mr. Morgan for several names. We could—"

Lordis lifted her index finger. "It's not up to me to decide. I can put the suggestion to Sally, but I don't think it will do any good. At least not for a month. Can you stay that long?"

John had yet to speak to Lordis about the idea Joseph Pulitzer had put forth of his dividing his time between New York City and Brunswick. If he did, he was afraid that Lordis would never agree to return to the South with him.

"Not even a week," he said, taking her hand. "In fact, Mr. Morgan has given me a date on which he is willin' to pay up his side of the bargain and sail me to Philadelphia. One solitary date, as his time is so valuable. That day is this comin' Thursday."

"Oh, my."

"Don't you say that *you* can't come," John fretted. "Didn't you tell me when we last spoke that you were movin' on Saturday?"

"Yes. I did. It's a nice three-room apartment over on Sixty-sixth, near the East River. It didn't take long, considering I only had one room to move." As she took back her hand, the charm bracelet tinkled.

"So, your belongin's are safe. But there's Sally and the children," John said, repeating the phrase that Lordis had used no fewer than twenty times that afternoon.

"And Neko San."

"We mustn't forget the cat. No one can feed it but you," he said, unable to keep the sarcasm from his tone.

"I am sorry. Perhaps I could come down to see you in a month. Or for certain when the weather cools."

"For certain," John echoed.

Lordis looked at her half-eaten sandwich. "I really should be getting back to the Topleys'. By now, Sally may need me."

John got up and held Lordis's chair so she could rise. His feet ached from the walk to the museum and then through its halls. "Why don't we take a carriage back?" he suggested.

THEY HAD NOT RIDDEN much farther south on Fifth Avenue than Seventieth Street when Lordis suddenly sucked in her breath.

"What is it?" John asked.

"My painting! In the rush to move my things, I completely forgot about my painting in the dining room. Sally wants the house sold as quickly as possible, and I'm sure the furniture will be auctioned first. I know how those estate people are when they come in; they take the good artwork right off the walls."

"Why don't we pick it up right now?" John suggested.

"Could we?"

John reached forward and lightly touched the driver's shoulder. "Turn in at Sixty-second Street, please, if you would." He patted Lordis's hand. "If you want, I'll go inside and get it. I imagine you're not real happy about your home bein' sold so precipitately."

"I'm not happy at all. My world is a small one. Of course that's my fault, but it's what I wanted. I see now how little is required to make a small world crumble."

As the landau turned east onto the street, Lordis stood from her seat.

"Sally! I think that was Sally."

"Where?" John asked.

She pointed at a hansom cab that was moving with speed down Fifth Avenue. "You can't see her anymore. I only caught a peek, but I could swear it was she."

"You have Sally on the mind," John fumed.

"I suppose I have," Lordis admitted.

Their cab stopped in front of the looming brownstone mansion.

"I'm sure she would have told you if she was comin' up to the house." John turned to the alert driver. "Wait here, please. We won't be but five minutes." He helped Lordis down to the sidewalk. Together, they climbed the front steps.

"It took me several visits before I noticed the W and H on these side walls," John revealed.

Lordis handed her parasol to him and dug into her handbag for her ring of keys. "Yes. Probably the most subtle thing about the house. I've tried to talk Sally into moving up here with the children. Far enough from her neighborhood to start again. I suggested she rechristen the place Whispering Hope. Like the hymn. That way, these letters would still make sense."

"She doesn't want the place."

"No. Most emphatically not." Lordis attempted to fit her key into the lock while John hummed the tune of the 1868 religious song. She tried several times.

"Problem?" John asked.

"Yes. That's strange. It doesn't want to go in."

John looked at the lock. "No wonder. It's from the same company, but this is a new one. Look! There are no scratch marks around the keyhole."

"You're right! Sally said nothing about having had the lock changed. Why would she do that?"

"Perhaps to keep out anyone that Hastin's might have given a key to."

"Perhaps." She turned and looked at the waiting carriage. "Oh, well. I suppose we should forget it for now."

"Not necessarily," John said. He walked down to the driver, apologized for the change of plan, and paid him for the short ride. The man shook his head and drove away.

Lordis came down the steps. "You're thinking about the side door. I have that key also, but what if she's had that lock changed?"

"Doesn't matter," John said. "Come around with me."

The change of the second lock was immediately evident.

Lordis made a tsking sound. "Well, that's that. Let's hike back to Fifth Avenue and hail—"

John dug into his trouser pocket. "I said that your key didn't matter." He pulled his lock-picking case out and selected the right pair of tools. "Here, hold my hat while I work," he said, handing over his derby and her parasol.

"This is breaking and entering," Lordis worried.

"Not breakin'. Just enterin'. You *are* the former chatelaine and the owner's best friend. And *I* am the temporary best friend of the local city detective. Relax." By the time John had finished his speech, he had the door open.

They entered the pantry and warming kitchen. Lordis set down her parasol. She dropped her voice to a whisper. "I still feel like a thief."

"We'll be in and out in two shakes of a lamb's tail," John responded, in an equal whisper. "To tell you the truth, I was kinda hopin' that you and I could give the place a final benediction. You know, on old Chriswell's bed?"

Lordis elbowed John in the ribs. "You sex fiend! Let's bring the painting back to my new apartment together. You and I can christen *that* bedroom."

"Deal."

They moved into the dining room. The enormous table and its twelve chairs were covered by white sheets. The paintings, however, remained uncovered on the wall. Lordis's was the largest and anchored to two sturdy hooks. Lordis worked off one side and John the other. They set it down carefully on the table.

"I'll get some butcher's paper and string from the pantry," Lordis said. "Only be a moment."

John contented himself with studying the painting up close, trying to see how the various pigments combined to produce such realistic effects. As he tilted his face downward, his derby slid off his head. He caught it in midplummet.

From the pantry came a bloodcurdling scream. John spun toward the noise. Lordis appeared through the swinging door. Benjamin Topley was directly behind her, holding her left arm twisted behind her with his left hand and pressing a revolver against her temple with the other.

"Slowly. Very slowly," Topley said to Le Brun. "If you make any quick move, I will shoot you first and then her. If you're thinking I won't kill her, think again. She's close to my wife, not me."

"And to think I defended you!" Lordis managed in a quavering but outraged voice.

John backed up. He made to set his hat on the table.

"No. Keep your hand filled for the moment," Topley commanded.

"Very well," John said. "Just stay calm." He moved his second hand slowly up to the hat and grabbed the opposite side of its narrow brim.

"Smart guy," Topley said. "Face the wall, and keep your hands on the hat. Over your head. Put your toes against the baseboard!" Topley grabbed Lordis by her hair and yanked her backward. He pulled out the chair at the table's head and pushed her onto it. He snapped his free fingers to fix John's attention, pointed, and said, "Lean your forehead against the wall where the picture was. Legs back. Spread them. Hands as high as they go. Legs wider. You just can't leave me in peace, can you?"

"This was purely unintentional. Miss Goode forgot her paintin'."

"Well, bad luck for both of you that she did. She surprised me so badly as I came out of the basement that I nearly dropped my gun."

In London, John had discovered he could face death with a sense of the comedic. He thought the music-hall impresario would appreciate a little gallows humor. "Nearly doesn't count. Want to go back down and try again?"

Topley did not laugh. "Shut up." Dividing his attention between the man and woman, Topley reached out and patted Le Brun from under his arms down to his ankles. "I'm surprised you're carrying no weapon."

"I'm retired," John replied.

Topley stepped back. "And why the hell didn't you *stay* retired?

Couldn't resist sticking your nose into one more investigation, could you?"

"I was invited. May I sit?"

Topley gestured with the gun as he went behind Lordis. "Slowly."

"May I put down my hat?"

"Slowly."

John eased out one of the chairs with the tips of two fingers. He sat and slowly placed the derby directly in front of himself. "And, then again, I came because you devised such a clever murder that I just couldn't resist admirin' it up close."

"You're a damned cocky number, aren't you? Well, maybe you figured out that I was behind it, but you didn't catch me."

"You're not Benjamin Topley's identical brother, are you?"

At this remark Topley laughed. "Funny you should say that." He circled the table so that he could watch Lordis and John at the same time. "I wouldn't say my plan was clever in retrospect. It was too contrived."

"True," John agreed. "A simple street robbery and murder of Edmund would have served better."

Topley wore plain clothes, such as John expected he donned when directing on the stage. His pants were baggy. Braces held them up, over a summer-weight negligee overshirt.

"Why *did* you make it so complicated?" John asked.

"I couldn't let those bastards over at the Metropolitan Club go unpunished when I saw a way to kill two birds with one stone," Topley revealed. "I had approached Edmund a few years ago about helping me fund a legitimate theater. He was flush with cash back then. He told me he knew nothing about theater, but he did hook me up with half a dozen men at his favorite club who professed to. One after the other, they set me jumping through their hoops. In every case, I would have broken my back and they would have extracted the lion's share of the profits. Always the same with those bastards. The golden rule: Them with the gold make the rules. Leeches. I hope the socialists and communists murder them all. Make the French Revolution look like a picnic."

John shook his head gravely. "One must never let emotions interfere with a good murder."

"*Now* he tells me," Topley said, bending slightly toward the shaking Lordis.

"How could you do this to your family?" she accused.

"How could I *not* do this *for* my family?" Topley countered. "Sally would have gotten nothing. She was less than dirt to all of them. Less than a servant. I figured out how to rectify injustice. And you? You threw in with the Pinckneys from the moment you came up here."

"I love your wife and children, and I was very fond of you," Lordis protested.

"Spare me. My absence defined your presence. You went out with Sally when I worked. You minded the kids when we went out."

"I merely worked for the Pinckneys," Lordis affirmed.

Topley took several steps away from Lordis, so that he would be able to catch her eyes. His raised gun hand, however, stayed pointed toward John. "And would you work for the devil? You could have gotten employment easily in another household. After Chriswell died, I offered to find you a good position through my contacts. Not once, but three times. But you wouldn't hear of it."

John's heart sank at the words.

Lordis gasped. "That *was* Sally leaving in the carriage!"

John nodded at her. "Probably droppin' off provisions. This should have been an excellent hidin' place, with all of the staff gone and new locks on the door. You want more proof it was your girlfriend? Look at his pinkie fingers."

Benjamin proudly held up the ring with the comedic mask and flashed it at her.

John said, "The police must have returned those pretty rings to her after she identified what was left of somebody else's body in the morgue. She gave them back to him."

"My God!" Lordis said. Her entire being slumped in the chair.

Topley said to Le Brun, "Don't get the wrong idea. I meant it when I told you in the theater that Sally knew nothing. At least nothing until this one showed up Tuesday afternoon."

John nodded his understanding. "She told Sally that I had asked her to set up Mr. Hastin's."

"That's right. Of course, I had no idea it was over the jewels. I was sure it was about the murders."

"It was both." John let his right hand down gently atop his hat. He tapped his middle and index fingers against its crown. "So, your wife wasn't that disappointed in you, was she?"

"That's not true. But Sally is a realist. She understood that I had done it for her and our children."

"Not to mention your own dreams."

"I won't deny it. She also understood that I only intended to have Edmund killed."

"I'm very curious about Tuesday night," John said. "What was that business with you callin' your wife and tellin' her to meet you at the theater?"

Topley smiled. "Purely an invitation for you and Detective O'Leary to witness my demise. Just disappearing wasn't good enough. After she put the children to bed, she sat by the front window and watched for your arrival through the curtain. The second she spotted you, she rang up the theater. I then waited five minutes for you to enter the house and called back. I was sure one of you would be listening in."

"And who was the man we found in your chair?"

Topley's smile turned into a grin. John realized that the man was a showman through and through and could not help reviewing his own performance. "You asked if I was my own twin? Well, it turns out that I once met a man in Stewart's department store who looked remarkably like me. We were so startled by our resemblance that we exchanged addresses. He worked on Wall Street."

"Him!" Lordis exclaimed.

Topley nodded in the housekeeper's direction. "She was there. I learned that Sally had planned a surprise fortieth birthday party for me. I turned the tables on all of them by having this fellow arrive in my place. He fooled everyone for about thirty seconds."

"He had a name," John said.

"Edward Karow."

"Good old Ed. So, you invited him back for a repeat performance?"

"Something like that. I was fortunately able to reach him Tuesday afternoon. Turns out he was a homosexual. Lived alone and used his good salary to buy the favors of young men. If he wasn't available, I don't know who I'd have found. A panhandler off the street, I suppose. Anyway, I asked him to tell no one that I was seeing him. I had a ticket for that night's show left at the box office. Afterward, he came back to my office. I waited until everyone had left, hoping that the phone wouldn't ring too early. I gave him a cock-and-bull story about doing another turn as me. He agreed. You see, at the past party he had met a fey chorus boy from the show I had running then. I suppose he was hoping that lightning would strike twice. He agreed to put on some of my clothes, to let me do his hair in my style. He even put on my rings. And then I stabbed him through the heart from the back."

"You monster," Lordis exhaled.

"And wouldn't you know, having lived for years with three monsters?"

John slowly raised his left hand to pinch the bridge of his nose. "The furniture."

"What?" asked Topley.

"I thought I heard you movin' furniture just before you set the fire. Then, when we returned the next mornin', there was nothin' in front of the door. I supposed that you had barricaded yourself in but that the firemen had moved it all after they broke down the door."

"Wrong!" Topley crowed with delight.

"A trapdoor," John said.

"Exactly. Under my desk. Once upon a time, where my office, the costume room, and the prop room were was the back of a much deeper stage. There are trapdoors all over that stage. It was created for vaudeville, after all. Where there's vaudeville, there must be magicians."

"Magicians," John echoed. He looked directly at Lordis and again drummed on the top of his derby. "I love magicians. Kellar. Malini."

"You know, I should have put a bullet into your head the moment I came through that door, Mr. Le Brun," Topley proclaimed. "You hit me when I was crossing the stage."

"I thought I had," John replied.

"I was very lucky. Just a piece of skin and a bit of muscle off my chest. If I'd been traveling slightly faster, you'd have killed me."

John refrained from antagonizing the man with a reply.

"As it was," Topley went on, "I bled like a stuck pig. It still burns. I had trouble sleeping for three nights. It's still infected. Sally just brought me a bottle of hydrogen peroxide. I was really afraid that blood would show through the fake police uniform I had changed into."

"How did you exit?"

"Through the orchestra pit." John remembered the locked pit door. "I waited until pandemonium reigned and played my part to the hilt. I could have been caught in the fire by waiting, but if I hadn't dared it I would have been dead anyway."

"So true."

"I'm also very vexed that you made such a big deal about those Colt revolvers. Who else but you would have noticed the difference of a few inches on the barrel?"

Lordis shook her head. John knew that she was busy castigating herself for having supplied the Topleys with so much inside information.

"Don't you pay attention to those potboiler murder plays?" John asked. "No killer can be so careful that nothing goes wrong. How could you know that Miniver Pinckney would choose to impersonate his brother that night?"

"I agree."

"Or that Witherspoon King would have an airtight alibi at an insurance banquet, right in this city?"

"More bad luck."

"Or that I would note the difference in the gun left on the bedroom floor?"

Topley leaned against the wall. "Absolutely. But I can't be entirely angry with you, Mr. Le Brun. After all, you did find the jewels that everyone else was sure had been sold off long before. We're twice as rich now. Sally will convert all her brothers' assets and sell this house as quickly as possible. She'll get what she can from what's left of the theater. Then she and the children will board a boat for England. I'll join her after a more circuitous route. We plan to open a truly great dramatic theater under assumed names, in one of the smaller cities. Even a second-rate English city respects good theater more than any American city."

John watched the revolver growing more and more heavy in Topley's raised right hand. He needed to keep the man talking for a minute or two longer in order to satisfy his plan.

"How long was Mr. Hastin's in your employ?"

"Since shortly after he read the brothers' wills. They really knew how to create enemies."

"Did you or Ogden kill Edmund?"

"He did that one also. I promised to double his pay. For a heavy man, he was remarkably spry, don't you think?"

"And your impersonatin' Maurice Van Leyden?"

"Again your fault. Although somehow I feel you planned it. His motive for killing Edmund seemed so good, I couldn't let it go unexploited. And, then again, he's one of the undeserving rich, so why not give him trouble?"

"You had his look and girth down beautifully," John allowed, "but you were too tall."

"I know. Again, too complex. I should have sent a note for Ogden to meet me near one of the piers for his payoff. Then I should have stuck him in the back, weighted him down, and tossed him in the river."

Lordis shuddered at the matter-of-fact manner of her best friend's husband's speech.

The gun wavered in Topley's hand.

"You can't kill us, you know," John said. "If you think you messed up with Mr. Ogden, we'll be twice as hard to explain away."

"I can't let you live."

"How will you get two bodies out of this house?"

Topley shrugged. "I won't. That's what that passage between the house and the drain is for."

"And what about Sally? She'll know you did it."

"With no bodies? She'll think you lovebirds decided to run away together."

"Lordis wouldn't leave," John stated flatly. "You really *don't* know her, do you? I've only known her a few days, and I understand that she'll never leave your family. Tie us up in the basement. Let Sally in on it. Flee with just the cash, bonds, stocks, and jewels. It's enough."

"No!" Topley cried out. "I am selling this house!" He realized just how tired his right hand was. He lifted his left hand and wrapped his fingers around the grip.

John drummed on the derby. "And then there's the driver waitin' outside for us."

Benjamin's head turned involuntarily in the direction of the front door.

Lordis collapsed out of her seat onto the floor.

John slid his derby toward himself, until the derringer he had long before transferred under it dropped into the space between the table and his waiting right hand. He half rose and shoved his chair away with the backs of his legs. The derringer came up just as his adversary had transferred the revolver and had his left index finger inside the guard. Topley attempted to aim at the figure that was sinking behind the table.

A small tongue of flame leapt from one of the derringer's barrels.

Benjamin Topley grunted as he was hit. Reflexively, his finger tightened around the trigger, and the revolver went off, sending a bullet a foot over Le Brun's head. Topley staggered toward the door that led to the foyer. He tried to find Le Brun past the sight of the revolver's barrel, but his adversary had ducked under the table, completely out of sight. Fearing to be shot in the groin from below, Topley lurched out of the room. From the foyer, he emptied his pistol into the center of the dining table.

An instant before the bullets began tearing under and over the table, John had rolled in the direction where Lordis lay. He came up on his knees between two of the chairs, his derringer pointed at the door. Lordis was moaning in terror. He hissed at her to be quiet.

For a moment, there was silence. Then, from a distance and echoing in the great open foyer, came coughing and then Topley's voice.

" 'A hit. A most palpable hit. I must declare it.' "

John rose into a squat. He grabbed Lordis's arm as he rushed toward the warming-kitchen door. He continued to pull her along until they came to the archway that divided the kitchen from the library. John shoved open the door, looked, and listened.

From even farther away came Benjamin Topley's voice, a rattle sounding through the shouting. " 'You have made worm's meat of me!' "

"I'll make meat of him!" Lordis pulled free and grabbed a butcher's cleaver from the cutting table. When she returned to the door, John beckoned for her to follow.

"He's dyin'. Just watch behind us," he said. "He's not dead yet."

"You've destroyed me, Le Brun!" Topley shouted. "I'm out of bullets. Come out and see the dramatic finale! It's not often you get to witness a man die twice. Well, where are you? God damn both of you and this house!" He coughed wetly several times.

"He's gone upstairs," Lordis said. "His voice is coming from the balcony."

Before the pair could move, a resounding crash echoed through the foyer. It was the sound of wood and glass shattering. Then there was a profound silence.

Step by step, John and Lordis advanced. They found the foyer pristine. Likewise, the grand staircase was devoid of debris. It was only when they had ventured halfway up the stairs that Lordis spotted the missing window above the front of the balcony. Benjamin Topley had hurled himself down onto the house's entry steps.

John opened the front door. Topley lay faceup among hundreds of bits of mullion and glass, as twisted as a rag doll. From the blood-circled hole in his shirt, John realized his bullet had struck about an inch below and to the right of the heart. A larger-caliber weapon would have killed the man in a few seconds.

Already, four people had rushed down the sidewalk from Fifth Avenue. Two carriages had come to a halt in the street. Lordis yanked off the sheet that covered one of the foyer lowboys. She brought it outside and laid it over the body. Then she turned to John.

"Thank you for my life. I'm so glad I told you that story about Malini and the ice under his hat."

"Not half as glad as I am. I couldn't use my gun while he held you so close." John stepped in front of the body and waved at the crowd. "Why don't you vultures fly somewhere else?" The group ignored him. Two servants hurried out of the house that stood directly across the street. John realized that if Benjamin Topley had failed in every other way, his final act would succeed in putting a stigma on Whimsy House that would never be erased. He walked around the body and back into the mansion. Lordis had retreated several steps. He closed the door, went to her side, and put his arm around her.

"We don't have to tell them about Sally, do we?" she asked.

"Yes, we do. Otherwise, we'd be guilty as well."

"But she didn't know until the last minute."

"You go take the rings off his fingers then."

"What about her children?" Lordis persisted. "Who will take care of them?"

John didn't bother to reply. They both knew the answer.

THURSDAY

J U L Y   5 ,   1 9 0 6

THE YACHT BASINS of Manhattan were all too small to accommodate J. P. Morgan's *Corsair*. The third of his yachts to bear that name, it measured 302 feet on the waterline. John watched from the East Twenty-third Street landing of the New York Yacht Club as the yacht's motor launch chugged across the green waters toward him. At his side stood Lordis Goode. Despite the turmoil of her life, she had insisted on seeing John off.

From her handbag she pulled a bottle of Napoleon brandy. "This is to keep you warm, because I can't," Lordis said, handing the gift to John.

"I won't need warmth in Georgia this time of year," he said. "Is this your way of sayin' you won't even come down in the winter?"

"We may," Lordis said. He realized that she was trying to keep her eyes from looking sad. He did not believe it was that great a task. For all the disasters that had touched her, much had gone well for Lordis in the past few days. Marie Van Leyden was not pregnant and therefore would have no child to claim part of the Pinckney estate. Benjamin Topley was dead, and his wife, Sarah, who had inherited the estate, would be going to prison for years. She had requested that Lordis supervise the estate and personally care for her godchildren. Lordis had told John that, in her estimation, Whimsy House had too much fresh death and scandal associated with it to fetch the money it was worth. She would continue to manage it, with the children occupying Miniver's and Sarah's bedrooms. With the money coming in from the jewelry alone, worry about the loss of a few thousand in selling the mansion was the flimsiest of excuses, John knew. The truth was that Lordis wanted her home back, and now she had it for years to come.

"I still don't know why we had to say anything about Sarah's involvement in the affair," Lordis lamented as the river breeze blew her wealth of hair smartly to one side.

"Because it was the honest thing to do," John said. "When I solved the Jekyl Island Club murders, I arranged it so certain people who were accessories wouldn't be punished. Similarly, with the Sceptred Isle Club murders, I helped one of the guilty ones lessen the sentence. In each case, I was actin' as judge and jury and makin' sure those I sympathized with didn't get the book thrown at them. It was not my place. I've lost many nights' sleep over it. I would not make that mistake a third time."

"But you don't know Sally," Lordis argued. "She's the most—"

"Precisely," John countered. "I do not know her at all. So even if I wanted to play God, I couldn't. Besides, you are aware that Kevin O'Leary is not a stupid man. Once he knew Ben Topley tricked us inside his theater, he could not help but know that Sally had helped. You're lucky I was able to keep him off your back. You had no right tellin' the Topleys all you did."

"I was sure they were innocent."

"And you were wrong."

Lordis looked away, upriver. John took her hand and squeezed it. "Ben Jr. and Leslie Lordis might not even have had a godmother to look after them. Count your blessings."

Lordis looked at John. "I do. And I know you are one of them."

John labored to keep the sadness from his face, but he was not as successful as Lordis. He had refrained from telling her about Pulitzer's idea for him to live in two cities. He was not enthusiastic about being her third love, after the children and the newly christened Whispering Hope on East Sixty-second Street.

The launch's mate had tied up and was approaching the pair. Lordis touched John's face affectionately. Because of her height, she had only to lift her chin to kiss him on the lips. Her charm bracelet tinkled softly. There was now a new gold charm on it. It was in the traditional shape of a queen chess piece, given to her by John.

"Until I see you again," she said.

"The invitation will always be open," he promised.

The mate grabbed the largest two pieces of John's luggage and grunted as he lifted them. Le Brun had bought a new suitcase and valise and had nearly filled them with books. John followed the young man to the end of the pier and climbed down into the launch. Lordis stood for minutes watching him motor away. From time to time she waved. When she was too far distant for him to read her eyes, he turned away.

John fixed his attention on the *Corsair,* which was anchored well out in the river. It was actually too large to be called a yacht. Yachts to him were sport boats invented by the Dutch for racing, craft that should not take more than three sailors to handle. This behemoth was an ocean-goer, with a crew of fifty-five. Moreover, it had an enormous back-raked smokestack, betraying the great engines below. There was no private vessel grander in the Americas. John smiled as he remembered reading the quotation from Morgan's lips about yachts: "If you have to ask how much it costs, you have no business owning one."

At lunch the previous Friday, Joseph Pulitzer had revealed that he knew about John's agreement with Morgan. "Don't step on that pirate's black scow," he had said. "I'll sail you down to Philadelphia on the *Liberty.* It's one foot longer than his, you know." It was one foot longer on purpose. Moreover, it was painted noonday white because Morgan's was midnight black. But it would not have been the same. Boarding and commanding the pirate's ship was precisely what made the trip so much fun.

John was reintroduced to Captain McKay. The man tried his best to smile, but he had been made a fool by the Georgian years before, and the incident still stung.

"Would you like to sit on deck or inside the salon?" McKay asked.

"On deck, thank you."

"And what would you like to drink?"

"Do you have Co-cola?"

"I fear not."

"What about iced tea?"

"I'm sure we do."

John listened to the anchor being weighed. "Is Mr. Morgan on board?"

"He is. He's below, working. I'm sure he'll be up directly."

John willed himself to relax. He basked in the morning sun that was trying to peek out from between hazy sheets of clouds. Not long after the ship got under way, he found the Statue of Liberty expanding beyond the starboard bow.

"Is she not the most beautiful sight?" John Pierpont Morgan asked, having come up quietly behind Le Brun.

"She brings a tear to my eye. But why does she face us? Shouldn't she face all those immigrants yet to arrive?"

Morgan eased himself down on the wicker deck chair next to his erstwhile nemesis. "I don't know. You should ask your friend Pulitzer. He was the one who led the campaign to finance the statue's base. I have no doubt he also controlled which way the lady faced."

John laughed.

Morgan said, "You know, as serious as we both are about our chess, we should begin immediately if we are to complete three games before reaching Philadelphia."

"Would you believe that *I* have the headache this time?" John said.

"I would not believe it."

"Then let us say that my mind is much too preoccupied for me to win against a man of your intellect and skill."

Morgan reached into his pocket and took out two cigars. He handed one to John and proceeded to light both. "That surprises me," he said as he was doing the honors. "I should think your mind would be at ease after having triumphed yet again. How could there possibly remain any detail unresolved?"

"You know that Miss Lordis Goode is the godmother of the Topley children?"

"That beautiful woman standing on the pier with you."

John was sure a telescope existed somewhere on the yacht. "Yes. She faces a fight over custody with Benjamin Topley's brother and sister-in-law, against the mother's wishes. They have seen the children exactly twice and only for a few hours each time. They live in Cincinnati, which would obviously uproot the children. Ben Jr. and Leslie Lordis would have great difficulty in visitin' their mother. Moreover, I have seen them with Lordis, and they love her."

"And if this were resolved in Miss Goode's favor, you would waive the three chess games?"

"I would."

"Isn't such a request in direct contravention of your philosophies?" Morgan asked. "I thought you deplored the ability of the powerful to bend the law for their own convenience."

Many thoughts collided in John's head. Making a deal with the devil. His resolve never again to play God or judge and jury. How he loathed the schemes and cabals cooked up behind the walls of places like the Metropolitan Club. But then he remembered Plato's benevolent dictator. He thought about J. P. Morgan's unprepossessing brownstone house, his presidency of the Metropolitan Museum of Art, his underwriting of the Players Club. Life simply was not simple.

"Sometimes it's not good for Miss Justice to wear that blindfold," he allowed.

The Titan of Wall Street smiled. "You're convinced you're asking for the right judgment?"

"I am."

"That's good enough for me. Consider it resolved."

"Thank you."

For several moments, J. P. Morgan contented himself with puffing on his cigar and watching the New Jersey shore. Then he turned toward his guest and confronted him with a serious expression. "So, how should we handle the Panama situation, Mr. Le Brun?"

Notes

All the clubs mentioned in the novel actually existed. Today, the Players Club and the Metropolitan Club still function at the locations described. The author was graciously allowed to tour the Players Club by its executive director, Mr. John Martello. He is especially grateful to have been allowed to see the private rooms of the great Edwin Booth. The management of the Metropolitan Club declined his request to walk through their physical plant. However, Paul Porzelt's excellent book, *The Metropolitan Club of New York,* provided an abundance of information on the club from its inception, into and beyond the first decade of the twentieth century. Likewise, John Tebbel's *A Certain Club: One Hundred Years of the Players* and Henry Watterson's *A History of the Manhattan Club* contributed mightily. Among other resources invaluable in helping to breathe accurate life into the novel were *American Heritage*'s *New York, N.Y.,* the Montgomery Ward and Company *Catalogue No. 57,* Spring and Summer 1895, Allen Churchill's *The Upper Crust: An Informal History of New York's Highest Society,* Time-Life's *The Progressive Era: 1901–1917,* and Moses King's *King's Views of New York: 1896–1915* and *King's Views of Brooklyn: 1905.* Items cited in New York newspapers were all accurate and occurred during the time span of the novel, with the exception of references to the fictitious Witherspoon King and the events of the Pinckney murders.

The Museum of the City of New York did finally open in 1932, on Fifth Avenue at 103rd Street. Among its many fascinating exhibits is the doll house collection, with every structure cited except the fictitious Whimsy House.

Finally, the character of Kevin O'Leary is largely based on the author's paternal grandfather, Patrick Monahan. He did in-

deed come to this country as a professional runner, became a
police patrolman, was cited for bravery under fire, and did rise
to the rank of detective. The author's grandparents' house did
have oriental carpets, hookahs, and parrots. However, his grandfather was born in 1890, so Patrick Monahan's period of service
began roughly a decade after the time of The Manhattan Island
Club murders.

About the Author

Brent Monahan lives in Yardley, Pennsylvania, with his wife, Bonnie, and children, Caitlin and Ian. He is the author of eight previous novels. The seventh was *The Jekyl Island Club,* the first novel featuring John Le Brun, and the eighth took Le Brun to the gentlemen's clubs of London. He collects chess sets and hardly beats anyone.